MARKETING CAMPAIGN

- National Digital Advertising
- Prepublication Trade Advertising
- National Print and Online Media Coverage
- National Radio and Podcast Interviews
- Outreach to Book Influencers on Instagram and TikTok
- Prepublication Online Buzz and Early Consumer Review Campaign
- Preorder Incentive Campaign
- Features in the *Harper Voyager* and *From the Heart* Newsletters
- Targeted Email Marketing Based on Consumer Browsing and Category Interests
- Features on the Harper Voyager, Avon Books, and William Morrow Books Social Media Platforms
- Ebook Backlist Price Promotions, with Teaser Excerpts from *Immortal*
- Library Marketing
- Reader's Edition Available
- Egalley Available on Edelweiss and NetGalley

IMMORTAL

Also by Sue Lynn Tan

THE CELESTIAL KINGDOM DUOLOGY

Daughter of the Moon Goddess
Heart of the Sun Warrior

Tales of the Celestial Kingdom

IMMORTAL

SUE LYNN TAN

HARPER Voyager
An Imprint of HarperCollinsPublishers

IMMORTAL. Copyright © 2025 by Sue Lynn Tan. All rights reserved. Printed in the United States of America. No part of this book may be used or reproduced in any manner whatsoever without written permission except in the case of brief quotations embodied in critical articles and reviews. For information, address HarperCollins Publishers, 195 Broadway, New York, NY 10007.

HarperCollins books may be purchased for educational, business, or sales promotional use. For information, please email the Special Markets Department at SPsales@harpercollins.com.

Harper Voyager and design are trademarks of HarperCollins Publishers LLC.

FIRST EDITION

Designed by Alison Bloomer
Map by

Library of Congress Cataloging-in-Publication Data has been applied for.

ISBN 978-0-06-326761-9

25 26 27 28 29 RTLO 10 9 8 7 6 5 4 3 2 1

TK

Map

PART
ONE

1

The God of War was famed for three things:
His unrivaled might. His devotion to the immortal queen.
And his heart of ice, devoid of all mercy.

⁂

FIRE RAGED THROUGH MY HOME, DEVOURING THE mahogany pillars and moss-green roof, the scroll paintings and silk carpets. In the gardens, magnolia trees, bamboo, and jasmine went up in flames, smoke lashing the air.

The God of War's heart might be formed of ice, but fire was his weapon of choice. The immortals had turned against us, and I did not know why.

My grandfather was the Lord of Tianxia, and until now a trusted and loyal subject of the Queen of the Golden Desert in the skies. Long ago, our kingdom was pledged to serve the immortals who protected us from a fearsome enemy, and they'd built a wall around Tianxia with their magic. Beyond these borders, the rest of our world was said to live in ignorance of the immortals—while we were the custodians of their secrets. Some might imagine we were favored to serve them. But though we lived in the shade of the gods, we felt no closer to them.

Tonight was meant to be one of triumph. After all these years, Grandfather had finally secured the precious treasure the immortal queen sought. And though many were eager for a glimpse of it, he had refused, keeping it safely locked away.

"Such a treasure is more trouble than it's worth. Greed turns too many honest men into thieves," he'd confided in me, adding darkly, "The immortals are not known for their mercy."

These last words echoed through me as cries of terror rang out from behind, accompanied by clattering footsteps and the frantic neighing of horses. As the thick scent of smoke clouded the air, I coughed loudly. My sweat-slicked hand was tucked in my grandfather's grip as he pulled me through the hallways of our palace. As we ran, my chest squeezed tighter until I thought it would burst, but I dared not falter.

I was not strong—possessed of a weak constitution, or so the physicians had claimed. When they thought I couldn't hear, they speculated at my condition in puzzled tones, unable to pinpoint it to any known illness. Grandfather hired private tutors so I could study at my own pace, though my best friend Chengyin often accompanied me. I wasn't ill, yet I never felt well either—constantly tired, a step behind the others. Nothing seemed to dispel the chill in my flesh, how it always felt like winter. After my parents had died, many urged my grandfather to marry again, or to adopt another heir—one stronger—but he'd refused.

"My granddaughter is not replaceable," he'd told them.

The court whispered behind my back, those crueler placing bets on the number of years left to me, while a few wiser but no less malicious bided their time in silence, eager for a rare chance at the throne. And maybe . . . one of them had tried to hasten my departure.

I remembered when the poison sank its claws into my body, just weeks ago. It struck like lightning, sapping what little strength

I had, my joy, my will to live. I became a shadow of myself, slipping in and out of consciousness. A lock of my hair turned white overnight—not the purity of snow, but the glitter of starlight. It didn't matter what tonics I drank, the medicines the physicians fed me, increasingly bitter and foul. Nothing helped, a relentless fatigue bearing down on my body until it felt like I was wrapped in a shroud. On the worst days, pain burrowed through my flesh like a vicious fever.

It was a soothsayer, an old crone, who claimed my condition was caused by drinking the waters of the Wangchuan River in the Netherworld. She'd pointed to my hair, nodding sagely as she said, "The waters of death are not meant for the living. There is no known cure."

Most scoffed at her; impossible that such a thing could be brought into our kingdom, if it existed at all. Grandfather was the only one who believed her . . . perhaps because no one else had an answer. Despite the grim prognosis, he kept searching for an antidote, offering a vast reward, though nothing had worked.

As we hurried along, I shivered, unable to recall the last time I'd felt warm. Grandfather's eyes darted around frantically, so different from his usual calm self. I wanted to ask what had sparked the immortals' anger but was afraid of distressing him further. His heart was weak; the physicians had warned him against straining it. As my anxiety spiked, I struggled to rein it in. Fear was a contagion that if left unchecked, would taint every spirit.

"Liyen, are you all right? Can you keep up?" Grandfather's voice was hoarse with urgency.

I nodded, though we both knew it was a lie. My breathing was ragged, pain puncturing my chest as I pushed myself onward. When we rounded a corner, I stumbled into an unknown courtyard. A wall ringed the garden, blades of grass grazing my knees, the branches of withered trees splayed wide. Neglect clung to the place like a fog. Grandfather fumbled along the wall, tearing away a curtain of vines to reveal a small door, latched with a rusted iron bar. A key gleamed in his hand that he slid into the lock. As it sprang apart, he tossed away the bar, pulling the door open to reveal the forest beyond.

"We need to run," he said.

"Yes, Grandfather." My voice was steady though my legs shook, light speckling my vision. "I . . . I just need a moment." I willed myself to move, even as I sagged against the wall.

Grandfather seemed to wilt as he reached into his sleeve and drew out a small flower. A shining lotus, its iridescent petals glittering like sunlit ice. "I was going to wait, Liyen—but I must give this to you now. Take it."

Something in his tone made me hesitate when I should have obeyed unflinchingly. "What is this?"

Grandfather clasped my shoulder, looking into my face. He did this whenever he had something important to say, when he wanted to be sure I was listening. "Liyen, you are dying. The waters of the Wangchuan are fatal to us mortals."

I recoiled from his words, shaking my head instinctively. While I'd heard this warning from the healers before, for Grandfather to say it extinguished any last flicker of doubt . . . and of hope. Death stalked us from birth, stealing even the strongest through its reaping—and though it was our fate, few went willingly.

As he blinked, his eyes suspiciously bright, my own grief spilled over. "I did as the physicians asked. I tried everything. I don't want to die, Grandfather. I don't want to leave you."

"This was not your fault, Liyen. Life is not fair. We cannot help how the dice fall, but it's our choice whether to keep playing." Grandfather looked old and gray in this moment, worn out. "The lotus is the antidote to what you suffer—the only one of its kind. Only this can counter the waters of the Wangchuan, as long as you want to live."

"Who wouldn't?" An ache swelled in my chest until it hurt, of *wanting* something so much yet fearing it was out of reach. Hope was an indulgence I rarely allowed myself. When your days are dark, you forget the existence of dawn.

Grandfather stroked the top of my head. "Accept the lotus. We'll flee then, returning here once it's safe." He spoke with the rhythmic cadence of recounting a tale.

A crash erupted in the distance, the roof of a nearby hall caving in. Grandfather didn't waver, pushing the lotus toward me. I hesitated, yet there was no one I trusted more. What did I have to lose? I was dying anyway.

I took the flower from him, cradling it in my hands. Warm to the touch, soothing the bitter chill in my body. The petals quivered, disintegrating into shining flecks that trailed toward me, vanishing into my chest. Warmth flashed, morphing into a feverish heat that surged through my veins. I buckled over, feeling as though the seams of my body were coming undone. A cry hovered but I bit my tongue, afraid to alert those we were fleeing from. One breath, then another. All the while, the blistering fire raged inside, followed by an icy numbness that left me unable to move or speak.

"Liyen!"

Someone called my name, Aunt Shou rushing into the courtyard. Part of her gray hair had unraveled from its coils, a jade hairpin dangling askew. Aunt Shou was one of my grandfather's trusted confidantes, my mother's closest friend—and another guardian to me after my parents' death from illness. Though I'd been too young then to fully comprehend my loss, the memories of my father and mother still hazy like a half-formed dream, it always felt like something was missing from my life.

As Aunt Shou pressed a cool palm to my forehead, her son, Chengyin, joined us. He crouched down beside me, his brown eyes clouding with concern. Aunt Shou had adopted him as an infant, abandoned, possibly due to the birthmark across his temple.

7

"Unlucky," the soothsayers had proclaimed him, but Aunt Shou had ignored them all. Chengyin was my best friend now, despite our contentious childhood when he'd pulled my hair and laughed at me without an ounce of respect for my position. Only later did I realize what a gift this was, that he'd always seen me for myself.

"What's wrong with Liyen?" Aunt Shou demanded. "Why can't she move or speak?"

"I gave the Divine Pearl Lotus to her," Grandfather said heavily.

The fine lines around Aunt Shou's eyes creased deeper. "I thought you were keeping it for Queen Caihong," she whispered. "Her Majesty is here for the lotus. She's furious that you ignored her summons and is waiting for you in the main hall with the God of War. The immortals won't cease their attacks until the lotus is surrendered."

I stared in mute horror at my grandfather, remorse clawing me. While I'd suspected the lotus wasn't of my world, maybe of magic forbidden to us . . . still, I'd taken it. I wanted to live. But I never expected it to have been stolen from the immortal queen.

Grandfather pressed a hand to his forehead. "Shou-yen, you've lost a daughter; you know the pain. Back then, if there was a chance of saving Damei—would you have hesitated?"

Aunt Shou closed her eyes. "I would have done anything I could."

"As I did," Grandfather said steadily. "I only learned about the antidote too late; the queen was already on her way. If I didn't take the Divine Pearl Lotus, the immortals would—and Liyen would die. She is the last of my line; I couldn't lose her, too."

"Why didn't you ask Queen Caihong?"

"When have the immortals ever weighed our desires more than theirs? Queen Caihong's command was clear; the lotus is precious to her. Moreover, her temper is volatile of late. If I'd asked, she would have refused, even been angered—and the chance to take it would be gone."

Aunt Shou clasped her hands, her body drooping. "The immortals will show us no mercy. Their God of War will burn Tianxia to the ground."

Grandfather lifted his head, silvered by moonlight. "I will confess and ask that the punishment falls on me alone. I was going to do so, after bringing Liyen to safety."

No! Mine was a cry with no voice; I was a ghost in this moment, a shell. It was like my mind was awake but my body pinned down, leaving me helpless.

Aunt Shou gripped Grandfather's sleeve. "You must be careful. What if they hurt you?"

"Then that is the price I'll pay for my theft." He patted her arm, then drew away. "I brought this calamity upon us. I will bear the penalty, even if it's my life."

"I spoke in haste. The gods will forget. They might forgive—"

"They will do neither." Grandfather's smile was so bright and resolute, it hurt. "You spoke the truth, my friend. You have always spoken the truth to me, even when no one else dared to—which is why your words bear weight."

"What of Liyen?" Aunt Shou was pale. "You have to think of her, too."

"I think of her *always*. It's why I did this—to give her a chance," he replied.

I flinched where I lay sprawled on the ground.

"What will happen if the immortals find her?" Aunt Shou asked. "What will they do to her if they discover the lotus?"

"You must hide Liyen until the Divine Pearl Lotus has merged with her body. Only then will its presence be concealed, and she can safely return here. Once the lotus has bonded with another, it cannot be seized—only gifted through a willing heart." My grandfather touched Aunt Shou's shoulder. "Can I count on you to look after her?"

I wanted to tell him to stay with us, that I'd gladly let the immortals pry their prize from my flesh if they'd let him go—but I had no voice to claim my thoughts, weeping tears that would not form.

"Yes." Aunt Shou's voice broke with emotion. "I will treat her as my own."

Grandfather nodded. "Take her with you. Now. A safehouse has been prepared, south of the wall. I will delay the immortals to give you time to flee."

As he folded me into his arms, a gray anguish clouded my heart. If I closed my eyes to this nightmare, I could almost imagine I was back in bed and he was bidding me good night—if not for the salt of fear that clung to his skin and the tears wetting the cheek pressed to mine.

Hate engulfed me at the gods who demanded our obedience yet did not answer our prayers, who threatened our lives for the slightest offense, lashing our world with misfortune when they were displeased. I cared not whether the rules were on their side this time, that their actions were deemed justified—

If they hurt my family . . . they would pay.

Grandfather bent to unfasten an ornament that hung by his waist, then tied it to mine. The imperial seal, the yellow jade carved with a round shield, said to be a sacred relic of our kingdom. My grandfather had never been without it, and for him to yield this now broke my heart.

"Live a good life, Liyen. Don't waste yourself in grief or vengeance. I want no regrets for you." Grandfather's words rang clear. "Watch over Tianxia: seek peace and happiness for our people, rule with compassion and strength. Serve the immortal queen loyally and maybe you can secure what I failed to—our people's freedom. We can't live behind these walls forever. The world beyond is part of ours too."

He hugged me tight, and when he released me and strode

away—such pain pierced me, worse than any poison. How I willed myself to break free to stop him, my pleas buried in the silence of my mind.

Aunt Shou took my hand in her papery one. "Liyen, you must be strong. Your grandfather knew the risks of stealing from the gods. If you offend the Queen of the Golden Desert, you will condemn not just yourself but your people, too." She closed her eyes briefly. "I hate this, but the price must be paid. Your grandfather accepted it, so must we. Whatever happens, I will honor my promise to your grandfather to keep you safe."

As Chengyin clasped my hand, my gaze beseeched him for aid. "I'm sorry," he whispered. "It's too dangerous here. We must get you to safety."

Aunt Shou nodded to Chengyin, and he hoisted me upon his back with ease. I had lost weight over the past weeks, my body frail.

"The Eastern Gate is closer," he suggested with a glance at me.

Hope flared, mingled with gratitude. We had to pass the main hall to get to the Eastern Gate. Chengyin was trying to help, bringing me to where my grandfather would be. As we hurried through the courtyard, I recoiled inwardly from the screams throttling the air, the drift of ash, the flames devouring the wooden beams—and most of all, from the gleam of the immortals' armor as they stalked through my home.

Closer to the main hall, Chengyin's steps slowed as he lagged behind Aunt Shou. He shifted so I might see within, to catch a glimpse of my grandfather. A tall immortal stood in the center of the hall, his black armor edged in gold, a cloak falling from his shoulders. The hilt of a large sword protruded from his back, carved of white jade and gold. Danger emanated from the tautness of his form, the weapons he bore—not just the sword, but the bow slung over his back, the daggers tucked into his waistband. The

God of War, the one who'd set my home afire. And seated behind him, upon my grandfather's throne, must be Queen Caihong, the ruler of the Golden Desert. Her shining headdress reflected glimmers of the flames outside, her dark-red lips pulled into a hard slash.

Grandfather knelt before them, his forehead pressed to the ground. Gray hair poked from his topknot, his robe wrinkled and stained. As he rose, he said something I couldn't hear. The God of War raised his hand, alight with a crimson glow—my heart quailing—but his magic streaked through the doorway, settling over the flames beyond, that extinguished as suddenly as they'd flared to life.

As the cries outside subsided, my grandfather's voice carried from where he knelt on the floor. "Thank you, Honored Immortal."

"You have surrendered. The people have done no wrong," the god replied, his voice resonant and clear.

Anger flashed. This was no mercy but to gild the image they wanted to portray, to parade the immensity of their power that we were helpless against. For the gods desired to be seen as great, just, and wise—thriving on worship and admiration. And they cannot bear insult or defiance, to be thought of as weak, infallible . . . or mortal.

"Zhao Likang." The queen enunciated each syllable of my grandfather's name. "Where is the Divine Pearl Lotus? When it bloomed on Kunlun Mountain, I ordered you to bring it to me. As the ruler of Tianxia, you are the only mortal who can enter there to harvest the flower, so it was you who'd plucked it. Yet now we can no longer sense its presence."

Kunlun Mountain? I'd wanted to go with Grandfather before, and now I knew why he'd refused. It was our kingdom's most important duty to watch over this place, as Kunlun was once the sole pathway to the heavens and to the Netherworld—though the immortals had sealed the way there.

"Your Majesty, I harvested the Divine Pearl Lotus as commanded and brought it here. It was closely guarded . . . but was stolen." Grandfather bowed his head. "I have failed you, and will endure any punishment you impose."

Grandfather lied so flawlessly, more in what he concealed than shared. While he disliked deception, it was a vital skill when dealing with the court. Once, he'd told me: *"There are lies of necessity and those of malice. Those you choose to tell will define your character."*

And now he'd done this to save us all, to ensure none suffered the immortals' wrath but him.

"Stolen? How did that happen?" Queen Caihong's voice sharpened. "Rise, and come closer so I can read the truth in your face."

Grandfather pushed himself slowly to his feet. He was afraid, of course he was. The immortal queen's displeasure had borne bitter fruit in the past, not just of fire but harsh storms, torrential rain, relentless floods. But his pallor sent a rush of unease through me, his movements uneven and halting as he walked toward her. A gasp tore from his throat as he collapsed—his hand pressed to his chest like it hurt.

His heart!

Terror choked me. I tried to cry out for a physician, struggling to move, to go to him. The God of War stalked forward and laid his hand on my grandfather's chest. As his fingers glowed like the burning tips of incense, I wanted to shove him away.

"Can you help him?" Queen Caihong asked.

"This injury can't be healed by us. It is bred by time, formed of the mortal body," the God of War said coldly, like it meant nothing to him.

"Find one of the mortal physicians," the queen ordered.

Aunt Shou was hurrying toward Chengyin and me. Her eyes rounded at the sight of my grandfather in the hall, a hand pressed to her lips. As she started forward, Chengyin caught her arm. "Mother, if they find us—they'll find Liyen. We must send a physician, then go."

Before Aunt Shou could reply, a frail cry slid from within the hall. Grandfather's head had fallen back, his body jerking, then going terrifyingly still. The God of War bent to pick up his hand. After a moment he shook his head, his palm brushing down my grandfather's eyelids.

"He is dead."

Grief wrung me, twisting my heart till it was shriveled, till I thought it had broken apart. I was screaming inside, though no one could hear.

The God of War rose, raising his voice to his warriors outside. "Seal the gates. None are allowed out until we find the Divine Pearl Lotus."

"Chengyin, hurry!" Aunt Shou tugged at him, tears running down her face. "We must go *now*."

Chengyin carried me away, following her. I didn't want to go, but there was nothing I could do now—whether to weep, rage, or even mourn.

As we slipped out the gate, a gong was struck, the bleak sound reverberating through the night. Four times it clanged, plunging through the stillness left in its wake. The end of a reign. A blink, a breath—a lifetime gone.

I would never see my grandfather again. All that remained were his words to me, unfinished lessons, unfulfilled dreams . . . those the immortals had crushed. Something hardened in my chest. I would not go the way Grandfather had, kneeling before the immortals, dedicating my life to their loyal service, fearing their merciless justice. He deserved better, as did our people. And I would forge a new path for us, to set us free of these ruthless gods.

2

The stillness of the forest was startling after the chaos of the palace. Above, the trees loomed like shadows of giants, blanketing the night. The darkness was eased only by the curve of the moon, the lantern of the skies.

I was crying, my tears soaking through Chengyin's robe. Tonight, the pillars of my life had vanished as though the earth had split apart and swallowed them whole. All that was left were fragments I was trying to pick my way through: heir to an uncertain throne, descendant of the dead.

I missed my grandfather—a bitter realization dawning, that I would miss him for the rest of my days. For so long, I had leaned on him, and now I was truly alone. It didn't feel right leaving his body behind, though we had no choice then. If we'd been caught, everything my grandfather had sacrificed would be in vain. The moment I returned home, I would prepare the offerings that would pave his journey to the afterlife, build him a great tomb, and lay his memorial tablet with our ancestors.

A drawn breath slid from me. At last, the effects of the Divine Pearl Lotus were wearing off. I could move a little, my voice frail. But what use was this now?

"He's gone," I whispered brokenly, my heart brittle with pain. If I said it again, would it hurt less?

15

"I'm sorry," Chengyin said quietly, shifting me upon his back. "I will miss him. He was stern but always fair. Kind, too, especially to those less fortunate."

"We all loved him." Aunt Shou's eyes were red, her voice raw with weeping.

"Grandfather is dead . . . because of me." Such heaviness sank over me, my grief bound with guilt.

"You can't blame yourself for being poisoned, you might as well blame the Divine Pearl Lotus for flowering," Aunt Shou said fiercely. "Your grandfather didn't do this because of you, but because he *loved* you."

I closed my eyes, unable to stop my tears. Aunt Shou stroked my head, brushing the lock of silvery hair from my face—the one some recoiled from, the mark of the waters of death. Most days, I preferred to tuck it beneath the rest of my hair to hide it, but nothing mattered anymore.

"I know it hurts. It will take time. Though the pain won't ever go away, it does get easier." Her eyes were haunted, as whenever she thought of her daughter.

"Does it still hurt when you think of her?" I asked haltingly.

"Every day," she admitted. "But it would hurt more if I didn't. And I'm blessed to have another child." She took Chengyin's hand, brushing her thumb across it.

Grandfather used to hold my hand that way, during those feverish nights when I'd been clasped in the poison's grip. *"If only I could trade my life for yours,"* he'd whisper when he thought I couldn't hear.

And now he'd found a way.

I closed my eyes, trying to breathe through the tightness in my chest. It would be easy to spiral into despair, festering in anger and regret—but I would not waste the life Grandfather had secured for me.

Live a good life . . . I want no regrets for you.

His last words were a comfort, except the thoughts in my mind were not those he'd have wished. I would find my peace *after* I'd secured our dream for Tianxia, after I made those who'd wronged him pay.

Yet a small voice inside me whispered that the immortals were not *wholly* to blame. My grandfather stole the lotus, and his heart was already weak when he faced them. They hadn't killed him . . . though it was easier to blame them, easier to hate than to bear the unadulterated sorrow. Still, his fear of them *had* caused his death; they weren't without guilt. A god's anger was far more dangerous than a mortal's, capable of inflicting far greater suffering. It shouldn't be this way; such power should be used to protect the weak instead of to harm them.

The immortals might not have been Grandfather's enemy, but they were mine. I did not possess my grandfather's calm temperament, his steady patience and devotion—only broken once through his love for me. Despite the misgivings of the court, he'd raised me to rule, entrusting the kingdom he loved into my hands. Our dreams were the same, for Tianxia to be released from the immortals' service, to bring down the walls that kept us in—yet our mind followed different paths.

What the gods did not give us, I would take.

My fingers curled, my strength returning in a rush, like falling headlong into a lake. My body tingled, my senses alive, the fog in my mind clearing. Something burned in my chest, searing against my skin. I rubbed it to find a hard ridge the size of a coin—a pale scar, newly formed. What did this mean? Had the lotus bonded with me?

Chengyin's pace was slowing; he was tired after bearing my weight all this while. I tapped his shoulder. "You don't have to carry me anymore. I can walk."

When he lowered me down, I weaved on my feet. Aunt Shou caught my arm to steady me, her gaze searching. "How do you feel?"

"I'm all right, Aunt Shou." I paused, trying to decipher these changes. It was like a shell around me had broken, and I was just beginning to emerge. The fatigue, the cold, my aches, were gone. It should have been a moment of joy and relief, but it was rife with bitterness. I would trade it all back for my grandfather, but death struck no bargains once its victory was sealed.

"Liyen, what do you want to do now?" Chengyin asked. "Rest here a while, or head to the wall?"

I straightened, raising my head. "We must go on. We can't risk being found yet." I wanted to delay the moment when I had to face the immortals, not just because of the lotus but until I could safely leash my anger and grief.

"Will we be safe by the wall?" Chengyin wondered. "It will be quiet, with only a few guards posted there."

What need was there for guards when none could get in or out?

"Maybe that's why Grandfather told us to go there," I replied.

We made our way as quickly as we could, and for once I did not fall behind. A gift, but at what price? In the distance, the wall towered, the red stone flecked with gold. If the heart of Tianxia was Kunlun Mountain, the wall was its body, fitted to the contours of our lands. It was said to be crafted by the immortals, for who else could have polished the stone until it shimmered like copper, enchanted to withstand any weapon, attack, or attempt to scale it. Nor was there any hope of tunneling beneath, for the magic of the wall seemed to extend into the very foundations of the earth— cleaving us from the rest of the Mortal Realm. The only way it could be brought down was if the immortals chose to do so.

Grandfather had told me the wall was built to conceal us from the outside, to protect us from those who desired our secrets. But I was starting to believe it was also to keep us in.

It was quiet here, not even a single guard present. Were they all asleep? Had they become lax in their duties, dulled by peace?

Shrines were built along part of the wall, the largest of which was painted bright ochre, the roof tiles gilded. A small statue carved in the supposed likeness of the God of War was housed within, wielding a spear in one hand and a sword in the other. While all gods were immortals, only those worshiped by the mortals were deemed a "god." The God of War was revered by those who strove to excel in his arts, warriors praying for his favor before any battle or skirmish. Offerings had been laid out of roasted meats, fruit, and small cakes. Before it lay a brass burner crammed with incense sticks, wisps of smoke spiraling to the heavens. The God of War reaped the finest of offerings, for the fear of death opened the purse strings of even the tightest miser.

The statues in the temples seemed so cold and distant, but as a child, it had comforted me to reach for them in times of need— when there were fears and wishes I dared not share with another.

"Do you pray, Aunt Shou?" I asked numbly.

"Not since my daughter died." She gestured toward the shrines, her lip curling. "The gods ignore these humble, well-intentioned offerings, those desperate for their favor. It is the slights to their pride that snare their attention, causing them to strike us with misfortune."

She faced me as she continued, "It was not prayers that saved you today but your grandfather's sacrifice, his bravery in defying the immortals' wishes. They would have killed him, had his heart had not given out first."

My chest clenched, her words resonating. "They didn't deserve Grandfather's devotion. Why do we still serve them, all these years after the war?"

Aunt Shou sighed, shaking her head. "Who will dare refuse? The immortals are selfish, showing little compassion or mercy when we falter—as they did with your grandfather today. They terrify, demand, and bend us to their will."

"Devotion should be earned, not demanded," I said bitterly.

"Yes, my child," she said sadly. "But it's far easier to demand it than to earn it."

Aunt Shou led us toward a small building, the tiles chipped, paint peeling from the walls. Yet the courtyard was newly swept, sacks of provisions stacked within.

"I hope we don't have to stay too long. I must see to Grandfather's burial. The court will be in chaos." Already the burdens of duty weighed a little heavier. Though I'd been the heir, I'd not liked thinking of ascending the throne, imagining my grandfather's death.

"We'll stay as long as we need to. As your grandfather said, we must be sure the lotus has bonded with you," Aunt Shou advised.

I touched the scar that had formed, the intensity of the heat mellowing to a soothing warmth. "I think it has."

Chengyin was staring at the skies, frowning as he gestured to me. A fragrance wafted in the air, sickly sweet with a sourish undertone like rotted plums. It was growing darker, like the moon had been swallowed—unease prickling across the back of my neck. Had the immortals found us? Tall forms appeared on the horizon, drawing closer with the velvet steps of a cat. Their faces were like ours, though I recoiled from the sharp points of their teeth and the waxy sheen of their skin. Claws arched from their fingers, and small gray wings flared from their backs, something bright shining from their foreheads like a yellowish gem.

"Who are you? Why are you here?" A tremor broke my tone.

"Why are *you* here, Lady of Tianxia?" one of them asked patronizingly, a glint in its eyes. "Are you fleeing from your new mistress?"

The title jarred . . . as did the realization that they knew who I was. Terror flared, even as their contempt seared me. "Our land is under the protection of the Queen of the Golden Desert," I declared. "Leave now."

Bold words, yet meaningless when we had little means of defending ourselves against such beings. We were a kingdom of warriors, trained to serve—yet mortal blades could not shed immortal blood, whether god or monster. The queen was reluctant to arm us with the tools that could wound them, too—relinquishing just a few weapons to us, barely enough to outfit a single troop. Grandfather had given a dagger to me and a sword to Chengyin, and I never imagined I'd see them used.

"What is the Queen of the Golden Desert's protection worth? Where are her soldiers?" The creatures grinned as they closed around us at a languid pace. No need for haste when we were trapped.

Chengyin moved in front of Aunt Shou, his sword drawn. My hand shook as I grasped my dagger. I was no warrior—unable to train as rigorously as the others in my childhood, with neither the appetite nor inclination for battle, the sight of blood turning my stomach. If I were honest, life in the palace surrounded by guards and attendants had draped me in an illusion of safety—one that had been swiftly ripped away tonight.

The creatures glided closer. Five, when one would have sufficed to end us. Light flared in their eyes, the stones in their foreheads—was it the excitement of the hunt? The prey within their grasp?

Something sparked inside me. It wasn't over yet.

I dove down, snatching up a handful of soil, then flung it into the faces of the monsters. A screeching erupted, their wings flapping wildly.

"Run!" I yelled to Chengyin and Aunt Shou.

We raced back toward the forest, hoping to lose them there. There wasn't much time; these creatures could outpace us at any moment. In the distance, moonlight glinted over the roof tiles of the shrines. A wild idea flashed through my mind.

It is the slights to their pride that snare their attention.

I turned sharply, running toward the shrines as fast as I could.

The monsters were gaining on me, one swiping at my legs with its claws. As I stumbled, I collided into the incense burner by the God of War's shrine. It teetered, then crashed onto its side—incense scattering like twigs, ash spilling like powder.

My insides twisted. This was the best and worst one to ruin. Dangerous, to summon the God of War—but choices were sparse when faced with imminent death. Yet the god didn't know I possessed the lotus they sought, and he wouldn't kill me without cause. As the Lady of Tianxia, I could claim the immortals' protection. Wasn't this why we served them?

I lunged toward the offerings laid out by a devout follower. As one of the monsters leapt at me, I swung aside at the last moment—the creature losing balance and crashing into the plates of food. Cakes crumbled, pears rolling away as the cups tipped over, spilling wine upon the earth.

Claws curled around my wrist, nails digging into my flesh. Blood oozed, leaking into the soil, forming a paste with the ash. As the creature's lips parted a tongue slid out, the shade of a ripe bruise. A scream erupted from my throat, shrill with fear. Chengyin fought his way toward me, hacking at the monsters, but he was too far away. I was trembling as I raised my dagger, slashing wildly at the one that held me, but it struck my arm aside with ease.

"Halt, or the old woman dies." A sibilant hiss. I turned to find one of the monsters holding Aunt Shou, a claw pressed to the vein in her neck.

I froze at once. "What do you want from us?"

A taunting laugh from the one who'd seized me. "Relinquish your weapons. Come with us; don't struggle, and you'll be safe. Fight back, and we'll dine on mortal flesh tonight."

The urge to retch crested. A hateful thing, this helplessness—to be at the mercy of these creatures. Could I trust them? I didn't want to; my instincts screaming, but was there a choice?

As I began to nod, Chengyin shouted, "No, Liyen! Don't believe them."

The monster beside him snarled, striking the side of his head. As he cried out, rage flooded me. With a burst of newfound strength, I swung my dagger at the creature restraining me, driving the blade into its neck. The skin gave way to a quivering softness, rust-hued blood oozing forth.

Monsters bleed as mortals do.

The thought gave me heart, even as the sight sickened me. As its hold on my wrist slackened, I tore free—but another grabbed me around the waist, lifting me until my head swam.

"You'll pay for that," it rasped.

I kicked wildly, trying to yank free. Grandfather hadn't saved me to be killed by these vicious beings. But they stilled abruptly, their heads darting up.

Fire carved the skies, seething and hissing. A blazing bolt hurtled down, plunging into the monster. Its shriek was like the shattering of glass, a hole gaping where its chest had once been— ragged flesh, quivering and wet. As the monster's grip around me loosened, I wrenched away. My body slammed against the ground, the breath knocked from my chest. The creature collapsed on the ground beside me, its blood muddying the soil.

The heavens blazed, molten flame now raining upon us. I crouched down, shielding my head with my arms—but nothing struck me. All around, the wind billowed stronger, tearing my hair from its coils. Loud cracks ruptured the air as shafts of crimson light speared the ground, caging the monsters. Above, a cloud swept from the skies, bearing a single figure upon it clad in black armor, a sword of white jade and gold slung over his shoulder.

The God of War.

3

The immortal's face was like winter, chiseled from ice and snow. At the sight of him, my body tensed, relief and dread twined so tightly together I couldn't pick them apart. I hated him, the memory he evoked of my grandfather kneeling before him—even though he'd just saved my life.

The god was watching me, his eyes alight as they traveled my length, pausing at my sash where the imperial seal hung. Ash and blood stained my robe, my hair spilling across my shoulders. I should be afraid of him—terrified, even—yet anger sparked at his intrusive stare.

"Why are you looking at me?" I demanded, like there was nothing to hide, even as I feared he could somehow sense the Divine Pearl Lotus. Fortunately, he'd given no sign of it, his expression unchanged—almost indifferent.

His mouth curled. "Curiosity, nothing more. Who are you?"

Was this a test? After all, the god had seen the seal. I dared not lie; the truth would emerge soon enough. "Zhao Liyen, the Lady of Tianxia—the last descendant of Zhao Likang." I claimed the title that was now mine.

"Lady of Tianxia?" he repeated slowly. "I thought the heir was dead. I didn't realize there was another."

"My father passed away. I am his only child, granddaughter to the Lord of Tianxia." Except Grandfather was dead. I swallowed, holding the god's gaze. It was no surprise that few outside the palace knew of my existence. Most didn't think I'd survive to claim the throne, and Grandfather was cautious with what he shared with the immortals, as were most of the people here.

"Why aren't you in the palace? Why are you here?" he asked.

"When my home was attacked, my grandfather ordered me to leave for my safety. Only later did I learn of his death." I tried to push down my grief and—far more dangerous—my rage. The god hadn't struck Grandfather, yet not all weapons were crafted of iron; not all wounds were of the flesh.

He said nothing, not even offering words of condolence. Immortals had no comprehension of death, of what it meant to lose a loved one. Maybe all of them were cursed with hearts of ice. As light flickered at the god's fingertips, Chengyin cried out in warning, rushing to shield me—but a shimmering barrier sprang up around him and Aunt Shou, keeping us a distance apart. The god didn't look their way as he reached for me. I darted back, but he caught my arm with surprising gentleness. A soothing warmth rippled from his fingers, healing the punctures gouged by the creature's claws.

I pulled away, stiffening from his touch. His eyes narrowed as they swung to my face. Was I being ungrateful? Rude? In the silence, I opened my mouth to thank him, then shut it again. He didn't deserve gratitude, not after what he'd done to my grandfather and my home.

"Who hurt you?" Softly spoken, yet rife with menace.

"They did." I nodded at the monsters still trapped in the god's fiery cage. Four left, one dead.

He unslung his sword, setting its point on the ground. "This land falls under Queen Caihong's domain. Winged Devils have no place here."

They bowed in unison. "We were mistaken, Great Immortal.

25

We will obey Queen Caihong's command, and leave."

The God of War tilted his head back as he studied them. "Do you still do the bidding of the Wuxin?"

I flinched, the word enough to make my blood run cold. It was the Wuxin who had invaded Tianxia, descending the skies through Kunlun Mountain, causing great devastation and suffering. The Golden Desert immortals had helped my people drive them away, which was why we served them now.

"How could we, when the Wuxin are sealed in the Netherworld?" one of the Winged Devils replied, a little too quickly.

"Then why are you here?" As the God of War's voice dropped ominously low, a chill glided through the air.

"To search for my friend," one said smoothly, gesturing at the body on the ground. "He wanted to visit this realm. We meant no harm."

Convenient, as the dead could not speak. "A lie," I said at once. "They attacked us together."

The God of War stepped closer to the Winged Devils. "Why did you attack the girl and her companions? Tell me now, else I will show you no mercy."

"You are not entitled to our answers." Gone was their respectful demeanor, their false subservience.

The four remaining creatures lifted their hands, a grayish mist swirling forth. As the god's barrier that held them broke—they circled us, eyes bright with malevolence.

Terror gripped me, but the god appeared unshaken. "Stay behind me," he commanded, with an almost infuriating calm.

"What of my friends? You're still holding them. Release them so they can escape."

"I will protect them."

Such confidence . . . I did not share it. Yet in this moment, the God of War that I loathed and feared was the only thing standing between us and death.

Without warning, one of the Winged Devils lunged toward us. The god unsheathed his sword swiftly, thrusting the blade into the creature's side—then drew back seamlessly to stab another Winged Devil. One sprang at me but I scrambled back, the god's sword arcing over my head, moon-bright, carving the creature's neck. Blood sprayed, warm droplets scattering across my face. I would have screamed if I were not half-frozen with fear. The god moved with deadly grace, dealing each blow with iron control yet unrestrained brutality. His expression betrayed neither strain nor fear, not even triumph or bloodlust. As the last remaining creature charged at him, the god lashed out, plunging his sword into the monster's chest. It reared back, staring at the blood that flowed forth, swiping curved talons at the god's face. But the immortal swung back, bolts of flame arcing from his palm to strike the creature, burning rivulets along its flesh. The creature shuddered in a grotesque rhythm, finally collapsing upon the ground.

Were they dead? One of them still writhed, a soft groan slipping out. The God of War crouched down, turning its head toward him. "Answer my questions and I will spare your life."

The Winged Devil bared its teeth as it raised a shaking hand, dragging a claw across its neck. Blood spilled, its body jerking violently and then going still.

I fell to my knees and vomited. Sourish and acrid, my throat raw, my stomach churning as I sank upon the grass. Reaching for the waterskin, I lifted it to my lips and took a long drink, then poured the rest over my face to wash the blood from it. When I looked up, the god was staring at me. Humiliation seared me at being seen this way. Did he scorn my weakness? I pushed my chin out as though daring him to mock me.

Instead, he sheathed his sword, his breathing a little uneven, his eyes pinched with strain.

"Are you hurt?" I asked, though it seemed impossible.

"No," he replied, his tone clipped.

"I see why they call you the God of War." It wasn't a compliment; it was no gift to possess an unsurpassed talent for killing.

"I don't like that name," he replied, though another might have reveled in the power the title conferred.

"Why?" I shouldn't have asked, I shouldn't care.

The eyes he turned to me were blacker than coal. "What is war if not suffering and death? Who would want to be the harbinger of such strife?"

"Doesn't the God of War thrive on power, fear, and glory?" I asked bitterly.

Dark flames leapt in his pupils. "You think there is glory in this? You think I feel triumph?" His voice was harsh as his eyes flicked across the bodies on the ground. "You speak from ignorance."

"Ignorance?" I repeated, fury seeping into every part of me. "How am I ignorant? Because I don't possess your infinite years?"

"Not quite infinite." His smile was vicious and mirthless. "Your ignorance stems from the fact you don't know me, yet are content to judge."

As remorse flashed through me, I stifled it. "I know that you burned my home. I know my grandfather is dead."

As he glanced at Aunt Shou and Chengyin, restrained a distance away, I was glad they couldn't hear me. Aunt Shou would have rebuked me for speaking to the God of War in this manner. My emotions were making me careless; I needed to guard my words better.

"I did not kill your grandfather," he said bluntly. "If you were told otherwise, you've been misled."

I couldn't tell him what I'd seen; it would lead to too many questions. "Then why did my grandfather die after earning the displeasure of your queen?" I said instead.

"Those who fail Her Majesty cannot be allowed to go unpunished—yet mortals are rarely sentenced to death," he said curtly. "Your grandfather's passing was unintended, caused by an existing illness of his heart."

"Should I be grateful that he was frightened to death?" My voice choked with anger.

"I'm not asking for gratitude," he said tightly. "Just don't misplace your hate."

I fell silent. Maybe he believed he'd done nothing wrong, but he had. Still, I reined in my temper; he held my life in his hands. Nothing would bring Grandfather back, but my actions could invite harsher reprisal on me, on my kingdom. And I didn't like speaking of my grandfather to him. My grief was my own, not for a stranger's speculation. It was too raw, too sharp . . . it hurt too much.

Stepping back, I found my shoes damp with the blood pooling from the Winged Devils' bodies. My skin crawled. "Why did he kill himself?"

"Perhaps they fear the consequence of betrayal more than death."

"What could be worse than death?" I asked.

"Many things."

"Only an immortal would think so." I smiled to conceal my scorn. "Immortals never fall ill or age. You've never been held back by the frailty of your body, the health time steals. You are the masters of your destiny, the keepers of your fate. No wonder you disdain death."

His eyes flashed. "We don't suffer from illnesses, but I have borne more wounds on my finger than you have in your lifetime. What do you know of the dangers of our realm, what we suffer?"

I looked at the creatures sprawled around us. "They come into our world, too, except we can't fight them as you do."

A brief pause. "What did the Winged Devils want with you?" he asked then.

"I know as much as you, Honored Immortal." I forced out the

honorific reluctantly. "There were a few rumored sightings close to Kunlun, but our soldiers found nothing. How are they connected to the Wuxin?"

"They were allies once, switching to our side when it was clear the Wuxin would lose the war. Since then, they've lived quietly among us—or so we thought." He frowned. "They can't be trusted, but Queen Caihong allowed them to keep their home in the Golden Desert, as long as they don't break the peace."

"What of tonight?" I asked. "What of this attack on us?"

"I will discuss it with Her Majesty. We will investigate the matter."

My hands clenched but I held my tongue. Mortals were dispensable, after all. If the Winged Devils had attacked the Golden Desert, Queen Caihong would have struck them all down without hesitation, without mercy.

"I am new to the throne, but always believed it was the immortals' duty to protect our kingdom against such enemies from the skies," I said carefully.

The god's gaze narrowed. "What of your duty to guard the Divine Pearl Lotus, the one your grandfather so carelessly lost?"

"He was not careless." I didn't dare say more, though it was a relief he hadn't disregarded my grandfather's claim. "If I don't know my duties, it's because Grandfather didn't have a chance to teach them to me."

"You are an adult. You should have learned your responsibilities by now."

How dare *he lecture me?* I wanted to strike this unfeeling immortal. But I was no longer a child—I was the Lady of Tianxia. I no longer acted for myself alone. Inhaling deeply to suppress my anger, I looked away, letting the god think I'd been rebuked.

"Did you know your grandfather was ill?" he asked.

"Yes. But he was still strong. He should not have died tonight." My chest ached. "You are fortunate that your people know little of such loss."

His jaw tightened. "We know more than you think."

I folded my arms across my chest. "Enlighten me."

"No," he said. "Not when your mind is set against us, your judgment clouded by prejudice, your heart shadowed with sorrow."

I didn't push further. I was tired, hollowed through after tonight. "Then let me go home, if you've stopped destroying it." There was no longer a reason to hide here. It was clear he could not sense the lotus; I'd already be in chains if he did.

He shook his head. "You should return with me. Every ruler of Tianxia must swear their loyalty to our queen before taking the throne. You may have the title, but only after your pledge to Her Majesty will you receive her mandate to rule."

I recoiled, unable to help myself, but I concealed it by smoothing down my bloodstained robe. "I'm not ready. This isn't a fitting way to introduce myself to the queen."

When I visited the Queen of the Golden Desert, it would be on my own terms. A chance to visit the realm of immortals was a rare opportunity. Grandfather's last wish was engraved in my heart, my resolve hardening with each moment. Our people should not be bound to the skies when our lives were *here*. I needed to find a way to set us free, or persuade the queen to do so.

"Will you disobey Her Majesty's command?"

"I'm only asking for time to make myself presentable, to set my affairs in order after the turmoil of tonight," I protested, refusing to let myself be daunted by him.

His gaze was penetrating. "Until you receive our queen's mandate to be acknowledged as Tianxia's lawful ruler, your position is vulnerable."

It already was, but not for the reasons he thought. Someone had poisoned me—but if I mentioned this, he might insist that I follow him at once.

"There is another reason," I told him heavily. "I must bury my grandfather . . . prepare the funeral and rites he deserves. You may not understand this, but it's important to me. My last chance to bid him farewell."

Silence fell over us. "I understand saying goodbye, perhaps more than you know," he said at last, his tone unreadable. Then he added abruptly, "One month."

More than I expected, but I'd learned to never take a first offer. As I opened my mouth to bargain for more, he raised his hand. "I won't allow more. During this time, your palace will be placed under my protection, and you must not leave its grounds. This is for your own safety," he added, looking at the bodies on the ground.

As I nodded stiffly, he continued, "In four weeks, an escort will be sent to bring you to the Immortal Realm. Any absence will be considered a grave insult to our queen. If you hide, I will find you. Run, and I will catch you."

A sliver of fear pierced me. *He'd said I don't know him*, I reminded myself. *Nor does he know me. I won't bow before them; I won't accept the fate they've charted for us.*

"You have my word that I will be there," I told him.

The God of War held his hand out to me. A slender sword lay across his palm, its scabbard carved of black jade, wrapped in silver filigree.

My pulse quickened. "An immortal weapon?"

He glanced at the dagger tucked into my sash. "It will be of more use than that fruit slicer you carry."

His disdain for my grandfather's gift angered me. "I stabbed a Winged Devil with this." I tilted my head up to him, wishing he weren't so damned tall. "Maybe you'd like to be next," I said lightly, though I meant each word.

"I think I might." His tone matched mine, then hardened once more. "You were reckless to challenge one of those creatures. Don't you know how easily your life could be snuffed out?"

"Fortunately, I'm alive," I replied, yet his warning resonated.

I was lucky that he'd come, but I would never admit it. "Why are you giving this to me?" I wanted the sword, yet was afraid of the unseen cost.

"It's rare for the Winged Devils to attack here. You need to be able to defend yourself."

He assumed that I could fight, as most of my people could. I didn't correct him. But while I lacked training, I had tried to learn what I could, even from watching the others.

I took the sword from him before he changed his mind. No matter how I felt about him, I wouldn't spurn this priceless gift. Pride could not slay an enemy; it would not keep me alive. As I unsheathed the weapon, a current darted through my fingers, the blade seeming to glow. A magnificent sword; light yet strong.

"Thank you." It was hard to utter these words, but I had to get used to saying things to him that I didn't mean.

His gaze was bright as he inclined his head. "Keep it hidden," he cautioned me.

With a flick of his hand, the shining barrier around Chengyin and Aunt Shou dispersed. A cloud descended from the skies and landed by his feet. I watched as he stepped upon it, then soared into the heavens. My hand tightened around the sword. For a fleeting moment I imagined plunging it through the god's chest, how easily it would slide through. What color would he bleed? There was little satisfaction in these thoughts. While the God of War was an enemy, he'd also saved my life—an unwanted obligation. Yet it wouldn't change how I felt about him or his kind. Immortals could not be trusted. Their selfishness went deep, their rare kindnesses were calculated or accidental. They didn't care about us; they'd never treat us as their equals. To the immortals, we were nothing but tools, tossed aside once we broke.

That was why they didn't deserve our service, why we had to be free of them. And they'd soon learn that mortals don't break that easily, that we are stronger than we seem.

4

"Long live the Lady of Tianxia, may she rule for a hundred years," the court intoned.

Liars, I thought as I stepped up the dais to sit upon the throne. A farce we went through each morning since my grandfather's death. A sea of faces looked back at me, most wearing expressions of bland civility beneath their long-tailed hats, though a few could not hide their displeasure. Aunt Shou had warned they were gathering, bickering among themselves to plot the way forward. Some were angling for position, seeking my favor—as many plotting my downfall. The more ambitious courtiers resented me, having imagined I'd be in a coffin than on the throne. Had one of them poisoned me with the waters of the Wangchuan? If I ever found out, they'd learn what a grave mistake they'd made.

Power bred enmity, the worst kind that kept to the shadows, waiting to strike unseen.

My lips stretched into a thin smile—any wider and it would appear weak, a desire to please. How I disliked having to watch myself this way. To be in power was to have a constant light shone over you. While it glittered from afar, any flaws or mistakes were magnified tenfold. As the Lady of Tianxia, I had to weigh my words before speaking, to guard my emotions from the many eyes upon me.

Weeks had passed since Grandfather's death, but his loss was still a nail in my heart. I'd arranged his funeral wearing a mask of calm, breaking down only in the solitude of my room. I wanted to plunge the kingdom into mourning, to command bright colors to be shunned, to cancel the festivities—but my grandfather's will had stipulated that the rules of mourning were to be waived, for life to continue unhindered. And so I'd honored his wish, though it seemed almost a betrayal that life could go on . . . that it had not ceased the day he died.

For so long I'd leaned upon him, and now—despite the attendants and courtiers who surrounded me—I was truly alone. For that is the real meaning of loneliness, being unable to share your mind and heart freely with another without the fear of being judged or found wanting, or that they might seek to use you.

I quelled the urge to fidget though my head ached beneath my headdress of sapphire butterflies. Gold was my armor. I gilded myself in precious metals and stones not to flaunt my status but to imprint upon others these symbols of power, to rouse awe rather than desire. Maybe it was also to suppress my own doubt that I might be unworthy of the position, though I'd never admit it aloud.

As I stared at the court, I remembered asking Grandfather once, "Why are you so stern to the courtiers? Aren't you afraid they won't like you?"

He had smiled, patting my hand. "Rulers aren't just meant to be liked. Loved. Feared. Hated, perhaps—but what's most important is doing what is right." His expression had turned solemn. "Never show your enemy your weakness, Liyen. The wolves are waiting to pounce. The only way to stop them is to be the greater monster."

"What if I'm not?" I'd asked.

He'd crouched down to meet my gaze. "Pretend."

I straightened now, lifting my head. Sometimes it felt like I was assuming a role in a play that was greater than my talent, thrust into an ill-fitting costume. But I wouldn't shirk my part, though the burden grew each day. I wouldn't give up, just as Grandfather never gave up on me.

We cannot help how the dice fall, but it's our choice whether to keep playing.

Minister Guo sidled forward with a scroll in his hand, an oily smile on his broad face. He was one of the most ambitious among the courtiers, and I stiffened instinctively. "Your Ladyship, now the period of mourning has been lifted, we must discuss the *urgent* matter of your betrothal."

He spoke in a blustery tone, more a demand than a request. I shrank back, catching myself too late as the minster's lip curled. I'd heard the nobles were jostling for a hand in selecting my consort. Suitors would soon be lining up, mouthing false words of devotion when all they wanted was to rule in my place—to sire a child from my body to secure the succession, with no blood spilled but mine.

I had few illusions about my marriage, but one thing was certain: I would marry when I chose, not because I was told to. "Minister Guo, your timing is inappropriate." My tone was cutting. "While my grandfather waived the official requirements of mourning, *I* am still grieving for him."

Instead of offering an apology, the minister began unraveling the scroll, speaking with a condescending air. "We are discussing the possibilities, not arranging a wedding yet. Your Ladyship can use the time to get acquainted with your suitors, of which there are many."

My fingers clenched the armrest of my throne. Did he think I was so easily overruled? I followed the minister's gaze toward the back of the hall, where the "suitors" lounged. Some wore expressions of indifference, a few smiling too broadly. Most were likely hauled here by their family elders in hopes of whetting my appetite. They were handsome in the forgettable way, dressed in fine garments, with the languid air of the prosperous. None had the presence of the God of War—an unwelcome thought that I furiously buried.

Minister Guo cleared his throat. "Lord Baoshu, the eldest son of the Bao family, is highly eligible. He—"

"Is your godson?" I interjected.

The minster blinked but recovered with admirable ease. "What of Lord Yang? He is capable and virtuous and—"

"Well connected, as your nephew," I added, grateful to Chengyin for having shared all he knew of the younger nobles.

"Lord . . . Hong?"

I hesitated, struggling to think of something against the handsome and well-liked noble. Minister Guo's chest puffed up as he prepared to push me further.

"The same Lord Hong who is in your debt, Minister Guo?" It was Minister Hu who spoke as he limped to the front of the hall. He suffered from an inflammation of the joints that had worsened with age. While he was one of the more reserved courtiers, I trusted his opinion; his loyalty wasn't for sale.

I inclined my head in silent thanks to Minister Hu. "I will hear no more of suitors. *When* I choose to hear about this, however, I advise you to find more suitable candidates—those who will enrich our kingdom and not your own treasury."

Minister Guo's eyes squeezed to slits. "What of your health, Your Ladyship? Your marriage must take precedence over all else, as your responsibility to Tianxia is to secure an heir."

As several of the courtiers nodded, a cold fury sank into me. "My responsibility is to the people of Tianxia, to guard their welfare and happiness, to keep them safe. I know my duty, *do not* dictate my responsibilities to me, Minister Guo"—my tone was soft yet needle-sharp—"else you will find yourself barred from court." I resisted the urge to punish him right there, still hopeful of securing compliance without drawing blood.

Minister Guo flushed, fighting to hold himself in check as he bowed—a triumph I keenly felt.

I addressed the court: "There is no urgency to my marriage. I am in good health and not in need of a spouse. I am strong enough to bear the burdens of the throne alone. If any doubt this, speak now."

A gamble, to toss this out. But those who schemed in the dark were cowards in the open, only moving once victory was assured. It was too early yet for any to have gained prominence, too uncertain to stick one's neck out in case it was cut off.

Silence followed as the court stirred, a few scowling. They definitely did not like me now, an almost liberating realization, even as I found myself tensing. The slightest weakness, and Minister Guo and his cohorts would swarm over me. If I did not assert myself, I risked being usurped, relegated to the shadows. By allowing them to speak for me, to dictate my actions—they would undermine me at every turn.

Once, I might have shied from the palpable displeasure in the room, wary of confrontation. But my grandfather had not sacrificed himself so I could lose his throne to another, unworthy and avaricious. If anyone thought I'd choose a life of ease as a puppet ruler, they were wrong. Grandfather believed me worthy to rule, he'd taught me against the counsel of his advisors, and I wouldn't let him down.

"Is Your Ladyship tired? Perhaps Your Ladyship should retire to your chamber and we can handle the petitions, to ease your burdens," Minister Dao, a grasping courtier, offered.

If I did, I'd return to find a third of the kingdom ceded to his sycophants. "Are you asking me to leave my own court, Minister Dao?" I said icily.

He blanched. "I would not dare—"

"I'm glad to hear it, Minister Dao," I said darkly. "It would be dangerous for you, if you did."

Aunt Shou cleared her throat from where she stood by the side of the dais. A sign that I'd pushed as hard as I could today. I was grateful for her experience and steadiness. Despite her refusal of an official position, she had been my grandfather's confidante, her astute opinion bearing as much weight as any minister's.

I gestured to the guards by the door, allowing the first of the petitioners in. Some sought aid, others wanting to resolve disputes. Hours passed as I listened and passed judgment when needed, at times deferring to the ministers with more experience. Part of me kept bracing for my fatigue to return, for my mind to cloud, my body to ache—marveling and grateful when it did not. The Divine Pearl Lotus had cleared all trace of my poisoning and more, somehow leaving me stronger than before.

As the sun dropped lower, some of the ministers began to shuffle restlessly, except for Minister Hu, who sat comfortably in the chair Chengyin had given him. I'd kept the court in session this long to prove I could bear the strain as well as them, to dispel lingering rumors about my health.

At last I rose, to sighs of relief. "The court is dismissed for today."

The minsters bowed as I strode from the hall, holding my head up until I reached my room and closed the doors after me. The lamps were already lit, hanging from carved bronze stands. Through the latticed window, the sweetness of jasmine drifted in, soothing my nerves. I could almost hear Grandfather's voice asking me to close it for fear I'd catch a chill. The mahogany desk in my study had belonged to him. I sat on the chair, remembering how he used to work here, my fingers brushing the mother-of-pearl pheasants and cherry trees inlaid into the wood. It was almost seamless but for the small drawer tucked into the side, one Grandfather had never let me open. I tugged at it now, finding just a thin book within, the cover weathered as though numerous hands before mine had leafed through it, the characters of Tianxia painted upon the cover.

I turned the pages, my fingers creasing the paper in my haste. As I read the first page, my heart leapt—this was written by Lady Zhirong, one of the earliest rulers of Tianxia, describing how the Wuxin had come to our kingdom.

Long ago, these creatures were little more than spirits, drifting unnoticed through the Golden Desert in the Immortal Realm. But over time, they developed appetites that helped them take physical form—not for food, but for emotions. When Queen Caihong ascended the throne of the Golden Desert, the Wuxin refused to accept her rule. A terrible war broke out between both sides that left the sands drenched with blood.

It was then the Wuxin descended to Tianxia. Devastation followed, our people helpless against their magic. What they craved from us most of all, what strengthened them—was our sorrow.

"Beautiful, vicious monsters," Lady Zhirong had written of them. *"Scavengers of joy."*

Countless lives were lost, much suffering inflicted, until one day, the immortals of the Golden Desert descended from the skies in their shining armor. A treaty was signed with Queen Caihong, who claimed our service in exchange for their protection during the war. The Shield of Rivers and Mountains, a sacred treasure of our kingdom, was surrendered to the immortals—enabling Queen Caihong to craft an enchanted wall that snaked around Tianxia to protect its secrets and prevent the Wuxin from infiltrating the rest of our realm. Once this threat was vanquished, our obligation would be fulfilled. Only then would the Shield of Rivers and Mountains be returned to us, and the walls brought down.

My fingers brushed the imperial seal I wore, tracing its carving of the shield. Why had Grandfather never mentioned this before? Maybe he believed he had time yet, or maybe he was afraid of awakening the ambition that was now stirring in my heart.

I turned the page, my eyes riveted to the words. The battle raged across the heavens and earth, with great losses on both sides. At last, the Wuxin were defeated—banished to the banks of the Wangchuan River in the Netherworld. However, before then, the Wuxin dealt a devastating blow to the immortals, killing the queen's consort.

It saddened me to think of her loss—though why should I pity the immortal queen? But after losing my own family, I could never wish such anguish upon another . . . not even my worst enemy.

My heart sank as I closed the book. A high price to pay, trading our service for our safety, isolating ourselves to serve the immortals. Yet when one was falling into the ravine, one would grasp at the slenderest branch. What did today's price matter when it would be tomorrow's debt? Except danger touched our lives still: not just illness but creatures like the Winged Devils, the storms that the queen's anger inflicted upon us. Grandfather had urged me to secure our people's future, and I believed that lay beyond our walls.

A knock on the door broke my thoughts. Yifei, my personal attendant, announced Aunt Shou and Chengyin, sliding the doors apart for them to enter. They were among the few who were welcome in my private rooms.

"Court always gives me a headache," Aunt Shou said, shaking her head. "You handled today well."

Chengyin grinned as he flicked a piece of lint from his brown robe. "Indeed. You were the perfect blend of cunning and intimidation. Few will dare gainsay you next time, for fear of losing their heads."

I scowled, hearing more insult than praise in his words. "You'd be wise to share their caution."

"I know you too well," he said with a smirk. "You don't have the stomach for beheadings, at least not yet. Better to start with a few imprisonments and beatings."

My nose wrinkled. "Are you volunteering?"

He shot me a look of exaggerated grief. "I would never dare to anger Your Ladyship."

Aunt Shou sighed. "Stop squabbling like children."

I swallowed my retort, nodding sagely instead. "Chengyin, listen to your mother. It's time to set aside these juvenile tendencies."

"She meant *both* of us," he told me with a glare.

"Are you prepared for your visit to the realm above?" Aunt Shou asked me.

My mood turned grave. "Yifei has readied my outfit. But I don't want to pledge my fealty to the immortals; I want us to be free of them."

"Your grandfather wanted that, too," Aunt Shou said. "He'd hoped—as did each ruler before him—that pleasing Queen Caihong would suffice to earn Tianxia's freedom."

"That she would return the Shield of Rivers and Mountains?" I asked.

Aunt Shou frowned as though surprised I knew of it, then nodded. "It was said when the shield was returned to us, the walls could finally be brought down. But they won't release us; they like having us on their string."

I ground my teeth at the thought. My kingdom was not an ornament, nor did we have infinite time. To an immortal, a hundred years was a blink in the span of their existence, while it was more than an entire mortal lifetime.

"If they won't return the shield, I'll take it back," I said with feeling.

Chengyin folded his arms across his chest. "Even if you find it, what will you do when the God of War attacks again, demanding its return?"

"How does one kill a god?" Even as I asked it flippantly, part of me wished I hadn't. The immortal had saved me from the Winged Devils. And while I wouldn't let this obligation hinder my plans, I wasn't sure I wanted him to die.

Chengyin choked back a laugh. "The gods might object to you killing them. They will fight back, and they do have a *few* advantages. Magic, for one, and the fact our weapons can't injure them. The few immortal ones in our treasury are nothing compared to what their warriors wield. The God of War's sword alone was said to have cleaved the Wuxin Army in half with a single blow—"

"Gross exaggeration, else the war would have lasted half a day," Aunt Shou scoffed.

I leaned forward, clasping my hands on the desk. "Nevertheless, we must arm ourselves better."

"Sure." Chengyin gestured to the window. "I'll leap on a cloud and fly to the Immortal Realm. Ransack their armory, then come back down."

It was what I most liked and disliked about him; that he had no reverence for my position, treating me as he did when we were children squabbling over the same toys.

"Just because something is hard is no reason to give up," Aunt Shou chided him. "If you don't believe in what you do, who will?"

"If we can reclaim the shield, it gives us the chance to cancel the treaty, to bring down the walls. We can even petition the Celestial Emperor for his aid. Aren't they the most powerful kingdom in the skies, and their emperor benevolent and wise?"

I'd read that long ago, when the immortals descended to our realm, they were bound by strict rules set by the Celestial Emperor to protect *us*. In Tianxia, the immortals had no such restraint.

Aunt Shou nodded. "The Celestial Emperor might also be keen to unite our world beneath him rather than sharing it with the Golden Desert."

Chengyin sighed loudly. "Mother, are you encouraging this madness? While Queen Caihong can be harsh, our kingdom has prospered in some ways, too—"

"It's not madness," I said firmly. "Over the years, Queen Caihong has grown more temperamental, erratic, and demanding.

When she is angered, we suffer treacherous storms, winds, and floods. We also have to deal with their enemies, the incursion of monsters like those Winged Devils."

"Life isn't perfect outside these walls either," Chengyin reminded me.

"I don't believe it is," I replied. "While no place is shielded from misfortune, at least it's not intentionally caused, imposed as a punishment. We shouldn't have to live within these walls when our world lies beyond them. Why must we set the immortals' wants above our own, especially when they care nothing for us? Don't you want us to live for ourselves?"

"What of Kunlun?" Chengyin asked.

"We will continue to keep watch over the place. We can protect Kunlun, with or without the wall," I replied.

A wistful look crept into Chengyin's eyes. "I've always wanted to see what lay beyond these walls."

"You will," I promised him. "We will."

"What do you propose, Liyen?" Aunt Shou asked, her brow creased.

"I don't intend to pledge us to another lifetime of service. I'll use my time in the Immortal Realm to search for the Shield of Rivers and Mountains," I said slowly. "To learn all I can about it, or anything that might help us stand against the immortals."

Silence fell. "If you do this, you must be very careful," Aunt Shou warned me at last. "Never forget what the immortals are capable of, the cruelty in their indifference. Our titles mean nothing to them; your rank there will be less than the lowliest immortal. Do nothing to earn their wrath, don't draw their attention. If you rely on their mercy, you will find none."

"Liyen, are you sure you want to do this—to challenge the immortals? We'll never be as strong as them," Chengyin said.

My hard smile hid my own uncertainty. "Then we'll just have to be smarter."

After Aunt Shou and Chengyin left, I lay awake in my bed for a long time, thinking of my Grandfather and how he'd tell me stories before I slept. My favorite tales were those of the Immortal Realm, which he'd visited after ascending the throne.

"Is it very beautiful there?" I'd wanted to know. "Did you want to stay?"

He'd laughed, rumpling my hair. "Why would I? The land of immortals is enchanting—but it's not home."

"Tell me about the realm above?" I'd asked eagerly. "Aunt Shou said there are eight kingdoms, and that the Celestial Kingdom is the most powerful."

"It is," he agreed. "The Cloud Wall is a close rival, and there is also the Phoenix Kingdom, the Golden Desert, and the Four Kingdoms of the Seas. The Golden Desert used to have no ruler, but they united under Queen Caihong—except for the Wuxin, which led to the war."

At the look of fear on my face, he'd patted my arm. "Don't be afraid. The Wuxin are sealed away in the Netherworld."

"What is so dangerous about them?" Maybe if I knew more about them, I wouldn't be so afraid. Ignorance often makes cowards of us all.

"It seems harmless that they thrive on emotions, yet it became dangerous when they wanted more than what one was willing to give—when they took what was withheld."

"How could they do that?" I struggled to understand. "Our feelings are our own."

"Our feelings are often a response to another's actions or words. We are happy with our loved ones, angry when disappointed. The Wuxin learned to harvest emotions . . . fear and grief above all."

I shuddered. "Why not happiness?"

Grandfather's eyes had creased, his cheeks sunken. He'd looked older than his years then. "Sorrow is powerful and unabating, more easily reaped than something as elusive as joy. With this, the Wuxin strengthened, gaining magic that even the immortals knew little of." He had pulled up my blanket and tucked it around me. "But you don't need to fear them anymore. The Wuxin are banished, and the immortals keep us safe."

I'd wanted to ask more, but he'd stood then. "Sleep now, child. The time will come when I'll share all with you, when you are ready to ascend the throne."

I'd nodded then, not knowing the day would never come— that I'd be floundering in the court I was meant to rule, grasping at any scrap of knowledge to stay afloat. Maybe it was better this way. A new beginning, unbound by the ties of the past . . . one that dared to imagine a new future.

5

The escort to the Immortal Realm was late, a discourtesy that was hardly surprising. A few courtiers exchanged impatient glances—their disdain for me evident in such looks, their shallow bows and increasingly brazen demands for lands and titles, anything they might grasp while the soil was still loose over my grandfather's grave. They would never have provoked Grandfather so, but a girl they had all but written off?

I was fair game.

They didn't care that my health had improved, that I was able to withstand a full day in court without flagging when I couldn't bear half a day of lessons before. They *wanted* me to be weak, it suited them to pretend nothing had changed, that I'd never recovered from the poisoning. On the surface, I looked the same—my skin more pale than radiant, eyes the color of ink, a heart-shaped face framed by black hair that curled at the ends. A few stared at the lock of white hair left by the waters of death, then looked aside like it made them uneasy. I should have tucked it away, as I did most days. But none knew how my chest pulsed with a new warmth, throbbing beneath the scar, or the way I woke feeling rested each morning, ready for whatever the day might bring . . . rather than being afraid I couldn't keep up.

I took nothing for granted, haunted by the times when the simplest things were a struggle. I went on long walks, grateful when I did not tire. Some evenings, I trained with Captain Li of the night patrol, learning the basics of weaponry and combat. While I'd hidden the sword the God of War gave me, it was now strapped to my side. No one seemed to notice it; perhaps it was enchanted that way. I'd never be a warrior, but I would grasp any chance to strengthen myself. Life felt new, alive with possibilities—more precious because I'd come so close to losing it. If only Grandfather were here. But all the wishing in the world would not turn back time, it wouldn't restore what had been lost.

"We wish you good health, Your Ladyship," someone called out from behind me.

I turned to see the crowd of people that had come to send me off—not the nobles or courtiers who were obligated to be there, but those who'd traveled from the towns and villages. They stood a distance away, behind the line of soldiers. I smiled at them, feeling lighter than I had in weeks.

As I strode toward them, Minister Dao moved into my path. "Your Ladyship, you should wait here in case the immortal escort arrives."

His authoritative manner annoyed me. "If the immortal escort is late, they cannot fault me for not being where they expect."

Turning back to the crowd, I greeted them warmly. "Thank you for your well wishes. My health is much improved."

"We prayed every day for your recovery," a woman told me, a sleeping baby slung against her back with a broad piece of cloth.

"And now we pray for Your Ladyship's safe return from the skies," a stout man dressed in the fine robes of a merchant chimed in.

"Don't let the immortals keep you in the heavens," an old man said with a grin, blackened gaps where his teeth should be.

"I'll be too much trouble for them." I returned his smile, but it faded as I took in his tattered clothes, the gauntness of his face. "Is everything well at home?"

The man's body sagged as he bowed. "A poor harvest in our village. Our crops were devoured by a plague of locusts." He added slowly, "I came to petition for aid, but was told Your Ladyship would be away and didn't have the time to see me."

A knot hardened within as I looked toward the ministers. "Who knew of this?"

"A small matter, Your Ladyship," Minister Guo replied, but not before I caught his scowl. "We didn't want to trouble you before your visit—"

"Starvation is never a small matter." My voice had tightened with repressed anger. "Minister Hu, open our reserves to send rice and other supplies."

The old man clasped his hands and bowed again, blinking away the brightness in his eyes. His gratitude did not lessen the burden that sank over me, knowing they'd suffered. This was more than a fleeting whim of mercy; the well-being of my people was my responsibility. As I stared at the faces around me, my mind drifted back to my grandfather.

"What do you see?" he'd asked me once, holding up a silver tael as our carriage rumbled over the uneven path. He liked to visit the villages when he had time, and sometimes he'd bring me along.

"Silver," I replied with little interest.

His smile hadn't reached his eyes. "For those in need, this is food on the table, life-saving medicine, a roof over a child's head. Those who have enough often forget those in need—not because they're unkind—but because it makes them uneasy, evoking guilt that they have so much while others, nothing. Life is inherently unfair." He had placed the tael into my hand, folding my fingers over it. "A piece of silver can change a person's life, while it will do nothing sitting in a miser's purse."

Filled with remorse at my earlier callousness, I tried to give

SUE LYNN TAN

it back. "Don't give it to me, Grandfather. Use it for something worthwhile."

"Why don't *you*?" he had admonished me gently. "It's our burden and our blessing to be in a position to help."

I'd been tempted to give the silver to the first beggar I saw on the street, a young man with a smooth stump where his right hand should be. But there were so many—their hungry, hopeful faces tearing at my conscience. Using the silver, I had bought bread and fruit that I handed to them, along with the leftover coins.

Even now I could recall the light in their eyes as I'd pressed the food into their hands, the tenderness that had kindled inside me— the guilt. How I'd wanted to help them all and yet there were so many . . . children, even. I'd emptied my purse that night and still it was far from enough.

A lesson I never forgot, one my grandfather had intended I learn that night—to walk among the suffering, to know their pain rather than sitting in the throne room surrounded by privilege, shrouded in ignorance. Life might be easier but far less meaningful.

I straightened, fighting back the prickling in my eyes, afraid the others would see. And I wondered, too, if this might be part of the problem between the immortals and us. Not that they were inherently cruel or vicious, but that they didn't understand our suffering because they so rarely walked among us or troubled themselves to learn about us.

My heart was heavy as I bid farewell to the people, heading back to wait for the immortal escort. The wind stirred then, teasing the hem of my robe. Silver phoenixes were embroidered on the white brocade, the sleeves encrusted with a border of seed pearls, my sash fringed with jade beads. I clasped my cold hands together, trying to warm them. I didn't want to go to the Immortal Realm, I didn't want to face the Queen of the Golden Desert, to swear my allegiance when all I wanted was for us to be free of them. But neither could I challenge her rashly, for fear of the misery she could inflict on us. I had to tread carefully, using my time in the skies to forge a path toward our freedom—impossible though it seemed.

On the horizon, a cloud appeared, its muted glow akin to a glittering breath. Finally, the escort had arrived. As the cloud swept closer, gasps rose from those watching its descent.

The God of War rode upon the cloud. He was not wearing his armor, but a gray robe embroidered with a pattern of pagodas and cypresses in gold thread. His great sword was strapped to his back—maybe he slept with it, too. My insides tightened at the sight of him. I'd have preferred anyone else; the journey would be less nerve-wracking.

I bowed formally to greet him, resenting the deference he was due. "We are honored by your presence. However, doesn't the God of War have more pressing matters to attend to than to serve as a mortal's escort?" My smile concealed the sting in my words.

He stared back at me stonily. "I do my queen's bidding. The Winged Devils have been trespassing more frequently of late." His gaze fell upon the sword by my waist. "The Lady of Tianxia's safety is of paramount importance."

"Yet you are late," I couldn't help remarking.

His eyebrows arched. "Are you displeased?"

"I wouldn't dare," I replied smoothly. "Any mortal should be grateful for the honor of your company."

"Such kind words." His smile was cold, as though he could see through my facade. "The Lady of Tianxia's grace is apparent to all."

As I glared at him, Chengyin smothered a laugh. From the side, Aunt Shou's eyes bored into me, a silent rebuke for my behavior. For some reckless reason, the God of War stoked my temper rather than my fear—but it would do no good to spar with him before the court.

I addressed the waiting courtiers. "Honored Ministers, in my absence Minister Guo, Minister Dao and Minister Hu will review the petitions, while Lord Chengyin will assume the role of First Advisor, providing the final judgment in all rulings."

The courtiers bowed as they intoned, "We hear and obey. Long live the Lady of Tianxia, may she rule for a hundred years."

Despite their words, their backs were stiff, their expressions sour. Such evident unease assured me of my decision. Minister Guo and Minister Dao were rivals. Given my precarious position, it was wiser to not favor any faction at court. Let them plot against each other rather than me. Chengyin would also ensure that my interests were protected, and he was only doing this as a favor.

He came forward, dressed in the dark-red robes of court, his black hat set with a piece of jade. Lowering his voice, he said, "Choosing sworn enemies to work together will ensure little will be agreed on while you're away."

"Maybe they'll leave the kingdom intact then, rather than carving it up among themselves," I replied. "I leave you to oversee matters, to ensure those that need attention aren't neglected. And keep watch in case of any unforeseen alliances."

Chengyin sighed in mock despair. "You've just ensured *my* workload will be the heaviest."

"Thank you, my friend," I said quietly.

He grinned at me. "Bring back a bottle of wine from the immortals as compensation and all will be forgiven. I hear they brew the finest wines."

"I'll bring two, and hide them from Aunt Shou," I promised, trying not to laugh.

The God of War was studying our exchange, his eyes narrowed. Did he think we were speaking of him? "We must leave now," he said abruptly.

For one with endless time at his disposal, he was impatient. As I stared at the cloud beneath his feet—pearl-white and petal-soft—I frowned. "Is this safe? It seems far too frail. Why not a chariot or flying mount?" Even walking would be preferable, if one could ascend to the skies that way.

"The clouds we travel on are enchanted. No harm will come to you while I'm here." A pause as the god's gaze flicked to me. "Now that I know your preference, I'll ensure we travel differently next time."

Was that a promise or a threat? I stared at his impassive face, deciding it was likely the latter. Holding my breath, I stepped upon the cloud, relieved to find it solid beneath my feet, cool tendrils curling around my ankles. As the god raised his hand, the wind swept us into the skies. My fingers curled as I glanced down, my head swimming. From up high, my home appeared no more than a pile of stone, forests shrinking to patches of moss, rivers dwindling to slivers of thread. Overwhelmed by the endless horizons, the vast emptiness beneath, I caught myself leaning toward the god. Silence fell over us but for the thud of my heart, the rush of air as it surged against my face. I peeked down again, glimpsing the red marble wall that snaked around Tianxia like a trail of blood. Mist cloaked the borders beyond, concealing it from sight—was it part of the magic that shrouded our kingdom?

The higher we soared, the more violently my stomach churned. As the cloud swerved, avoiding a flock of birds, I stumbled, treading upon the god's foot. His arm ringed my shoulders to steady me, his touch ice-cold. At once, I pulled away, thinking of how he'd slain the Winged Devils and how easily he could kill me should he choose.

"Is something wrong?" he asked.

"No." I smiled tightly, leashing my emotions. Alone at night was when I unraveled, though even then I pressed a fist to my mouth to stifle my grief.

He tilted his head to one side. "Yet your smile is false."

"You don't know me well enough to judge that."

"We don't need familiarity to sense falseness," he replied.

"Do you really want to hear a mortal's thoughts?" I asked sharply.

"All you will tell me, and more." He examined my face, adding, "You seem surprised."

"It doesn't fit with what I've heard of you," I said stiffly.

"They also say I have skin the color of blood, fangs for teeth, and that I carry a polearm taller than a cypress," he scoffed. "Don't just choose the stories you want to believe."

The way he spoke . . . for some reason, I flushed. A ridiculous impulse that I quelled; *he* should feel ashamed for what he'd done.

"Did you accomplish all you'd wished during this month? Your grandfather's funeral?" he asked.

I remembered how Grandfather had looked in the coffin, the hollow in my heart when his body was lowered into the earth. Unable to speak, I nodded in reply.

"I know you're grieving," the god said quietly. "I know what it's like having part of your heart wrenched away—how hard it is to pretend life is normal when your world has fallen apart."

Was he confiding in me? Or trying to learn my mind, to test my loyalty to the queen? "Why are you telling me this?" I asked cautiously.

He shrugged. "Because I'm tired of you looking at me the way you do."

"How should I look at you? My grandfather died because of you." I couldn't help saying, though it was rash, unwise. A little unfair.

His mouth drew into a thin line. "We did not kill him, nor was it in our power to heal him either."

"Would you have saved him if you could?" *Why did I ask?*

"Yes."

Against my judgment, his unflinching answer moved me. I stared at him, trying to uncover the lie in his words, but found none.

Unsure of what to say, I fell silent, unable to shake the unwanted revelation that he might not be as heartless as I wanted to believe.

Our cloud approached a peak of blue-white stone rising from the glistening sands. In the distance, a mansion of dark wood and gleaming stone sprawled over the grounds, tucked within groves of bamboo and flowering gardens.

"Is this Her Majesty's palace?" I asked.

"No," he replied. "Intruders tried to break into the Palace of Radiant Light earlier today, causing my delay. Queen Caihong commanded that you are to remain in my house for now, until the palace is secure. Accidents here can have dire consequences for mortals."

"Why not send a messenger to delay my departure?" I demanded, forgetting to soften my tone.

"Her Majesty wanted to keep you close, in case of other attacks—whether here or in Tianxia. While your palace is guarded, the rest of your kingdom is not. She might also summon you at any moment."

"I am at Her Majesty's disposal," I said tersely. "Can I send word to my people? I don't want them to worry at my absence."

"I will send a messenger." His gaze was piercing. "If you wish to return, I won't hold you here against your will."

I wanted to go home, but this was a rare chance that I'd be stupid to cast away. The Shield of Rivers and Mountains was here, maybe even in the God of War's home. And if it wasn't, I might be able to learn where it was instead of returning empty-handed.

"Will I be safe in your home?" I asked, as though considering my decision.

The god's eyes flashed. Had I slighted his honor? If he was this easily offended, it was fortunate he couldn't read my mind.

"Do you think I brought you here to harm you?" His voice was low, like he was holding his anger in check.

"I meant safe from these other dangers. If you wanted me

dead, you'd have killed me before."

"You should be more careful with your life," he chided me. "Just because someone didn't kill you yesterday is no assurance they won't today. Alliances change, priorities shift, intentions are thwarted with ease."

I quashed a spurt of fear. "I value my life greatly. If you prefer that I not stay with you——"

He made an impatient sound. "It was advice, no more. You are overly careless with your safety. Rest assured, no one has ever invaded my home. You will be safe there—as long as you obey me, and do nothing to endanger yourself."

I nodded, even though the commanding way he spoke made me grit my teeth, even though I had no intention of obeying him.

"Give me your hand," the God of War said abruptly.

Instinctively, I tucked it behind my back. "Why?"

He held out a strand of red thread with a gold bead in the middle. "Mortals are not allowed into the Immortal Realm. Her Majesty summons the rulers of Tianxia to visit her for the pledge of fealty, so an exception is made as part of our agreement with the Celestial Kingdom—but only once in a mortal's lifetime. While you are in our realm, you are *our* guest, and your actions are our responsibility to bear. Once your time here ends, the bracelet unravels."

"What happens if a mortal stays beyond that?" I was curious about these rules set in place to keep us out. Maybe the Celestial Emperor was concerned at the precedent this might set if every mortal under his domain wished to visit *him*.

"They die," he said flatly. "There are no exceptions, and neither Queen Caihong nor I can do anything to prevent this."

He knotted the string around my wrist, but not tight enough to cause discomfort. As his fingers brushed my skin, our eyes met—a shiver running through me.

I drew away at once, raising my chin. "Then it's fortunate that I don't intend to stay."

6

The cloud set us down by tall ebony doors, inlaid with an intricate mosaic of mother-of-pearl. Gold-flecked lapis tiles lined the rooftops, with sculpted dragons and phoenixes rearing up from the ridges. The pathway was flanked by pear-blossom trees, their branches laden with tiny white flowers. An ebony plaque hung above the towering entrance, engraved with the characters: "Silver Willow Manor."

I didn't want to admire the God of War's home; I wanted to despise it, as much as I did him. But against my will, I was enchanted, unable to look away from the ethereal vision. Immortals were rumored to carve jade from stone, weave silk from rain, and pluck flowers from the clouds—and only now did I believe it. Yet this magnificent place was a jolting reminder of how shallow the god was beneath his harsh exterior. How could one who thrived on destruction live in such gloating, ostentatious splendor? It was clear the god didn't care what became of his victims and the families he tore apart. How easily he must set them from his mind once he returned to his shining abode, where he evidently indulged his every whim.

"Does my home displease you?"

I swept the frown from my face. "It's not as splendid as I thought a god's home might be," I lied, to annoy him. "The stone is a little dull, the wood too dark, the carvings lacking in originality."

"The Lady of Tianxia has discerning taste." His tone was glacial. "Perhaps you might invite me to visit your home, to show me what impresses you."

"Of course." I was fenced into a corner of my own making, provoked into a reckless invitation. My home might be a shadow of his, but I loved it regardless—each worn tile and faded painting a precious memory of my past. "When we return to my kingdom, you must be my guest."

"I look forward to it."

"But only if you have the time," I hedged.

"I will make the time."

His lips curved into a smile that I returned in force. This was courting danger but I wouldn't back down, a current sparked in my veins.

"What would you change about my home?" he asked.

I didn't answer right away, surprised by the question. "It's beautiful," I admitted grudgingly. "Yet if beauty is so common, what is rare?"

"There is beauty everywhere if one looks hard enough."

His gaze was piercing, almost unnerving. I looked away, studying the guards in black-and-gold armor, attired differently from the queen's soldiers. They bowed as we approached, opening the doors that led into a wide courtyard. Camphor trees flanked the pathway, red silk lanterns hanging from their gnarled branches. A thick hedge of jasmine ran along the walls, the sweetness of its fragrance reminding me of home. The God of War strode toward a large hall flanked by teak pillars. Large porcelain jars filled with water lined the stairs, lotuses blooming upon the surface. As we entered, two immortals hurried toward us, clasping their hands as they bowed formally to the god.

"Rise," he told them. "There's no need for such ceremony."

"But we have a guest," the taller one said by way of explanation.

As they straightened, their wide eyes remained on me. Their fair skin was the delicate shade of magnolias, their black hair held up with tortoiseshell sticks. They were beautiful, their movements graceful. Were they his wives? Concubines? The God of War was believed to be unattached, though the lavishness of this place made it clear he indulged his desires. I found myself wondering where his preferences lay: did he treasure beauty more, or intelligence or temperament? Almost at once, I cast the thought aside, a needless distraction.

"Lord Zhangwei, your bath has been prepared. Would you like to eat here or in your room?" the tall one asked.

"My room," he replied. "The mortal may—"

"My name is Liyen," I said pointedly. "Not 'the mortal.'"

"Liyen." He uttered it softly, drawing out each syllable. I flushed, realizing I'd inadvertently given him leave to call me by name.

"You may call me Zhangwei," he told me.

"Lord Zhangwei," I said carefully, preferring the formality of his title. It made him feel more distant, less real—easier to scheme against. As he frowned, I turned to the others. "May I know how to address you?"

"I am Ningxi, the head attendant here," the taller one said, then gestured to the other. "Weina will attend to your needs while you are here."

"Lord Zhangwei, the real question is who is *she?*" Weina asked, her cheeks dimpling. "You've never brought anyone—"

As Ningxi nudged her sharply, Weina closed her mouth. I wanted to ask what she meant—surely the God of War must have countless visitors, those eager for his favor, the relationships he needed to cultivate to safeguard his position. One could not exist alone at court. There were rivals or allies, and those without either were of no importance or would be soon forgotten.

"Her Majesty commanded that the Lady of Tianxia is our guest, for now. Inform the household, and prepare a room for her in the West Courtyard. She is to be provided with anything she needs."

"What of her meals, Lord Zhangwei? Will she have them in the dining hall?" Ningxi asked.

"Have them sent to her room."

As he strode away, I called after him. "What if I want to eat here?" He might be used to ordering his attendants around, but I wouldn't let him dictate to me.

"Eat wherever you wish," he replied without turning.

"Does that mean I can go wherever I want?" My calm tone concealed my eagerness. If so, I'd be free to search for the shield, for anything that might be of use to my kingdom.

He halted, his back still to me. "The South Courtyard is forbidden."

"Why?"

"Because I said so." His hand strayed to his waistband, brushing a red jade ornament that was carved with a flower—or possibly, a star.

As he strode away, I stared daggers after him before realizing the attendants were studying me in turn.

Weina cleared her throat. "My lady, did our queen really invite you on Lord Zhangwei's behalf, or are you his bed—?"

"Weina!" Ningxi admonished in a shrill tone.

"No!" I snarled at the same time.

Weina drew herself up. "You would be the most fortunate of mortals should Lord Zhangwei deign to honor you so," she said with a sniff. "There's no need to be small-minded when some of the other nobles have an entire courtyard of concubines."

"Enough, Weina," Ningxi rebuked her again. "Bring the Lady of Tianxia to her chamber and hold your tongue. She doesn't want to hear your chatter."

Oh, I did want to hear it—my anger at the dubious "honor", drowned by curiosity But I had to be patient. We headed down the corridor in the opposite direction from where the god had left. Was he in the East Courtyard? Had he placed me as far from him as possible? An insult and a relief.

The evening sky was swathed in rich violet, speckled with starlight. With each step we took, oblong lanterns upon wooden pedestals flickered to life, illuminating the pathway. As we passed a fountain, shining rivulets of water arced from a stone crane. A large building in the distance caught my eye, set back from the pathway, encircled by bamboo.

"That's the library," Weina told me helpfully. "You may visit whenever you wish."

"Why is the South Courtyard forbidden? What's in there?" I tried to keep my tone light. "A monster?" *Like the one that dwells in the East Courtyard?*

"I don't know. Only Lord Zhangwei is allowed to enter," Weina said. "It's been this way since I entered his service."

Something of great worth must be kept within—why else the secrecy? "Aren't you curious?" I probed. She seemed more inclined to gossip than Ningxi.

Weina shook her head. "A little curiosity makes life more interesting, but too much could get you killed. I value my life too much to disobey His Lordship. As should you, Mortal," Weina told me somberly.

The way she said the last irked, but I recalled Aunt Shou's caution. I searched for another question, something to dispel her suspicion. "How did you come to serve Lord Zhangwei?"

"It's a great honor," she said with pride. "Lord Zhangwei is the greatest warrior in the kingdom, despite his youth."

"Is Lord Zhangwei considered young?" It seemed impossible to tell as the immortals appeared ageless.

"Yes, for our people, though we don't count the years as you mortals do. It ceases to matter once we reach adulthood."

"How fortunate that Lord Zhangwei is so accomplished at his age." I wanted to draw her out, to learn more about him. Part of me still hated him for the destruction to my home, for terrifying Grandfather—but for now, my safety lay in his hands.

"He may be young, but no less wise and respected than those centuries older. Our queen holds him in the highest regard, valuing his opinion above all others."

Weina quickened her pace until she was ahead of me, a useful way of evading the rest of my questions. She stopped by a circular red door that she pushed open. "This is your courtyard."

A grove of mandarin trees was clustered at the far side, the fruit hanging like luminous globes. More jasmine bloomed in thick rows along the wall, its sweetness melding with that of the mandarins. The lanterns here were set upon carved rosewood stands, their glow infusing the night with warmth.

I followed Weina into a large room furnished in green, white, and gold. A bed lay at the end of the room, its curtains tied back with braided cord, the sheets gleaming invitingly. Exquisite paintings of mountains and forests were mounted on stiff brocade and hung on the walls, thick carpets covering the wooden floor.

"I thought you'd prefer to eat here tonight. You may choose where you wish tomorrow." She gestured toward the round wooden table, already set with food: Glazed pork ribs, crisp fried fish, braised vegetables, and rice. There was a jug of wine, a reddish-gold liquid poured into a porcelain cup. I lifted it and inhaled its aroma of osmanthus, cloves, and an undefinable spice.

She smiled. "If you can't sleep, I suggest the wine. Some dreams turn so pleasant, you might never want to awaken."

I resisted the urge to tip the jug onto the floor. Was this how they dealt with unwanted guests, letting them slumber away once their welcome was worn out?

She opened the closet and gestured to the garments folded

within. The material shone brighter than the finest silk, the weave so delicate it was almost seamless. "All these are for your own use. Anything else you require can be provided."

At the end of the room, a four-paneled screen was laid out, carved with the flowers of the seasons. A bronze bath lay behind the screen, already filled with water, steam thickening the air. Rose petals were scattered across the surface, floating amid the perfumed oils.

"Thank you. I am grateful for your hospitality," I told her, already eager to sink into the water.

She inclined her head. "You are Lord Zhangwei's guest."

Without another word, she left the room. I waited until her steps had faded before closing the door. For want of a lock, I dragged a side table across the entrance and set a porcelain vase upon it, where the slightest jostle would cause it to crash. None of this would yield any protection in a household of immortals, but it offered the illusion of safety.

Alone, I sank onto a stool, my heart racing. It didn't feel real that I was here. It was wondrous, as my grandfather had said, but I understood now what he meant—for despite the extravagant beauty here, I still longed for home.

Shaking my head, I pulled myself up. The Queen of the Golden Desert might summon me tomorrow, and I could find myself home by nightfall. I wouldn't waste my precious time among the immortals. I had to find a way for us to be free of them, and it would start here. Guilt pricked me at my plans to violate the god's hospitality, but I extinguished it. No matter the glimpses of consideration the God of War had shown, I couldn't forget how Grandfather had died trying to protect us from the immortals' wrath. Bitterness surged as I unsheathed the sword that Lord Zhangwei gave me, angling the blade to catch the light. I'd almost been afraid he'd ask for its return. Maybe to him it was a common weapon, maybe he believed I was no threat to him, yet this meant I was no longer helpless here, for only an immortal weapon could hurt a god.

7

I spent the next morning exploring the buildings clustered around the main hall, connected by the pathways through the gardens. The flowers and trees were immaculately tended, the ponds filled with glistening carp. While there were fewer rooms than my home, each one was beautifully furnished. To the east were the God of War's quarters, while the rooms in the west were vacant except for mine. The library, kitchens, and attendants' quarters were situated in the north.

As for the South Courtyard—I headed there the first chance I got, surprised to find the place unguarded. The grounds were surrounded by a high wall, one without an entrance or window. Gilded stars, intricately carved with eight points, were set evenly in a single row. Peach-blossom trees towered from within the courtyard, their blooms clustered along the branches like rose-tinted clouds.

My pulse quickened, my senses alight. Something vital lay within, something the god wanted to hide. An enemy's secret could be a powerful weapon. I dug my fingers into the stone crevices, as slippery as half-thawed ice. Was this some magic to deter trespassers? I scrambled up a short way, clawing at the wall—but slipped, falling against the grass. A bruise darkened my knee, yet I was lucky to not have broken anything. From the pouch by my sash, I pulled out a small porcelain jar and applied some of the ointment to the swollen flesh, a blend of aloe and pomegranate. As the ache eased, a memory drifted back of how the god had healed me before, though my wounds then had been far worse. How easy everything was for the immortals, with the effortless power they possessed.

As I studied the wall again, one of the gilded stars gleamed brighter like it was polished more often. I traced its carving, which was set a little deeper than the others. Was this intended for a key? When the God of War forbade me from this place, he'd touched a carved ornament by his waist, one that just might fit here.

After dusting the soil from my robe, a light-gray silk embroidered with birds, I headed to the library. There were no guards, just a pair of stone lions flanking the entrance, their bulbous eyes gleaming as I walked past them to enter the chamber. Wooden pillars stretched from the tiled floor to the ceiling, inscribed with the characters of a poem. Lanterns with colored tassels hung from the beams, low tables skirting the walls, each one stacked with paper, inkstones, and bamboo brushes. A painting mounted on black brocade hung in the middle of the room—an elaborate scene spanning palaces on clouds, pagodas on earth, mountains and waterfalls, phoenixes soaring in the skies. As a breeze darted through the windows, the delicate tinkling of a windchime broke the silence.

All around were wooden shelves crammed with books and scrolls, each promising a safe escape to magical realms, a glimpse into the mysteries of our world, excitement and wonder in their pages. *This* was wealth. Eternity would be well spent within these walls. My eyes darted around, unsure where to start, afraid to miss something. It would take more than my lifetime to read everything here . . . and I had days, at most, or as long as the red thread remained knotted around my wrist.

"Knowledge is one of the greatest weapons," my grandfather had told me. *"Arm yourself well, for there are times words can reach where*

a sword cannot."

I picked up a book from a nearby shelf, flicking through its pages before laying it aside. Then I reached for another, finding it to contain poetry. More followed, books piling on the tables around me. I almost resented the urgency of my search when all I wanted was to run my hands over each volume and slowly unravel its secrets. If only I had a month here, a year, a decade. If only this place did not belong to the God of War so I could admire it without feeling this spike of resentment.

I lingered over a book that detailed the magic of immortals known as Talents. Their powers intrigued me, aligned as they were to the elements of Fire, Water, Earth, and Air, with some even possessing the ability to heal. The God of War must be skilled in Fire, I guessed, my home still bearing the marks of his assault. According to the book, there were also several things that all immortals were able to do regardless of their Talent: flying on clouds, healing minor wounds, summoning small objects, and shielding themselves from harm.

The doors creaked open, as someone strode into the library. I looked up, expecting a guard or Weina, but it was the God of War in a robe of midnight brocade, his long hair gathered into a silver ring. His sword was slung across his back—it shouldn't be a surprise that he carried it even in his own home. At the sight of me, he stilled, as I did at him.

"I didn't expect to see you here." I gestured at the books, feeling a little foolish given this was *his* home, his library.

"Why? Because you didn't think I could read?" he asked coolly.

It was a little close to the truth. "I didn't think you *liked* to read."

He folded his arms as he leaned against a wooden pillar. "What did you imagine I liked to do?"

Fight. Hunt. Kill. I couldn't say that aloud, my mind searching for a more suitable reply. As his gaze slid to the piles of books scattered around, a frown creased his face.

"I'll put everything back," I said at once, flushing at my thoughtlessness.

"Do you know how?"

His question seemed almost a challenge. Sensing an opportunity, I said, "Yes, if you'll tell me how the collections are organized."

"By color." He plucked a book from a shelf, angling it to reveal a green streak at the base of its spine, then glanced at the tassels of the lanterns hanging above.

"What do the colors mean?" This would make sifting through the texts much easier.

He nodded at the painting I'd admired when I entered. "Use that as the guide."

Only now did I notice the characters inscribed above each section in different colors. As I studied the details of a painted dragon, I asked, "Blue is for mythical creatures?"

"Mythical?" A note of amusement rang in his tone.

"Of course they are real here," I corrected myself, wonder battling with fear. Dragons were revered by my people for their wisdom as much as their power, but they were still frightening to behold with their fangs and claws.

"Red is for warfare, yellow for poetry?" As he nodded, I continued, staring at the illustration of a courting couple, "Violet would be for romance?"

His mouth thinned. "I don't read all the books here. Some are for my guests."

Guests? According to his attendants, the God of War had none. "If I were immortal, I would read everything here. Your library is beautiful."

A long pause. "That is high praise, coming from you."

His tone lightened, almost teasing. But I ignored it, refusing to be drawn in. "I give praise when it's due."

"Then it means something." He gestured at the shelves. "You may read anything you wish from here."

I smiled as was expected, trying to remain unaffected by his generosity. "Can I take them with me to Tianxia?"

"Only if you promise to bring them back."

The gravity in his voice struck me. Did he expect me to return? Even if I wanted to, it would be impossible, according to the rules of his realm. "Then it's safer that I leave them here," I replied.

"Do you have everything you need?" he asked.

"Yes. Your attendants are most helpful. I am glad for the clothes, as I brought none with me."

"They fit well." His gaze traveled over me as he reached out to straighten my sleeve. The embroidered birds fluttered their wings, one soaring through the gray silk.

I started, pulling away from him. The birds stilled at once, one frozen midflight. "How did you do that?"

"The finest garments here are crafted with magic," he said. "But only those with a strong lifeforce, the root of our power, can bring them to life."

No wonder the birds had never moved for me. "I appreciate your generosity, Lord Zhangwei."

He inclined his head. "If you need anything else, you have but to ask."

The key to the South Courtyard? But his offer was a meaningless formality, just as I was his guest only at the command of his queen. My gaze strayed to his waist, the jade tablet that hung from it, carved with a star. This must be what I sought. Out of caution, I averted my eyes—inadvertently looking into his. I reminded myself, this was also a valuable opportunity to speak to the God of War, one high in the queen's favor. An urge rose to ask him about the Shield of Rivers and Mountains, but I had to conceal my intent to deflect suspicion.

"Lord Zhangwei, I was wondering where you keep the tributes from your victories. The weapons for your soldiers, perhaps?"

"A curious question," he said slowly. "Why do you ask?"

"I am keen to learn more, to ensure my soldiers are adequately equipped." I held his gaze steadily. After all, our soldiers fought for them, too.

"I keep no store of weapons here," he replied.

"But . . . you're the God of War."

"The soldiers serve Her Majesty, except for those who guard my home. Their weapons and armor are in the Palace of Radiant Light. Any tribute or trophies remain there, too. I don't do any of this for myself, but to protect my kingdom and those I care about."

His loyalty to the immortal queen was known to all. My heart dipped that the shield was likely in Queen Caihong's palace . . . but that didn't mean there was nothing of use here. He might even be lying, to keep me in the dark.

"Your concern for your soldiers is admirable. Few rulers think of those who shed blood to keep them on their thrones." His words deepened with intensity like this mattered to him.

"Does Her Majesty think of the soldiers of Tianxia, too?" I kept my tone soft to avoid a direct challenge, though my hands curled at my sides.

"We value their efforts to keep the Mortal Realm safe—"

"Then, why not support us a little more?" I suppressed the urge to raise my voice. "The greatest threats to my people are those from *your* realm—immortals with ill intent, monsters like the Winged Devils, or the Wuxin from the past. Our own blades can't harm them. Against such foes, Tianxia soldiers will fall like rice before the sickle."

To my surprise, he nodded. "I have broached this with Her Majesty. However, she believes the time is not right; there is no imminent danger on the horizon. Rest assured that we are considering the matter."

"We don't know when danger will strike—isn't it better to be prepared? Or does Her Majesty doubt our loyalty?" I laughed in seeming disbelief. In all honesty, I didn't want to hurt the immortals or challenge their might—I just wanted to be free of them. "Even with your weapons, we have no magic. We are no threat to you. All we want is a chance to defend ourselves, should the need arise."

"Her Majesty desires your kingdom to prove its devotion before—"

"We have been loyal," I burst out, my temper slipping.

"The loss of the Divine Pearl Lotus is a grave matter," he reminded me somberly. "If it is found, it would alleviate some of Her Majesty's unease."

Half-promises that offered nothing of worth. Even if I surrendered the lotus, it would just turn the queen against us more because it would reveal my grandfather's lies—and mine.

"Thank you for speaking on our behalf." I restrained myself from pushing further when his position was clear. While I wouldn't thank him for anything he did for me, his support for my kingdom was another matter. It struck me then: the God of War could be either a dangerous enemy or a powerful ally. According to Weina, his voice carried the most weight with Queen Caihong, whom I needed to persuade. It didn't mean I had to like him, but I should conceal my resentment. Such pretenses turned my stomach, but I couldn't afford a rigid sense of honor when dealing with the immortals—they already had far too many advantages over us.

There are lies of necessity and those of malice. I would do this for my people, for my own survival.

Feeling his gaze on me again, I looked up into his face. There was a cut just above his eye—not deep, but bleeding a little. "You're hurt."

"I was training with the soldiers."

"Who inflicted that on you? Did someone manage to best the God of War?" The question slipped out before I could stop it.

His expression darkened. "How can you determine who won without watching the fight?"

There was an edge in his tone like he was irked at my assumption that he'd lost. I blanched, imagining his opponent's wounds. "Why don't you heal yourself?"

"A small matter," he said with a shrug. "There is a cost to magic. Every time we use it, it drains our energy a little. I've grown used to ignoring the things that don't need to be healed."

I recalled how he'd healed me without hesitation when we first met, the warmth of his magic as it knitted my torn flesh together. Something tightened around my chest, another strand of obligation that I must rip away. An inconvenience to be indebted to the one I was determined to hate. I wanted to use him, not to like him—though I had to feign one to achieve the other.

I pulled out my jar of ointment, offering it to him. "Apply a little to your face. Not everything has to be done by magic."

He did not take it. "Why don't you show me how to use it?"

Did he want me to serve him, or was this some game? As his mouth curved, I glared at him, tempted to refuse. But it would be ungracious after his hospitality.

I pulled out the stopper, the herbal fragrance soothing my nerves. Then I leaned toward him with deliberate measure to brush a thin layer of the ointment across his forehead—trying not to flinch from the touch of his cool skin, how the cream mingled with the dried blood.

"Thank you." His voice was a little rougher than usual.

Something stirred in my chest, something I forced to still. I looked around, seeing a weiqi board on a nearby table. "Do you play?"

"Would you like a game?" he countered, his eyes alight.

I wrinkled my nose. "You're the God of War; strategy is in

your blood." While I had played often with my grandfather and Chengyin, I wouldn't underestimate his talent in this game.

"I'll offer a handicap and play the first move," he said, already moving toward the board.

I paused. "Nine stones might rebalance the odds—but only slightly."

In reply, he held up three fingers instead.

"Nine," I repeated.

"Don't you understand how negotiations work?"

"I state what I want; no less. You have many centuries of experience ahead of me in this game," I argued.

"Not *centuries* more." He sounded offended. "Very well. Six stones."

"This isn't a game of chance but of skill and experience," I said brightly. "Or are you afraid I'll win? Do you only play when there is no risk of losing?"

The corners of his mouth tightened. "Very well. Nine."

I smiled, reminding myself that it didn't matter if I lost, beyond the blow to my pride. But I couldn't yield too easily. Someone like him would relish a challenge more—and I also didn't want to appear a fool.

As we sat down by the board, he handed me a bowl of rounded white stones, then began placing the ones I'd negotiated from him along the star points.

"You may change them as you see fit," he said. "Though I think you're not as unskilled as you'd have me believe."

"Skill is one thing, but immortals have the advantage of age."

"Age does not always bestow wisdom." Zhangwei picked up a black stone and placed it on the board. "While time allows one to accumulate knowledge, it's what one does with it that sets them apart. It doesn't matter how many years one studies if one remains closed to learning."

In my realm, age mattered: Respect was yielded to an elder,

and tolerance to the young. Maybe it was because the years etched their marks upon us—unlike the immortals, whom it left untouched. It was easier to disregard time when one did not suffer its scars.

"At least you have the chance to seek all the knowledge you wish," I argued. "Moreover, the endless years aren't the only advantage you possess. You have magic, nor does illness touch you."

"Do you envy us?" he asked quietly.

A dangerous question. "These gifts make you more powerful than us, but not necessarily better."

"Do you think your people are as capable as us?" It wasn't disbelief or condescension in his voice, but curiosity.

"I daresay our hearts and minds are as strong as yours," I said carefully. "Given the same opportunities, we'd be more than a match for your kind."

"Would you wish to be immortal? To have these advantages?" he asked.

I studied his face, wondering if there might be something more sinister behind these questions. Who wouldn't want to live forever with their loved ones, to never fear illness and death, to have the time to read every book ever written, to listen to music without end? To be beautiful, powerful, and *eternal.* But even as I envied their gifts, I did not want to become like them—jaded and careless, almost cruel in their callousness to those they deemed "less." What use was a gift if it wasn't treasured? But I needed to guard myself not to reveal my ambition, my resentment of their kind.

I placed my piece on the board, no longer thinking about the game. "Maybe, if there was someone to share it with. Eternity might be lonely otherwise." A safe answer.

He set another piece on the board, laying an elaborate trap as I smothered a curse. "Are you lonely?"

At his question, the hollow in my chest gaped a little wider. "My grandfather is dead. I have no family left."

He paused. "He was a good ruler."

"He was a better grandfather." My voice thickened with emotion.

"Do you still grieve for him?"

"Of course. How long do immortals grieve for?" I asked, a touch bitterly. "There is a hole in my heart. I don't know if it will ever close or if anything will fill it—but I also don't want it to. I want to miss him, to never forget."

He reached out, brushing away a tear that I'd not known had fallen. His touch was unexpectedly gentle for one who wielded a sword with such violence.

"I am sorry. I hope you will find the peace you need."

His words seeped into the silence between us, my cheek burning from his touch. Was he apologizing for my grief? The fear his people roused in us? Or how my grandfather had died: afraid for his life, his loved ones, and his kingdom? It shouldn't matter, yet it did—a little—that he cared.

This felt too real, unsettling, and I sought safer ground. "Grandfather was loyal to Her Majesty. He served her to the best of his abilities." It was the truth, until he'd disobeyed her.

"Did he speak of the Divine Pearl Lotus to you?"

Inside, I stiffened, even as my brow puckered in seeming confusion. Had this all been an act? Was this why he'd sought my company? As I was trying to draw information from him, he was doing the same with me. A relief that he was ignorant about the lotus, that what he sought lay inside me. I resisted the urge to rub the scar, picking up another weiqi piece instead.

"Grandfather said the lotus was greatly treasured by Her Majesty. He guarded it with care but warned me that many desired it, too." I stared into the god's face, keeping my tone as steady as I could. "Why does the queen want it? What does the Divine Pearl Lotus do?"

"That is for Her Majesty to disclose," he replied shortly. "Do you share your grandfather's loyalty?"

There was only one answer, if I wanted to live. I placed my next move, barely looking at the board, a chill crystalizing in my veins. The stakes of this game were higher than I'd thought—not the pieces on the board but those played with words. I needed to convince him of my loyalty, that I knew nothing of the missing lotus.

"Of course, I do." I spoke with as much sincerity as I could muster. "I remember my grandfather's lessons. Tianxia is loyal to Her Majesty."

A brief pause as he contemplated the board. "It's not been an easy time for your kingdom or ours," he admitted. "We suffered great losses in the battle with the Wuxin. Her Majesty in particular, with the death of her husband. She has not recovered from her sorrow."

My kingdom had suffered from it. "Have you served Her Majesty for long?" I asked.

"She is my queen. I am her loyal subject."

"What if Her Majesty errs? What if she's in the wrong?" I smiled like it was a joke.

"Right or wrong is often a matter of perspective."

"A villain's defense," I scoffed.

"Or a hero's excuse," he returned. "Which do you imagine in this case?"

"Neither." I would not be trapped.

We continued playing in silence. Words could be treacherous, as slippery as the riverbank, where one misplaced step could plunge you into waters too deep. Once spoken, they could not be forgotten, imbued with an unpredictable power that blurred fantasy and reality, spinning lies into truth. I had risked too much already.

He made his moves more swiftly now, moving to encircle territories and capture my stones with appalling ease. I played halfheartedly, neither attacking nor defending with care, instead studying his technique for another day. When our game was over—a frown crossed his face. Was he disappointed? I'd been a poor opponent, but I'd also barely tried. Maybe one day I could show him what I was capable of. He would learn not to underestimate me then. For now, it was safer that he did.

As I rose to leave, he glanced up at me. "I will be away tomorrow morning. Would you take your evening meal with me? Maybe we could play again?"

I did not want to eat with him, much less lose another game. But one thing Grandfather had taught me was that my wants could not always govern my actions. I had to think beyond myself to what my kingdom needed. I could refuse under the pretense of an excuse, remaining confined to my rooms. Or I could use this opportunity to find out what I needed, to cultivate a powerful relationship that might help my people. Maybe it was time to stop being afraid of the immortals—to see them as equals, whether as villains or allies. Maybe it was time we used *them*, rather than seeking their approval.

He drew back, his expression shuttering. "It's an invitation, not a demand. If you prefer otherwise—"

"I would like to." My answer was wooden, but I hoped he wouldn't notice.

"Till tomorrow."

A shadow of a smile played on his lips as he turned away. At least with him gone tomorrow, I could explore his home in peace. I should be relieved at his absence, yet when he left the library, for some reason it felt a little emptier.

8

The next day, I woke early, taking my meal in the hall. As I sat by the round marble table, Ningxi served me enough food for four. Silken congee cooked with prawns, small plates of preserved vegetables, tea eggs, pickled ginger, and fried dough sticks. The food was good, yet the silence was unnerving.

"Has Lord Zhangwei left?" I asked Ningxi, careful not to appear too eager.

"Yes. At dawn," she replied.

My fingers tightened around my cup. To conceal my excitement, I took a long drink of tea, warm and fragrant. "Do you know when he'll be back?"

"In time for the evening meal. Lord Zhangwei instructed us to make the preparations, and to aid you with anything you might need in his absence. Shall I help you select a suitable dress? Maybe one Lord Zhangwei would like?"

As her lips formed a knowing smile, I swallowed a sharp retort. "I have a dress in mind," I lied, hoping to divert the slant of her mind.

"He likes red," she suggested helpfully.

I sighed in false regret. "Unfortunately, I don't wear bright colors."

"The cook is planning a special meal," she told me with great satisfaction. "All of Lord Zhangwei's favorites: roasted quail, braised pork—"

"I can't eat quail." Another lie. It annoyed me that to them, only Lord Zhangwei's preferences mattered.

Ningxi continued, oblivious to my worsening mood, "I will tell the cook to avoid the quail. For the wine, I have a rare one in mind that will stimulate—"

"Ah, there's no need for the wine," I interjected. "It makes me break out in rashes."

Her mouth pursed. "There's no need to be nervous about tonight. Though Lord Zhangwei is much admired, you're the one he invited into his home."

I stifled a protest. It was safer to lean into their suspicions, to better conceal my intent. The immortals were so arrogant, they'd readily believe us fools for love for them. "It was only because he was commanded to do so by Queen Caihong," I said, as though uncertain. "Even in Tianxia, we've heard of his devotion to Her Majesty."

Ningxi shook her head. "No one can make Lord Zhangwei do anything he doesn't want to—not even Her Majesty. Lord Zhangwei could have found rooms for you in the palace or sent you to live with one of his many subordinates. For some reason, he wanted you here."

My curiosity was sparked, though it was not for what she implied. Was the queen's hold on him weaker than I'd assumed? If so, I might be able to persuade him to aid us. Our kingdom must be a burden on the God of War, who had to protect us, unless he thrived on the worship of the mortals.

Ningxi was waiting for my response. "How do you know Lord Zhangwei is much admired?" I asked quickly.

"Do you have eyes?" She grinned, continuing what seemed to be a favorite subject. "Everyday gifts and tributes arrive for Lord Zhangwei, hoping to win his favor—"

"Or his mercy?" I couldn't help adding.

"Some, to be sure. But many are from those who hold him in high regard, the families hoping to secure a union." As a choked noise slipped from my throat, Ningxi glanced at me. "You seem surprised."

"No, Lord Zhangwei is . . . attractive," I managed to say. Beneath her scrutiny, I found myself thinking of the God of War— not just the weapons he bore, though he never seemed to be without them—but the black of his eyes, the sculpted planes of his face, his thin lips that yielded an air of gravity even when he smiled. A flush crept up my neck; suddenly this claim didn't feel like the lie I'd thought it was. He *was* handsome—just as this place was beautiful. But that didn't mean I wanted to stay here, nor did it mean I wanted him.

Ningxi scowled, disdaining my lukewarm praise. "His Lordship has been courted by almost every eligible person of marriageable age—"

"You are right, Lord Zhangwei is handsome and intelligent and . . . powerful." I took a gulp of tea to wash down the bitterness, eager to end this discussion. "And let's have the wine tonight." I wouldn't drink it, but it was a useful distraction for Ningxi as she headed toward the kitchens.

At once, I made my way from the hall. I'd already explored most of the grounds but found nothing of use. All that was left was the South Courtyard and the God of War's private rooms. Maybe he'd left the red jade ornament there. And if he was away, there was no better time to search his quarters—as long as I could find a way in.

High walls cleaved the East Courtyard from the rest of manor, the red lacquered doors closed. The threat of discovery flashed across my mind, but I ignored it, pushing at the heavy wooden panels. I was growing impatient, afraid that despite my grand ambitions I'd leave this place with nothing. As the door creaked open,

I slipped into the courtyard. Bamboo shaded the stone pathway, sunlight filtering in watery shafts. To the side lay a large pond circled by willows, their delicate leaves gleaming silver as they trailed through the glistening waters. Smooth, flat stones formed a path that led to a black-roofed building flanked by mahogany pillars.

My heart raced. If I could find something of use here, it might change the course of our future. As I drew closer to the building, a melody sprang to life—achingly poignant, the strings reverberating with emotion. The qin was my favorite instrument, its sound solitary yet rich in depth. While I'd taken lessons as a child, my playing often made my tutors wince . Fortunately, there were always musicians at court.

Caution reared as I spun around, seeking this talented musician. The music drifted from a pavilion nestled in a corner, behind a grove of trees. A man sat there with his back to me, his unbound hair flowing down his back, his plain gray robe pooling on the floor.

The song soared, a sweeping melody of yearning, of loss. The musician could not be the god. An immortal might master technical perfection over the years, but not the passion that flowed through these notes. They whispered of a reverence for life, a sensitivity that a brutal killer could not possess, a tenderness that made me ache for some unknown reason. I slipped back among the stalks of bamboo, their shadows falling in slivers upon my face. Was this stranger why the god chose to keep to his rooms? Was he a friend, or the god's lover? The thought pricked, but I forced myself to think how to shift this to my advantage. Could I make an ally here? Or should I flee, to avoid discovery? The latter seemed safest—as I took a step back, treading over a twig that crackled faintly.

The music stopped. A loud twang erupted as a gold cord snapped free from the qin and sprang toward me, swifter than a striking snake. I gasped, darting out of the way as its end sliced my cheek, blood oozing from the cut. The cord curved back, flying toward me again, but I dropped down—just as another cord tore free, wrapping around my ankles. As I staggered, trying to catch my balance, a third qin string shot forth, coiling around my wrists.

I fell, crashing against the stone path, pain flaring along my body. As I continued struggling where I lay, the thin cords bit deeper into my flesh. *So stupid—so careless, to end up bound and helpless!* Fear slithered down my spine as I turned onto my back, a shadow falling over me. I squinted, trying to make out the face against the glare of the sun—

"You!" I seethed.

The God of War crouched down, the loose strands of his hair sliding down to graze my cheek. Silken soft, even as his gaze speared me, all trace of the courteous host gone. "You dare much, coming here uninvited."

Mustering my courage, I shoved my wrists at him, glaring though I had no right. Safer to attack, than to admit wrong. "How dare *you* tie me up?"

His eyes narrowed. "How should I treat a trespasser?"

"I did *not* trespass," I said boldly, widening my eyes. "You said I could go where I wished. You only forbade me from the South Courtyard, not your quarters."

"Isn't it common courtesy to not invade a host's rooms?" As his tone lightened, a little of my tension eased. "Had I known you desired a private encounter—"

I laughed aloud, even as my face burned. "Do you think everyone desires you? I don't—not now, not ever," I declared rashly, something about him stirring the reckless devil within.

As his eyes blazed, I cursed myself for baiting him. He bent closer then, the coolness from his body flaring across mine. My limbs froze, snared by the predatory gleam in his gaze, the harsh slant of his lips. As his fingers brushed my cheek, something sparked at his touch—something that frightened me. His hand slid lower to clasp my neck, his hold light yet intent . . . as though wanting to disprove my claim, as though knowing he could make me want him. He was wrong, I told myself fiercely, fighting a wave of doubt.

As he lowered his face to mine, sweat broke out across my skin. "I'm here upon your queen's command." I hated the quiver in my voice. "You promised I'd be safe."

"Don't be so stupid to trust fully in another's word, especially a stranger's. Learn more caution if you want to survive here. *Safe* just means I keep you alive. I could imprison you in your chamber. I could bend your mind to my will, to obey my every command with utter delight. I could keep you in a state of endless slumber, safe—yet some might argue, better off dead." He remained as still as a statue, restrained power pulsing in his fingers, the dangerous glitter in his eyes holding me fast. "Be more careful in your demands, be more discerning in *whom* you trust."

"Are you so deceitful? Can a god's promise be broken?" I demanded hoarsely, refusing to cower.

"*Anything* can be broken. The question is whether it can be remade." He released me, tracing the cut on my cheek, tingling with the now-familiar sensation of his healing.

I twisted away from his touch, refusing to show my fear; someone like him probably thrived on it. "Are you done trying to terrify me?"

As I struggled to my feet, he grasped my arm, pulling me up with ease—then propped me gently against a flowering tree. Soft petals drifted down, one gliding across my face. Unlike those in my world, these were not edged with brown but veined with gold. There were no reminders of death here, and I didn't know if that enhanced or diminished its beauty.

I held out my bound hands. "Release me."

"The Lady of Tianxia is meant to be gracious." There was a lilt in his tone, akin to a laugh.

"Oh, I am, to those who deserve it."

The god scowled as he reached for the cords around my wrists, unwinding them until they slithered to the ground. I rubbed the grooves embedded in my flesh, trying not to wince.

He made an impatient sound at the back of his throat. "Give me your hands."

"I would rather—"

He did not wait for me to finish. With a deep sigh, he caught my wrists. A current pulsed from his touch, light streaking across the marks, which subsided along with the discomfort. "I'm not your enemy," he said quietly as he let me go.

"Of course not," I replied cautiously. "It's an honor for Tianxia to serve the Golden Desert."

His eyes flicked toward me. "Save the flattery for Her Majesty. You don't need to say such things to me; I'd rather you say what you mean."

A terrifying thought. Thankfully, his attention slid to the welts that ringed my ankles. His eyebrows drew together as his fingers grazed my leg, his touch like a breath of winter. The pain vanished, along with the swelling.

"Your skin is cold," I blurted without thinking. "Are you ill?"

How foolish I sounded. Immortals were untouched by such suffering and vulnerabilities—those that plagued us. Maybe their ignorance made them seem cruel, though it was no excuse.

"No," he said. "But there are times when I'm tired and just want to rest like today, without anyone knowing I'm here."

"I understand." I wanted him to continue, to pry apart this rare window into his heart. "Everyone needs time to themselves. Even the strong are weak sometimes, even the powerful need someone to care for them."

Silence fell over us, his gaze deepening. "There aren't many who would say this to me. Most expect me to protect them."

I didn't draw away, making myself shift closer. "You must

look after yourself, too. It must be hard to bear the responsibility over so many."

"As do you, Lady of Tianxia." The gravity of his tone mirrored mine. "Especially when there is no one to share it with."

And though I'd hoped to snare him with my words, *his* drew a string around my heart. I tried to cast it away, to snap it— reminding myself why I was here. These dreams could not be allowed to form; they had no right to exist. I couldn't get caught up in this farce, pretending he was someone other than what he was: The God of War. Immortal. Cruel.

"I hope you find that person." My words rang hollow, the intimate spell broken.

He sensed it, too, as he folded his arms across his chest. "Why did you come to my courtyard?"

"Can't a guest seek out her host?" I asked evasively. "I was curious about you, about where you stayed." It was wiser to follow the train of his suspicion rather than attempt a clumsy deflection.

As he straightened, the ornament by his waist caught the light, the slender tablet of red jade—the key to the South Courtyard. How could I steal it? I was a terrible thief; unable to even slip into his garden without being discovered. If the god caught me groping at his waist, what would he think? What might he do?

But I couldn't afford to be cautious. The South Courtyard held something precious, the only reason it was protected so well. Taking a step toward him, I feigned a stumble—falling against him with my full weight. A low breath rushed from his throat as we went sprawling to the ground, his arms encircling me as a shield. His embrace seared, my mind clouded by his touch. As I lay on him, my eyes flew to his—as wide as mine. I struggled in his arms to distract him, my fingers closing around the tablet, unfastening it swiftly and tossing it into the grass. I dared not take it yet, trembling all over—was it from what I'd done, or the intimacy of our bodies pressed together? Was this fear, revulsion, or something else entirely?

He was breathing as heavily as me, his hands still clasped around my waist. "First you force your way into my quarters. And now, this?"

My mind went blank at his teasing, my guard springing up. I pushed myself upright, anger crowding out the rest of these unsettling emotions. "You're an arrogant beast to imagine I'd ever want this."

He sat up, resting an elbow on his knee, his jaw clenched. "I've been called many things before, but never a beast."

"How surprising." I would have gladly called him more names, many of which I was certain he'd never heard, those that would make a bandit blush. "Maybe most are afraid to tell you what they think to your face."

Something flickered in his gaze. "Yet you aren't afraid of me."

I lifted my head. "Should I be?" I didn't think he'd hurt me, but I was afraid of what he might do to my people if angered. I didn't know him yet or understand his mercurial moods. He wore a mask that I was curious to look beneath, yet equally afraid of what I'd find.

"It depends. What have you heard of me?" he countered.

"All mortals know the God of War possesses a heart of ice, a desert of a soul." As soon as I spoke, I wished I could take it back. But once uttered, words take on a life of their own, sometimes detached from their meaning. I'd told him exactly what he'd asked, yet I'd not been kind—wanting to strike at him because I was afraid. Because I didn't like how he made me feel: vulnerable and uncertain.

His face darkened. "If you think that of me, you should leave."

A dismissal. My heart twinged at his expression but I hardened myself, stalking purposefully toward the jade tablet I'd torn from him earlier, that was lying in the grass. Sensing his watchful gaze upon me, I bent to adjust the hem of my skirt—then surreptitiously slid the ornament into my palm. As I rose, I tucked it into my sleeve. My breath caught as I braced for accusations, but there were none. Triumph reared, yet it was tempered by a lingering heaviness from our encounter, an unfamiliar weight.

The God of War might not be the monster he was rumored to be, but that did not mean he wasn't dangerous. Part of me wanted to retreat from this perilous game—yet the stakes were too high, I could not give up. He held many things in his palm, including the safety of Tianxia. If I wanted to gain anything of worth, I needed to push the door between us wider to win his trust, to hide my resentment and loathing, to make him think I cared.

And above all . . . I must *never* forget that I was pretending.

9

I stood before the South Courtyard, glancing around to ensure no one had followed me after leaving Lord Zhangwei's quarters. Eager to return the jade tablet before it was missed, I pressed the carved star into the gilded hollow. It slid in with a soft click, a perfect fit. Light rippled in waves across the wall as a section of it vanished, large enough for one to walk through. Holding my breath, I stepped inside.

When the god had forbidden me from the South Courtyard, I imagined it housed a trove of magical artifacts, weapons to pierce immortal flesh, potions to drain their might. Maybe prisoners who could be turned to allies once I'd helped secure their freedom. And in my wildest imaginings, the Shield of Rivers and Mountains itself.

Not this exquisite, useless, taunting beauty. My insides knotted; something about this place setting me on edge. A shimmering lake took up most of the courtyard, lotuses blooming in a violent riot of color. The water was calm, not a single fish breaking the surface, not even the flutter of a dragonfly's wings. Encircling the lake were willow trees, the namesake of this place—their slender vines billowing in the air like silver ribbons. A stone bridge arched across the lake, leading to a hall that rose from the water. The deep-green roof was curved at each corner, the ridges adorned with gilded sculptures of phoenixes.

The stillness sank deep, like an unearthly slumber. Despite the tranquility, my breathing hitched as I crossed the bridge. Who lived here? This place was too lovely to be uninhabited, such care taken with every detail. Sliding the doors apart, I entered a magnificent chamber, rosewood pillars soaring from malachite bases. The ceiling was an intricate mosaic of turquoise, gold, and mother-of-pearl, resembling the sky. A wide bed was placed in the middle of the room, the gauze curtains tied to the posts, the blue brocade covers neatly tucked under the mattress. A table at the far end was crowded with small wooden boxes. As I opened one, jeweled ornaments glittered: amethyst hairpins, sapphire earrings, lacquered combs, ropes of pearls.

I tugged open the doors of a cupboard, smothering my conscience at this violation of privacy. Silk and brocade were piled in rich hues of emerald, topaz, and lapis. The robes were embroidered with silver and gold, pearls studding the sashes and the hems of cloaks. Exquisite garments that even a queen would have delighted in.

A lacquered qin rested on a table, flowers carved into its wooden frame. As my fingers brushed the taut strings, a memory flashed of the haunting melody Lord Zhangwei had played earlier—of the way his body felt against mine when we'd fallen together. A tremor coursed through me as I set the qin aside and turned to search the rest of chamber.

Everything gleamed as though newly polished, yet an air of abandonment shrouded the place. These beautiful quarters must have belonged to someone cherished—a family member, or a beloved concubine, perhaps? One who had fallen out of favor, which might explain the desertion of this place and the god's grim demeanor.

Perhaps *here* lay the God of War's weakness.

I continued my search with newfound enthusiasm, yet gleaned no clue of the occupant's identity or why this courtyard had been forbidden. Beyond the jewels and fine clothes, there seemed to be nothing of note, or maybe I hadn't found it yet. As I left to search the gardens, the air outside was suffused with the heady fragrance of lotuses.

One of them caught my eye—a soft rose, the tips brushed with white. It reminded me of the lotuses in Tianxia, those that bloomed wild over the lakes and ponds. As my fingers brushed it, the petals shriveled, leaving a shimmering powder on my hands. The other flowers shuddered in eerie unison, a whispering rush gathering in force. Terror snaked around me—was this a trap?

I turned to run, but vines sprang from the waters, scattering droplets like rain. Tendrils coiled around my ankles, binding me fast. My heart thudded, the air choked from my lungs. What magic was this? I pulled out my dagger and slashed at the stalks, but it was as tough as cutting through wood. Tiny, needle-like thorns dug into my flesh as a thick brownish sap leaked through the sliced stems, searing me. Tightening my grip on the hilt, I slammed the dagger down again, sawing through the thick stem until it broke, freeing one of my ankles. The skin was torn, the wound burning like fire. Grinding my teeth, I slashed the binds on my other leg with renewed vigor, severing the remaining vines. Relief surged as I raced away, ignoring the pain in my legs. Behind me, the rustling thickened as more vines broke the pool's surface, lashing toward me—

A rumble crackled above, clouds moving swiftly across the heavens. Was it a storm? A bolt of light struck the path ahead, erupting into thorny plants that blocked my path, glinting menacingly. As I staggered to a halt, staring in horror—clouds descended from the skies, bearing soldiers in gold armor. A woman flew alone, her cloud sweeping down to land before me. She was clad in violet brocade, pearls the size of my thumb dangling from her ears, framing her angular face. A gold headdress studded with amber glittered from her black hair.

She was studying me with her wide eyes, her lips pinched into a knot. "This place is forbidden to all. Who are you?" she rasped, her tone reverberating with fury.

Fear shrouded my mind. "I am the Lady of Tianxia," I said at last. "Lord Zhangwei's guest, upon the order of Her Majesty Queen Caihong. I am here to pledge my fealty to her."

Titles were useful as a shield from danger. Maybe they'd help temper this woman's wrath—except it struck me then, she was the one who'd sat on my grandfather's throne: Queen Caihong, herself.

The queen's eyes thinned to slits. "Is this how you greet me, Lady of Tianxia?" she seethed.

I was still standing, looking her in the face. It wasn't easy but I lowered myself to the ground, bowing my head as Grandfather had—though anger twisted and writhed within.

"Your Majesty, I am honored to meet you." I spoke stiffly, resentment weighing my tongue. The intensity of her stare unnerved me, as did her rage. She appeared quick to anger, though it should come as no surprise when my kingdom bore its marks.

"Who permitted you to enter these quarters? Confess now, or your punishment will be tenfold worse."

Punishment?

My mouth went dry. Was *she* the mistress of this courtyard? I kept my head down; it was easier than looking into her face. "No one gave me permission, Your Majesty. I was told not to come . . . but I was curious." I wasn't trying to protect the God of War, but lies would gain me little. As a taut silence fell over us, I added with more prudence than sincerity, "If I caused offense, I ask your pardon, Your Majesty."

The corners of her mouth dipped as she examined me, appearing deep in thought. If these were her rooms, how else was she connected to the God of War? I'd thought the god's dedication stemmed from loyalty to his monarch—but was it something more that bound him?

Something slithered between my ribs at the thought, my chest squeezed tighter. I dared not move or speak, acutely aware that I was hovering on the brink of disaster. Another wrong move and the pledge of fealty would be the least of my worries, the queen demanding my head instead.

The queen's gaze fell onto my fingers, coated in the gleaming powder from the lotus. "You *plucked* the flowers," she accused venomously. "You dared to steal one."

Her tone was laced with triumph; she was looking for a reason to punish me whether I deserved it or not. "I only touched it," I protested. "They were so beautiful. I didn't know they belonged to you."

"Guards—seize the mortal." Her face was a stony mask. "Bring her back to the palace for her punishment."

Two soldiers moved toward me, grabbing my arms. Fear was ice in my stomach, hardening along my veins. "Wait!" I cried out, my voice breaking. "Lord Zhangwei said I was under his protection."

She stilled at once, an odd light flaring in her eyes. "If that is true, then let Lord Zhangwei come and collect you himself."

Would there be there anything left of me after my "punishment"? I struggled violently against her guards. I wouldn't go willingly, not this way—a victim of her wrath. The God of War was ruthless and cold, but compared to his queen, he was the incarnation of kindness.

One of the soldiers shoved my back and I fell onto my palms, scraping them against the stones. Another started toward me—but then light struck the ground between us, waves of fire arcing wide to form a ring around me.

"Step away from her."

Lord Zhangwei stood a short distance behind me, his command uttered with such authority, the soldiers froze at once. Before their queen, they wrapped their fists in their palms to bow to him, their reverence clear to all.

I exhaled with relief; I could have wept with it. The God of War wore no armor, clad in the same gray robe as earlier. His jade-and-gold sword was clasped in his hand, his hair pulled back into a silver ring. All the while, his flames circled me like a shield, one I welcomed now.

"Lord Zhangwei, you've been careless," Queen Caihong admonished him bitterly. "This place is forbidden to *all*."

Her hostile manner was surprising. After her rage at my presence, I'd imagined them more intimate. Was I mistaken? Were these not her quarters?

Lord Zhangwei bowed to her. "The Lady of Tianxia is my guest, under my protection. If she has displeased Your Majesty, I will bear the consequences."

"You are protective of the mortal." Her mouth curled into a mirthless smile as she raised her hand, white light streaking forth to engulf the flames around me. They shuddered, dying abruptly. "Given your negligence, she will return with me now."

Mutely, I shook my head. If she took me, I was as good as dead. The way she looked at me . . . I was a splinter in her finger, a thorn pricking her heel. And she wanted me gone.

As the soldiers moved toward me again, the god drew his great blade and hurled it toward us—its tip plunging into the stone path, fracturing it into a web of cracks. The soldiers stepped back, exchanging uneasy glances.

It was not an attack but a warning.

"She is under my protection," the god repeated calmly as he strode forward to stand beside me. "No one will take her from me."

"Are you defying me, Lord Zhangwei?" Queen Caihong's voice dropped dangerously low.

"I am obeying your previous command, Your Majesty—to

bring the Lady of Tianxia *safely* to court, to pledge her loyalty to you," he replied without flinching. "Nor am I asking you to rescind her punishment, but to allow me to bear it, since she is my responsibility."

"No." The protest fell from me, stupid though it was. I should let him do this, let him suffer—hadn't he caused enough strife in the world? But deep down, I didn't want this. Was it the obligation? How it muddied my feelings when I so desperately needed the clarity? I should hate him, I needed to. Moreover, this was my fault. I'd defied his order, stolen the key to enter. I should accept the punishment myself . . . except I didn't want to die. And it dawned on me, too—this wedge between the queen and her God of War could be beneficial to us. Let the immortals play their own games; it was better for Tianxia if they turned on each other.

The queen drew herself up, her amber headdress catching the light. "Think carefully, Lord Zhangwei. Do you truly wish to bear the mortal's punishment? Her offense is grave, as you know."

"It was a single flower," I protested. "It withered when I touched it."

"You entered where you shouldn't have, you touched what you had no right to," she said harshly. "You have disrespected our rules and violated the hospitality of your host."

I bit my tongue, suppressing a flash of shame. She was right, and yet her anger and threats seemed disproportionate. "I apologize for offending you, Your Majesty. I meant no disrespect." These conciliatory words choked me, but I hoped they'd be enough. I didn't want anyone to be punished on my behalf, not even *him*.

As Queen Caihong stared at me, unspeaking, the God of War stepped forward. "I will bear her punishment," he said, more forcefully than before.

I tried to read his expression, to understand why he was doing this. But whether his protection of me was bound to duty or honor . . . I wasn't indifferent to it, an unwanted warmth spreading through me.

A brittle smile stretched over Queen Caihong's face. How did she feel, her general protecting a mortal? "Lord Zhangwei. I summon you to the Palace of Radiant Light to receive your punishment tomorrow."

"What is the punishment?" I asked, half-expecting her to ignore me.

"Four strikes on the Dragon Platform."

The soldiers shuffled anxiously, but Lord Zhangwei bowed without hesitation. "Yes, Your Majesty."

The queen's face was a mask of cruel indifference, as though the God of War was not her most loyal warrior. When she spoke, her voice rang clear. "Bring the mortal. Let her see what her actions have wrought."

10

Since Queen Caihong's visit, an uneasiness festered inside me. The queen was every bit as merciless as I'd expected—even to the one who was high in her favor, a pillar of her kingdom's might. Dread sank over me at the thought of going to her palace despite the lure of what I might find. And something else gnawed at me—the God of War's protection. Though I hadn't asked this of him, my guilt did not lessen. I needed to harden myself; I had to learn not to care.

I pulled on a white robe embroidered with orchids, then headed to the hall for breakfast. I'd missed dinner—too tired to spar with the immortal, my mood bleak. He was likely glad for it, maybe resenting me for forcing him into a confrontation with his monarch.

The God of War was sitting at the table, dressed formally in a black brocade robe, embroidered with a pattern of squares in gold. His hair was coiled into a topknot, the severity of the style somehow enhancing the sculpted planes of his face. As he lifted a cup to his mouth, Ningxi set the food before him: bowls of steaming soybean milk, crisp pancakes filled with sweetened bean paste, and glutinous rice dumplings wrapped in bamboo leaves—my favorite type, cooked with pork, mushrooms, and salted egg yolk.

I stilled, contemplating flight, but the god's eyes flicked toward me. "Running away again?" he asked, an edge to his tone. "I didn't think you were a coward."

Squaring my shoulders, I stalked into the room, taking the seat across from him. "Don't call me a coward. After yesterday, I thought you'd prefer not to see me."

"I invited you to dine because I wanted to see you," he replied. "I don't change my mind that easily."

His answer surprised me. In the silence, Lord Zhangwei placed a rice dumpling onto my plate, cutting the string that bound the leaves together. As his long fingers deftly unwrapped it, I imagined them curled around the hilt of a sword.

I didn't want his courtesy; I didn't need my resolve blunted. It was safer if my emotions remained untangled. Even though Lord Zhangwei had saved me, he was an immortal, not a friend . . . and certainly not someone I could trust. Despite the seed of obligation that had sprouted—I must yank it out, discard it before it grew into a hindrance.

I lifted the teapot and filled his cup. While I didn't want to serve him, I'd repay each kindness with one of my own. It might lessen my confusion to think of it as a trade; it might make me care less.

As I ate, I suppressed the urge to ask him about the South Courtyard—afraid of stirring his anger, of reminding how I'd stolen the key. A memory flashed of how I'd fallen on top of him, heat creeping over my face.

"It is too warm here?" His tone was soft, his gaze riveted on me.

"Yes, it's grown stifling." I took a sip of tea, ignoring the coolness of the morning air.

He smiled, a knowing one that chafed at me. "The Dragon Platform is set outdoors. If you don't like the heat, you should join the spectators in the shade."

"No." I looked at him then. "I will stand with you."

Something flared in his eyes. "Why?"

"Why did you accept the punishment on my behalf?" The question slipped out, one I shouldn't have asked.

His fingers toyed with the rim of his cup. "Would you rather I let Her Majesty punish you? One strike upon the Dragon Platform could flay the flesh from your bones."

"I'm not afraid," I lied, recoiling inside.

"You *should* be." He took a bite of a pancake, the edges crackling. The impending punishment seemed to have little effect on his appetite. "Our realm is dangerous for mortals; a slight injury for us could be your death. You must stay on your guard, be cautious—be afraid."

An unexpected sentiment from the God of War, one that pried a little of me apart. "I am afraid," I admitted in a low voice. "I wish I wasn't."

"You gave no sign of it. Not yesterday, not even when we faced the Winged Devils," he said. "Hide it if you must, but don't be ashamed of it. Fear keeps you safe, it keeps you alive."

I met his gaze. "Are you afraid when you face an enemy? When you fight?"

He didn't answer right away. "Sometimes you learn to hide something so well, it's lost even to yourself," he said slowly, like he was sharing something intimate.

My pulse quickened for some reason. I looked away, using my chopsticks to break the rice dumpling into chunks. "When do we leave for the palace today?"

"Soon." His mouth slid into a hard smile. "Such events are typically held before the afternoon meal. It whets the appetite."

"You make it sound like entertainment."

"Many find pleasure in watching blood spilled when it's not their own."

I took a bite of the rice dumpling, though my appetite had waned. "Have you been punished on the Dragon Platform before?"

"No."

Of course not. He was the queen's most trusted and respected warrior, now brought low because of me.

"Is it dangerous, for an immortal?" I asked.

"It depends on the severity of the strikes, the element channeled. Lightning is the harshest. After that would be Fire, Water, then Earth."

I set my chopsticks down, my desire for food gone. "Which will be yours?"

"It depends on Her Majesty's mood."

Queen Caihong might want to humble her God of War, but she wouldn't harm him—it would only hurt herself. Yet when I recalled the queen's rage, fear gripped me again. "What if you die?" I asked hoarsely.

His expression shuttered. "I don't intend to."

When he rose to leave, I caught his sleeve, unintentionally brushing his wrist. His skin was cold, or was mine too warm? The heat of the Divine Pearl Lotus pulsed through me constantly. I'd grown used to it; a familiar presence.

"That doesn't answer my question." If only my voice didn't shake.

Anything that weakens these immortals, strengthens us. If the Golden Desert is in turmoil, maybe Tianxia can break free, a voice inside me whispered. But one thing emerged clear amid the chaos of my mind: No matter what . . . I didn't want the God of War to die.

When his gaze fell to my hand, I dropped his sleeve as though scalded. "Are you concerned about me?" he asked, a small smile playing on his lips.

Did he expect a heartfelt confession? Tears of gratitude? Such arrogance, as was the way he seemed assured of the answer he was casting for.

"Of course," I replied, wide-eyed. "If anything happened to you, who would bring me home?"

I'd have said anything to wipe the pleasure from his face, but as his smile vanished, the small victory left me hollow.

"My attendants will escort you back should anything happen to me. Her Majesty will also ensure your safety."

"It's more likely Her Majesty will send me home in pieces," I said, forgetting for a moment to whom I spoke.

His brow furrowed as he said sternly, "Don't speak this way of Her Majesty. Don't judge her."

His anger sparked my own. "Why? Because I'm mortal?"

"Because you know nothing."

Such condescension stoked my fury. How I wanted to strike out at him, to hurt him the only way I could.

"One thing I *do* know," I hissed, rising to my feet, "is that I'll *relish* watching you get humbled today. I hope the punishment hurts. I hope it brings you to your knees." Wicked words, but a devil possessed me in that moment, one with a knife for a tongue and a stone for a heart.

His eyes blazed, turning into those of a dangerous predator I'd made the mistake of baiting. "It will take more than a few strikes to bring me to my knees. Take a front seat and enjoy the spectacle. I'll be watching you. If you flinch, I'll know you for a coward and liar."

As he stalked from the room, I found my hands clenched. Our masks had slipped. While it was better to have my path cleared, a line drawn in my mind—I couldn't indulge my temper again. I had to earn his trust, not push him away, though he excelled at infuriating me.

I followed after him reluctantly, grinding the grass beneath my feet with each step—coming to an abrupt halt in the courtyard by the entrance. The God of War was standing beside a magnificent creature, caught between a dream and a nightmare. Fiery feathers curled from a wide body, a spiked crown springing from its forehead. Curved talons dug into the earth, crumbling the immaculate lawn. And those eyes . . . I suppressed the urge to shy from those luminous orbs as the creature cocked its head at me, its beak parting as though anticipating its next meal.

"You didn't like flying by cloud," Lord Zhangwei said stiffly. "I thought you'd prefer riding a phoenix to the palace. Your natures are somewhat similar."

As the phoenix reared back, to swipe at me with its claws, I scowled, burying my surprise at the immortal's consideration. "Will it eat me?"

"Not unless you antagonize it." Lord Zhangwei stroked its head with a sure hand.

When the phoenix lowered itself to the grass, the god climbed upon it, then extended a hand to me. I grasped it and scrambled upon the creature, pulling away the moment I could, my body tense. The phoenix's feathers were soft, despite their needle-like barbs. As I bent to examine them, they glinted like iron.

Lord Zhangwei leaned forward to take the reins, his chest pressing against my back, hard and cool. I shifted slightly, trying to ignore the way his arms enclosed me—how safe I felt, in spite of all I knew of him. Our earlier quarrel replayed through my mind, my anger unquenched.

We flew a short distance, a sea of glittering sand stretching beneath us. Turquoise stone sloped up from the desert, forming a ridge of mountains, their peaks cresting like waves. A magnificent palace was sprawled upon the highest one, all white and silver like it was carved from ice—the Palace of Radiant Light. From a distance its beauty was all the more startling when surrounded by the untamed majesty of the desert and mountains. Delicate aquamarine bridges arched across the skies, linking the buildings like a finely spun spider web.

We landed on the outskirts of the palace. Peonies bloomed alongside jasmine and azaleas, in the shade of plum-blossom trees. The flowers here defied the seasons of my world, infusing the air with a heady fragrance, one that stirred something inside me—was it the remembrance of my gardens at home? A sense of peace stole over me; a desire to linger, if only I could forget why we were here.

"Why not land inside the palace?" I asked.

"This is an added precaution since the attempted attack. Whether we fly or ride through the skies, all must now walk through the main entrance," he explained.

He kept a discreet distance between us as we walked. Some silences were comfortably rounded at the corners, but the one that cloaked us was jagged and sharp.

The guards at the entrance bowed to him. "Lord Zhangwei," one of them said, "Her Majesty reminds you that the main wing of the palace is still under repair, and to use the pathway through the new wing."

Was the damage to the palace caused by the attack he mentioned? Was that why I had been ordered to stay with him?

When Lord Zhangwei nodded, the other soldier cleared his throat. "Her Majesty also commanded that you attend to her on the Dragon Platform the moment you arrived. The hour is near."

"I will go at once."

As the god strode away, I followed him through a courtyard of pine trees, down a long corridor lit by lanterns. My mind was whirling, barely noticing my surroundings. The attendants we passed looked at us curiously, the courtiers inclining their heads to Zhangwei, some exchanging sly smiles. Were they savoring the thought of the god's impending torment—someone they had probably envied and undoubtedly feared?

As it turned out, vipers existed in all courts.

Twin doors of dark mahogany loomed at the end of the corridor. Dragon heads sculpted from gold formed the handles, a thick ring clasped in each of their jaws.

As the god grasped one of the rings, he stilled. "Fight me in all else but trust me in this: keep your head down, and do not draw any attention to yourself. The court only knows you as the mortal from Tianxia, and many have a bloated sense of their own superiority. If you offend them or the queen, if you give them cause to fault you—whether by accident or design—Her Majesty will have no choice but to punish you."

I nodded, not so stubborn to ignore good sense. The Queen of the Golden Desert would also be keen for an excuse to chastise me after I'd escaped her clutches yesterday. As he looked at me, an apology hovered on my lips for causing his punishment, for my cruel words earlier. I'd lashed out at him because of my own guilt and fear. But I suppressed the impulse, afraid to open another window between us.

With a tug of the god's hand, the doors swung open, sunlight spilling on the floor like molten amber. He strode onward without hesitation, his silhouette soon consumed by the brightness.

And then, just the silence remained, taut with dread.

11

I waited a moment, gathering the courage to follow the God of War. Yet voices from behind startled me, drifting from those who hadn't turned into the corridor yet.

"Hurry, else we'll miss the show," a woman urged.

Show? My hands clenched in disgust.

"A rare event. Lord Zhangwei's position is no longer as secure," a man noted in a pleased tone.

"Our esteemed God of War has grown arrogant," the woman added. "He doesn't obey our queen as readily as he used to. I heard he defended a mortal against Her Majesty."

"Maybe Lord Zhangwei will come to heel after this." A derisive laugh.

I should be glad they spoke disdainfully of him, yet a sourish sensation writhed in my stomach.

"Maybe I should pay Lord Zhangwei a courtesy visit after his thrashing," the man mused.

"What can you do that the healers have not? You just have a soft spot for our God of War," the woman replied snidely.

"Indeed, I would loath to see such physical perfection marred." He lowered his voice as he added, "I hear his old wounds are still troubling him, those from the war with the Wuxin."

I smothered a laugh. Clearly this pair had never seen Lord

Zhangwei in battle. He fought with such vigor and force, it seemed impossible he could be doing *more*.

They turned into the corridor, a man and woman in ornate brocade robes hurrying toward the doors. Rings glittered from their fingers, a necklace of plump jade beads around the throat of the lady. Their eyes flicked toward me, then to the red thread bracelet around my wrist—stark evidence of my mortality. Their lips curled as they strode past like I didn't exist. How their scorn stung, but I had to swallow it. The weakest among the immortals could kill me with ease, an infuriating and frightening thought.

Alone now, I was tempted to remain in the shadows—but I wouldn't be a coward, hiding while the God of War was dealt the punishment that should have been mine. Bracing myself, I stepped out onto a circular stone platform that was wider than the main hall of my home. A thick stone column towered from the center, carved with a majestic dragon. Its head was flung back, whiskers flaring, its bulbous eyes crafted from onyx. A long tail curled on the ground, the end tipped with spikes that glinted in the sunlight.

Clouds ringed the platform, bearing the nobles of the Golden Desert in their fine garments. Some were dark-skinned, others fair, generously curved or slender. While many were striking, with their ageless skin and clear eyes—they did not possess the God of War's startling beauty that I'd assumed most immortals were gifted with.

Queen Caihong sat on a throne at the front of the platform, her gold brocade robe shimmering. Guards surrounded her, their weapons drawn. As Zhangwei bowed to her, then straightened, his eyes searched the platform until they fixed on me.

Take a front seat . . . I'll be watching you.

My breathing hitched as I walked toward him. The crowd's gaze shifted to me, some curious, others impatient.

"Kneel to greet Her Majesty," someone hissed from the side.

I hesitated, then lowered myself to the queen, recalling Lord

Zhangwei's warning to guard her pride.

"Maybe the mortal should leave the platform," another suggested cuttingly. "There is no room here for Lord Zhangwei's pet."

I gritted my teeth but kept my head down. The arrogance of immortals was hard to stomach; if only I had the power to repay them in kind.

The God of War's face seemed hewn from stone as he slanted toward the rude courtier. "Watch your tongue. By offending her, you offend me, too—and I am not as tolerant."

Brief words, curtly spoken, yet the courtier hastily stepped back. I smiled as his friends shifted away from him, as though afraid of the association.

When the Queen of the Golden Desert rose, a hush rippled through the crowd. Her face was grim as she stared at the God of War. Did it vex her to punish him, the leader of her army, when it should have been me? In this moment, I could almost understand her. Rulers were not infallible—they could err, lose their temper, or be tricked. The pressure was immense to do what was right, not just for themselves but for their kingdom, a delicate balance that was so hard to get right.

Her court leaned forward eagerly, their eyes bright. After all, there was neither glory nor sport in punishing a mere mortal, but to bring the God of War to his knees . . . that would be a rare spectacle indeed.

"Lord Zhangwei, are you ready?" Queen Caihong called out, her voice clear and resonant.

A chill twisted down my back, leaving me cold. If he changed his mind after what I'd said, I could not blame him.

"I am." The god unfastened his sword and laid it on the ground, then stretched out his arms, his hands fisted. Crimson sparks shot from Queen Caihong's fingers, arcing toward the stone pillar. As they sank into the carved dragon's eyes, it shuddered, then reared as though come to life. Its claws splayed, then clamped around the god's wrists with an ominous click, binding him fast. Lord Zhangwei did not flinch. As the dragon's eyes glowed, light crackled along its form, its spiked tail undulating. Warmth flooded the air, the dragon's scales aglow like embers.

A thick rope of flame surged from the stone column, seething and crackling as it sprang forth—lashing the God of War in the chest. I gagged, fighting the impulse to retch as the hot scent of blood snaked around us. A jagged hole was torn in Lord Zhangwei's robe, which now clung to him, wet with blood—yet the dark color hid the stains. Was that why he'd chosen it? His head tilted back, the cords along his throat straining, yet not a sound emerged.

Even in my worst nightmares, I'd not imagined such brutality. This debt . . . how could I ever repay it? But I met his gaze, my nails cutting into my palms, in this small way trying to offer a shard of solidarity. Despite my merciless words earlier, my resentment of his kind—there was no pleasure in his torment.

The dragon stilled, the light fading from the stone. Lord Zhangwei closed his eyes briefly as his chest rose and fell. Queen Caihong's expression was more resigned than triumphant as she raised her hand for the second strike, while I bit back a cry of protest. Once more the flames surged forth, hotter this time, sheathing the god's body. He sucked in a harsh breath, his lips parting to reveal clenched teeth. I was trembling, my stomach queasy, but I forced myself to steady. Later, I could fall apart—but not here before these uncaring immortals. Years of shoving myself into an ill-fitting mold were now of use. It came almost naturally, like putting on a cloak, one I could not let fall. I kept my eyes on the god, no longer knowing who was tethering whom in this nightmare.

Once more, the stone creature reared upon the queen's command, fire erupting from the pillar, coiling around Lord Zhangwei like a serpent. As the flames pressed tighter, searing his flesh,

I curled inward, squeezing my eyes shut. *Coward*, he'd mock me later. He was right; I couldn't bear this any longer. Even if he was my enemy, *my* heart was not made of ice. In the sudden quiet, my eyes flicked open. Somehow, he remained standing even as he swayed. How could he endure another blow?

His robe was plastered to him like he'd been caught in a storm, blood trailing from the hem, leaking upon the stone floor. Yet the God of War stood unbowed, his head raised. What he had borne would have killed me thrice over. Except the crowd was still hungry, their appetite unsated. A vicious lot to revel in another's pain—was it sweeter when drawn from one more powerful?

Despite the crisp air, sweat broke out over my skin. The god's face was ashen, yet his lips curved in the semblance of a smile. It struck me then, he was looking at me. Tears were falling from my eyes . . . I was crying, despite my earlier claims. Not for him, I told myself wrathfully—but from remorse, from causing such anguish to *anyone*. At once, I lifted my chin, willing the wetness in my eyes to vanish. How weak I was. Where was the satisfaction, the sense of justice fulfilled? The immortals had threatened my grandfather and hastened his death, brought storms and floods and suffering to my people. Shame scorched me at these conflicted emotions for the God of War, and most of all—I hated that I cared.

As Queen Caihong raised her hand for the final strike, a sigh rustled from the god, shattering my mask of calm. Something stirred inside me, raw and fierce—an almost visceral response to his torment. Was it guilt? Shame? I was no longer thinking, my legs carrying me forward. I couldn't watch any longer; it had to end.

But I was too late, the red sparks were hurtling from the queen's hand toward the stone dragon again—toward me. Dazzling, blinding, like bloodied stars of heaven.

"Move aside!" Lord Zhangwei shouted.

Such fear in his voice—I froze, then darted aside—but one of the lights buried into my shoulder, a scorching pain erupting like my flesh was ripped apart. As blood spilled down my arm, I stared at it numbly, shocked that so small a thing could wreak such harm. The imbalance of power was startlingly unfair, that the immortals' slightest actions bore such grave consequences for us.

Queen Caihong was staring in my direction, such fury in her gaze, I shied from it. But I was alive, relief flooding me. I wasn't trying to be a hero—still unsure of what I'd intended, only that I wanted this to stop. A dizziness cloaked me as I dug in my heels to keep standing, but then my legs buckled and I collapsed to the ground.

"Release me, Your Majesty. I must see to her," the God of War said in a terrible voice, straining at his bonds.

"Lord Zhangwei, your punishment is not complete," a courtier reminded him sharply.

"Then finish it, Your Majesty," he snarled.

I pushed myself up slowly, glaring at him. Had he lost his mind? He was ignoring his own advice, earning another thrashing. Facing Queen Caihong, I clasped my hands and folded over in a bow, trying to ignore how my wound seared.

"Lady of Tianxia, you may leave the platform," Queen Caihong said brusquely. "A physician will see to you."

"I thank Her Majesty for her consideration," I said in a hollow tone. "But I humbly ask for Her Majesty's mercy, to forgo the God of War's final strike—to accept my blood in repayment." I touched the wound on my shoulder then, letting the blood stain my fingers.

Silence descended. But then, someone laughed. "A girl, defending the God of War?"

"Not just a girl," his friend replied, "but a mortal."

I groped for anger, but there was nothing—my body afire with agony. Lord Zhangwei was watching me, an unexpected softness in his face, his eyes so dark they might drown me.

Queen Caihong's gaze thinned. "Why would you do this for him?"

"I have my honor to uphold, too, Your Majesty." I was breathing heavily, my words disjointed. "Lord Zhangwei has borne more than enough for me."

"Indeed, he has." Queen Caihong's voice turned cool. "Very well, I accept your request. Lord Zhangwei, your punishment is served in full. You may leave the platform."

The stone dragon's claws snapped apart to release him. We stood there a moment, staring at each other, before he bent down and helped me up, the coolness of his touch as startling as his gentleness. A wetness was spreading across my chest, blood blossoming across the silk as the pain knifed deeper, like a dagger buried in my flesh.

"Let me carry you," he said, already reaching for me.

But I shook my head, wanting to walk from here, refusing to let them see me fall. With Lord Zhangwei's arm around my waist, I stumbled through the entrance, clinging to consciousness. As the doors closed behind us, only then did a ragged sigh slip from my throat. Lord Zhangwei's hand caught mine. I would have pulled away had I the strength, but his touch was oddly soothing.

"Why did you do that?" he asked quietly. "Why take the blow? Why did you speak for me?"

I should admit that I hadn't intended to get struck . . . but the wiser part cautioned silence, to let him think this if it would bring him closer to Tianxia's side. And so I looked into his face, uttering half a truth: "I didn't want you to be hurt any more."

His hand tightened over mine. "I'm not used to another stepping in for me, asking mercy on my behalf. Much less—"

"A mortal?" I finished the sentence for him, managing a small smile, though it was becoming harder to remain standing. "Why did *you* take the punishment for me?" I repeated his question to him, my self-control unraveling.

"Because I didn't want you to be hurt either."

My mind clouded. This moment between us . . . what was it? All I knew was that I wasn't just pretending anymore. And whatever this was, it might be more dangerous than any punishment the queen could devise.

The God of War clasped my arms gently. How I wanted to lean on him, to draw from his strength when mine was almost spent. I should pull free, but I was tired, my legs crumpling. He caught me, his hands sliding around my shoulders to steady me, a moan breaking from me as he accidentally pressed on my torn flesh. Without a word, he swung me up, my head falling back, my hair trailing over his arm. At his touch, a tingling coursed through my veins like the tender graze of snowfall—his magic healing me before he'd even healed himself. The agony subsided, fading to a throbbing ache.

"Sleep. I'll look after you now," he whispered.

A command that I readily obeyed, a mercy to succumb to the dark—devoid of pain, hurt, my warring emotions . . . and the fear that I could not hate him as I should.

12

Shafts of light slipped through the latticed windows, my mind stirring as my body shifted. Instinctively, I braced for pain, but there was none—my palms brushing the covers of an unfamiliar bed. I pushed myself up and looked around the chamber, small but beautifully furnished. Paintings of forests hung from the walls, a pair of rosewood chairs flanked a marble side table, a miniature tree set upon it.

The door swung open. Weina entered, carrying a tray with a bowl and a pot of tea. "You're awake. Are you feeling better?"

I nodded, rubbing the back of my neck, wondering at the absence of discomfort. "Did the healer visit me?"

"Lord Zhangwei tended to you himself. It isn't easy to heal mortals, particularly if your injuries are severe. Caution is needed, as your bodies aren't accustomed to magic."

I bit the inside of my cheek, imagining him here while I slept, touching my wound, watching me. "How is Lord Zhangwei?" I asked.

"It would take more than a few strikes to bring down our God of War," Weina replied as she handed the bowl of soup to me. Despite its light color, the flavor was rich, teeming with herbs.

"Weina, are we still in the palace?"

She nodded. "You've been asleep since yesterday. Lord Zhangwei asked me to accompany you so you wouldn't be among strangers."

"He is considerate." If she heard the hitch in my voice, she gave no sign of it.

"I'm also here to help prepare you for the pledging ceremony," she added. "Her Majesty commanded that it take place in three days."

My fingers crumpled the bedsheet. Time was running out. I had to find the Shield of Rivers and Mountains soon, or at least secure Lord Zhangwei's support—someone who would speak for us here. After what I'd seen, no other immortal would be willing. A strange twist of fate, that the God of War was now the only one I trusted here.

"Is Lord Zhangwei in his room?" I asked.

"Yes. Shall I bring him here?" she offered. "He asked to be informed when you woke."

"I will go to him, if you'll tell me the way." A useful excuse to explore the palace.

After Weina left, I dressed quickly in a light-yellow robe, tying up my hair with a long ribbon. In the mirror, I examined the reddish welts left on my shoulder where a wound had gaped yesterday. They stung as I touched them, though nothing compared to the blistering pain of before. Without the God of War's healing, such an injury would have taken weeks to recover from, maybe months.

Leaving the room, I followed Weina's directions, crossing a bridge that arched across the sky. I took a winding route to cover as much of the palace as I could, taking care to map the place in my mind, especially the paths leading to the entrance. Whenever any immortals passed by, I dropped my head, the memory of the Dragon Platform still fresh in my mind. In this realm, the slightest mistake could have dire consequences.

After some guards cast suspicious looks my way, I headed to

the God of War's chamber. Outside his room, I knocked on the door. When there was no response, I tried again—the panels gaping like they'd not been properly closed, like he'd left in a hurry. If he was out, this would be a chance to search his room. I buried a twinge of guilt and fear. After all, there was nothing to hide; I'd told Weina I was coming here.

Quietly, I slid the doors apart and stepped inside, then pulled them shut after me. The god's chamber was far larger than mine, a round table in the center with six stools around it. Silk-lined lamps were hung upon ebony stands, a tall brace of unlit candles in the corner. Something clinked in a gentle rhythm—a wind chime—one of the windows thrown opened. A carved rosewood screen was spread out at the end, its panels inlaid with gold. Steam drifted around its sides, infused with the scents of flowers and herbs, the fragrance almost intoxicating. The curve of a bronze bath peeked from behind the screen. Lord Zhangwei was lying there, his back to me. His arms were spread around the rim, his head flung back, eyes closed like he was asleep.

My heart almost stopped. I cursed myself for this intrusion, yet he had not stirred; I could still leave unseen. Holding my breath, I turned toward the doors. Water gurgled, droplets scattering. A strong hand clamped upon my arm, spinning me around and pushing me against the wall. The breath was knocked from me as the God of War caught me in his firm hold. The ribbon holding my hair up came undone, my hair falling across my face as I struggled to wrench free. Our eyes collided, his flaring in recognition—but I shoved him away as hard as I could.

He released me, though his hands slid to the wall, his arms trapping me in place. As I glared at him, my throat went dry. He'd pulled on a thin inner robe, almost translucent as it clung to his damp skin, water beading in the hollow of his neck. Heat surged through my veins from his nearness, the scent of him filling my senses, mingling with the fragrance of flowers.

This was wrong, foolish, and above all, dangerous. While I wanted him to grow closer to me to secure his support, since yesterday something had changed. There was a new awareness of him now, tangled with something that went deeper that I did not understand . . . that I must be wary of, suppress and lock away, for such weakness led to ruin.

He was still staring at me, a slow smile spreading across his lips. "Have you looked your fill?"

"Don't flatter yourself," I scoffed, forgetting myself for a moment.

"Why are you here?"

I breathed deeply to compose myself, trying to soften my manner. "I was concerned about you; your injuries were worse than mine. I didn't realize I'd be attacked."

The back of his neck reddened. "I didn't know it was you."

"Why don't you lock your doors the next time you don't want to be disturbed?"

He grinned. "Maybe you should stop coming into my quarters without an invitation."

"If I'm unwelcome, then let me leave." I tapped his hand, still pressed against the wall, but he didn't lower it.

As he leaned toward me, his mouth formed a single word. "Stay."

A glittering current rushed through me; I found myself unable to move—or maybe, I didn't want to. It wasn't his arms that held me in place any longer but the intensity of his gaze, the low pitch of his voice. I made myself pull away, ducking beneath his arm to stalk to the garment rack. Picking up the robe slung over it, I handed it to him. "You should cover up before you fall ill," I said without thinking, repeating what I'd been told most of my childhood.

He didn't laugh at me as he shrugged the robe on, fastening it with a belt. His hair hung straight down, still wet from the bath.

We were so close, the chill from his skin drifted across mine.

As a breeze darted through the window, I shivered. "Are you cold?" I asked.

His eyes flicked to mine. "With you, I am warm."

The words resonated, my heart quickening. He said things sometimes that I didn't entirely understand, that reached deeper than I wished—that I was afraid to examine. It was becoming far too easy to see him as someone other than the God of War who'd burned my home, who struck such terror into the hearts of mortals, immortals, and monsters.

But I was *not* here for him. My smiles, my words, were for my kingdom—and how he could help us. I had to regain control of myself, else I risked being swept away.

"How are your injuries? Do you need to rest?" I was trying to blunt my earlier rudeness when I'd been caught off guard.

"You are one of the few who ask such things," he said. "Most think I feel no pain."

"Then they are wrong," I replied. "No one is invulnerable. Those stronger, suffer too—maybe they hide it better but their pain is as real."

He tilted his head back. "How are your wounds?"

"Healed, as you saw to them yourself." I added awkwardly, "Thank you. For healing me . . . for bearing the punishment on my behalf."

"I would do it again." He brushed a lock of hair from my face, his touch lingering on my cheek. "I've been meaning to ask, why is this white?"

Careful, I warned myself, my body tensing. If he knew I'd been poisoned with the waters of death, would he suspect what Grandfather had done—what now lay inside me?

"It's always been this way," I lied. "Grandfather said it was from my mother's side of the family." A safe answer, one he could not disprove.

His expression was inscrutable as his hand fell away. "After yesterday, it would seem you're in my debt again."

"What will it cost?"

"I am feeling generous—and bored. Just your company, to entertain me."

"What entertainment do you expect, Lord Zhangwei? I don't play music or tell stories." His title was a familiar barrier, one that was becoming more necessary.

A slight pause. "For the remainder of your visit, shall we dispense with the formalities?"

I nodded reluctantly. Such intimacy was dangerous. The more time I spent with him, the more confused I became. What I *should* do and what I *wanted* to were slipping further apart . . . and I was beginning to fear they might never come together again.

"You owe me a meal after abandoning me for our last one," he reminded me. "There is a place I'd like to show you outside the palace. We can eat there tomorrow, if you'd come with me?"

"We could go today?" There was little time left; I was afraid to waste it. While I preferred to stay in the palace to learn its secrets, spending time with him was also vital to securing his trust— his support could be as valuable as the shield. I was beginning to loathe myself for such calculation, as deceitful as those courtiers I disliked.

He shook his head. "You need to rest today. Your wound was severe; I dared not use too much magic." He hesitated, adding, "A scar will remain."

"I'm lucky to be alive," I said with feeling, as I made my way to the door. "Till tomorrow then."

There was a lift in my heart that I tried to stifle, an anticipation kindling within. It was a struggle to feign this closeness with him, essential to win him to my side—yet to keep myself safely locked away.

What if this was real?

Impossible. There was no future for us, at least none I would accept. To him, this was a brief interlude, a blink in his immortal existence. Whatever lay between us, even *if* it was real—it was not meant to last. And no matter the temptation, I would never trade my kingdom for my heart.

13

My reflection in the mirror was clear and sharp, unlike the yellowish tinge of the bronze mirrors in my realm. My eyes appeared darker after I'd lined them, and my lips were painted red. The pale lock of my hair gleamed, framing the curve of my face. I didn't tuck it away as I usually did—this was a part of me now. Plum-blossom trees were embroidered on my pink robe, a blue sash wound around my waist. Soft colors, pretty ones—chosen to lower the god's guard. The first bright colors I'd worn since Grandfather's death.

It didn't feel right, but I had to overcome my unease. Queen Caihong had sent a magnificent dress to my room for the pledging ceremony tomorrow, one I had no choice but to wear. I was running out of time. Regardless of whether I found the shield or won Lord Zhangwei's support—I couldn't pledge myself and my kingdom as things stood. My people needed to be freed of our obligation, to have the choices the other mortals did, not confined within our walls.

It was early yet, but Zhangwei was already waiting outside my room. His white robe shifted in the breeze, the light color startling against his tanned skin. Red hawks were embroidered along the hem, their wings seeming to flutter, one taking flight toward the wide black sash that was knotted around his waist. A jade ring bound the immortal's long hair, which fell across one shoulder to frame his coldly beautiful face. Despite his lack of armor, his sword was slung across his back.

"You always carry your sword," I remarked. "Are you planning to fight someone today?"

"No. But danger often comes without warning, causing most harm when unexpected."

"Should *I* bring my sword then?" I was still unused to carrying one around, just my dagger.

"I will keep you safe," he told me.

I shouldn't rely on him; I shouldn't trust him, nor feel the warmth that I did at his assurance. Yet being with him made me careless, stirring unfamiliar emotions that were becoming harder to suppress . . . to pretend they didn't exist.

I smiled instead. "Then I'll leave mine. Who would harm me with you here?" Flattery, woven into a claim to his protection that I hoped to extend to my kingdom.

He returned my smile, then let out a sharp whistle. His phoenix descended toward us, the one we'd ridden before, its rainbow-hued tail flaring wide. Zhangwei helped me onto its back, then climbed up behind me, leaning forward to stroke the phoenix's head. The magnificent bird spread its wings as we took flight, the wind surging into my face. My initial fear had vanished, a wild exhilaration seizing me as we flew. This time, when his body pressed against mine, I didn't lean away even though it would have been wiser to.

A growl rang out behind us, frantic and low. I twisted around to find an enormous creature flying toward us, even larger than phoenix we rode upon. Silver antlers reared from its head, its body covered in coppery scales. A red mane encircled its face, from which curved tusks emerged. Black hooves gleamed at its feet, curled beneath the creature as it soared with swift grace.

Fear flickered, underscored by something else—was it curiosity? Fascination? This being was otherworldly and magnificent—a mystery—unlike the dragons and phoenixes I'd often read about. "What is this creature?" I wanted to know.

Zhangwei's eyes narrowed. "A qilin. She should not be here."

"Why? Are they dangerous?"

"They can be," he replied tersely.

Was the creature more vicious than it appeared? Before I could ask more, Zhangwei raised his hand, the tips of his fingers aglow with his power. The air thickened with a tension I was growing attuned to, a translucent shield sweeping around us that rippled with the wind. The qilin howled as it flew past, like it could no longer see us. The fury in its tone unsettled me as I instinctively covered my ears with my hands.

"It's gone now. Don't be afraid." Zhangwei caught my hand, his touch searing me.

"Why did you hide us from the qilin?" I asked.

"You mean instead of killing it?" He paused, then replied, "Violence should never be the first answer."

"Sometimes, not even the last," I agreed, glad he could not see my face. Maybe it was time to stop making assumptions about him when I was so often wrong. "Violence should be avoided at all costs, the reckless reaping of innocent lives."

"Yes," he agreed. "Yet there are rare times when the lines are blurred, when it's your life against your enemy's, when you need to protect those you love." His voice rose above the wind, clear yet low. "I didn't want to hurt the qilin. They are wondrous creatures: powerful, intelligent, not prone to aggression—though they can attack when challenged or provoked."

"It flew so swiftly," I said. "Can the qilin be ridden as the phoenixes?"

"Many have tried. But the qilin have little interest, the few who allow riders preferring to choose their own."

Beneath us, the mountains rose like a ridge of islands from

the glittering sand. The sun beat down upon us, a pleasant heat that glided off one's skin rather than settling like a cloying weight. Emerald-green forests loomed on the horizon, a steep cliff appearing from their midst, its sheer face gleaming like beaten copper sliding into the azure ocean. Flowers bloomed from the branches, vivid reds and yellows, until they seemed afire from a distance. As our cloud descended, an exquisite melody filled the air—pure, sweet, and strong. Such lightness filled me, unseen burdens falling away. Here I could *breathe* easier, smile without restraint, a rare peace stealing over me.

We landed upon the grass, silken-soft beneath my feet. After Zhangwei helped me down, he unfastened a basket from the phoenix's side. A breeze sprang up, infused with the warmth of summer. As a shadow swept over us, I looked up to find a phoenix soaring above, its bright tail rippling through the skies. Another flew alongside it, spiraling through the air—this one with a scarlet crest and silver-tipped feathers.

How easy it would be to lose oneself in wonder, to forget why I was here. Yet those soft feathers came with talons that could rend flesh like silk, and a mortal here was nothing but prey.

"This is the domain of the Phoenix Kingdom," Zhangwei said as we walked. "It's a privilege to hear their song; not many beyond their borders have the opportunity. Their songs possess a rare quality that aids in healing, especially the mind—the wounds that can't be seen."

"Do you come here often?" I asked.

"The Phoenix Queen doesn't look kindly upon trespassers, but she granted me permission to visit when I wish."

"She must think highly of you."

"It was more a repayment of a debt." His tone hardened. "The Golden Desert bore the brunt of the war with the Wuxin. We protected the Immortal Realm when the other kingdoms did not, claiming it was an internal conflict within our desert. Maybe they believed it was safer to not take sides—to wait until the dust settled, until it became clear who would win."

My anger flared. "A costly mistake that both our people paid for."

"The other kingdoms underestimated the danger of the Wuxin, not knowing enough of them," he said. "They only became a threat under their new ruler—one who taught them to seize, to destroy."

"If the Wuxin had won, the other immortals would have been next," I said bitterly. Selfishness lay at the root of this, those who jostled for gain rather than for the good of the realm. "Why didn't your allies help you?"

"Our kingdom was newly formed, without allies, those willing to help shoulder the burden of war."

Unlike Tianxia. "Why did Queen Caihong decide to unite the Golden Desert?" I asked.

"Back then, the Golden Desert was the only domain in the Immortal Realm without a ruler. It isolated us, keeping us friendless, weakening us with petty infighting and rivalries. We've learned that we're stronger together. Since then, the other kingdoms have also welcomed us." He looked around. "I was glad to be able to come here. This place was vital to my recovery after the war."

While I'd heard murmurs of his injuries, this was the first time he'd spoken of them. "Were you badly hurt then?"

"Yes," he admitted slowly. "Some days I still feel its shadow."

He appeared so strong and indomitable, it was hard to imagine him weakened. "Is that why your skin feels cold?" I asked.

Zhangwei reached out, lacing our fingers together, his touch no longer startling me. "I'm not cold anymore," he said in a low voice.

Nor am I. But I didn't say it aloud as I drew away, my heart beating far too quickly.

It was easier to examine our surroundings, the phoenixes

perched upon the trees, their beaks tearing through a reddish fruit as they dug out wedges of ripe flesh. "I'd imagined their diet to be more hearty."

"I wouldn't anger a phoenix," he warned. "They might eat fruit from the trees and drink the purest water, but they won't hesitate to rip your head from your neck if they think you're a threat. Or a nuisance."

As we sat on the ground, Zhangwei lifted the food from a basket: a roasted duck, its skin carved into slices, thin flour pancakes, a small dish of plum sauce, and curls of spring onion. Hungry now, I folded the pancake around the duck, dipped it into the sauce, then took a bite. The crisp skin melded with the sweet plum. I chewed slowly, savoring the taste as Zhangwei filled my cup with tea.

"My mother taught me to serve the guest first." With the barest glint of humor, he added, "Though she didn't say what to do when the guest served herself so quickly."

I laughed, folding another slice of meat into the pancake. How strange to imagine him as a boy, learning manners from his parents, those that stayed with him today. "Where are your parents?" I asked.

"They live in a small village far from the palace. They don't enjoy court life," he told me.

"You are lucky that you can see them whenever you wish." A trace of envy slid into me. This was the greatest blessing the immortals possessed—not their magic or the riches of their world— but that they weren't destined to be parted from their loved ones.

"I know," he said gently. "I am sorry for your loss."

I swallowed, fighting down my emotions. "Is there anyone you miss? Anyone you've lost?" I wanted to shift the discussion away from me.

His gaze turned up to the skies, shrouded in memory. "Just one."

"How fortunate that immortals don't die as easily as mortals,"

I remarked, a little too sharply.

He shook his head. "That is not why. You have to love someone to miss them."

A shiver ran through me at the emptiness in his words. "All these years . . . and you've only loved one person? What is the point of eternity?"

A beat of silence. "I didn't say I only loved one person, just that I lost them," he corrected me gravely. "One is enough, if they are the right person. It doesn't matter how often you love, but how well."

I was breathing deeply, trying to suppress the ache in my chest. Was this jealousy? Envy? Regardless, it was stupid and futile.

"You're not who I expected," I admitted after a pause.

"Maybe you should look a little deeper," he suggested. "Don't just see what you think you should."

I had known him as the God of War even before I'd known his name. Maybe that had colored my perception of him. "Have you killed as many as they say?"

"It depends on what you've heard." His voice dropped. "Maybe more."

"Monsters? Villains?" What was I hoping for? A reason to not be afraid . . . or one to stay away?

"Some; not all. But never lightly." His voice was raw, like the ghosts of those he'd killed haunted him still.

I softened my tone. "Is it hard?"

"There is no joy in the taking of a life. But my people are safe," he said. "If your loved ones are threatened, if it's between you or them—would you choose otherwise?"

Was I not doing the same? Making hard choices, those that went against myself, for the sake of my people? Was I not playing on his emotions though it hurt me, too, because I needed his support for Tianxia? And what of my grandfather? For my sake he had betrayed the queen he'd dedicated his life to serving, by stealing what she desired above all.

Maybe we were all monsters inside, waiting to be unleashed if pushed too far.

I wouldn't run from it. I would embrace it, hone it into a strength as he had done. Steeling myself, I looked up at him. "When you took the punishment for me, was it out of honor? A sense of duty?"

"No."

"Then why did you do it?" My heart raced, my throat tightening as I pushed each word out. Part of it was to edge him into an admission, but I also simply wanted to know.

His head dipped toward mine until I could see myself in his eyes, a lock of his hair brushing my shoulder. "I think you know. Isn't that why you're asking?"

We were both hovering on the brink, neither willing to fall first . . . or were we just waiting for a reason to?

I lifted my wrist with the red thread—the constant reminder that I did not belong here, and only death awaited me should I stay. "I will be leaving your world soon. Will I see you again?"

"If you want to see me, nothing will keep me away."

How bright his gaze was. Until now, I'd never known the shades of black that existed in his eyes: the sharp glitter of onyx, the tender brush of ink, the unfathomable depths of midnight. Each one drawing me closer, fraying my restraint.

I leashed my thoughts. It was not about what I wanted but what I needed from him. This was the moment to be bold, to claim what I sought.

"I would welcome you to Tianxia," I told him. "For myself, not from duty. Not because we are bound in service." I let my face fall then, my voice trailing away. How I hated this pretense, such low trickery.

"What is troubling you?" he asked, as I knew he would.

I waited a moment like I was afraid to share my mind. "While it's our honor to serve the Queen of the Golden Desert, it was my grandfather's wish—and mine—that Her Majesty will free Tianxia of the obligation we've borne since the war, to bring down the wall so we can rejoin the world we belong to."

He didn't pull away, nor did he appear shocked. "If you serve Her Majesty well, she might be persuaded to consider it."

I shook my head. "Every ruler before me has tried. Nothing ever sufficed."

"Why not broach a smaller request first, a loosening of the binds?"

His advice was sound—but I didn't want the binds loosened, I wanted them gone. The path ahead would be difficult, not the life of ease I might have chosen—but I knew deep down, that this was right.

"Instead of the pledge, I want to ask Her Majesty to release my kingdom, to return the Shield of Rivers and Mountains to us." I studied him carefully. If he recoiled, if he refused to help, it would be far harder to convince Queen Caihong.

"These are difficult things you ask for," he warned. "What do you offer in return?"

Of course the immortals would demand payment; they do nothing without gain.

The only thing I possessed that they desired was the Divine Pearl Lotus. Yet if Queen Caihong knew I'd had it all this while, that Grandfather had lied to her—she would be enraged, she might take my life. It comforted me that the lotus could not be seized, that it was mine until I surrendered it.

I hid these perilous thoughts. "The Golden Desert is strong and powerful. What more do you need from us?"

"It is not that simple."

"Maybe it should be." The fact he'd not refused outright gave me the courage to plunge onward. "Would you speak for us? Her Majesty values your opinion; you are much respected at court."

"You don't need to flatter me," he said. "I've been thinking on the matter. After all, the Wuxin are sealed away, and it would ease tensions with the Celestial Emperor, who prefers the Mortal Realm to be united. We have also formed strong alliances with the other kingdoms that will help keep us safe." He added firmly, "But Kunlun must still be protected; this duty cannot be shirked."

"We will; we want to keep our realm safe, too," I assured him. "Though our people should be armed to face any danger that might emerge from Kunlun."

He looked into my face like he was studying it. "I will speak for Tianxia," he said.

Excitement surged, entwined with relief. "Thank you," I said fervently, meaning it more than anything I'd said to him before. "I will never forget your kindness and generosity."

"I have something else for you, a token to remember me by." His expression was grave as he reached into his sleeve and drew out a comb of lacquered sandalwood. Gold filigree adorned the frame, studded with small red stones.

"It's beautiful, but you don't need to give me anything. You've already given me so much." I felt like a thief, having already won what I most wished from him.

Zhangwei's gaze darkened. "I want to. Will you wear it?"

As I nodded, he slid the comb into the side of my hair. My skin burned, bright with the awareness of his touch—so assured yet gentle, his hand sliding down to graze my neck, to smooth my hair away. A fire kindled inside me that I fought to tether. The God of War awoke a dark craving within me of desire edged with fear— one that threatened to set everything ablaze.

He tilted his head back, his tone lightening. "It is customary among my people to exchange tokens to mark a promise. Do you have something in exchange for mine?"

My mind went blank. Nothing belonged to me here, neither my clothes nor ornaments.

"What about a lock of your hair?" he suggested, perhaps realizing my predicament.

I nodded, pulling out my dagger to cut my hair. As the black strands fell away like shorn grass, he gathered and bound them with a silk cord, then tucked it into the folds of his robe.

This simple exchange seemed to bind us closer, startling in its intimacy. Something shifted in my heart, the intensity of the heat softening to a radiant warmth that spilled through me. I would have given him almost anything he asked for, as long as he kept his word to help Tianxia.

What were we now? What was he to me? I no longer knew, just that this moment felt real, precious . . . and, weak creature that I was, I did not want it to end.

14

The day of the pledging ceremony dawned pale and gray. Rain fell in an incessant sheet, so light it appeared a weaving of mist.

"Does it rain often here?" I asked Weina, who was pinning up my hair with sticks of jade.

When she was satisfied, she slid a comb into the coils, the one Zhangwei had given me. "Only if Her Majesty wishes it."

The queen's mood must be grim indeed if the skies were any reflection, and I hoped my kingdom would remain unscathed. My hands were cold as I clasped them together. Today, I must set myself against Queen Caihong, to defy her command by withholding my pledge—a terrifying thought. But if I did not, nothing would ever change.

My people could not afford the endless patience of immortals; we didn't have the time.

Weina picked up a robe and shook it out. As the silk billowed, the fragrance of sandalwood suffused the air. The cloth was the hue of dawn, with shades of rose and vermilion melding into each other, tiny gold stars embroidered on the skirt. When Weina draped it over my shoulders, the hem fell to my ankles. I was no stranger to extravagance, but these garments possessed an ethereal beauty that could not be achieved by mortal hands.

"The dress suits you," she told me.

"Her Majesty is generous," I intoned, then added with more sincerity, "Thank you for your care of me."

"It's my duty," she replied.

I thought of the scorn the other immortals had shown me. "Kindness is never a duty."

Weina smiled as she picked up a lacquered box and flicked its clasp open. Strands of pearls twined among rubies and sapphires, jade bangles as translucent as ice, diamond rings that glittered like wintry rainbows. Just one of these might have fed a family in Tianxia for a decade, but here they were strewn as carelessly as pebbles.

"Are these jewels mined from your realm?"

She nodded. "There are mountains of jade in the Phoenix Kingdom, the Eastern Sea cultivates coral and pearls in their gardens. Gold and silver are gathered from riverbeds that never run dry. While such treasures are rare in your world, here they are cherished simply for their beauty."

With their abundance of wealth and power, the immortals did not need us. My resolve hardened as I glanced at my sword, wishing I could bring it. But only the God of War was allowed to bear a weapon to meet the queen.

I picked up a pair of tourmaline pins, their pointed ends glinting as I slid them into my hair. Weina frowned; I'd marred her immaculate work, but this would be a useful tool if all else failed. Outside the room, Zhangwei was leaning against the wall. A black brocade coat was layered over his robe of silver and white. His long hair was pulled into a jade headpiece, his sword strapped to his side. As his gaze swept across my dress to my face, lingering on his comb—a fierce light shone in his eyes.

The space between us seemed to tighten. A flutter stirred in my chest, so different from just days ago, when he'd evoked dread. His words from yesterday echoed through my mind, his promise to support my kingdom more valuable than any treasure here. My lingering resentment and hostility had faded, along with my suspicion—any attempt to cling to them now felt hollow. There was a new closeness between us, an awakening trust. These feelings were unfamiliar: warm and bright. I didn't understand it all myself . . . except it made me feel alive. Maybe the best things in life had no reason and we should just cherish them as the gift they were.

But the dangerous thing was, I was beginning to want more—to reach for him without guilt, to touch him as I desired, listening out for the sound of his voice, the tread of his step. Was this love? I cast the question aside, suddenly afraid. To win the God of War's support was wise—to fall in love with him would ruin me.

As he came toward me, I smiled at him. "Doesn't the God of War have more pressing matters to attend to than to serve as a mortal's escort?" It was what I'd said to him the day he took me from Tianxia.

"No," he said, coming to my side. "I want to escort you."

Was it because I was leaving soon? I couldn't dwell on it, not with everything at stake. We walked in silence toward the throne room, yet I was acutely aware of his presence, his every move, the way his eyes darted around to assess each room for danger, and how they returned to me each time.

We crossed a bridge, aglitter in the morning light. From here, the Dragon Platform gleamed below—deserted—the crowd gathered in the throne room instead. Today, I was the planned "spectacle," and they would be getting a performance they did not expect. I stiffened at the thought but made myself keep pace with Zhangwei.

Soldiers flanked the doors that led to Queen Caihong's hall. The closer we drew, the heavier I felt, each step leaden and graceless.

"Don't be nervous," Zhangwei said.

"I am," I confessed. "I don't want to anger Her Majesty, but I can't keep silent—I have to try. Nothing will be the same after this."

"Change is always frightening." He turned to look into my eyes. "But trust in what is real. Trust in me."

He took my hand, pressing it against his chest. Through his robe, his heart thudded against my palm—my skin, for once, as cold as his. The soldiers were all staring at us, some openmouthed, but he ignored them. He did what he wanted, regardless of what others thought. I envied such assurance, recalling the mask I wore in my own court—but he had earned this respect, while I was still unproven.

Someone cleared their throat. As I pulled my hand away, a soldier stepped from the line, his brown eyes crinkling as he grinned. "Lord Zhangwei, you are setting the gossips afire today."

Zhangwei returned his smile. "Let them talk, Lieutenant Yang. There is nothing to hide."

"Are you Lord Zhangwei, or has a Wuxin taken over your form?" the lieutenant joked with more bravery than wisdom. Was this soldier his friend?

Zhangwei brushed the hilt of his sword. "Care to test me on the sparring field?"

Lieutenant Yang shuddered as he turned to me, greeting me with a bow—an unexpected courtesy from an immortal. "Lady of Tianxia, I'm pleased to meet you. I remember your grandfather when he visited our palace, and I was sorry to learn of his passing."

His compassion touched me. "Grandfather spoke highly of his visit to your realm. I'm sure he would have remembered you, too."

Lieutenant Yang inclined his head, then tapped Zhangwei on the shoulder. "Her Majesty grows impatient. She's already dispatched messengers to find you."

"I trust you devised a suitable excuse on my behalf?"

"Lord Zhangwei, I dared not speak on your behalf, nor did I wish to anger Her Majesty out of self-preservation." Lieutenant Yang winked as he whispered, "Reap what you sow."

At Zhangwei's scowl, I laughed—a welcome release to my coiled tension. But it returned in force as we entered the throne room, the doors closing after us with a decisive thud. A single lantern the size of a drum hung from the ceiling, crafted of rosewood, the silk panels painted with clouds and stars. The hall was flanked with turquoise pillars, set into the gleaming marble floor. A thick yellow carpet was thrown over it, shining as the sands of the desert.

At the far end, Queen Caihong sat on a luminous throne, carved from a single block of polished quartz. Her brocade robe gleamed like beaten gold, a thick strand of pearls clasped around her throat. On a table beside her lay a small bottle and a gleaming bronze shield. It was exquisitely crafted; one half inlaid with sapphires that formed a river, the other a mountain set with amethyst and pearls—the Shield of Rivers and Mountains, the key to Tianxia's freedom. Was it part of the ceremony today? My heart raced, my fingers digging into my skirt. It was so close . . . if only I could take it.

I leashed my rising excitement as I bowed to the queen in greeting. She gestured to Zhangwei who ascended the dais, speaking to the queen in hushed tones, while I waited below, wishing I could hear what they were saying.

The immortals were staring at me like I was a wild animal stumbling among them. I would have staked the gold in my treasury that not one knew my name—to them I was just "the mortal." A hollow feeling, to be among strangers, many of whom felt I was their inferior. Kindness would have been so easy to extend—a smile or greeting, as from Lieutenant Yang. In times like these, those who possessed true grace were shown from those who didn't know its meaning. But I stood straighter, holding my head high;

they would not bring me down.

When Zhangwei returned to my side, Queen Caihong faced me. At her stern expression, dread knotted in my gut. "Lady of Tianxia, are you ready to pledge your fealty to me?"

Now the moment was upon me, I found myself tongue-tied. Afraid. But I thought of my grandfather's patience and dedication, his years of loyal service to the immortal queen—and how he'd been repaid. A spark of fury flared, igniting in me the courage to speak. "Your Majesty, I am honored to stand before you. I have a proposal that I hope you will consider for Tianxia." My words were not eloquent, but they emerged with an unexpected calm.

Queen Caihong's eyes narrowed, the courtiers whispering among themselves. Zhangwei's face was unreadable, though I held his promise in my heart.

"A *proposal?*" The queen drew out the word like an insult, the embroidered phoenixes on her robe tilting their heads mockingly.

My pulse was erratic, my breathing growing ragged. A negotiation need not be defiance, except this was only true for those the queen believed her equals, not those whose service she expected as her due.

"Your Majesty, Tianxia was pledged to your service after the war. The wall was erected to keep us apart from our realm—"

"I do not require a history lesson," the queen snapped.

Her condescension riled; it helped me hold my ground, when a small part of me wanted to fall to my knees and plead for mercy. To her, these events seemed like a few years ago, but to us, several *lifetimes* had passed.

"The Wuxin are no longer a threat," I said. "In accordance with the treaty, we ask Your Majesty to begin the proceedings for the return of the Shield of Rivers and Mountains, for the walls of our kingdom to be brought down, to allow us to rejoin the rest of Mortal Realm."

As Queen Caihong's eyes blazed, I rushed onward, "We will

always honor Your Majesty, and will remain your loyal *allies* in our realm." A slight emphasis on the word, but a world of difference—to be treated as equals, with the respect we deserved.

"Impossible," she said harshly. "Tianxia is needed to guard Kunlun. The Wuxin can never be allowed to invade again."

"Your Majesty, our soldiers will continue to guard Kunlun—"

A courtier scowled as he stalked forward. "It is a great privilege to serve Her Majesty. Your kingdom is honored above the rest of the Mortal Realm."

Maybe it would be, if Queen Caihong had *earned* our service rather than claimed it as a trophy, left to tarnish untended. Such close-minded arrogance to believe otherwise. How did some immortals live for so long yet possess so little wisdom or empathy? Maybe their time was squandered because it held no value to them, while us mortals chased each day as though it might be our last. Immortality was their legacy, while we had to fight to leave our mark or be forgotten.

"Your Majesty, the Lady of Tianxia's concern is valid." It was Zhangwei who spoke. The court shifted, all attention on him. "The initial treaty was spurred by the urgency of war—the Shield of Rivers and Mountains should have been returned once the Wuxin were exiled to the Netherworld. The mortals have done their part, more than fulfilled any obligation to us. Moreover, our kingdom is stronger now, secure in alliances. Tianxia should be allowed to rejoin the Mortal Realm, whether the threat resurges or not, and we can explore a different agreement to both our benefit."

I stared at him, wide-eyed. He'd kept his word; he'd spoken for us, despite the queen's disapproval. Relief filled me, and something more . . . something precious, fine and fragile. The manner of the courtiers was markedly different now—their expressions attentive, a few even nodding. Yet Queen Caihong's mouth remained pursed like a prune.

"Lord Zhangwei, we've all heard the rumors of your closeness with the Lady of Tianxia. Are you speaking with your mind or your heart?" she asked scathingly. "Keep them separate in my court."

"Your Majesty, I would never compromise my loyalty to my kingdom, nor will I be afraid to speak for what is right," he replied gravely. "The people of Tianxia should be released from their obligation. They should be allowed the same freedom as the others of their realm, to go where they wish—not confined within walls because of us."

"We will speak later, Lord Zhangwei," Queen Caihong said tightly, then turned to me. "I ask you once more: Will you pledge your loyalty?"

The flash in her eyes fractured my calm. But I'd come this far; I wouldn't back down now. "Your Majesty, a pledge of loyalty should be offered, not claimed."

The queen clasped the armrests of her throne. "Only the weak imagine it so. Favors and alliances can be rescinded upon a whim, whereas a pledge is binding."

"Something forced will never be as strong as that which was earned," I countered.

"Yet you are the Lady of Tianxia, your subjects do your bidding by virtue of your title," the queen said cuttingly. "You did not earn the throne but were born to it."

Her assumptions stung. "I serve my kingdom, I seek my people's happiness. Every day, I think of them—of how to make their lives better."

Her laughter was derisive. "Idealistic child. You should rule your kingdom, not let it rule you."

I shook my head, rejecting her advice. "I don't believe we are entitled to our positions, but should strive to be worthy of them."

The queen's cheeks hollowed with rage. "Enough with this. I refuse your proposal. Tianxia has not fulfilled its obligation to us."

"What more can we do? Tell us, Your Majesty—set out a

plan." Despair welled up within. "My grandfather served you loyally all these years, obeying your every demand—"

"All but the most important one."

Her voice rang out, a jittery unease settling in the pit of my stomach. The scar over my chest throbbed, the warmth of the Divine Pearl Lotus pulsing through me. Dare I mention it? Would it enrage the queen further? Could I even relinquish it without harming myself? I didn't want to, but it was the only thing I had left to offer . . . unless I could somehow secure the shield.

"Your Majesty, I urge you to reconsider the Lady of Tianxia's proposal." Zhangwei's harsh tone was one I never thought he'd use with his queen.

A long silence fell over us, of the rough and prickling kind. "Very well, Lord Zhangwei, I will *consider* it, after today," the queen said at last in a glacial tone. "Enough with the delays. You know what must be done, though I dislike this as much as you."

What did she mean? Her consideration was a victory in itself, yet my body braced instinctively. Zhangwei's eyes were cold, his jaw clenched. When he looked at me . . . he was the God of War once more. A stranger.

As I backed away, he caught my arm. I tried to wrench free, but his hold was like iron. He'd never gripped me with such force—my fear spiraling, unbound. "What are you doing? Release me."

He didn't reply, instead raising his other hand. Light flared from his fingers, sheathing me in a wintry embrace. I'd seen him attack others—but fool that I was, I never thought he'd unleash his magic on me. A sharpness pierced my chest like needles, a gasp torn from my throat. My scar glowed, visible now beneath the silk of my robe. I could not move, his magic holding me captive, as helpless as a butterfly pinned by its wings.

"Why?" A haze descended over me as I tried to cage my rising terror, blinking away the evidence of my hurt.

"Because the Divine Pearl Lotus is inside you." The queen rose, stalking toward me. "Your grandfather gave it to you—the lying traitor."

She knew. I should have been afraid, tried to deny it, yet the proof shone like a beacon over my heart. And the way she spoke of Grandfather wrenched me; it made me mad.

"Don't call him that," I snarled. "He was good, loyal and kind. He only did this to save me."

"Why did he not confess?" Zhangwei demanded.

Except he wasn't "Zhangwei" to me anymore . . . but the God of War, the queen's devoted general, a hateful, cold and deceitful immortal. I was stupid to believe he could have been anything else.

"Because he knew he would find no mercy." I stared at the queen's pitiless face, despair coiling around me like a snake. The warmth of the lotus wavered, as terror flooded me. Were they trying to steal it?

"The lotus cannot be seized by force," I told them fiercely. "It must be—"

"Gifted of a *willing* heart." The Queen of the Golden Desert finished my sentence, her gaze sliding to the god who held me captive.

She knew—they knew. Nothing had been a coincidence; they had plotted everything that led me here.

I was shaking all over, wrenched with anguish, my chest aching so hard I could hardly breathe. "You knew I had the Divine Pearl Lotus all along . . . you pretended to be ignorant. Why?"

The God of War did not reply. Was it remorse that shone in his eyes, or triumph? Did it matter? How did I ever imagine he could care for me? He'd *never* seen me as an equal, just a tool to be used, a fool to be tricked. Such bitterness crawled up my throat, choking me. I was tired of fighting, of scheming, hoping against the odds. But I would never forget what my life had cost my grandfather, and I would not waste it.

"It was all a lie," I said slowly, my mind scrambling for a way to delay him. "The time we spent together, your interest in me, your protection from the Dragon Platform—*everything* was false." My voice rose, thick with rage. I almost shouted the last.

He looked away like he was unable to hold my gaze. There was no satisfaction in being right—only pain.

"Lord Zhangwei, complete the ritual," the queen commanded.

Ever obedient, the God of War opened his hand. In his palm lay the strands of my hair, those he'd claimed yesterday. "A token of the heart, given of your free will."

An icy fear engulfed me now. "Your magic is vile, as are all of you," I raged, struggling against my bonds. Anger was the only tool left to me—futile against my captors, yet vital to preserve a sliver of hope. "You *can't* take the lotus from me." Yet nothing seemed impossible for the immortals.

Zhangwei wrapped my hair around the hilt of a dagger. The black strands fragmented, pooling into an inky sheen that coated the blade. He'd trapped me well, the heartless villain. The Wuxin weren't the worst monsters in the realm. Memories flooded me of how he'd watched over and healed me, of his consideration and care, playing on my emotions with the same skill he used to pluck his qin—

Lies. All lies.

"Now, Lord Zhangwei." The queen's voice rang with sudden resonance. "Claim what you need."

The Divine Pearl Lotus was for *him,* not the queen? The rumors of his injury flashed through my mind, the startling coldness of his skin, his own admission.

Some days I still feel its shadow.

"The Wuxin attack—you never recovered from it," I said slowly. "All these years, you've been suffering, hiding your condition. Seeking the one thing that can save you."

With you I am warm.

When he'd said this, I thought it meant something more, the glimpse of a declaration—but it was the stark truth. He didn't want me, but the power of the Divine Pearl Lotus. And he would stop at nothing to claim it.

"I'm sorry," he said hoarsely. "I must do this."

His remorse meant nothing. It was worse that he understood the anguish he'd inflicted on me and still chose betrayal. I would *never* forgive him. Rage and shame swept over me along with a bitter, clawing hate . . . the hate I should have felt for him all along; it would have kept me safe.

The God of War's gaze shuttered like he was blocking something out, his viselike grip locking tighter around me. There was no mercy in him, just the unyielding force of his might. His eyes blazed until they appeared all white, as clear as the ice in his heart.

Then he raised the dagger and thrust it into my chest.

15

My body splintered with pain. Shadows blotted out my consciousness, but I fought to stay awake. The God of War did not drive the blade deeper, leaving just its tip buried in my flesh, yet the agony did not lessen. Numbly, I stared at the blood trickling from the wound, the red lights of his magic coursing from the blade into me. Something wrenched from my chest, surging free—a glittering trail of stardust, flowing toward the god. The immortals were as vicious as their magic. Somehow, they'd found a way to steal the lotus from me. Bound by his accursed power, I glared at the god who stared back at me with unrelenting, despicable calm. All I wanted now was to hurt him as he had me.

"Why did you do this to me?" I'd make him spell out his treachery, to destroy any last remnant of emotion I might still feel for him.

"The lotus was the only cure to what ailed him," the queen answered, her eyes fixed on the God of War. Was he so precious to her?

"Immortals never share, you only take." Venom laced my words, if only they could draw his blood.

The color leeched from the immortal's face like this was draining his power. I hoped he was suffering, I hoped it hurt. The force restraining me vanished abruptly, like he could no longer sustain it. Without it, I lost my balance—but Lord Zhangwei's arm slid around me, holding me fast, yet not loosening his grip on the dagger in his other hand. I recoiled from his touch, struggling in his grasp, a sparrow in the merciless claws of a tiger.

His eyes were black as coal. "Trust me—"

"Never again," I swore. "They were wrong about you. Your heart isn't made of ice—you have no heart." *This* was his true self: selfish, cruel, and ruthless.

He didn't answer, maybe he didn't care. "Will I die?" I asked.

"No, I won't let you," he said fiercely.

"My grandfather gave me the lotus because I was poisoned. If you take it, aren't you killing me?" I wouldn't let him cower behind meaningless assurances, those that veil his villainy.

He nodded at the dagger. "I am only taking what remains, *after* the lotus cured you. What was healed will not be undone. You won't retain the other traits it might have yielded, but you will live."

"What traits?" Maybe I could learn something that might stop this.

But the God of War did not reply, too cautious to surrender any advantage. "Why the elaborate pretense if you intended to use force anyway?" I asked him.

"For this to work, your feelings had to be real, the magic would not work any other way—using a token of love in place of consent. Once the Divine Pearl Lotus bonds with another, its power must be freely relinquished, willingly gifted."

"I am *not* willing," I seethed.

He looked into my face, his expression grave. "Sometimes we don't even understand our own hearts."

I shoved at him with my free hand, but it was like striking stone. How I burned with fury to have fallen for his wretched scheme. But regret was useless; I needed to get even. I *couldn't* let him win.

"How could you be so confident of my feelings?" Knowledge was a weapon, as Grandfather had said—the only one left to me now.

The queen sighed. "You are clever, child, but I've seen the finest of the mortals live and die, endured more than you know. In gratitude lies the swiftest route to trust. Guard your heart with more care next time."

I flushed as I glared at the God of War. "I wish I'd never asked for mercy for you on the Dragon Platform; I wish you'd suffered *worse*."

"He didn't know what I intended then," Queen Caihong said. "It was a plan that formed after you trespassed where you shouldn't have."

Sounds of a scuffle erupted through the closed doors behind: muffled shouts, a frantic clash of weapons. As the queen's gaze flicked toward the entrance, she frowned.

"Is it done? Have you claimed the Divine Pearl Lotus?" she asked the God of War.

"Not yet, Your Majesty. This is more complex than anticipated." His forehead creased as light blazed brighter from his fingertips, surging along the dagger—yet the glittering trail of the Divine Pearl Lotus stilled in the air like time itself had frozen.

Hope flared. Something was wrong . . . something I might turn to my advantage. "Why didn't you ask me for the lotus?" I said to distract the immortal.

"Would you have agreed?" he countered. "Wholeheartedly, of your own will—without bargains or threats? You resented us, blamed us for your grandfather's death. Even if your mind agreed, your heart was closed to me then. You'd suspect my intentions and actions, imagine everything I did was just for the lotus."

"I would have been right." Yet there was truth in his words. I'd never have let my guard down if I'd known what they wanted of me. And now . . . even as I hated him, even as his deceit was laid bare—the fact I hurt meant that I'd cared.

"We're not so different," he pointed out bluntly. "You planned no less, using your words and charm to gain my support for Tianxia."

"It is not the same," I retorted. "I wanted to use you, but not by hurting you. I wanted your support, while you schemed to steal my heart."

"I didn't want to hurt you either—if only there could have been another way. But there was no time." He sounded unsteady, like he was struggling, too.

Memories surfaced of how he'd spoken to me, all he'd done—the God of War had been courting me all this while. He'd wanted me to fall in love with him so he could take what he needed from me. Except their spell was not working, the warmth of the Divine Pearl Lotus burning unwaveringly in my chest. My heart was bruised . . . but unbroken.

They were wrong. I did *not* love him—not then, not now.

I could have laughed from relief. There had been attraction. Gratitude, desire, even—but not love, the all-consuming emotion that would have yielded my heart and the lotus to him irrevocably, sealing my doom and their triumph. The immortals were too impatient, too arrogant, thinking we would fall at their feet if they showed us a little attention. He'd known my intent to use him and was still confident of winning me. Maybe I'd tricked him, too, as I played on his emotions. Maybe I'd led him to believe my feelings were stronger than they were.

If he'd been patient, waited a little longer—I would have succumbed. And though he'd hurt me more than I'd thought possible, it was not over yet. I would not be their victim; I would fight back.

His eyes narrowed, staring at the dagger between us. He sensed it; that his magic wasn't working as planned. What if I could muddle his mind as he had mine? Stir his emotions to lower his guard? Buried beneath the lies, a spark might ignite—a chance to turn his deception against him, to escape.

"You said I made you feel warm." My heart was beating far too quickly as I brushed the hair from my face, my fingers closing around a hairpin that I tucked into my palm. Only now, did his eyes return to my face. "I felt your touch, saw the way you looked at me." I pushed onward, my cheeks burning from such boldness. "In deceiving me, you ended up deceiving yourself, falling into the trap that you laid. You care for me, too."

He didn't deny it, his gaze boring into mine unrelentingly. "Why does it matter, if you hate me anyway?"

I smiled with all the malice and pride I could muster. "Because then, I can hurt *you*."

I rammed the hairpin into the god's hand, the one that held his dagger. As the sharp point pierced his skin, I ground it deeper, suppressing an urge to be sick. As he flinched, I shoved his chest with all my might, tearing his blade from my flesh. His dagger clattered on the floor, splattering it with my blood.

"You're wrong about me," I snarled. "I'm *not* in love with you. I will *never* love you."

His eyes widened, ink-dark and soulless. As he staggered back a step, I ripped out the other pin from my hair and thrust it at his face—but he swung aside, the tip scratching his cheek. Furious now, unthinking, I grasped wildly at his sword—sliding smoothly from its scabbard to come away in my hand. I froze, stunned by the enormity of what I'd done, the impossibility. The God of War's sword was said to strike fear in the hearts of monsters, to leech life as easily as a sponge soaks water, a weapon that would only answer to its master. And yet, it was in my hand . . . and I was still alive.

Gasps rippled through the court, a hand pressed to Queen Caihong's mouth. I laughed recklessly as the God of War stalked toward me, his face strained.

I pointed the sword at him, though it shook a little. "Stay away from me."

He did not pause as he extended his hand. "Return my sword."

As my answer, I swung it at him with both hands, though it was far heavier than the one he'd given me. The sword whistled through the air, whispering of death. A thrill coursed through me when the god halted, his eyes blazing. How enraged he would be to see his weapon in the hands of a *mortal*.

"Release it before you hurt yourself. My sword is dangerous for a mortal to wield," he warned.

More lies? "Maybe you've underestimated us all." I slashed clumsily at him, yet my palms tingled with a strange energy, emanating from his blade.

As the God of War moved toward me without warning, I thrust the sword at him again, my arms already tiring, unused to the weight. He dipped back, the blade slicing the air above his face.

"Guards, stop her!" Queen Caihong's voice rang out, sharp with urgency.

"Don't hurt her," the God of War commanded.

As I pointed his weapon at them, sparks scattered from it. The soldiers leapt back, exchanging frantic looks. What magic was this? If only I could summon it again, if only I knew how. Fear clutched me as the soldiers surrounded me again, their expression grim—but they wouldn't kill me yet, not until the God of War had taken what he wanted.

Behind me, the entrance doors shuddered violently. Cries rang out, a moment before the doors were flung open, crashing against the wall. Lieutenant Yang stumbled into the hall, blood spattered across his armor. He sank to his knees before the throne. "Your Majesty, the Winged Devils have breached the palace!"

Chaos erupted. Guards rushed toward the entrance, courtiers swarming for safety. The Winged Devils crowded into the chamber, some with swords, others using their claws to flay the soldiers.

The yellowish gems on their foreheads gleamed with malevolent light, their skin glossy with a waxy sheen. I froze at the sight of them before my instincts kicked in, forcing myself to move—to follow the attendants who were streaming through a small doorway at the back covered by a thick curtain.

"Liyen!"

The God of War roared my name with such urgency—I stilled, glancing behind. Our eyes met, the heat of his gaze scorching me. But then a spear hurtled toward him—my fingers instinctively tightening around the sword. He evaded the attack deftly, then spun to knock away a blade swung at his head. Three Winged Devils closed around him, the god's face dark with frustration. As one of his soldiers tossed him a sword, I pulled aside the curtain and raced down the narrow corridor, suppressing the flicker in my chest. A last glimpse of the Shield of Rivers and Mountains left on the table filled me with regret, but I had to save myself first.

Hurrying down the corridor, I pushed my way through the crowd of immortals. None glanced my way, all as eager as me to save themselves. Only the God of War and Queen Caihong would be stalking me now, the thought spurring me onward even as my calves burned.

My robe was damp with sweat as I ran through a narrow passageway that opened to a bridge, trying to recall the pathways I'd studied, those that led outside. An entrance loomed, one that I recognized, leading to the back of the palace. The glimpse of sky beyond sent a jolt of relief through me, though I hadn't the faintest idea how to get back to Tianxia.

One step at a time.

As I dashed across the garden, a rushing sound snared my attention. A Winged Devil was chasing me, gliding forward with startling speed. Terror clawed me as I plunged into a thick grove of bamboo—just as something hissed through the air. I ducked instinctively, evading a streak of grayish mist. More followed with an eerie rush, but I swerved abruptly to evade them.

I was shaking, clinging to the God of War's sword though it weighed me down. Temptation struck to fling it away, but it was the only thing that might help me. *Monsters bleed as mortals do,* I reminded myself. They were stronger, but not invulnerable. And this time, I had a sword.

Gritting my teeth, I forced myself onward. As another dark bolt of magic hurtled toward me, I swung at it with the sword. The bolt shattered abruptly, a strange tingling crawling over my hand. The sword glowed in my hand yet seemed diminished— unlike when the God of War had drawn it. A deep exhaustion was spreading over me, one that sank into my core.

The sun hung low, a crimson disc crowning the heavens. The bamboo grew sparser, barely concealing my presence. I ran through a grassy field, an easy target for the monster chasing me. Ahead, the garden seemed to end, merging into the sky. My heart plunged. Was there nothing beyond? A shadow fell over me, a swish rippling through the air. The creature was closing in; there was nowhere left to run. Tightening my grip on the sword, I spun around—my feet stumbling to a halt.

An enormous creature swooped down before me, magnificent and terrifying. The qilin who'd chased the God of War and me, its antlers shining, its scales gleaming copper. As its great jaws parted, its head lowering toward me—I flinched, suppressing a cry. Yet it nudged my shoulders, rubbing its forehead against me, its mane surprisingly soft. Such affection emanated from the qilin, I could have wept with relief . . . from the unexpected calm that spread over me after the anguish of today.

A furious cry rang out, shattering the brief tranquility. The Winged Devil had almost reached us. I raised the God of War's sword as I pushed the qilin aside—but it lunged in front of me. Was it protecting me? Without hesitation, the qilin hurled itself against the creature—thrusting its antlers into its chest. The

Winged Devil screamed, blood streaming from its wounds. Without another word, it turned on its heel and darted away, likely to find reinforcements. The qilin flew back to me, then lowered itself on the ground, its head tilted in an unspoken invitation. My pulse raced as I climbed upon its back, wrapping my arms around its neck. I didn't know what I was doing, except this felt right.

The qilin let out a huge sigh as it bounded into the air, its wings spread wide as it bore me away. It was so fast, faster even than the phoenix—the breath struck from my lungs. I should be afraid of the creature, afraid of falling—but I felt safe for some reason, even as the bitter taste of treachery was still raw in my mouth.

"Home. To Tianxia," I whispered as I stroked the qilin's head.

It nodded like it understood, flying lower at once. Tears of relief fell from my eyes as my mind slipped briefly to Zhangwei. Was he still battling the Winged Devils? Could he protect himself without his sword? I mocked myself for this remnant of stupidity. If he was hurt, I shouldn't waste any pity on him.

Together, the qilin and I soared through the skies. Clouds flew against my face, billowing soft and gray. The silence was welcome now, this brief peace to unravel my thoughts and the tangle of my emotions. Yet my chest ached with a different type of loss—of betrayal, that hurt no less. I rebuked myself for mourning something false and unworthy . . . but our minds are often wiser than our hearts. Anger seared me that I'd been such a fool, my spirits sunken that I'd failed in what I sought.

I was lucky to have escaped, though I was far from safe—it was not over yet. The God of War knew I possessed the Divine Pearl Lotus and his sword. He would come for me; he would stop at nothing to get what he wanted.

But this time, I would be ready for him.

PART
TWO

16

In the distance, Tianxia gleamed like a jewel amid the clouds—the violet mountains and glittering rivers, the red wall that snaked around the land. When the qilin landed just outside my home, I slid down from its back. Such lightness swept over me at the feel of the earth beneath my feet, at the glimpse of the dark green tiles of my home. Despite the wonders in the realm of immortals, nothing could compare to this fullness in my heart, the one of belonging.

"Thank you." I hugged the qilin tightly, wishing I knew its name. I would have died but for the creature's compassion.

I released it, expecting the qilin to take flight again—but it followed me as I walked toward my home. Its presence comforted me, but once the God of War subdued the attack on the queen's palace, he would come here. He seemed to mistrust the qilin, and I wouldn't endanger the creature.

"I wish you could stay, but it won't be safe here. Don't you want to go home?" I asked, sensing it could understand me.

The qilin bent to nuzzle my hand, its weight pushing me back a step. Then it straightened, springing into the air. Its wings flared wide as the qilin soared gracefully back through the heavens. I stared after it until dusk crept up around me, the first glimmers of starlight peeking through the darkening skies.

Alone now, I pressed a hand to my chest. The scar was still there, no longer aglow, bearing no trace of the God of War's dagger. Just the blood remained, which I wiped away, but what he'd done could not be erased. The Divine Pearl Lotus pulsed within me with its familiar warmth, a fierce gladness filling me at the immortal's failure to seize it. While it was a relief that I wouldn't die even if I relinquished it, what else might I be surrendering?

I inhaled deeply, shifting my mind to more immediate matters of home. What welcome would I receive? There would be questions, some I couldn't answer—the most pressing being whether I'd received the Queen of the Golden Desert's mandate to rule. No ruler of Tianxia had ever returned from the skies without it. How could I tell them I'd failed, and that the God of War was hunting me? No, not hunting, for he knew exactly where to find me—it was only a matter of time. Part of me wanted to flee, but where could I go? We were all trapped within these walls, those of the immortals' making.

I wouldn't run like a coward. This time, the stakes were in the open. When I next faced the God of War, it would be among my people, in the security of my home—though he could incinerate my hall to ashes should I push him too far. He was good at setting things on fire.

But his mind was sharp; I'd seen how he played weiqi, planning each move far ahead. He would be furious, but he wouldn't let it govern him. He might rage at me, but he wouldn't hurt me— not when I possessed what he most needed. There was only one way to secure the Divine Pearl Lotus . . . and that was if I gave it to him.

Yet I needed something from him, too, even though I wished I didn't. The thought of Queen Caihong's anger sickened me: the catastrophic form it might take upon my kingdom, whether in torrential rains or violent storms. Did she realize how she was hurting us? Did she care? And though I wanted little more than to run the God of War through with his own sword, I had to extract a compromise from him rather than incite a confrontation that I'd surely lose. We were bound by need, by necessity: the God of War who so desperately needed the lotus was also the only one who might protect us from his queen's wrath, who could persuade her to reach an agreement with me.

How could I share this with the court? I'd be handing the ambitious Minister Guo and Minister Dao a knife to plunge into my back. I had to tread carefully until I'd unearthed the identity of my real enemies—those who schemed in the dark, who'd poisoned me before, who weren't afraid to get blood on their hands. If one of them ruled Tianxia, the people would be doomed under such tyranny. I could not let this happen.

As I approached the entrance, the guards pulled apart the sturdy wooden doors. I thanked them, entering my home. While I'd only been away a week or so, it felt like years. This place was at once familiar—and different, my mind crowded with new memories. Now I saw the withered flowers scattered across the grass, the parts of the trees cut away when they'd sickened, as I breathed in the lingering scent of decay that twined with new life. So different from the ageless perfection of the skies, its ceaseless fragrance— yet a reminder of how precious our lives here were. A fallen blossom would never bloom again, just as a moment lost could never be regained. Each one had to count.

Heads turned as I stalked through the main courtyard. Attendants bowed, some retreating into the shadows—either alarmed by the urgency of my stride or, more likely, bribed to divulge news of my return to their paymasters.

I stopped one, asking, "Where is Lord Chengyin?"

"In the throne room, Your Ladyship."

"At this hour?" I was surprised.

"Lord Chengyin usually keeps such long hours," she told me with another bow.

I frowned, wishing I could have met him alone, eager for news before facing the court. But word was already spreading of my return. I could not appear apprehensive, to give rise to gossip that would weaken my precarious standing.

I went to my rooms to change quickly, my stained dress would stir too much curiosity. Glancing in the mirror, I yanked out the sandalwood comb from my hair and dropped it to the ground. The ornament was as worthless as the sentiment behind it. Then I wrapped the god's sword in a piece of brocade and locked it into a cupboard in my study. It was safer out of sight, though I didn't like leaving it here.

I strode to the main hall, my brisk pace concealing my nerves. The court typically grew restless long before dusk. Yet when I entered, the calm was startling. The ministers stood before the throne, heads turned up attentively. Chengyin sat on a polished wooden chair beside my throne, dressed in formal robes of deep red and gold. They suited him well, enhancing his fine features.

When those closest to the entrance saw me, whispers of "Her Ladyship" drifted through the hall like an unwelcome chill. Chengyin's head swung toward me. Did he resent my return? A vile suspicion that was swiftly banished as a smile lit his face. He hurried down from the dais, clasping his hands to bow low.

"Welcome home, Your Ladyship."

With this, he declared his allegiance before all, quelling any consideration that he might supplant me. Following his lead, the court bowed, intoning a greeting. Minister Guo and Minster Dao hesitated before bending their heads, their expressions sullen.

I climbed the dais and settled into my throne. It felt unfamiliar, the seat too wide—yet I didn't want to be anywhere else. "What news during my absence?" I spoke decisively, thwarting any attempt to question me.

"Your Ladyship, a few days ago there was severe flooding in the east," Chengyin replied formally.

"Has there been much rain?" Unlikely, as it was the dry season.

"Yes, Your Ladyship," Minister Hu answered, leaning heavily on his wooden staff as he hobbled to the front of the hall. "Relentless rain, without pause. The rivers swelled, bursting through the barriers, destroying the crops."

I recalled the gray skies in the Golden Desert—Queen Caihong's fury when she found me in the forbidden courtyard. Despite the deception, her anger then had been real. Was the storm the mark of her displeasure, spilling over to us? What else might be inflicted on us once she learned of my escape?

I hid my anxiety, gesturing to an attendant to bring a chair for Minister Hu. "Has aid been sent?" I asked.

"Yes," Chengyin replied. "Food and provisions. Shelters are being built for those who lost their homes."

"Later, they will need support for replanting their crops." I hesitated before asking, "Were there any fatalities?"

"Several villagers were swept away," Minister Hu replied somberly. "Most are presumed dead."

"Send more soldiers to help search for the missing; prepare aid for their families. We must help bear their burdens. Inform me as soon as we have more news," I told him, my voice leaden.

"What of Your Ladyship's news?" Minister Guo's smile masked his malice. "How was Your Ladyship's visit to the Immortal Realm?"

"Everything proceeded as planned," I lied with a straight face. "But I was forced to leave earlier than intended, when intruders attacked the queen's palace."

"Who would dare attack the immortals?" Minister Hu asked.

"They are called the Winged Devils. But the immortals' forces are strong, they are in no danger." Against my will, the memory of how the God of War fought slid into my mind, his ferocity and grace. How would he fare without his sword? The thought pricked, when there should only be glee.

Shaking myself, I said, "For now, I only want to learn of any urgent matters here that require attention."

"The court has managed exceedingly well in your absence, Your Ladyship," Minister Guo said silkily.

Minister Dao added, "If Your Ladyship is satisfied, we would be honored to continue sharing your burdens at court—to handle the petitions so Your Ladyship may pursue other matters that she enjoys more."

A flagrant attempt to grasp power. Had the ministers found a way to work together? More than greed, this was an intended slight, one I would not meekly ignore. Not *today* of all days, after confronting the immortal queen, being stabbed by the God of War, then chased by monsters.

"Minister Dao, I want to be here," I said decisively. "Don't presume to know my preferences. Your duties will revert to what they were, and all past petitions will be reviewed when I have the time." My tone emulated the way Queen Caihong had spoken to me.

His face twisted with anger, but he folded into a bow. "Forgive me, Your Ladyship. I only have your best interests at heart."

Behind him, his accomplices exchanged furtive glances, their lips pursed. They thought me weak and malleable before; now they judged me as vicious and sharp-tongued. It was better this way. From the side of the hall, Aunt Shou cleared her throat, a warning to remain calm. When had she entered? It was a delicate balance, weaving one's influence over a reluctant court but not yanking the threads hard enough to tempt rebellion. While I was far from perfect, I was beginning to believe that I'd find my own rhythm.

I straightened, almost wishing I'd worn one of my gold headdresses. Clothes, crowns, and ceremony helped imbue one with the illusion of power. But wearing a robe embroidered with dragons did not endow one with their might; a cloak of feathers did not enable one to fly.

Grandfather would have frowned at such ostentatious displays, but he'd always been secure in his position, possessing an innate dignity and charm. If only these might be inherited along with blood. The court had willingly yielded to his will, unlike now. To many, I was a custodian of power, a temporary inconvenience. The worst imagined me a vessel for breeding the next heir, to be bundled away either as a powerless consort or in a shroud.

Minister Guo cleared his throat. "What of the mandate, Your Highness?" he prodded as though scenting weakness.

I met his stare steadily. "Would I have returned without it?"

The minister opened his mouth, but before he could speak, Chengyin raised his voice to proclaim, "We are pleased to hear of Your Ladyship's success."

I shot him a grateful look as Minister Guo glared at him. "The position of your imperial consort still lies vacant," the minister informed me in a ringing tone. "Now that Your Ladyship has the mandate, allow us to propose some candidates for Her Ladyship's selection? More than one, if you prefer?"

My hand itched to slap the leer from his face. But I smiled widely. "Of course, if there are enough desirable candidates." I leaned back against my throne. "We must prepare a courtyard to be fitted out for my consorts after I select them." Hollow words to silence the minister, to throw him off guard.

Minister Guo's eyes rounded. Maybe he'd hoped to embarrass me with his crude suggestion, but after today few things could shake me.

Minister Dao sidled forward. "Would Her Ladyship share her plan to choose her consort?"

I glanced at Chengyin, but his expression was blank as he studied me curiously. He'd never seen this side to me either—harder than when I'd left, sharper around the edges. A thought struck, part inspiration, part recklessness.

"*When* I choose the imperial consort"—I took care to emphasize the word—"the person will be the one most capable and worthy of serving Tianxia, by my side.

"A lofty ambition, Your Ladyship." Minister Guo's tone dripped with condescension. "How will you determine this paragon?"

"A competition." I was pulling ideas from the air. A useful distraction from unwanted questions. "We are a land of warriors, most trained regardless of status. Those who are eligible will compete for my hand. But all entrants must be willing, none forced."

While I had no plans of holding this event, even if I did, I wouldn't want anyone coerced to enter. I wanted someone who'd want me for myself.

Minister Dao blanched. "Such a thing has never been held before."

"If we cling only to tradition, we will be left behind," I said firmly.

"You will marry the winner? Regardless of their appearance or situation?" Minister Guo probed pointedly. "Even a stranger?"

I blanched inwardly, imagining him scouring the land for the most brutish and vicious warriors, bribing them to his side.

"*If* he is worthy. Everyone will be given the same opportunity to participate, the same weapons and challenges. A warrior is valued not just for their physical form, but also the sharpness of their minds." I swiftly conjured rules to give the impression I'd thought this through, rather than it being a haphazard plan cobbled together.

"Weapons?" Minister Chen repeated shrilly. He was a thin man with a straggly mustache, and—if memory served me right—three children of marriageable age.

I leaned my head upon my hand, dealing the final blow, one to ensure this plan never saw the light. "It will be a fight to the death. The winner will be the last one remaining."

Maybe *this* bloodthirsty suggestion would finally deter them from the prospect of my marriage. Fewer suitors would be willing to enter the fray once a deadly price was attached to the crown.

Or it might leave those more determined, my mind reminded me drily.

Faces paled, whispers slithering around the hall. I'd caught them off-guard. The thought that I'd even consider this would make them hesitate, doubt their assessment of me as a puppet, easily led. If they couldn't read me, they could not trap me . . . and maybe I would keep my throne a little longer.

I'd meant each word I'd said to Queen Caihong. I wanted to be a good ruler, to earn my place. But first I needed the support of the court—and if I couldn't secure it by playing by their rules, I would make my own.

17

Night had fallen when I left the throne room, the moon illuminating my path. As I entered my courtyard, I plucked a handful of jasmine from a bush, inhaling its rich fragrance. A relief to discard the mask of decorum here, the need to guard every word.

In my study, I sat behind the mahogany desk, recalling how Grandfather used to sit here as he worked tirelessly into the night. This was how I liked to remember him, in these quiet moments— not the chaos and anguish of the night he'd died. My breathing hitched as I lay my head down against the cool wood. Remembrance was both the solace and bane of the living.

The doors slid apart, Yifei ushering in Aunt Shou and Chengyin. As I straightened, they sat across from me. Yifei set down a tray with walnut cakes, winter-melon pastries, and a bowl of mandarins. She poured the tea, then nudged the fruit closer to me, ever concerned for my health since the poisoning. Even now, the memory of it made me shudder: the bone-deep weariness, the feverish pain that burned yet left me cold. A familiar anger rose at the unknown enemy who'd inflicted this upon me.

"Being the First Advisor is more a punishment than an elevation," Chengyin said with a sigh. "Now that you've returned, I gladly surrender my position. My ears hurt from all the 'advice' the ministers have been trying to dispense. I would rather spend my afternoons—"

"Drinking wine and spouting bad poetry with Minister Xiao's eldest son?" Aunt Shou interrupted, glaring at him. "Or is it his sister you're casting your eyes at?"

Chengyin flushed. "Our poetry is not 'bad.' Besides, he's one of the few around here who don't say one thing and mean another."

"Surprising, given his father," Aunt Shou remarked with a sniff. "Minister Xiao is one of Minister Guo's closest allies. Who knows what his children have been taught."

"Children shouldn't be held accountable for the bad choices of their parents," Chengyin replied with an irreverent grin.

"Children should respect their elders," Aunt Shou chided him, yet there was a tenderness in her eyes when she looked at him.

"Chengyin, could you bear it a while longer?" I asked. "There aren't many I can trust at court who are also capable. Once things are stable, I'll find you a new position where you can host all the questionable poetry-reciting banquets you wish."

"Can I be the Minster of Revelry?"

I frowned. "Do I have one?"

"You will soon." He grinned as he lifted his cup to me. "I accept your proposal."

I laughed, raising my own cup to him. As Chengyin picked up a pastry and bit into it, Aunt Shou smacked his arm like he was a boy once more. "Remember your manners. Serve Her Ladyship first."

He shot her an aggrieved look. "Mother, this is the same shameless person who used to snatch my favorite books and toys, who broke your precious porcelain vase. She even gave me this." He pushed his sleeve up to show a scar on the underside of his wrist, one familiar to me.

"You deserved it," I said loftily. "We *both* broke that vase, and you were just clumsy enough to cut yourself on the pieces."

"You pushed me into them."

"Because you shoved me in the first place," I retorted, restraining the urge to laugh.

He scowled. "You shouldn't have wailed so loudly, then. Mother heard you, when we could have swept up the pieces and buried them in the garden like I wanted to."

I looked at Aunt Shou, shaking my head in mock disgust. "Parents shouldn't be held accountable for the bad choices of their children, either."

"Traitor," Chengyin muttered, even as his lips twitched.

The bond between us was forged through such remembrances. Chengyin and Aunt Shou were my only family now, not through blood but affection, and yet as close and vital. I wished they would accept the gifts and honors I'd gladly bestow on them, but they'd refused everything except when it would aid me, as Chengyin did with the position as First Advisor. While this denied me one of the keenest pleasures of power—to reward those loyal and deserving—it was also a precious thing to be loved for oneself.

"Enough," Aunt Shou said wearily, pressing a hand to her forehead. "We can't have the Lady of Tianxia and her First Advisor bickering like spoiled children. If any of the minsters heard—"

"She can just order their heads cut off," Chengyin interjected.

I smiled sweetly. "I might start with yours."

"There will be no executions," Aunt Shou said sternly. "Liyen doesn't have the stomach for that; moreover, ruling by fear is ill-advised. Silencing worthy ministers, only rewarding advice that pleases the ear, cultivates a viperous court of bootlickers where nothing of worth gets done."

I nodded. "I don't want that, either, though it might make life easier."

"The idea about the betrothal competition was shrewd. They didn't expect that," Chengyin told me.

"Unpredictability will keep them on their toes, but it won't earn you their loyalty or respect," Aunt Shou observed bluntly. "Right now, they fear the unknown more than you. It will take a while to change their opinion, but prejudices aren't overcome in a day."

"Are they plotting against me, Aunt Shou?" I asked.

"There are always plots when a throne is at stake. But they won't dare move against you when you have the mandate from the Queen of the Golden Desert," Aunt Shou said firmly. "With her favor, your position is stronger than before."

When I didn't reply, Aunt Shou's eyes narrowed in that knowing way—the one that made me feel like a child again, caught doing something I shouldn't have. "Liyen, what's the matter?"

"I don't have the queen's mandate," I said slowly.

Chengyin frowned as he glanced at Aunt Shou. "What happened?"

"The God of War tried to take the Divine Pearl Lotus from me. He failed."

He drew in a long breath. "It's a wonder you're alive."

The wrinkles across Aunt Shou's forehead deepened. "The immortals knew about the lotus? I thought it was concealed."

"As did I," I said darkly. "Maybe he sensed it when he healed me? Magic seems unpredictable. We can never assume we know how it works."

"Those monsters who attacked us before—the Winged Devils? Were they after you, for the lotus too?" Chengyin probed.

"Maybe, but I hope not." An uneasy feeling to be a target, hunted by both immortals and monsters.

Aunt Shou shook her head. "Your grandfather said the lotus couldn't be seized; it had to be gifted. How did the immortals try to take it from you?"

"An enchantment. They needed my trust for it to work." I wouldn't say more of what he'd done. "Love" had no place between the God of War and me, nor would it ever.

"How did you escape?" Chengyin asked.

Quickly I told them of what had transpired: Queen Caihong's anger, the attack in the palace, the flight with the qilin. I said little of my time alone with the god, of the ceaseless ache in my chest now.

"The immortals won't let you go," Aunt Shou said somberly. "They will come here."

Chengyin sighed. "We haven't recovered from their last visit."

I simmered, recalling the fires that had raged through my home, the ruin left in their wake. If the God of War intended to repeat his destruction, I'd throw his precious sword into the forge— *after* I'd run him through with it.

If you can, that unhelpful voice in my mind added.

I smothered it; I had to think clearly. "I won't let them hurt anyone. The immortals need me alive—at least for now. They've learned that they can't just *take* what they want from me. They need my cooperation to secure the Divine Pearl Lotus, else I wouldn't have dared to return here."

The god's sword hidden in my study was a secret I was reluctant to share. This would attract more thieves than the lotus, both mortal and immortal, and I didn't want to endanger anyone with it.

"What will you do?" Chengyin asked me.

"I won't serve Queen Caihong like Grandfather did—devotion and obedience has gained us nothing so far. After what they tried to do to me, it shows they'll never treat us as we deserve."

Aunt Shou nodded. "I didn't expect the immortals to be so cunning and underhanded. They spout virtues like honor and valor, yet are quick to turn their back on them to get their own way. If I'd known, I would never have let you follow him to the skies—God of War or not."

Her protectiveness moved me. "There was no choice; I had to

go. But now, they are forced to negotiate. I have an opportunity that no ruler of Tianxia has had before—a chance to reopen negotiations, to forge a new treaty . . . one without walls."

"A new future." Chengyin's eyes were bright. "No matter how large a place, to be fenced in makes one feel small." He frowned then. "These negotiations only work if both sides are willing and able to trade. Will giving up the lotus hurt you?"

The thought troubled me more than I cared to admit; I was no sacrificing heroine. "The God of War said I wouldn't die. Though we can't wholly trust him, I don't think he'd lie about this." I fell silent, unwilling to explain. Because deep down, I think the immortal cared for me, too—just a little, but enough that it had enabled me to break free.

"What will you ask from them?" Aunt Shou wanted to know. "We must keep the terms precise and clear."

"To end our obligation to the Queen of the Golden Desert, for the return of our shield. To rejoin the world beyond—it's *ours*, too," I said fiercely. "We would still guard Kunlun. It keeps us safe, too."

"Queen Caihong will not want to relinquish Tianxia," Aunt Shou mused. "Having the worship of the mortals also elevates her status, bringing her closer in prestige to that of the Celestial Emperor."

My hands curled on the table. "We aren't a prize to be traded or won. We deserve more than to be a jewel in the queen's crown."

"And we will be." Aunt Shou's eyes were as bright as the silver in her hair. "But this negotiation will be delicate; agree to nothing without consulting me. We must ensure your safety alongside Tianxia's future."

Chengyin was studying me, rubbing his chin. "If the Divine Pearl Lotus is a part of you now, do you have magic?"

I recalled the tingling as I gripped the god's sword, the fear in the soldiers' faces. That was what power felt like, though I didn't know how to grasp it. "If I did, Minster Guo and Minister Dao would have found themselves transformed into crickets," I replied evasively.

"This is a serious matter," Aunt Shou reminded me. "The immortals will try to retrieve the lotus at any cost. If you have magic, you can stop them."

"I don't," I said heavily. "At least, nothing I can use. Why don't we have magic, Aunt Shou?"

"It's the way of life," she said, her gaze distant and almost sad. "Mortals can't channel magic, just as rabbits cannot fly. I've read that mortals lack the lifeforce that enables the immortals to channel their power. It's a vital part of them—if their lifeforce is extinguished, they die just as we do."

The thought didn't bring me the satisfaction it should have. I straightened, clasping my hands. "We must prepare for the God of War's arrival."

"You seem certain *he* will come," Chengyin said. "Why not Queen Caihong? After all, it was she who wanted the lotus."

"It's the God of War who needs it."

They stared at me. "Why?" Aunt Shou asked.

"He was injured in the war with the Wuxin but is still powerful."

"An injured God of War," Chengyin remarked. "They must be guarding this secret from their enemies."

"From us, too." They didn't trust us, or maybe they didn't think we were worthy of the knowledge. I added wrathfully, "I hope his wounds *hurt*."

"You are vicious today, Liyen," Chengyin said. "Did the great God of War offend you during your visit, beyond his attempted theft? Did his handsome form fail to win your good opinion?"

I scowled, resenting how close he cut to the truth. "Self-preservation. If he's more focused on his wounds, he won't inflict more on me."

At once, his face clouded. "We won't let him hurt you. Guards will accompany you at all times, armed with any of their weapons we can gather."

I did not like being shadowed, and having seen the God of War fight, this seemed futile. Yet any blade was better than none.

Aunt Shou pressed her lips together. "We must keep this from the court. We must maintain the pretense that all is well and that you have the queen's mandate," she advised. "Too many are still eyeing your throne. They would leap at any chance to displace you."

I nodded as Aunt Shou and Chengyin rose. It was well past midnight, too close to dawn.

After they left, I headed to my grandfather's altar in the corner of the study, crafted of ebony and mother-of-pearl. I brushed away the incense ash that had fallen over his ancestral tablet, replacing the flowers in the vase with freshly cut ones. Yifei could have done all this, but it was a privilege to care for his memory. Lighting three sticks, I knelt down and whispered a prayer, not to those undeserving gods—but to wherever my grandfather's spirit was, a wish for him to find peace, to lend me strength for what lay ahead. My grief had not lessened but was changing—growing gentler, weaving nostalgia to blunt the sharpness of loss. Rising to my feet, I pressed the incense sticks into the brazier. Could Grandfather see them or smell their fragrance? Or did we perform such tasks for ourselves, a frail comfort to lessen the guilt that we still lived?

I didn't have these answers. But as though *someone* had heard me, a gentle breeze darted through the window, the wind chime breaking into a delicate melody. I stood straighter, my resolve hardening. This was not a game I could sacrifice; winning was more than a matter of pride. The immortal had underestimated me; he didn't know what I was capable of. This time, I would show him, and victory would not be claimed by the God of War.

18

Sleep eluded me as I tossed on my bed. When I closed my eyes, the God of War's face flashed through my mind—the unrelenting darkness of his eyes, the slant of his lips, the sharp planes of his face. It was safer to be awake; I could guard myself better.

He would come soon. The thought twisted me into knots, even as a restless anticipation built. I was no longer the ignorant mortal to be duped, no longer trapped in his world. Here, he would be in mine. All my efforts should be set on plotting against him, preparing for every eventuality. What if the God of War was crafting another plan? Another spell? The prospect of his nefarious schemes burrowed through my mind like a nail in my shoe.

I shifted in bed, pushing the covers down. It was too warm, too stifling with the windows closed. The air thrummed constantly with a faint energy, that I only noticed when all was quiet and dark. The God of War's sword. A powerful weapon that could shift the balance in our favor, if only I knew how to use it. What use was power if one could not wield it? The finest sword left in its scabbard could strike no blow.

When I finally slept, it was uneven and fitful. I awoke later than usual to ashen skies, my mind gritty and drawn. As I pulled myself up, something fell from my wrist. The red thread bracelet

Lord Zhangwei had tied around me, the bead broken, the thread snapped. My time in the skies was over; I could never return. My heart sank when it should have soared. Even though there was no one I'd miss there—life had become a little less wondrous, a little more gray.

At least today was one of rest for the court, though many would attend the afternoon meal with me. Yifei had laid out a set of clothes as I preferred to dress myself, unless more elaborate attire was required. I tied a yellow sash around the fern-green brocade, then sat down by the table to comb my hair.

Footsteps sounded along the path outside, the assured stride . . . almost familiar. The doors were pushed apart without a knock. I stood up, anger flaring—my gaze colliding with the God of War's. His black robe was color of my mood, his belt accented with jade. I hadn't expected him so soon, with the tumult in the Palace of Radiant Light. Had the Winged Devils been subdued so quickly? As he stalked toward me, I opened my mouth to call for the guards—

"If you scream, if they come—I just might kill them."

I didn't think he would, yet he spoke the words with such menace, I closed my mouth instinctively, a shiver darting across my back.

"Are you done uttering pointless threats?" I asked, infusing my tone with scorn.

"Not by half."

"The guards wouldn't have let you in unannounced. Did you hurt them?" I demanded.

"No," he ground out. "They are asleep."

"At this hour?" I frowned, the truth setting in. "You did this. Wake them at once."

He shook his head, moving toward me. "I'll wake them once I get my answers."

Fear spiked, but whether he liked it or not, he needed me alive.

"You'll get no answers from me unless you improve your manners."

"Such arrogance." He tilted his head back, raking me with his cold eyes. "Has Tianxia forgotten its obligation?"

I smiled. "Have you forgotten I haven't pledged my loyalty to your queen yet? I am not bound."

We glared at each other, my fear forgotten in the rush that swept over me. His presence set me on edge—inside, I was seething at his arrogance and presumption, after all he'd done.

"I have come to propose an agreement," he said finally.

A small triumph that he'd been forced to speak first. "What terms do you offer, Lord Zhangwei?"

His eyebrows raised. "Is there need for such formality? Don't we know each other well enough?"

"*Lord Zhangwei*," I repeated with deliberate emphasis, "as it turns out, I never knew you at all."

His mouth tightened. Let him be angry; I was angry, too.

He took another step forward, towering over me. "You have a vile temper, little thief."

"Don't call me that," I snarled.

He tapped his chin contemplatively. "What should I call you when you took something you had no right to."

"You stole from me first." I folded my arms. "And if I'm a thief, what are you?"

"Not a good one. I came out poorer from our encounter."

There was an edge to his tone; he didn't like losing. I laughed tauntingly. "Don't underestimate mortals next time."

"You were far more cunning than I gave you credit for."

"And you were infinitely more treacherous."

His eyes slid down my neck to my chest. "Does it still hurt?"

"Do you care?"

A pause before he answered. "You said that I had no heart. It turns out you are the same."

His audacity was breathtaking. "*You* stabbed me."

"You were never in danger. It was necessary to forge the connection—"

"I'm so glad I now understand *why* you stabbed me," I said cuttingly.

"What about you? You sheltered beneath my roof as you plotted against me, watched me get struck as I bore your punishment, all the while pretending to care." He spoke tightly as though restraining his fury. "Was it all for Tianxia? Did you *only* want to use me, nothing more?"

"Yes," I claimed furiously. "What other reason could there be? Why would anyone care for the God of War? Your hands are soaked in blood." Anger made me cruel. It made me reckless and unkind . . . saying things I didn't always mean, things I wished I could take back.

He closed the distance between us, my body alight at his nearness. As much as I wanted to back away, my pride wouldn't let me—and deep down, part of me still craved this feeling his presence stirred. Let me be a fool in my mind, as long as he never knew it.

"If so, why did you plead for mercy for me on the Dragon Platform? Why defend me if you didn't care at all?"

"Because, as your queen puts it so well," I said bitterly, "'In gratitude lies the swiftest route to trust.'"

His gaze seared. "Yet how ungrateful you are. Without me, you would have died twice over."

"Oh, I'm very grateful that you did all this to preserve the Divine Pearl Lotus, and your own life. I will strive to repay such generosity in kind." I spoke through clenched teeth and only a madman—or an arrogant immortal—might imagine I meant it.

As light flared in his eyes, I stepped back, suddenly afraid of myself as much as him. My heart was beating too quickly, it was becoming harder to breathe. "Enough with the 'pleasantries,'" I said. "I know you want the lotus and your sword. What will you offer in exchange? Speak honestly, for the first time since we met."

He didn't reply right away, his throat convulsing. "That's not all I want from you."

"Immortals want everything, don't they? Was your pride hurt that your plan didn't work? I don't intend to be another trophy for you." I lifted my chin. "I've told you all I offer; no more. What are your terms?"

He smiled with such assurance, I resisted the impulse to strike him. "Let's start with an easy one. Return my sword that you stole."

"How interesting, that you'd choose your weapon over your life." I couldn't resist mocking him.

"I'm not choosing one over the other. I want both, but the sword is the easier one, since the Divine Pearl Lotus requires—"

"Me to be a greater fool than I've already been?" As my fingers curled, his gaze slid to them like he was attuned to my every movement.

"Strike me, if you want." He leaned toward me. "If it will make you feel better. If it will help us get past the sniping and onto how we can help each other."

I started toward him, not needing another invitation. As I flung my palm at his face, he caught it effortlessly—then spun me around, my back pressed to his chest as his other arm locked me across my waist.

"You . . . *liar*," I gasped, struggling to pull free. "You said I could hit you."

"I didn't say I would *let* you."

The press of his chest, his hand clasped around mine, his breath against my ear—I was trembling from rage, fighting the heat that swept through me, hating how I both wanted and loathed this with every fiber of my being. Of far greater danger was the way something about him called to me still, evoking emotions that should have died the moment his dagger slid into my chest. I couldn't undo the time we'd spent together—where in trying to draw him closer, I'd lost a little of myself, too. I had to guard myself better . . . until I could hate him as I needed to.

"Let me go." My voice was harsh.

He released me then, his face somber. "One day, you will want to stay."

Those words pierced me, but I hardened myself. "I'll *trade* your sword back to you for the shield that belongs to Tianxia," I offered coldly. "One weapon for the other."

He tilted his head back. "Is that all?"

"I wasn't finished. I want your queen's assurance of my safety and the mandate to rule. While you are here, you must do or say nothing to indicate there is a rift between Tianxia and the Golden Desert."

His eyebrows lifted. "Are you having trouble at court? There is no rift except between you and me, you and Her Majesty."

I ignored his taunt. "Do you agree to these terms?"

"No. But I look forward to a long negotiation."

Before I could reply, someone knocked on the door. Yifei entered, halting at the sight of the God of War. Her hands shook, jolting the tray she held, a few lychees falling from the bowl and rolling toward him.

"I'm sorry," she stammered as though afraid.

He bent down to gather the fruit, then placed them back on her tray. "There is nothing to be sorry about."

He spoke as gently to her as he did to his own attendants, and I hated that I knew this about him.

As Yifei smiled at him, wide-eyed, I cleared my throat meaningfully. At once, she spun to me. "My lady, the First Advisor is waiting for you to join him for the afternoon meal."

Chengyin was being thoughtful, sending her to remind me. "Tell Chengyin—tell the First Advisor, I will join him shortly."

As she bowed and left, the God of War faced me, a dangerous glitter in his eyes. "Why does the First Advisor presume himself entitled to your company?"

"Why shouldn't he? He is more entitled to it than you." My answer was intended to infuriate, though it might have worked too well, the heat of his anger surging through the air.

As I turned to leave, he moved to block my path. "We must speak."

"Later." I resisted the urge to snap. "I must go. They are waiting for me."

His lips pressed into an uncompromising line. "Then I will accompany you."

"I don't recall asking you to," I said.

"I claim the privilege of a guest."

"Guests have to be invited."

He smiled widely, devastatingly. "You invited me, did you forget? Twice, as a matter of fact. The first time when you disparaged my home, and the second . . . only a few days ago."

I would welcome you to Tianxia.

I cursed myself—aloud. He was right; I could not refuse. Moreover, he'd hosted me once, although his motives had been self-serving. As Zhangwei looked around my room, his eyes slid over my dressing table strewn with discarded ornaments, the clothes I'd worn last night slung over a stand, then lingering on my bed, the sheets still rumpled.

His gaze darkened—an answering heat rushing into my face. He shouldn't be here. These were my private rooms where I slept, bathed, and dressed, where only Yifei and those closest to me were allowed in. A thought unsettled me—could he sense the sword? While it was hidden in my study, I dared not take the chance. He strode to a corner of the room, picking up the comb I'd tossed aside—his gift. As he brushed the dust away, magic flickered from his fingers, repairing the scratched lacquer.

He handed it to me, but I shook my head. "Not everything can be fixed that easily."

His expression was unreadable as he tucked the comb into his belt. I suppressed the twinge in my chest. "You may stay as my guest," I told him grudgingly. "Explore the grounds as you wish, with one exception. This room." I was starting to enjoy setting rules for him, though no one could bind him to them.

He strode to the door and held it open it for me, a mocking lilt in his tone as he said, "I thank the Lady of Tianxia for her gracious hospitality."

19

As we walked toward the dining hall, those we passed turned to stare, more at the God of War than me. Even without his armor, he cut a striking and forbidding figure, moving with predatory grace. He didn't speak but studied everything we passed. Did my home appear dull to him, used to the perfection of his realm, the effortless opulence? I loved my home, yet could not deny the wear in the buildings, the faded paintings, the chipped tiles that hadn't been replaced. Was he judging us, finding us wanting? Grandfather preferred to channel our limited funds into strengthening the kingdom rather than gilding our domain— but what would an immortal know of that with their mountains of jade? Moreover, the God of War's attack had left far too many things in need of urgent repair.

"What are you thinking about with that look on your face?" he asked.

I pointed at a charred pillar ahead. "Whether you're admiring the marks of your rage."

His gaze followed mine, his jaw tightening. "It wasn't because of anger."

"Then why? To punish us? To force us into submission?" My voice cracked as I fought for calm.

"Your grandfather failed in his duty. He ignored Her Majesty's command. Such defiance could not go unpunished." He paused, then added, "Only later did I realize he did it to save you."

"Would it have made a difference? Or would you still have attacked and burned my home?"

His expression was grave. "Buildings can be repaired."

It struck me then, he hadn't hurt my people that day. There had been fire and smoke, terror and chaos . . . but no blood spilled. Only Grandfather had been lost—my heart clenched at the thought—and even then, I could not wholly blame the immortals for his death. I used to think the God of War relished bloodshed, that he thrived on it—but now I wasn't so sure. It didn't matter; this changed nothing of what he'd done to me.

"It will cost us more than we have to restore it all," I told him. "We have no magic, no endless source of treasure. Everything here has a price; the gold to fix a roof could have been put toward a new school."

"I will pay for the repairs," he said with hesitation. "This was my doing."

My pride wanted me to refuse, but why should my kingdom suffer? I wouldn't thank him though; this wasn't kindness, it was guilt. "You may discuss the reparations with my First Advisor," I said coldly.

"Stop acting like this." He moved toward me. "I know you're angry with me, that you've been wronged, that you might even think you hate me—"

"Oh, I do," I interjected, raising my chin.

Small creases formed at the corners of his mouth. "You have every right to feel this way, but I hope you will listen with an open mind."

My eyes narrowed. "If this is your 'apology,' it's wholly inadequate."

"What do you want of me?"

"Nothing from the God of War. Why should I listen, when

you don't offer the same courtesy?" It was becoming harder to speak, like a vise was tightening around my chest. "You immortals lash out when you feel slighted or wronged, but what of the times you fail *us*?"

"I do listen; I'm trying. I don't want us to be at odds." He held my gaze. "Believe me when I say we want the same things—we just need to figure out how to get them, together."

I didn't reply, as we reached the dining hall, yet his words resonated. As I entered, the courtiers rose, intoning a greeting. Minister Dao was still holding a roasted quail leg but I ignored the disrespect; there was no need to reveal how little regard he had for me. As Chengyin came forward to greet me, his eyes darted to the God of War, widening in shock.

Chengyin recovered swiftly, clasping his hands and bowing. "We are honored by your presence, Great Immortal. If we'd known in advance, we would have prepared a banquet to welcome you."

He smoothly offered the courtesies that I should have. I kept a meaningless smile on my face to appease those staring at us—even as the thought of holding a banquet to celebrate this wretched immortal choked me like a bone stuck in my throat.

Several tables were arranged around mine on the dais, all of which were occupied. The nearest available one was halfway down the hall, which suited me well. I gestured toward it as I took my seat. "Why don't you sit there, Lord Zhangwei? An attendant will bring you the finest—"

He stalked toward me before I'd finished, his teeth clenched as he said, "Your Ladyship is most kind. However, as I came to see you, I will sit by your side."

"There is no space," I told him flatly. "Perhaps another time."

The God of War turned to the man on the other side of me—Minister Guo—who shot to his feet at once. Muttering an unintelligible apology, he scrambled away as though I had the plague.

His dining partner, Minister Xiao, also rose and left—followed by a swift vacating of the other occupants on the dais. Soon, only Chengyin remained, his expression decidedly pained.

Lord Zhangwei's lips slanted into a mirthless smile as he took Minister Guo's seat. "Your court is most hospitable. There is ample space now."

"You have a wonderful way with people," Chengyin remarked in a strained voice. "If only I possessed that skill."

"The ability to terrify with a single look?" I replied. "You'd need to have done a lot of terrible things to earn a reputation like that."

Chengyin grinned. "Imagine how useful it would be for us at court."

"Us?" Lord Zhangwei repeated in a deceptively light tone.

An idea sparked. One that might offer a veil of protection from further entanglements with the immortal—and as importantly, from my own wavering heart. I cleared my throat, casting a meaningful look at Chengyin. He frowned but nodded, offering his support though he didn't know what it entailed. A decision he might soon regret.

"Chengyin is my betrothed." I spoke swiftly, not giving myself time to doubt, dropping my voice so no one else could hear. Chengyin went pale but inclined his head shakily, in acceptance of my claim.

"I ask for your discretion, Lord Zhangwei," I added. "This news has not been shared yet with the rest of the court—a secret. However, our engagement was planned long ago; Chengyin and I have been close since we were children."

Lord Zhangwei's gaze slid to Chengyin, then back to me. "Is this true? You are engaged?"

I braced at his tone, both silken and deadly. "Maybe it's different in the realm above, but it is a mortal custom to congratulate a betrothed couple."

"Except you have *not* been behaving like someone who is betrothed," he lashed out.

His anger fed my own. "How dare you imply that I've done anything inappropriate? What about *your* behavior? I owe you nothing; you have no claim over me, and I couldn't care less what you do."

A deathly silence fell over us. "Congratulations," the God of War said at last, his eyes ablaze. He leaned forward then, to whisper into my ear, "But I don't give up that easily."

I stared ahead like I hadn't heard him—even as something kindled inside me, something I swiftly smothered.

Chengyin spoke, filling in the silence. "We accept your good wishes," he said weakly, gesturing for an attendant to pour more wine. I was tempted to ask for a cup, though I tended to abstain from it. In my position, the barest slip of control could have dire consequences.

I'd hoped the immortal would leave after my announcement, but he remained beside me as an attendant hurriedly cleared his table, another bringing fresh food and wine. He lifted the wine cup to his lips and tossed down its contents—then once again, after the attendant refilled it.

Chengyin tugged my sleeve. "Why did you tell the God of War we're betrothed?" he whispered urgently. "Why does he look like he wants to throttle me?"

I shrugged. "Killing runs in his blood."

"That's not funny." Chengyin scowled. "You're going to have to find yourself another fiancé. Or rather, another victim."

"Don't you dare." I smiled widely for Lord Zhangwei's benefit. "I won't let him hurt you."

"I'm not sure you can stop him." Chengyin sighed as he began filling my plate with food: thin slices of beef, tender pea shoots, noodles garnished with shrimp. "Since we're doing this, let's make it look good."

"Thank you," I said gratefully.

"Our esteemed God of War looked ready to flay someone from the moment you both arrived. What did you do to provoke him?" Chengyin asked.

"Maybe he provoked me?" I retorted.

"Your temper is undoubtedly shorter than usual."

I let out a drawn breath. "Chengyin, are you on his side or mine?"

"A hard question. Both of you possess the power of removing my head from my neck. I like it where it is."

"Your Ladyship," Lord Zhangwei drawled from beside me, the wine cup in his hands. "Perhaps we should begin our negotiations?"

I glanced at the court. Even though it was just the three of us on the dais, all eyes were upon us. "Later. In my chamber," I said unthinkingly.

"Is that an invitation?" His smile was knife-sharp. "I wouldn't want to trespass."

"To talk, nothing more." I enunciated each word.

"A pity," he murmured, his gaze pinning mine.

Against my will, a memory surfaced . . . of when he'd placed the comb in my hair, his fingers gliding down the curve of my neck, his breath against my ear. My throat went dry. "Why do you keep playing this game? You know none of it was real," I said in a low voice.

"What if it was?"

We stared at each other in silence. Was this another trick? Chengyin cleared his throat then, a fortunate distraction. "What brings you to our realm, Honored Immortal?"

"A delicate negotiation. If I can come to terms with the Lady of Tianxia," he replied.

Chengyin nodded sagely. "I defer to Her Ladyship in these matters."

"A most accommodating consort." Lord Zhangwei's tone reminded me of silk yanked taut.

"Yes, he is. Unlike others I can think of." I searched the hall, seeking a way to loosen the coiled tension, to divert the guests who were staring at us. "Do we have any entertainment planned for tonight?" I asked aloud.

A musician came forward, a slender woman in a peach robe. Her instrument was shaped like an elongated pear, lacquered in black. As she took the seat in the middle of the hall, her hands plucked the strings of her lute with the skill of a true master.

The God of War's attention shifted to the musician, and I hated how acutely aware I was of it. A vigilant attendant was refilling his cup that he'd emptied with startling speed. My chest tightened. Was he attracted to the lute player? He was not the only one; the crowd watched her with reverence. Moreover, as an accomplished musician, it was natural to admire the talent in another.

"Would you like an introduction? Perhaps you might join her in a duet?" On the surface, I sounded like a solicitous host, yet it was plunging the knife in deeper.

"I can introduce myself." He rose and walked over to the musician, indifferent to the attention he was stirring.

The musician started at the sight of him, her fingers halting mid song. But then she rose and greeted him with a graceful bow. He spoke to her in hushed tones, gesturing for an attendant to bring another chair and instrument. As he arranged the qin across his lap, the musician stared at him, her turn to be transfixed. The melody they played rippled forth in seamless unison, a joyous one. They played exquisitely, his hard features a foil to her delicate loveliness.

As though enchanted, the guests smiled as they stared at the pair. I fought to remain indifferent. Once I had let the beauty of his music cloud my mind, imagining there were other layers to the God of War. A costly mistake. Let him be attracted to another; it was better this way.

Yet how it rankled, how it gnawed at me. At the end of the song, the guests rose, clapping in earnest. Lord Zhangwei invited the musician to sit beside him at his table—it was his right as a guest, though how it stung. I buried the sensation, smiling until my jaw ached, wishing I were anywhere but here.

20

After the last course was served, Chengyin and I left the hall, walking in silence to my courtyard.

The moment the door closed behind us, he turned to me. "Cancel our 'betrothal.'"

"Why?"

He shuddered. "Didn't you see the way the God of War glared at me throughout our meal? Nothing is worth the end he's planning for me for having a claim on you—even an imaginary one."

"Don't be a coward." His insinuation rankled. Even now, the immortal might be leading the musician to his room. The thought seared like a hot coal in the pit of my stomach.

"Oh, but I *am* a coward." Chengyin grinned. "Very much so, and I'm proud of it. It's kept me in good health all these years."

I looked at him, *really* looked at him, for the first time in a long while: taking in his large brown eyes, wide mouth, high forehead, the mark on his temple. He was no longer the scrawny boy I'd squabbled and brawled with. For those closest to us, we no longer saw them clearly, relying instead on familiarity to fill the gaps. Chengyin was handsome, though I didn't desire him—nor did he want me that way. But he was my best friend, someone I trusted, someone I could be myself with. I had no illusions of love. The one I married would be wedding the throne, and the most I could hope for was an ally who had no desire to supplant me . . . and that children would follow to secure the line of succession. Could I ask for more in a life partner?

So much more. My traitorous mind conjured unwanted flashes of memories: the frantic beat of my heart, the ache of desire, the heat pulsing through my blood that I fought to smother. Dangerous for anyone—more so with a kingdom at stake. I needed someone who would support my reign, not destroy everything I'd fought for.

"Would you marry me? For real?" I asked Chengyin, ignoring the way my chest constricted.

His burst of laughter died when he looked at me. He reached out and took my hand, his gaze thoughtful. Maybe he sensed my hurt and was being kind, even as he shook his head. "I'm not the one for you, as you're not for me. I want more, Liyen. I want love."

Relief swelled at his rejection. I'd asked as the Lady of Tianxia, not for myself. "You don't love me?" I asked lightly.

"Not that way," he replied. "I love my friend. You are my family, but I don't love you as a husband should."

I didn't love him that way either. Yet my mind still argued that this was an ideal solution, ignoring the protest of my heart. "I would like to be married to my friend. Love can be . . . complicated." *Fickle. Vicious. Treacherous.*

"Then it's worth having because it means something, because it makes you feel."

"We like each other well enough." I was being selfish, convinced this was the answer. A quick resolution, a cowardly one. Once I was safely married, maybe the hollow in my chest would vanish, along with the fevered dreams of a false future.

"'Like' and 'love' are not the same, though the happiest unions often have both."

"I don't need love. It makes you weak. Stupid." I spoke more vehemently than intended.

"Yet there is much wonder in it, and strength—when you aren't just fighting for yourself but for another." He peered at my face. "What happened in the Immortal Realm? You aren't the same as when you left."

"I'd rather not talk about it."

"Who hurt you?" he asked penetratingly.

"It doesn't matter." I smiled, burying my feelings. "I never took you for a romantic."

"Maybe it just takes finding the right one."

I sighed. "How did you become so philosophical?"

"Wine." Chengyin grinned conspiratorially. "I've had many a deep and meaningful conversation with myself over a cup."

I laughed. Maybe it was better that he wouldn't marry me; I might have throttled him myself. "Have you found this person?" I asked. "I've seen you with Minister Xiao's son . . . but you've also been very attentive to his sister. Whom do you like?"

"Both?" He winked as I swatted him.

"Don't be greedy. You're stirring enough trouble in their family—" I stopped, imagining Minister Xiao's fury, my smile widening. "Chengyin, I give you my blessing to continue."

"I strive to obey, Your Ladyship." He bowed mockingly, but then his expression turned serious. "What about you? Was it the God of War? He wanted to draw my blood the moment he heard of our engagement."

"If anything, his pride was hurt," I scoffed.

He tipped his head back, a speculative glint in his eyes. "You're wrong. He wants you." He let the words sink in before adding with a laugh, "You'd think an immortal would have better sense."

Anger rushed through me. Chengyin had teased me countless times before, but this struck deep. My hand shot forward to push him, like we were children again, all decorum forgotten. He caught my arm, his reflexes ever quick. As I kicked at him, he struck my foot aside easily—but then the door to my room flew open and slammed against the wall.

The God of War stood in the doorway. Without a word he stalked toward Chengyin, pulled him away from me, and hurled him against the wall. Chengyin gasped, his face twisting as he slid down, rubbing the back of his head.

"Is this how you treat your betrothed?" Lord Zhangwei demanded.

"Leave him alone!" I cried, stepping between them.

"Leave me out of this," Chengyin groaned, so softly only I heard.

"I'm sorry," I whispered as I helped him up, then rounded on the immortal. "Apologize to Chengyin. Your blow could have killed him."

"If I wanted to kill him, he'd already be dead," he snarled.

"Ahh, there is no need for any demonstration." Chengyin had gone pale. "I have complete faith in your ability."

I jabbed Lord Zhangwei's chest. "How dare you attack an innocent?"

"He attacked *you*."

Chengyin released a long breath. "You're wrong. She attacked *me*."

"I did," I said at once. "While you hit him without reason."

"He struck you," the god said grimly.

"We were sparring."

His jaw tightened, but then he inclined his head to Chengyin. "I misunderstood—"

"An apology is not necessary," Chengyin said hastily, raising his hands. "I will settle for you not wanting to kill me.

Lord Zhangwei glanced at me. "I would like to speak with you—alone. As promised."

Chengyin cleared his throat. "I just remembered I must be elsewhere. Unless . . . you need me to stay?" The last was spoken in a pleading tone.

I hesitated, then shook my head. Chengyin left at once, closing the door after him. Being alone with the God of War made the room seem smaller, or maybe I was acutely aware of his presence—my senses alive, like awakening to the first day of spring. How I wished it were anyone but him who roused these feelings in me.

"Why are you here? You seemed engaged with your guest earlier."

"She was certainly more agreeable—"

"Go back to her then," I retorted.

"Agreeable, but not preferred." A thin smile played on his lips. "Much of my pleasure came from your evident discontent."

His unexpected admission loosened a knot inside me. "Stop playing these games. Why pretend that you care? I'm not so stupid to fall for the same trick twice."

"I'm done playing games." He moved toward me, slowly, like he was afraid I might bolt. He stood so close, the air between our bodies seemed to tighten. It was becoming harder to feign indifference, to keep myself in check.

"Stop fighting me; let us help each other. Right now, both of us have more to gain from working together," he said steadily.

"What do you mean?" I would make him spell out his intent; I would take nothing for granted with him.

"Only I can give you what you want, while only you can give me what I need." A pause, his eyes shifting toward my study. "I could take back my sword now—but I can't do that with the Divine Pearl Lotus."

I reined in the impulse to refuse, to deny anything he wanted—making myself acknowledge the sense in his words. Right now, he was the only one who could help Tianxia. This might work if I could shape the terms to bind him. Dare I trust him again? Was there even a choice?

I needed time to think. "You shouldn't be here, alone with me.

Others might talk."

"Your betrothed gave us permission." One of his hands folded into a fist. "I wonder why he feels comfortable in doing so."

"Because our relationship is built upon trust, not like—"

"Ours?" he asked.

"We don't have a relationship."

He didn't answer right away, his gaze sliding to my mouth. "I think of it, too. How you feel. How you would taste."

My lips parted involuntarily, a treacherous warmth flaring across my body. As he lowered his head to mine, I should have moved but didn't—trapped in the spell he was weaving with his voice, his words, his nearness. As his hand brushed my waist, the touch jolted me.

I wrenched away, shaking my head. "Don't do this."

"Why not? You want this, too." He spoke without triumph, just a gentle knowing that was infinitely worse.

"I may want candied hawthorns, but eating too many will make me sick." My breathing was uneven. "I *can't* let myself want you again."

Silence fell over us, the brittle kind. The light dulled in his eyes as he nodded, something about his expression tugging at me. I almost missed the heat of our anger, the sharpness of hate . . . they were easier to bear.

The air turned cool, wavering like it was caught crosswind. A tremor ran through his body, lines creasing his face before they were abruptly smoothed away.

"What's wrong? Are you in pain?" My voice hitched, though I tried to stem my concern. When he didn't reply, I added, "If you want us to work together, don't hide things from me."

He looked away like this was hard for him. "My cure is long delayed."

"What injuries are you suffering? Why do you need the lotus?" There were no visible wounds on him unless they lay beneath his clothes—nor had I seen any sign of weakness, beyond glimpses of fatigue after battle, the time he was resting in his courtyard.

Maybe not all wounds left scars that could be seen. Maybe I'd been wrong in thinking the God of War wore no mask for the others, and sometimes we all had to feign strength we didn't have.

"In the war, the Wuxin unleashed a forbidden magic, a powerful and insidious poison that damaged my lifeforce. Our healers could not cure me, they were only able to delay its advance—the song of phoenixes helped, too. Yet these could only slow the symptoms, they don't heal the root cause. The Divine Pearl Lotus is the only cure, and there is only one in the world."

If their lifeforce is extinguished, they die just as we do.

"Are you dying?" It felt almost absurd to ask this of him, one of the most powerful immortals in their realm.

"Yes," he replied unflinchingly, like it was a truth he faced every day.

And though I'd suspected it, his admission pierced me deeply. If I were stronger, I'd have been glad, seeking the opportunities in his vulnerability. But even now . . . I didn't want him to die.

"If we are in this together," I said slowly, "no more lies or secrets."

He held my gaze. "No more lies."

I glared at him, but I had secrets, too, that I didn't want to share. "No secrets that will threaten me or my people," I stipulated. "If I learn that you've deceived me again, I'd rather destroy the lotus than give it to you."

He nodded gravely, "I swear, you will not have cause."

"Let's lay out the terms. In return for your sword and the lotus—you will secure Tianxia's freedom, return the Shield of Rivers and Mountains, and bring down the walls."

"Tianxia will still guard Kunlun," he stated. "This will be important to Her Majesty."

"A separate alliance can be negotiated. Those who guard Kunlun must be appropriately armed to face any threats." I steeled myself to add, "I will only give you the lotus if it doesn't endanger me; I will not trade my life for yours."

"I would never want that." He stretched out his hand, his palm turned up. "Are we in agreement?"

I hesitated, then laid my hand over his, letting his fingers close around mine. As my gaze met his, a luminous warmth kindled despite the chill of his skin. It was not magic . . . yet something close.

I pulled away, cautious now, unwilling to yield anything that hadn't been agreed. "How do I give you the lotus?" I asked uncertainly. "I can't govern my heart."

"All I ask is that you try." He spoke almost gently. "It must be given without thought of gain. You must *want* to heal me."

"But I'm doing this because of what you're offering," I said, unwilling to mislead him. "I can't promise more."

"I don't expect more," he assured me. "Just a chance."

Was he hoping for my gratitude? To find another way into my heart after his last attempt had failed? Whether it worked or not, my conscience was clear.

"Where is the Shield of Rivers and Mountains?" I asked.

"In the palace treasury. During the attack, all precious artifacts were sealed there as a precaution, until the Winged Devils were captured. We didn't know what they sought. Their attack was well planned, except they lacked the forces to secure victory—like they were a diversion. While they are generally close-mouthed, some were angry enough to confess they were waiting for reinforcements that never came, though they wouldn't disclose who. We are hopeful that a peaceful solution may eventually be sought, though it will take time."

"Reinforcements? From the Wuxin?" I made myself ask.

"They were allied once. We thought it had ended after the Wuxin were sealed in the Netherworld." He sounded like he no longer wholly believed these claims.

"No walls last forever," I told him.

Silence fell over us. "I will retrieve the shield for you; your people will be free." He spoke intently. "But this must wait until I can speak with Her Majesty. She was injured in the attack and is in seclusion to recuperate. It could be a week or more until she emerges."

I abruptly doused a flicker of concern—not for her, but how this would affect my kingdom. I never thought the immortal queen could be hurt, but then again, I'd not imagined the God of War could be either. Maybe deep down, we were not so different after all . . . just bound by different rules.

"What if Her Majesty refuses? We're both offering things we don't know if we can deliver," I said in a low voice.

"Nothing is assured in life. Sometimes we need to just believe—whether in destiny, or each other."

My mouth curled. I didn't believe in destiny—that my parents were fated to die young, that Grandfather's heart would give out the way it had. But I would believe in what I knew: that the immortal needed me to live, and the Queen of the Golden Desert needed her God of War.

"Will you give me the lotus first?" he asked.

I shook my head. "Not until you give me what was promised."

It wasn't easy to refuse, but I wouldn't relinquish my greatest advantage. I'd rather be mercenary than a fool. Without trust, promises were just words strung together—easily broken.

"Don't you believe me?" he wanted to know.

"I believe you, but I don't *trust* you," I said bluntly. "Trust goes deeper, aligned to one's character rather than the stakes. We need each other now, but after that—I can't trust what you'll do." I raised my chin. "I've learned that gods can lie as easily as mortals."

"Then I will wait."

His unflinching response took me by surprise. "Will you return home?" I asked.

"No." His gaze dropped to my wrist, now bare, after the red thread had fallen off. "You can't enter my realm anymore, so I will stay here with you. While you have the lotus, you are in danger. These attacks can't be mere coincidences. They were looking for you; they must know what you bear. Magic calls to its own—and here, where your realm is barren of it, its scent rises like smoke. You don't know what other predators you'll attract, what they'll do to take the power inside you."

"But they can't take it," I said. "You tried and failed."

"I'm not arrogant enough to believe I know everything about magic. There are forbidden arts that I'm ignorant of, those that might succeed in ripping the lotus from you, willing or not—if they don't care whether you live or die. That's another difference between them and me. I'd rather you remain alive."

"Why?" I'd wondered before why he'd not chosen violence.

"Dawn would be dark without you." He smiled. "You make life more interesting."

I shouldn't care, yet what were these feelings that wrapped around me, just when I thought I'd broken free? But I wouldn't reveal my weakness; I'd keep it folded tight. "If these creatures can trace magic, will they sense your presence?" I asked instead.

"I've shielded myself." He unslung the sword from his back, the one sheathed in a black jade scabbard that he'd given me before. "This is yours. Will you return mine?"

It was a fair demand, especially if he was keeping me safe. Moreover, the most vital thing he needed was still in my keeping. After I retrieved the god's sword from my study, I handed it back to him.

"How could I take your sword?" I asked curiously. "It was said no one could wield it but you."

"When we were connected by the enchantment, I channeled my magic into you. A trace must have remained, why my sword recognized you."

A shudder rippled through me as I recalled his dagger in my chest, my hand rubbing the scar. "How could it remain if I don't have a lifeforce? Is this because of the lotus?"

"Maybe," he said carefully. "But you can't channel it without a lifeforce; it's too dangerous for a mortal."

"Why?"

"Because you can't control it. If it surges unexpectedly, it could alert our enemies to where you are—it could drain your strength." His gaze flicked to mine. "You will die then, just as us, should our magic be exhausted."

Our enemies. How strange to imagine that the God of War was now my protector. Though it made me feel safer, his presence bore a different kind of danger. It was also sobering to realize that once I relinquished the lotus, I'd lose this sliver of magic, too. But if the God of War fulfilled his promises, if he kept me safe—it was a small price to pay.

"Why do the Winged Devils want me?" A frightening thought, that I might be their prey.

His lips pressed thin like he was deep in thought. "It could be their own scheme to gain power. Or they could be working with another—the Wuxin, possibly, as you mentioned."

My insides churned. Even though they were sealed away, their threat always hovered at the edge of my mind. "Are the Wuxin worse than the Winged Devils?"

"The Winged Devils' ambitions are smaller—they serve rather than seeking to rule, choosing masters who possess a similar appetite for chaos and destruction. There is still much unknown about the Wuxin, except they feed on suffering. Some can see into your darkest secrets, turning them into weapons against you," he said grimly. "The most powerful Wuxin can even steal another's form."

I shrank back, my eyes going wide. "Then how do we know

who is real?"

"We are more than our appearance. If you know someone, you can easily discern the true from false—as long as you're looking," he said.

"How can I guard myself?"

"Mortals are the most vulnerable. You have no magic to protect yourself, only your strength of will. But even then, it's not easy for a Wuxin to possess your body—you must first surrender, allowing them to. They will offer false promises or threats, anything to secure their way. Many are skilled in divining the secrets of the heart, plucking out the root of desire and of fear, even those we are ignorant of."

My fingers curled, unknown terrors crowding my mind. "I don't ever want to meet one."

"It may not be them," he reminded me. "We don't know yet who is behind this, who our enemies are. It's why I came as soon as I could; we can't take any chances."

My gaze flicked up to his. "Then train me. Teach me to keep myself safe."

Light flared in his eyes. "I can't train you in magic. If you die, I die, too."

"I hate feeling helpless." A moment of vulnerability to share something real. Death was not something I took lightly, especially after escaping its merciless clutches. I wanted to fight for my own life rather leaving it in another's hands.

"There are other things that I could teach you." He touched the hilt of my sword. "There is strength in this, too."

"Then teach me," I told him. "I want to learn."

He slanted his head back, studying me. "I can't instruct you if you question everything I say. Will you listen to me?"

"Yes, but only as far as the lesson," I agreed.

"Will your betrothed object?" he asked, a taut smile on his face.

"He lets me decide for myself. He doesn't dictate what I should do. He respects my wishes."

"He sounds as docile as the silk rug beneath your feet." Zhangwei spoke with equal parts venom and anger as he headed to the door. "We begin tomorrow."

21

Someone was knocking on my door. Was it Yifei? It was still dark, too early to rise. My mind was fogged with sleep, drifting off once more—but then the doors were pulled apart, someone entering my room. My eyes flew open, staring into Zhangwei's, as black as midnight.

"Why are you here?" I scrambled up, glaring at him.

"You asked me to train you." He pulled a robe from my wardrobe, tossing it onto my bed. "Get dressed."

My fingers crumpled the silk, resisting the childish urge to fling it back at him. "Don't tell me what to do."

"Today, all day, I will be telling you *exactly* what to do." He leaned against the wooden bedframe, a slow smile spreading across his face. "If you prefer not to get dressed, I have no objection, though you might scandalize your court."

As his eyes flicked toward me, then traveled down my robe—I grabbed the covers, yanking them to my neck. All I had on was a thin garment, as I'd slept with the windows closed.

"Vile wretch," I swore.

He cocked his head, adjusting the sleeve of his robe. "Is this how you greet your teacher? Shouldn't you call me Master?"

"Never," I flung back. "Now, get out so I can dress."

He stalked to the end of the room, turning his back as he looked out the window. Quickly, I thrust my arms through the dark-blue robe, knotting a sash around my waist. I cleaned my face and teeth, then combed my hair and tied it back with a ribbon.

"Is there a place we can train around here?" he asked. "Somewhere secluded?"

I bent to slip on my shoes. "One of the old practice grounds for the guards. It's not been well tended; we'll have to make do with the weeds. But it's outside the palace, so we won't be disturbed—yet close enough, so we'll be safe. Some of the guards will follow us, too." An almost foolish consideration when I was with him.

He shook his head. "Leave your guards here. This will be pointless if you keep crying out for help."

I picked up my sword from the table, the black jade scabbard cool to the touch. It felt right in my hand somehow, like it fit. "I will *not* cry," I told him.

"Then you're not trying hard enough."

YELLOWING BAMBOO TREES RINGED THE ABANDONED grounds, their stalks sloping at the top. A wide river ran along the edge, the rush of water a soothing murmur. I'd heard the soldiers used to swim there after a grueling day, the waters deep enough. A red-roofed pavilion had been built in the middle of the field, where the instructors would stand to observe those training. After years of neglect, the wood had weathered, paint peeling from the columns.

Zhangwei examined the place, hands clasped behind his back. Raising his arm, sparks scattered from his fingertips like a drizzle of rain—a whisper of magic compared to the surge I'd sensed from him before. As the lights faded, so did all sound beyond: the rustle of leaves, the thrum of the river.

"This way no one will hear us," he explained.

"Can such magic be sensed?" I didn't want to draw any monsters to my home.

"If enemies are close enough to detect this, then it's already too late."

Fear pooled in my gut. My gaze shifted to the sword he carried, the one I'd returned to him. "Shall we begin?"

He gestured to me. "Show me how you hold a sword."

I unsheathed mine, holding it as firmly as I could, its tip pointed at him.

"Now, attack me."

I thrust the sword toward him, the point quivering as it halted just before his chest. Zhangwei didn't bother to flinch or evade. Next time, I just might run him through—not all the way, but a little.

He grinned. "That's a fine move if your enemy was a tree, considerate enough to stand still while you attacked."

"Then teach me how to do it better," I snapped, lowering my hand. "Why do you think I asked you to?"

He frowned. "Weren't you trained in combat, like most of your people?"

"I didn't learn as quickly as the others," I replied stiffly. "I wasn't born strong like you; I can't run as fast, nor could I hold a sword for hours on end."

"I didn't know." A brief pause before he asked, "Was your life here hard?"

"No," I said at once. "I don't need your pity or anyone else's. I was *lucky*. I was not as strong as the others but had family who loved me, a secure place in the world. Since I was young, I've had a dream, something to live for. Some people go their whole lives looking for these things, never finding them. Nobody's life is perfect, it's just what we choose to see when we look at ours."

"You are wise," he said in a quiet tone.

"I've been called many things before, but never wise." I smiled, repeating what he'd said to me once when I'd called him a beast.

"Then you're surrounded by fools."

His stare unnerved me; I looked down at my feet. Careless, to lapse back into speaking to him in this familiar way. It was easier when we were fighting . . . because then, I wasn't fighting with myself.

"Did taking the Divine Pearl Lotus strengthen you?" he asked.

"Yes." I turned back to him. "I'm also aware that may change once I give it to you, but I've accepted the price."

"What's cured will not be undone," he assured me. "But any other advantages the lotus yielded will disperse. If you change your mind—"

"I won't."

He straightened, moving toward me. "Then let's continue. If you could hurt a Winged Devil with a dagger, you have some skill—but while such a weapon might work for the element of surprise, you'll lose against the reach of a sword." He tapped the hilt of my blade. "Show me your stance again."

As I held the sword, he stood behind me, leaning over to adjust my grip. He seemed unaffected by our closeness like he'd slipped effortlessly into his role of the queen's general, training me as one of the troops. Except I was struggling to set him from my mind, to ignore the brush of his chest against my shoulders, his hand clasped over mine.

"Don't grip the sword with all your fingers like you're clutching a stick," he told me. "Wrap your thumb over the middle two— your remaining fingers should be used to support and guide, but not to grasp."

The sword slid from my hand to the ground, narrowly missing slicing my toe. "Isn't it less secure this way?" I asked, picking it up again.

"You need to be able to *use your sword* against an opponent. By clutching it so tightly, you can't wield it as well—and when you lack flexibility, it becomes easier for an enemy to disarm you. To block or strike, you have to react quickly," he explained patiently. "Holding it this way, the hilt glides in the hollow of your palm while still in a steady grip. Practice this until it comes naturally to you, until the weapon becomes an extension of your arm. Don't worry about using it to attack just yet—that will come."

I did as he instructed, repeating the moves. It was easier to listen when he spoke in this manner, his measured tone that of a teacher.

Once he was satisfied, Zhangwei stepped back, spreading his arms. "Attack me."

I lunged at him at once, not wasting a moment. My sole advantage lay in surprise, though I doubted my blow would land—already flinching as the sword hurtled toward him. Zhangwei held his ground till the last moment, spinning aside—until somehow, he was behind me. His scent suffused my senses, his robe brushing mine. A moment's distraction was all it took as he caught my wrist and flipped it up, my sword falling to the ground. I snatched my hand back, glaring at him.

"Don't be upset, whether with me or yourself," he said. "When I trained, I was knocked to the ground countless times."

Satisfaction coursed through me at the thought. "Who knocked you down?"

"My teachers. Other students." A smile lit his face, one that irked me for some reason. He continued, "Failing is an essential part of learning. Each time you're beaten or outmaneuvered, study why, learn the signs—you won't be as easily defeated next time."

Zhangwei picked up my sword and handed it back to me. "You can wield a weapon well enough, but you're still treating it as a tool. When you hold your blade, it should be a part of you, each movement connected to your body. Don't doubt yourself. If you believe you'll lose, your arm will falter. Don't depend on luck, a fickle ally. All you can trust is your hand, your strength of mind, your own resolve."

I nodded, trying to remember all he'd said.

"Most of a fight is in here." He tapped his head, then his heart. "Be ready for the unexpected. You imagined that I would evade; you didn't think I would counterattack without a weapon. Yet in a real battle, a moment's carelessness can be fatal, and second chances are rare. A strong opponent is never a predictable one."

He moved behind me again and caught my wrist. His fingers closed around mine, guiding it to swing the sword in a series of strikes—his other hand splayed against my ribs, moving my body to the pace of his footwork. His rhythm became mine, both of us locked in synchrony like a dance, but far more intimate.

Zhangwei seemed aggravatingly unaffected, even as this strained my concentration to the brink. My body was afire, his touch searing through my robe, my heart racing. If he'd released me, I might have fallen. If an enemy affected me so, I would be dead.

Again and again I repeated each move, mimicking his stances—swinging the sword until my arms were throbbing, every bit of me aching.

Finally, Zhangwei nodded in approval. "Are you ready for the next lesson?"

I was not, unused to such exertion. "You've ordered me around a lot but have yet to show me what you can do." I spoke this as a challenge, while seeking an opportunity to rest. Part of me also hoped he wouldn't be *that* good. Reputations were hard to live up to, particularly the God of War's.

He lifted his sword over his head, the blade aligned with his other arm, held straight. The pose was graceful like a dancer's, if not for the deadly calm in his gaze. His eyes narrowed as he spun, his sword sweeping through the air, darting as quickly as a fish in water. Sunlight glinted over his blade as he sprang up, diving with his arm outstretched—flying forward as he drove his blade into an old archery board. The thick wood cracked, then splintered apart loudly. It was fortunate we were shielded, else my guards would have rushed over at once.

He continued, his sword spinning and weaving like a living creature, his breathing calm like this was no exertion. "When you attack, focus your strength, keep your weapon aimed at your enemy—but always out of their range," he said. "Move with purpose, deal each blow with an aim. It's a delicate balance to always know exactly what you're doing, yet to never lose awareness of your enemy."

I was hanging on his every word, unable to take my eyes from him, attuned to the sound of his blade slicing the air, the forceful grace of his every move. Something shifted in my chest like a piece dislodged, then forgotten abruptly, as he swung his sword back again, the flat of the blade now aligned to his face. His body dipped back without warning, the weapon falling seamlessly into rhythm as he plunged through the air, the length of the sword across from him like part of his arm.

"A sword isn't just for attacking but is vital as a shield," he told me. "To defend yourself, wield your weapon with intent to deflect each blow, and guard yourself at every moment. Your body must flow like water, no matter what lies beneath the current. Master this skill, and not even the rain can touch you."

As he lowered his sword, turning to me, only then did I realize I had been holding my breath. I buried my admiration, feigning indifference. "A fine display. However, the wooden board was hardly an inspiring opponent, just as much as a 'tree' would be."

His eyebrows lowered ominously. "Set your challenge."

I strode to the riverbank and gathered a handful of gleaming stones, each roughly the size of my thumbnail. "Are you ready?"

As he nodded, I drew my arm back and smiled. "You spoke of rain . . . then let it hail."

I threw the stones at him, all at once. As they flew toward him, he didn't flinch. I found myself bracing, not wanting him to be struck—almost as much as I wanted him to be humbled. Zhangwei's sword spun so quickly, it was a blur as it struck the stones down with dazzling speed. They fell to the ground, each marked with the force of his blade, some cleaved apart, until the earth beneath him shimmered darkly.

It was over in barely the amount of time it took to draw a breath. Such speed, such precision, to not miss a single one—even among the gods, there could be no one his equal.

Slowly, I brought my hands together and clapped. He'd earned this respect, the sheer mastery of his swordplay shining through, unmarred by threat or danger.

He strode toward me, his eyes bright. "I like the way you're looking at me."

I shook myself from the stupor, folding my arms across my chest. "You were showing off."

"You are hard to impress." He grinned, not denying it. "Now, show me what you've learned."

"I could never do what you did." After his demonstration, it felt impossible. And I was already tired, aching all over, my spirits low.

"Try what you can; not everything at once. Break a problem into smaller pieces and it won't intimidate you anymore."

"How can I do this—whether here, or in a real fight?" I looked down at my sword, hating this doubt. "I'm not a warrior like you, staring danger in the face. I just want to run from it."

"Yet you don't," Zhangwei said gravely. "You asked me to train you. You chose to defy tradition, challenging our queen for a better future for your people. You are stronger than you think." He lifted a hand to my face, and this time I didn't draw away.

"Heroes are not born but made through their choices. One could be given the greatest gifts in the world and choose to do nothing with them. Or someone with nothing could forge their way to the pinnacle of power. Whether mortal or immortal, our destiny is in our hands."

His words struck a chord that reverberated inside me. "I don't believe in destiny either—that it's been set or determined from our birth. I don't believe it is written in the stars."

His gaze was that of an endless night. "Then write your own."

22

week passed, each day like the one before. I rose early,
spending my mornings at court hearing from the ministers, going through the petitions, mediating the disputes
that cropped up. In the afternoons, Chengyin would take over as
the First Advisor, leaving me free to train with the God of War.
When I returned late at night, I would pore over the scrolls and
notes that Chengyin had left in my study, for those matters that still
needed my attention.

The hours flew by until I barely knew when the sun rose and
set. My eyes closed the moment my head dropped on the pillow,
and I woke each morning feeling like I hadn't done enough the day
before. I was beginning to regret my decision to train with the God
of War at his unrelenting pace. Maybe it was enough if I left my
protection to him, to my soldiers—but a voice whispered: *What if
they're not there? What if you're alone?*

It wasn't just my body that was tired, but I was emotion-
ally drained. Each day as we trained, spending hours with each
other—an intimacy was forming, even as I tried to fight it. To learn,
I had to listen to him without suspicion, and there was much to admire in his lessons. When he touched me to adjust my posture—his
hands on my arms, shoulders, and neck—it was like he was setting
my body alight. It frightened me, yet I was beginning to want this;

I'd never felt so alive.

There was so much I was learning about fighting, about magic, too. Though it was of little use to me, Zhangwei indulged my curiosity, teaching me about the different elements of magic: Air, Water, Fire, Earth.

"Some immortals possess more than one Talent," he'd said. "Some are also skilled in Life and Mind, specializing in healing injuries or even influencing thoughts. Often, the magic we are most proficient in stems from what is inherent in our surroundings."

I recalled what I'd heard of his realm, all I'd read. "Are those from the Sea Kingdoms more skilled in Water enchantments? And do those from the Phoenix Kingdom possess the most powerful Fire magic?"

"In a way, but neither is it so simple. While magic has its rules, what can or cannot be done may simply be undiscovered. Those from the Golden Desert are strong in the elements of Fire and Earth. Yet immortals of the Celestial Kingdom do not follow a set pattern, drawing magic from across the elements."

"How are some immortals more powerful than others?" I wondered.

"Why are you the Lady of Tianxia, and why do the people obey you?" he'd countered.

"Because of my family name, my birthright."

He nodded. "Just as some are born with more power than others, whether by heritage or by chance."

"I didn't earn the throne, but I want to be worthy of it." It was a fear of mine that I didn't deserve this honor, that I would fail those who depended on me. And I didn't know why I was sharing this with him.

He regarded me intently. "Then you already are."

Silence fell between us then, something fluttering in my chest. Why did his praise affect me so? I made myself pull away, though I'd regretted it. This wouldn't last. Once our pact was over, once the God of War had gotten what he wanted from me, he would return to the skies and I'd never see him again. The more I guarded myself now, the less I'd hurt later.

It was a rare chance though, to learn from the God of War. Under Zhangwei's tutelage, my skills vastly improved. While I would never be a celebrated warrior, I could hold my own in a fight. And at night, when it was quiet and calm—I began to wonder, was he helping himself, too? He wanted the Divine Pearl Lotus, but my heart had been closed to him. Yet now, after spending time together, things were shifting once more. I found myself thinking of him more than I should, anticipating our sessions, even craving his touch. We had grown closer . . . and this time, it felt different, more real—and because of that, far more dangerous.

———————— ❈ ————————

THE MORNING DAWNED CLEAR AND BRIGHT. AS there was no court in session, I could spend the whole day training with Zhangwei. Yifei brought a tray of food to my room: a bowl of noodles steeped in chicken broth, a side dish of eggs and one of beansprouts, along with sliced watermelon. I ate alone, resisting the urge to invite Zhangwei. It was wiser to keep a little distance between us, though my restraint was rapidly crumbling.

From outside, footsteps drew closer; Zhangwei's decisive yet quick tread. He was earlier than anticipated—and it struck me, was this our last day? Once Queen Caihong emerged from seclusion, the God of War would return to the skies to confer with her. Our time together was ending.

My heart sank as I picked up my sword and left the room. An urgency filled me to not waste a single moment. Outside, Zhangwei was leaning against the wall, his black hair held up by a jade ring, silver mountains embroidered on his charcoal gray robe. His dark eyes went to my face, then moved down my dress. It was a soft lilac, a color I rarely wore. My hair was pulled high, a flower-shaped pin tucked into one side, a mother-of-pearl comb tucked in the other. As his gaze shifted to it, his mouth tightened. Was he thinking of the one he'd given me? The one I'd discarded?

The skies were still cast in rose and gold, the last breath of dawn lingering. We walked in silence to the training field, except this time, Zhangwei led me down to the river that bordered the grounds. It was wide and deep, flowing into the vast lake at the heart of Tianxia. This was a rich source of food for us, and pleasure, too—where I'd first learned to swim, one of the few activities that hadn't tired me too much before, that I could enjoy at my own pace.

Zhangwei pointed to a flat rock in the middle of the river. "That is your training ground today. Practice your stances on the rock."

I stared at him blankly. "Why?"

"You've made good progress learning the different positions. However, fighting a real opponent—one who wants to hurt you—is much harder. It's crucial to keep steady under strain, to avoid mistakes. Precision and balance are vital." He grinned as he dipped a hand into the river. "Nothing makes you more aware of it than the prospect of falling into cold water."

While I could swim, it was a cool day, one of the last few of spring. I scowled, wanting to refuse. But I'd asked him to teach me, and this was the price of his aid. I stepped gingerly upon the stones, making my way to the one he'd pointed out. My robe fluttered as shards of sunlight glinted over the water.

"First stance. Point your sword out and lean forward," he called out.

I did as he instructed. He was right that out here in the open, with the water rushing all around, I felt more vulnerable, uncertain. My senses were alert, the stakes higher. How would it be when survival was on the line?

Zhangwei leaned against a tree, his eyes fixed on me. "Now, stand on one leg and thrust your sword forward."

I swallowed, struggling to keep my balance as I lifted one leg up and pushed my sword out. I'd done this pose countless times over the past week, though not like this, balancing on an uneven rock.

"Good," he said. "Now, sweep your sword to the right."

I cursed him under my breath, not daring to look at him this time, all my attention on holding my balance. As he called out another command, I shifted again—then once more.

The sun beat down on me. I'd lost track of the number of stances Zhangwei had made me do. Sweat poured down my face, my robe sticking to my body. But I hadn't fallen once, triumph surging. If he'd intended to make a fool of me, he would fail. Yet my limbs were aching, my head beginning to spin. I'd been holding one position for a while: my sword arm thrust straight, my left leg lifted high off the ground. Something buzzed around me—a fly, landing on my nose. It tickled, snapping my focus. I blew at it, the fly flitting away only to return. Annoyed now, I shook my head to dislodge it. Zhangwei shouted a sharp reprimand as one of my legs wobbled, my body weaving to try to regain balance—but then I tumbled headlong into the river.

The water was ice-cold and stinging, almost welcome after the heat of training under the sun. It rushed up my nose, searing my throat before I remembered how to breathe, kicking wildly to stay afloat. Just as I was about to resurface, I swam away, burning with humiliation at my fall. Would Zhangwei laugh at me? A rash impulse stirred to drag him into the water, to get him as thoroughly soaked as I was—it would serve him right for his smug commands.

"Liyen!" He called my name, then again, more frantically than before.

I ignored him, waiting for him to come closer, holding my

breath though it felt like my lungs were about to burst. A shadow fell over the river: Zhangwei's. But before I could pull him in, he dove into the waters—churning with his weight. He hadn't seen me yet, and I quickly broke to the surface for a gulp of air, then dove back down. I wanted to swim away; he would be furious once he realized my trick. But something wasn't right . . . his arms and legs flailing like he was struggling in the water, only to sink deeper.

He couldn't swim. Immortals wouldn't need to, when they could fly. As I recalled the chill of his skin, the poison in his body, a new terror clutched me. I swam toward him as fast as I could, my heart pounding. Zhangwei had gone limp, his eyes closed, his skin almost bluish through the haze of water. At once I swam to his back, sliding my arms under his shoulders, struggling to drag him up. He was heavier than I expected—but I pulled harder, refusing to let go. I kicked violently with him in my arms as I fought to reach the surface, the sunlight glimmering above almost tauntingly—

He spun around swiftly, breaking my hold as his arms slid around my waist, clasping me to him before I could dart away. His eyes met mine, flaring with intent, as he lowered his head—and kissed me. Fire shot through my veins, searing every part of me. I was shattering, coming apart, even as he held me together. One of my arms went around his neck and I was holding him, too—my caution, suspicion, and resentment melting away, leaving me lightless, adrift, untethered . . . but for the feel of his lips, the tangle of our breath.

Such madness, yet why did it feel so right?

He pulled me effortlessly through the water, his arms still wrapped around me. We stumbled to the bank, and then somehow I was lying beneath him on the grass. As the weight of his body sank over mine, an ache swelled within, a hunger that silenced the murmurs of my heart, casting the last of my restraint aside. His mouth pressed hungrily against mine, his hands cradling the curve of my face.

The chill of the air was a shock, sanity returning in a rush. I pushed him away, suddenly afraid. As I wrapped my arms around myself, the wet silk of my robe clung to me—yet he looked only at my face, his eyes black with desire . . . and something more, something I couldn't read.

"We can't do this." My words tumbled out. I was grasping for reason as he remained silent, just staring at me intently. "I'm betrothed."

"You don't love him," he said flatly.

The certainty in his tone angered me. "You know nothing about Chengyin and me. Our bond goes deeper than you will ever know."

"If you loved him, you wouldn't have kissed me back."

"I was caught off-guard," I said quickly, trying to deflect the undeniable truth. "I thought you were in danger. Were you pretending to drown?"

"As much as you were." He thrust a hand through his wet hair. "I don't want to talk about this; I'd rather talk about us."

"There is no 'us,'" I said harshly. "You are immortal, I am mortal. We have no future together."

"Don't you believe that our destiny is in our hands?" He held his out to me as his voice deepened. "Let's make ours together."

How he tempted me, but it was not enough—not for my kingdom, and not for me. Even if I could consider what he asked, I wanted to be more to him than a season in the span of his existence.

"No," I said adamantly, though it was hard to refuse.

"What are you afraid of?"

You. How you make me feel.

"What future would this be?" I asked him bluntly. "I would age while you remained the same, the years marking me as they left you unscathed. I want to be with someone as an equal—to be their life, their great love as they are mine. I don't want half a life with you, knowing you'll forget me—"

"I will *never* forget you." He spoke with such intensity it bordered on fury. "No one will ever replace you, whether you live for a hundred years more or ten."

"But that's the thing," I said slowly. "I don't have a hundred years, no matter what you or I do." A sadness filled me suddenly, my shoulders folding inward. "This ends here. We have a deal; we'll both get what we want, then we won't see each other again."

How bright his eyes, how his expression hurt me. Part of me wanted to take back my words, to let the moment carry us into the unknown, borne along the current of desire. But I couldn't be reckless; I wasn't just a girl in love with a boy. I was the Lady of Tianxia and he was the God of War. There was no happy ending in our story, and I wouldn't let my kingdom pay the price.

"As you wish." He dropped his hand, looking away. "I will return to speak to my queen. When I come back, we will fulfil our obligations to each other—repay our debts."

A sharp suspicion slid into my mind as I pulled my robe tighter. "Was this another scheme? Are you afraid I won't be able to give you the lotus, and you were trying to convince me? I already promised you I'd do what I can."

He moved toward me so swiftly, he caught me unaware. Though he didn't touch me, he was so close, his coolness radiated from him. "Did it feel like a trick? Did any part feel false?"

No.

"Pretend to yourself all you want," he said wrathfully. "But don't presume to read my mind, to make me a villain because it would be easier that way. I've given you my word: no more lies."

The air around us seemed to contract, not the way it felt when Zhangwei's magic flowed. In the distance, something gleamed, streaking across the skies like a fallen star. Zhangwei's shield around us vanished abruptly, the sounds from outside rushing though, the sudden cry of birds jolting me. A flock of them darted through the heavens—unfamiliar ones, their pale feathers glinting, their crests a fiery orange. I was shivering in my sodden clothes, only now aware of how cold I was, inside and out.

Zhangwei's face darkened as he gazed toward Kunlun, the silhouette of the mountain looming ahead.

"What's wrong?" I asked. "What do you sense?"

"This magic—I've never felt anything like it before," he said, looking up into the night. "Someone is coming . . . but I don't know who."

My throat went dry. "Do they know you're here?"

His face was grave. "If they do, then they know where you are, too."

23

We raced back to the palace, the wind strengthening, dust and leaves swirling in the air. A shadow fell over us as clouds descended from the skies, bearing four immortal soldiers clad in the gold armor of Queen Caihong's army. Relief filled me, yet I couldn't help recalling how I'd fled from them before. The soldiers leapt to the ground, bowing to Zhangwei. One of them turned to greet me with a warm smile—Lieutenant Yang—Zhangwei's friend, whom I'd met in the palace.

"Her Majesty has just come out of seclusion. She commands your immediate return, Lord Zhangwei. A great disturbance was sensed here, and your counsel is needed," the lieutenant said.

"We sensed it, too," he replied. "I will return as soon I've secured the Lady of Tianxia's safety. She can't come back with us."

Lieutenant Yang's gaze shifted to my wrist, the red thread bracelet gone. "A pity," he murmured. "Her Majesty would like to speak with you, too."

I suppressed a ripple of unease as I faced Zhangwei. "Even if I could leave, I wouldn't. What about my people's safety? Will you protect them, too?"

"We can't remain here," he said grimly. "The presence of other immortals will be sensed, if these enemies haven't detected me already. By staying, we'll draw them here, risking those you want to protect." He glanced at the birds circling the skies. "We can't let them find you. We must be cautious until we know who our enemies are, and what they are planning."

He was right; I couldn't risk my people. "Where should we go?"

"Kunlun Mountain. I know a place where you'll be safe, as long as we can reach it."

I nodded. "I must tell the others: Chengyin, Aunt Shou, the ministers."

His expression shuttered. "Of course, you must inform your betrothed."

His tone rankled. "He's also my First Advisor," I reminded him.

Lieutenant Yang cleared his throat, his eyes bright like he was enjoying this. "Lord Zhangwei, your hands appear full. Shall we remain with you until you're ready to return?"

"What were your orders from Her Majesty?" Zhangwei asked.

"To head back after delivering her message, unless you needed our aid," Lieutenant Yang said. "There are fears another attack will be launched by those conspiring with the Winged Devils."

Zhangwei frowned. "Then you should return at once. We have no need of a guard here; I will protect the Lady of Tianxia."

The lieutenant laughed. "We meant no disrespect, Lord Zhangwei. I'll confess I wanted you to protect *us*."

Zhangwei's grin erased the harshness of his features. "You are every bit as capable as I am, Lieutenant Yang," he replied. "We won't keep you from your duties. Please inform Her Majesty that I will return as soon as I can."

Lieutenant Yang bent his head in acknowledgment, as did the other soldiers. The clouds at their feet shimmered as they stepped upon them. A moment later, they were soaring into the skies, the wind roiling around us.

"Liyen, we should head to Kunlun now," Zhangwei urged.

"For Queen Caihong to send a messenger, the danger must be great. Once I've escorted you to safety, I will return to learn more."

"I can't just disappear," I protested. "I have responsibilities, I must warn the others of the danger. It won't take long."

He hesitated, then nodded. "Be careful what you share."

A thunderous crack shattered the stillness. We froze, our gazes darting in unison toward the skies—glazed with a haunting shimmer like moonlight gliding upon a lake. Those strange birds shrieked, circling once, then soared toward Kunlun. Light ruptured the heavens in bursts of vermilion as four fiery comets plummeted through the skies.

Zhangwei's hands flew up, his magic pulsing through the air. What did discovery matter when the skies blazed with it? Glittering strands shot from his fingers, weaving a luminous net above us. The flaming remnants hurtled down, caught by the net before they crashed to the ground. Ice glazed my insides, my heart constricting at the sight of the four charred bodies within—those of the queen's soldiers, Lieutenant Yang among them. Deep gashes were carved across their faces, streaking down their necks beneath the twisted remains of their armor, now blackened and gnarled. They'd been alive a few moments ago—immortal and powerful— and now, they were snared in the eternal clutches of death.

The urge to retch swelled inside me. I fought it, trembling from terror and revulsion. Zhangwei crouched down beside Lieutenant Yang, gripping his limp hand. A tremor ran through his body, his knuckles white with strain. If he wept, he hid it well.

After a long moment, he pressed the lieutenant's hand to his own chest, then laid it back down. "Sleep well, my friend."

"I'm sorry," I said hoarsely. "I'm so sorry for your loss."

"If only I had accepted their offer." Zhangwei's voice was raw, racked with anguish. "If only I'd returned with them—"

"Then you would have died, too." I was grasping to find a

way to ease his burden, wishing I had more than these inadequate words.

I drew a long breath. "When Grandfather died, I blamed myself, wishing I hadn't needed the lotus. But you didn't cause their deaths any more than I asked to be poisoned. Don't let your grief turn inward; don't let it hurt you."

He remained silent, yet his breathing seemed to steady a little. "Was Lieutenant Yang a good friend?" I asked. Grief was awkward and frightening; some thought it was unwelcome to speak of the dead to those who loved them. But when I lost my grandfather, I didn't want to stop talking about him. For those we loved, the greatest disservice was to forget them.

"We met while training together in the army. He was one of the few who did not care who I was, or what I could do." His voice was hollow, but calmer than before. "I will miss him."

I hesitated before saying, "We have a tradition here, to build an altar to the fallen, to honor them with offerings of food and wine. If you wish . . . I will build one here in their memory."

"Thank you." His eyes were bright as they met mine. "It would be fitting, given where they lost their lives. For our kind, we have few rites for the fallen, fewer physical remembrances."

"Be glad for it." I spoke quietly, thinking of the inevitable fate of my people, the cemeteries that sprawled our land. The soft cries during the Tomb Sweeping Festival, when the dead were remembered and honored through their descendants' offerings.

As Zhangwei laid a hand on Lieutenant Yang's chest, sparks scattered from his fingertips, falling over the body. He went to each of the soldiers in turn, performing the same rite. "Their bodies are preserved until I can return them to their families."

He stood now, a hard look in his eyes. As he raised his arms, red light surged from his fingers into the heavens, his magic swelling like cresting waves. In the distance, something glimmered yet held fast. Zhangwei's chest rose and fell, his face taut with concentration—yet he did not stop, his power intensifying until the air shuddered with it, until the heavens themselves blazed.

Lines deepened across his face, growing ashen, sweat streaking from his brow. He was not well; already weakened. If he exhausted himself . . . he might die. Pain struck my heart at the thought, but I told myself any concern was for my kingdom and what he had promised us.

"Stop, Zhangwei," I said forcefully. "You're hurting yourself."

He didn't turn, he did not reply like he was ensnared in the throes of his spell, too far gone along this path of destruction. I grabbed his arm, as cold as ice, but I didn't let go.

My voice shook as I let my fear spill free, hoping it might reach him. "You promised to protect me. If you die, what will happen to me?" I would say anything to stop him.

He stilled then, blinking as he lowered his hands, his breathing ragged. "The skies are sealed. This must have just happened—the moment my shield broke."

"Someone wanted to isolate Tianxia," I said numbly. "They wanted to make sure the immortals could not reach us."

"This is forbidden magic. With most of the Winged Devils captured, this must be the doing of another. Only the Wuxin would have such power." His hands balled into fists. "I can't break this enchantment alone. I can't warn Her Majesty or ask for reinforcements. For now, we are trapped here."

"Then there is no time to waste. I must return to the palace."

His eyes locked onto mine, his jaw tightening. "I need my strength for what lies ahead. Would you give me the lotus? I will keep my promises to you—*all* of them."

Something writhed inside my chest, my resolve faltering. I'd had denied him outright before, but it was harder now. He was right; he needed his power—we needed the God of War to keep us safe. This danger threatened us all. And as I looked at the bodies on the ground, fear gripped me that Zhangwei might be next.

Yet if I gave it to him, I'd have nothing to hold him to his word. I might lose the only chance Tianxia would ever have to break free of the immortals. It wasn't just my future at stake . . . and I didn't trust him enough yet.

"I can't," I said haltingly. "If I agree now, it would be out of fear—not because I want to."

He nodded slowly. "Then it wouldn't work anyway. Don't apologize, it's my fault that you don't trust me yet. But one day, you will." He didn't rage, threaten, or attempt to persuade me— which was worse, somehow, my remorse thickening.

As he extended his hand to me, I took it, a shiver running through my body that had nothing to do with the cold. And as his fingers closed around mine, a warmth unfurled within, an anchor amid the rising dread.

24

The entrance of my home was abandoned, the door swinging ajar. Frost glazed the wood like rivulets of salt that crept over the metal grates.

"Where are the guards?" It was hard to keep calm, my nails digging into my palms.

Zhangwei pressed a finger to his lips as he pulled me to a grove of trees, his tense expression sending a spike of fear through me. "The Wuxin. They're here."

The words sank in like a curse. How quiet it had grown, the chill sharpening like a scythe carving the air. Translucent forms appeared in the main courtyard, just beyond the entrance—twelve or more of them, their flesh no more substantial than breath fogged against porcelain. I'd expected monsters with fangs and claws, scales and wings. Yet these wraithlike creatures seemed fragile, likely to dissipate if one blew upon them. I was not stupid enough to imagine them weak, not when the God of War braced at their approach.

With each passing moment, their bodies solidified more, as though a painter had begun filling in the lines of their work. Were they feeding on the fear they roused? Or was this form how they'd slipped through the gateway? Their robes flowed in shades of gray, a bronze bell the size of a loquat dangling from their waists, eerily silent as though hollow within.

As the Wuxin took shape, they began to look like the immortals—ageless, without blemish—yet their hair was a shining white, draping their shoulders like pale shawls. Some were fair and others dark, yet all their eyes were ringed with copper. They crossed the courtyard, moving with swift purpose, heading deeper into my home. Dozens of Winged Devils trailed behind them, their claws gleaming, a cloying fragrance of spoiled fruit wafting in the air—they *were* working together.

Zhangwei and I remained still until they'd gone. It was dark now but for the curve of the moon, casting our surroundings into ash. I hugged myself, trying to banish my dread, the heaviness stealing over me. This was a hopeless battle against so powerful an enemy. We were doomed. But I shook my head, chiding myself. The Wuxin were said to leech one's strength and hope; they would not take mine.

"Don't let your mind wander." Zhangwei brushed a light finger across my forehead. As a shimmering heat slid into me, my heart lightened at once. "This will help protect you from their influence, but you must also guard your emotions. The Wuxin draw your misery from you like smoke winding to the skies. The more you yield, the worse you'll suffer, falling deeper into their clutches."

"How did they change their appearances?" I asked.

"Their natural forms are those we saw in the beginning, akin to spirits. Once they gain strength, they gain substance."

I shuddered. "I thought they were sealed away in the Netherworld."

"They are," he said grimly. "I don't know how they got out. I must inspect the gateway."

"Who are they looking for?"

When he didn't reply, I pressed further, "No more lies, remember? Not even those that make me feel better."

He sighed. "It's no coincidence that they're here in your home. That all this began—"

"Once I took the Divine Pearl Lotus," I finished his sentence, trying to keep calm.

Zhangwei's head dipped toward mine, his presence helping to drive away my frantic fear. "I won't let them hurt you," he told me.

Of course—if I died, he died. And I almost hated myself for the way I twisted his words around. But while he was protecting my body, I had to protect my heart.

His hand tightened around mine; only now did I realize he hadn't let go. "I must get you away. There are too many of them."

But a new terror was beginning to stir, one I couldn't ignore. "If they don't find what they're looking for, will they hurt the others? I must warn—"

"We have to go." He was still pale, his breathing uneven since his attempt to unseal the skies. Could he be on the brink of exhaustion? Was he afraid he couldn't protect me now?

"I want to go," I admitted; it took all my self-control to remain here, surrounded by these monsters. "But I can't, not until my people are safe. I won't let them be hurt because of me. If you won't help, I'll go alone."

"If the Wuxin capture you, if they take the lotus—"

"It's just about the lotus, isn't it?" I shot back. "You're afraid I'll lose it, that you'll die."

His face clouded as he glanced at the skies. Was he thinking of Lieutenant Yang? The dead immortal soldiers? "I'm afraid for *you*. I can't risk them hurting you. What other magic do they possess that we know nothing of?"

"But you'll risk everyone else?"

"Once you're safe, I'll return for them—"

"After they've killed everyone here? My soldiers aren't equipped to battle such creatures. I must help them." My hand gripped my sword. "We need every weapon we can gather."

"They are searching for you for a reason. If they find you, *they win*, and your kingdom will be the first to suffer."

His voice roughened with intensity, but I couldn't let myself listen to him—I would flee if I did, my resolve worn thin. What did I know of monsters except those the immortals had let into our world? Neither of them had any place here.

I rounded on him, holding onto my anger—it was of more use than my fear. "My people are in danger *now*. If they're hurt, I don't care what happens to your precious lotus. Let me go; you have no right to stop me."

When he didn't release me, I drew my sword with my other hand, spurred by anger and fear. *Move*, I urged him in my mind. But his eyes blazed as though challenging me, as though *daring* me to strike like he didn't believe I would. My rage flared, eclipsing all else as I swung the sword at him. He didn't evade, maybe underestimating my resolve—his gaze pinning mine as my blade sliced his arm. Inside, I recoiled, my chest caving—sick at the sight of his blood, though it was a shallow cut. But I didn't pause, wrenching free to stalk away, resisting the urge to turn. I wouldn't be a coward. I was no longer helpless, an immortal blade in my hand . . . and a heart that was slowly hardening to stone.

I RUSHED TOWARD THE TRAIL OF CRIES, THE CLASH of blades, the cold that knotted the air until it became a struggle to breathe. In the square ahead, just outside the hall where I held court, my soldiers were battling the Winged Devils. Their faces were pale but they fought bravely—even as their weapons gave way and shattered beneath the claws and blades of these creatures. Bodies lay on the ground, limbs splayed, blood oozing from their wounds.

I couldn't look at their faces, I would break if I did.

The Wuxin were surrounded by soldiers, but they were no prey. While they bore spears and swords, they didn't draw their weapons like they disdained our might.

"How dare you trespass here?" Captain Li, the leader of the night patrol, demanded.

One of the Wuxin stepped forward, her skin the shade of magnolias, her white hair brushing her shoulders. "Where are the immortals? Where is the Lady of Tianxia?" The delicate peal of her voice reminded me of a flute.

Captain Li kept her sword raised, though her hand trembled. "You are mistaken. No immortals are here."

A tall Wuxin with light-brown eyes and a narrow face drew a curved dagger from his waist, brushing a finger across its tip. "Confess, and we will spare you. Lie, and you will die."

I was afraid, but now I was furious. Slinging my sword behind me, I stepped out from the trees. Heads turned my way, Captain Li hurrying to my side.

"Your Ladyship, you can't be here. Let us escort you back to your rooms."

I looked at the soldiers, their tired faces bright with courage. "My place is with you."

"Is this the Lady of Tianxia?" A laugh rose from the tall man. "A frail thing. She will be easily subdued."

"Captain Rao, insults are not necessary," the woman admonished him.

I seethed, gripping the sword tighter behind my back. There were only a handful of immortal blades among the soldiers here, including mine. Each had to count. Doubt clouded my mind, whispering this was futile, that it was safer to surrender—but I smothered it. Was it the presence of these beings or my own innate cowardice, my desire to survive?

As the one called Captain Rao stalked toward me, a young soldier from my army leapt between us, thrusting his spear forward.

Reckless and rash . . . and in my defense. The spear tip drove toward the captain's shoulder, yet he did not evade. As it touched his skin—the sharp point broke away, leaving just a jagged wooden stump. Against these creatures, our weapons were as much use as porcelain blades.

The soldier's eyes widened as Captain Rao cocked his head. "My turn," he rasped.

"Don't hurt him!" I cried. The soldier was so young, younger than me.

I lunged forward, but Captain Li blocked my path. "It's too dangerous," she said, though her throat convulsed.

From behind, Chengyin was hurrying toward me, his robes in disarray like he'd just pulled them on. "Liyen, stay back," he called out. "We can't let them take you hostage."

My protest was drowned by a piercing cry. I spun to find the Wuxin captain's hand thrust into the young soldier's chest. Blood oozed, trickling down his wrist to blot the earth. The soldier's eyes bulged, strangled sounds slipping from his mouth—as the Wuxin plucked his heart out as effortlessly as a ripe plum from its stem. With a malevolent grin, he dropped the heart, striking the ground with a wet thud.

A scream erupted from me. I was frozen with horror as the soldier's lifeless body crumpled to the ground. He had died protecting me . . . and I didn't even know his name.

"You're despicable," I spat at the Wuxin captain. "Every vile story I've heard about your kind is true."

The captain's mouth twisted in anger. He moved toward me, but another of my guards leapt forward, slashing at him. As the Wuxin reached for him with a cruel smile, something broke inside me.

They would not take another.

I shoved my way to the front, pulling away as Chengyin tried to seize my arm. Rage burned through me—all my caution, my fear—like fire devouring paper. As I swung my sword, the silver filigree shone like a piece of the moon. A Winged Devil aimed a spear at me—but I ducked, spinning around to plunge my blade into its chest. The creature grinned, maybe expecting my sword to break as the others before—but it sank deep. As I yanked it out, the Winged Devil staggered back, its fingers groping the hole in its flesh.

"What weapon is this?" the creature hissed. "I thought the mortals were poorly equipped."

"More lies?" another Winged Devil accused Captain Rao. "Just as your promised reinforcements that never came when we attacked the immortal queen's palace? My people are imprisoned—"

"We will rescue them," the short-haired Wuxin woman replied firmly. "Our leader needs a little time; our plans are underway."

I was listening intently, trying to learn more. Sensing my distraction, Captain Rao sprang toward me, his daggers drawn. Just in time, Chengyin dragged me back to safety. My soldiers rushed forward, forming a barrier between the Wuxin and me.

"Captain Rao, you were not authorized to attack. Killing the soldier was excessive," the woman admonished him.

Her reprimand surprised me; I'd believed them all eager to murder without cause. Was this an act, or were there some who didn't share these bloodthirsty appetites?

Captain Rao scowled. "Miss Lin, matters of combat are my domain."

"Much as you relish violence, Captain Rao—this is not the time for it. Lord Dalian entrusted this task to me. *I* determine our course of action. Cross me again, and I'll report you for insubordination, for disobeying our leader's instructions."

Lord Dalian? Was he the ruler of the Wuxin?

Captain Rao's face darkened, but he fell silent. Miss Lin faced me now, her gaze dropping to my blade. "Where did you get this sword? It's a powerful weapon."

I raised my chin defiantly, trying to steady my shaking hands. "I'll tell you nothing." Did Zhangwei regret giving me the sword after I'd cut him with it? How furious he must be. Furious enough to let me die?

As Captain Rao moved menacingly toward me, Miss Lin tapped his shoulder in warning. "Lord Dalian wants her alive. Unharmed."

"What if we remove her tongue from her mouth?" Captain Rao offered as he raised his dagger again.

"Then *you* can explain her inability to speak to Lord Dalian."

Captain Rao flinched. Whoever he was, their leader must be terrifying indeed.

Miss Lin gestured toward me. "Mortal, if you surrender and come with us, no one else will be harmed."

Her tone was soft, her smile warm, but I would be a fool to believe anything they said. "What do you want with me?"

"Answers."

"If I don't have them?"

"If you don't *share* them," she corrected me, her voice hardening, "you'll wish you had." She shrugged, her smile widening. "Meet us with an open mind; you might find an ally in us. Not all of us are like him." Her gaze slid to Captain Rao, then back to me.

A chill glazed my skin, a prickling sensation that faded abruptly. Was she trying to secure something in me—something she had no right to? Had Zhangwei's shield protected me? I wouldn't let myself wonder where he was, though part of me couldn't help worrying for him as I recalled his pallor and the ice of his skin. Miss Lin lied well. A stranger might believe her, one who didn't know about the Wuxin, who hadn't just seen them rip out a young man's heart, leaving the bloodied hole in his chest. His family would weep over his body tonight.

Could such monsters be reasoned with? Could I ally myself with such brutal killers? Never—but I had to pretend to. "Do you swear you won't harm me or my people?"

"Not unless you act foolishly."

"Will I be a guest or a prisoner?" I asked like I was considering it, when the very thought sickened me.

Miss Lin inclined her head. "You will be accorded the honors of a guest, as long as you abide by the rules of one." She was shrewd, not giving anything without taking something in turn, weaving threats within silk.

"You can't go." Chengyin pushed his way to me, his own sword drawn. "What if they hurt you? What if they never let you go?"

Captain Rao snorted, his head tilted to one side. "Who are you to speak for your ruler?"

Chengyin straightened. "Her betrothed."

Fortunately, only a handful of my soldiers heard him. They exchanged guarded looks, knowing better than to question it now. As Captain Rao's eyes gleamed, fear burrowed into my chest. I wanted to silence Chengyin, to conceal him from the Wuxin's avaricious eyes—just as my friend was trying to help me, claiming a position he did not want.

"If I refuse, they will kill us all," I told Chengyin in a low voice. "If I'm forced to go with them, send word to the God of War." He would come for me, if only to retrieve the lotus.

I didn't give Chengyin a chance to reply, instead turning toward the Wuxin. If I delayed, my false veneer of bravery would crack. They parted, forming a pathway, my spirits leaden as I took a step forward—

The air crackled, bolts of flame slamming into the ground before me. Fire erupted, scorching and bright, forming a blazing barrier between the Wuxin and me. As a gale surged through the garden, dust scattered like a storm, my hands flying up to protect my eyes.

Zhangwei emerged from the trees. His sword was drawn, shining like ice. Even without his armor, danger emanated from him—no sign of any weakness, though I knew the toll this took on him. Had he been gathering his strength for this confrontation? At the sight of him, a strange feeling caught at me, a shred of remembrance. It was like the first night I'd met the God of War . . . and here he was again, burning my home. Such terror I'd felt when I saw him then, such despair and loathing—yet now, there was only this fullness in my heart.

"The Wuxin were banished to the Netherworld. Do you not fear retribution by returning?" His voice was not the one I was accustomed to: cold, unearthly, seething with power and wrath. The voice of the God of War.

Captain Rao's cheeks mottled. "Banished upon whose orders? The Queen of the Golden Desert's command means nothing to us. The day is drawing closer when you immortals will kneel to us."

"Never." Zhangwei's face seemed hewn from stone. "Tianxia is our domain, under our protection. Leave now."

One day, Tianxia will be no one's domain, I vowed to myself.

A cunning smile spread across Captain Rao's face. "Since when is the God of War so merciful? Why have you not struck us down? Where are your soldiers?" He looked up into the night with knowing, his tone laced with malice. "Or are they already dead?"

Zhangwei's blade gleamed as he swept it forward, its point aimed at the captain. "Your little trick with the skies will not hold," he said coldly, as though he'd not already tried to break it. "Queen Caihong's soldiers will soon arrive. Do you wish to face her wrath?"

The Wuxin shuffled nervously, except for Captain Rao who was studying Zhangwei.

"How did you escape the Netherworld?" Zhangwei demanded. "How did you seal the skies?"

"Why should we tell you?" Captain Rao replied insolently.

He lunged at Zhangwei abruptly, his twin daggers thrust before him—long and curved—whirling till they were a blur. The God of War's sword flew up, deflecting each blow with startling swiftness.

Not even the rain can touch you.

The captain fell back, facing Zhangwei, arms outstretched as he circled him. He was panting, his expression cautious now. Without warning, his daggers swept up, the curved blades arching toward Zhangwei's throat. A scream hovered on my lips as Zhangwei flung his sword up, thrusting it between the daggers, sparks scattering from the force of his blow. As the immortal twisted his arm deftly, he swept one of the daggers from the captain's grip, flinging it away. The Wuxin dove forward, his teeth bared as he thrust his remaining dagger forward—but Zhangwei dipped back, then kicked the captain in his side, knocking the dagger from his grip.

The Winged Devils were advancing on my soldiers. Before I could rush forward, something gleamed between them, shining like a curtain of stardust. As one of creatures clawed at it, a hissing sound erupted, fiery welts streaking across its arm. Zhangwei had erected a shield of protection around us, a further strain on his power as he was forced to fight and defend us, too. Fine lines creased around his eyes, his breathing shallow, my own heart thudding like a drum.

The Winged Devils charged forward, hacking at the god's barrier. Just Miss Lin stood apart, watching the events unfold, maybe trying to determine who had the upper hand. This was not an even battle, most of our weapons unable to pierce our enemies' flesh, Zhangwei's power was stretched thin, straining beneath the weight of the attacks. Light streaked through the air, bolts of fire hurtling down to strike the Winged Devils like molten rain. They cried out, shields forming around themselves as they stumbled back.

A greenish light arced from Captain Rao's hand now, plunging toward Zhangwei, but he swung aside. With a swift sweep of his arm, Zhangwei drove his sword into the captain's shoulder—yet the captain laughed as he wrenched free, blood trickling from his wound.

"God of War, why have you not unleashed your full might? You did so before to mercilessly destroy so many of my kin. What is staying your hand now?"

Zhangwei's expression was inscrutable. "I don't need magic to defeat you."

"I'm starting to think you *can't* use it—at least, not as before. Are you unwell, Lord Zhangwei? Still suffering the effects of our curse?" Triumph surged in Captain Rao's voice.

They knew.

I drew closer to Zhangwei, my mind working quickly. Captain Rao scented victory; he wouldn't back down. And if the God of War revealed his vulnerability, it would embolden our enemy; they'd never leave. The Wuxin would overrun my kingdom—they'd nearly destroyed us once. I couldn't let it happen again.

Something slipped into my mind then, something Zhangwei had told me once . . . that I was only now beginning to understand.

With you, I am warm.

I'd thought them tender words to lower my defenses, yet his skin had warmed at my touch. Did the presence of the Divine Pearl Lotus help him in any way? Could I channel part of it to him, lending its strength even if I did not yield it? I couldn't use its power to save us . . . but the God of War might.

I gestured to Captain Li and whispered a quick command. At once, she ordered my soldiers to form a close circle around Zhangwei and me, facing away from us. To the Wuxin, it appeared like they were guarding me, when they were concealing us from sight.

Captain Rao bared his teeth as he advanced, but Miss Lin seized his arm, whispering into his ear.

"What are you doing?" Zhangwei asked in hushed tones.

"Helping you."

I moved behind Zhangwei, sliding my hand over his, not giving him a chance to protest. A wild guess—this need to touch him as he'd touched me whenever he'd healed me. His body stiffened, but he did not move away, his tension seeming to ease. Drawing a breath, I reached inward for the lotus, seeking the heat that pulsed in my chest—trying to recall the little he'd taught me of magic, how it felt when he'd tried to take it from me. Gritting my teeth, I grasped at this unseen thing within, as hard as trying to catch a snowflake before it thawed. I strained against an unseen barrier, not to push it from me but to channel it—toward my hand that was locked around his. Somehow, Zhangwei's skin was already warming beneath my fingers, the color returning to his face.

Heat surged through my blood now, more slipping through the barrier in my chest. Sweat broke out over my body, yet I shivered despite the unrelenting warmth that flowed through me, my fingers gleaming against Zhangwei's skin. Something bound us in this moment stronger than chains, more intimate than a kiss. We moved in unison, my body attuned to his: I could feel the warmth seeping through him, the power building in his grasp. My lungs tightened as I struggled to breathe, exhaustion looming over me. My instincts rebelled, screaming caution—yet I couldn't stop. Our lives depended on this.

"This is your final warning. Leave now, or I will show no mercy," Zhangwei commanded, his voice taking on a new resonance, thrumming with unbound power.

As Captain Rao sneered—Zhangwei's sword flared to life like living flame, the air writhing around us in the rhythm of a storm. The power torn from me was like my heart was being wrenched apart. As I gasped, Zhangwei moved away, breaking the contact.

I slumped back with relief. Was it enough? I didn't know if I could do more.

Cries erupted among the Wuxin, the Winged Devils scrambling away. Miss Lin grabbed Captain Rao's arm. "You're *wrong*, the God of War is as strong as before."

"No," Captain Rao snapped. "We must continue our attack—"

"Then stay here yourself," Miss Lin snarled. "I won't risk us all to fulfil your bloodlust."

Captain Rao's gaze slid from Zhangwei to me, narrowed with suspicion. My insides clenched—but then he turned away reluctantly, the monsters gliding away from my home as silently as they had entered.

25

I was shivering, the cold startling after the warmth of the bond with Zhangwei. As I swayed, Chengyin slid an arm across my shoulders, steadying me.

"Are you hurt?" he asked.

I shook my head. Yet part of me would never recover from the brutality of tonight, the young soldier's death.

"We must go. The Wuxin will return in greater force." Zhangwei's tone was curt as he looked at Chengyin and me.

Chengyin angled himself to shield me from Zhangwei's sight. "Do you want to go with him?" he whispered.

"No, but—"

Before I finished, Chengyin straightened. "The Lady of Tianxia needs to remain here until the physicians assure us of her health. Her well-being is of the utmost importance."

Zhangwei's eyes narrowed. "Yet you allowed her to fight at the front?"

"Chengyin knows that I can take care of myself," I retorted.

"Oh, I know you can." Zhangwei's gaze flicked toward the cut on his arm, the one I'd inflicted.

I repressed a flash of remorse—morphing into a grimace at the sight of Minister Dao and Minister Guo striding toward me, eager to stake their presence now the danger had passed. Somehow, they'd found the time to dress in their official robes of state. Other courtiers and ministers followed them, including Aunt Shou—though she remained at the sidelines, unlike those who were pushing their way through the soldiers.

I turned from them deliberately, facing Captain Li and the soldiers. They had fought valiantly, risking their lives. More than anyone, they deserved an explanation.

"You must have many questions," I said to them.

Captain Li clasped her hands and bowed. "Your Ladyship, Honored Immortal, if those creatures were the Wuxin, how did they escape? We'd believed them locked away."

Whispers coursed through the crowd, quietening when Zhangwei raised his hand. "They are sealed in the Netherworld with our queen's most powerful enchantment. We will examine the gateway to learn more, to stop the Wuxin from entering again."

"Will Queen Caihong send reinforcements?" Captain Li asked.

I glanced at Zhangwei, unwilling to hide the situation—it would be more dangerous to rely on aid that never came. As he nodded, I cleared my throat. "The skies are sealed; no one can cross them. Until this is resolved, we can't get word to the immortals, nor can they descend here."

Gasps broke out, louder this time. Minister Guo stepped forward, bristling as though someone was to blame. "How could this happen? The immortals have abandoned us—" His voice trailed off abruptly as Zhangwei straightened to his full height.

"You have not been abandoned. Queen Caihong would send aid at once if she knew," Zhangwei said sternly.

Minister Guo bowed swiftly, mumbling an apology as he slunk back into the crowd.

"No one is to blame," I said slowly, trying to sound calm when inside, I was as frightened as all of them. "However, we cannot expect the immortals' help for now. We must protect ourselves should these enemies return."

"Why did they come?" Captain Li asked.

"I don't know." I couldn't mention my suspicion about the Divine Pearl Lotus; too many were present for secrecy.

"The Wuxin have always coveted the Mortal Realm," Zhangwei said, "It is the greatest source of their strength, where they feed best."

"What do they feed on?" Minister Hu asked, raising his voice from behind.

"Misery."

Silence fell, woven with dread.

"A poor diet," Chengyin said weakly.

"To those who have to provide it," I agreed.

Zhangwei glanced at the silhouette of Kunlun, almost drowned in the dark. "The Wuxin believe they have found the ideal victims among your people. A wealth of emotion, in a land devoid of magic—unable to withstand their attacks. Prey who cannot fight back."

Captain Li shook her head, and when she spoke, her tone was respectful but firm. "Honored Immortal, we aren't victims, nor are we prey. We are well trained in combat, adept at weaponry and fighting. Now that we're aware of the danger, we will prepare accordingly. They will not take us by surprise again."

Pride surged through me at her words, underscoring our strengths rather than our weaknesses. Some believed the ruler needed to be the pinnacle of wisdom, but the truth was, I was learning from my people every day. Captain Li was braver than most; it was no easy thing to correct the God of War.

Zhangwei inclined his head, not reprimanding her as I almost expected. "Your training is evident, as is your courage. You have much to take pride in. But it's not a fair fight if one side possesses magic and the other does not. While you can undoubtedly hold your own in combat, what can you do against spells of fire, wind, and ice? What if your weapon cannot inflict harm on your enemy? You will fall, through no fault of your own."

I hated the truth in his words, how vulnerable we were. Tianxia should not be the stage for the battles of gods and monsters, ill equipped as we were. My people would suffer, they would die, all for a war we'd never sought. A reminder of what was at stake for our future, and what I was fighting for.

"What can we do?" I asked. "We may be weaker, but this doesn't mean we've lost—just that the battle is harder."

Zhangwei inclined his head to me, then Captain Li. "Make what preparations you can. I will craft a barrier to help protect those within the palace that will give you a little time."

I stared at him, a little of the wall I'd built around my heart falling away. This couldn't be easy for him, already much weakened. I'd thought mortal lives mattered little to him, and yet he was risking himself to help my people.

"How can we prepare? What about those outside the palace?" Chengyin asked.

"Gather all the immortal weapons we have. Send more patrols out, closer to Kunlun to watch for any unrest. Each must carry at least one immortal blade," I instructed. "While the danger is present, any who wish can shelter within our walls."

"We need more weapons from your realm, Honored Immortal," Captain Li said gravely. "With this attack, we are at the brink of war, if not already knee-deep. We must be able to protect ourselves—to better guard Kunlun, to keep the realms safe."

"I have reached an agreement with the God of War," I assured her. "He will speak on our behalf."

"Things cannot continue as they have," Zhangwei agreed. "Once the skies are unsealed, I will confer with Her Majesty. For now, we must make do with what we have."

"Will your queen agree?" I asked.

"Her Majesty is wise; she will listen to reason. Peace spoils the victor. We grew careless, content with the way things were—believing the enemy safely locked away while they were hard at work, gaining on us. Strengthening your kingdom will help us, too." Zhangwei addressed the soldiers now: "Rest assured, I will do all I can to keep you safe."

"Thank you, Lord Zhangwei," I said. This time I didn't use his title to set him apart but to honor the God of War who protected us.

"There is no need to thank me," he said softly. "I'm not doing this just because of our pact, but because it's right."

"I know," I replied. "And that is why I'm thanking you."

It was like everyone else had faded away, and it was just us in that moment. His eyes had never seemed so dark, so unfathomably deep—and though I might drown, I didn't want to look away.

Zhangwei raised his hands, shimmering with his power. Band of crimson light surged forth, knitting together. They circled us, stretching wider across the grounds, shining like sunstruck copper. His breathing was uneven, but when he spoke, his voice remained steady. "This barrier will guard the palace. It will hold against minor incursions and alert you should the Wuxin attempt to enter again."

As my people bowed to him, Zhangwei held out his hand to me. "Come, we must leave now."

"Where are you going?" Minister Dao asked, his voice shrill. "Will the God of War not stay here to defend us?"

He shook his head. "The Lady of Tianxia must come with me to Kunlun, to secure the safety of the realms."

The ministers stared at me, afire with curiosity, yet none dared to question Zhangwei.

"Let me come with you, too," Chengyin offered. From the side, Aunt Shou was scowling—she didn't want either of us plunging into danger.

"I must do this alone. No other mortal is allowed into Kunlun," I reminded him.

"A troop of soldiers is always stationed close to Kunlun, to patrol the foothills and surrounding areas. More can accompany you from here, Liyen." Chengyin dropped my title in his urgency. "They can help protect you if need be."

"His attentiveness is beginning to grate," Zhangwei said icily.

I glared at him. "Chengyin is right. Who knows what enemies lurk? But we can't wait. The soldiers can follow after us and catch us on the way."

"I'll make the arrangements," Chengyin said. "I can accompany them—"

"I need you here, as does your mother," I told him, though I wished he could join me. "As the First Advisor, I grant you the mandate to rule the court in my absence."

Chengyin hesitated as he studied me, but then he bowed. "As you wish, Your Ladyship."

I crouched down by the bodies of my fallen soldiers, beside the one who had died defending me. I made myself look at the gaping wound in his chest, his vacant gaze. I would never forget this; his death wouldn't be in vain. An unspeakable weight fell over me as I laid my hand over the soldier's eyes to close them. How tired I was, wishing I could fold over and weep. But with everyone watching me, I had to be strong.

"What was his name?" I asked Captain Li hoarsely.

"Wang Pengyu."

"Does he have family?"

"A wife. A daughter, just turned three."

A child too young to understand his loss. A widow struggling to make ends meet. My hands balled into fists, anger searing at this needless death, at how little these monsters cared for the life they'd snatched tonight.

"Grant them a generous pension. I will bear all funerary expenses—not just for him but for those who lost their lives today." It would not replace a beloved member of the family, but it would secure their futures, allowing them to grieve unhindered.

"When will you return?" Chengyin wanted to know. "Will you be safe?"

"Right now, no one is," I said in a hollow voice.

Except it would be safer for everyone once we left, drawing the Wuxin away. A chill shrouded me at the thought. How bleak it was to be surrounded by enemies, with little hope on the horizon. Yet as I looked up at the God of War, I found myself remembering that at the end of every night, no matter how long, comes the rise of the dawn.

26

According to the ancient tales, the path to Kunlun once lay unhindered. Any adventurer could attempt the journey, and many had, seduced by dreams of eternity. Most failed to find it, some perished on the ascent. As for the few who vanished without a trace—it was whispered that they'd died at the threshold of the Immortal Realm, divine punishment for daring to reach above themselves. How cruel this would be, destroying a dream at the cusp of its fulfilment.

Back then, the Celestial Emperor had commanded the immortals to distance themselves from our world. Magic had upended too many of our lives, ruining some upon a whim while elevating others without merit. The immortals who ventured to our world were governed by strict rules of conduct, those that kept them hidden, that kept us safe.

But everything changed when the Wuxin invaded, sowing catastrophe and chaos. It was the immortals from the Golden Desert who saved us, driving the Wuxin away. Queen Caihong banished them to the Netherworld, crafting a powerful spell to seal the gateway that lay in Kunlun. Since then, Kunlun was barred to all except our ruler, the only mortal permitted to enter its grounds. It had been Grandfather's duty to watch over this place—and now it was mine.

Zhangwei and I rode in silence. My face was numbed from the wind, my head throbbing from the incessant clomp of hooves striking the ground. I had learned to ride as a child, a skill one didn't forget. How did Zhangwei ride with such grace, his horse obeying his every command? When he'd suggested this means of travel, part of me had hoped to see him fall flat on his back.

We halted by the edge of the forest, bordering the foothills of Kunlun. The trees towered, folding into one another like the bars of a cage. "I didn't think immortals knew how to ride," I said as we dismounted. "Are there horses in your realm?"

"No." As he stroked the stallion's mane, the creature leaned into his touch. "But I find joy in the sport, beyond its need. A slower pace allows one to appreciate the passing scenery." He looped the reins loosely around a shady tree. "It would be a waste of eternity should one choose to stand still in life. Few things are more satisfying than the pursuit of knowledge, to better oneself through study or reflection."

"The God of War possesses the heart of a scholar," I remarked after a moment's pause.

His eyes slid to mine. "You sound surprised. What did you think of me?"

Warmonger. Killer—

I flushed, quelling such thoughts. I was wrong, used to thinking of him within such narrow confines, filling in his character with my own prejudice and the tales I'd heard. There was a time all I did was look for his flaws, to ignore all he was. Ill-advised, for it meant I'd underestimated him.

"Silence is an answer in itself." He sounded amused rather than angered.

"My grandfather taught me courtesy."

"Yet you've shown no restraint, insulting me to my face."

Laughter crept up my throat. "I had good reason."

As he grinned, an unexpected lightness filled me. I was still unused to these rare moments when we let down our guard . . . at how they felt so right.

"This is the first time I've been here," I admitted to Zhangwei. "Grandfather always came alone."

His eyes held mine. "Does it look different from how it was afar?"

"Everything looks different when you take a closer look," I said quietly.

Even now it didn't seem real that I was standing in the shade of Kunlun. A towering mountain of bluish-purple stone rose from the jade-green grass. Snowy mist embraced the slopes, clouds enveloping the peak. The ground was carpeted with tiny flowers, the petals pointed at the tips like stars. Cypress trees lined a narrow pathway that wound up the mountain, then vanished from sight.

"My soldiers should be near." I looked around, but there was no sign of them.

"They are further west," he told me.

Suspicion stirred. "You knew where they were all this while," I accused him. "Did you take this route to avoid them? Did you maintain this relentless pace so the guards from the palace couldn't catch up?"

"Of course," he replied unrepentantly. "My time alone with you is precious. And we are also in a hurry."

I scowled but couldn't fault the latter. "Where do we go from here?"

"First, to the gateway. The way to the Ancient Grandmaster's place lies there too."

"Who is he?" I asked.

"One of the oldest and wisest immortals. His place is well hidden, as the way there changes—few find it, unless he wishes them to. He can help us get word to Queen Caihong."

"Perhaps he can help us against the Wuxin," I said hopefully.

Zhangwei shook his head. "He doesn't like to involve himself in such matters."

"But this affects us all."

"The Ancient Grandmaster has lived unscathed through countless wars; he will emerge untouched from this one. His greatest love and only care is the Tree of Everlasting Life."

"A tree?" I asked in disbelief.

"This tree existed long before the immortals. Some whispered that it was first spark of life, but who knows? Regardless, it possesses great power—not as a weapon but of protection."

As we walked up the slope, Kunlun seemed a wilderness, shaded by unkempt stalks of bamboo, the pathway pitted and worn, wildflowers blooming in tangled profusion. Yet with each step, my spirits lifted, the rich fragrance of flowers and herbs invigorating my senses, a rare tranquility filling me.

The rough stone beneath my feet morphed to amethyst, veined with iridescence. The bamboo grew more evenly, tall and straight, interspersed with clusters of peonies. Ahead, the trail forked, the wider path on one side broken in the distance, large cracks running through the stone—while the other led to a narrow opening in a stone wall. A strange energy thrummed from it, my chest pulsing with sudden awareness.

"This is where the gateway lies." Zhangwei's voice dropped in warning. "Be on your guard."

I pointed to the other side. "Where does this lead?"

"Once, toward the skies," he said solemnly. "But after the Wuxin descended to your world, the Celestial Emperor decreed this pathway too dangerous and it was destroyed. Now it leads nowhere. You could wander these mountains for eternity and never find your way out."

I shuddered as Zhangwei and I turned onto the smaller path, slipping through the gap in the stone. It opened into a wide clearing, the soft ground blanketed by moss, glistening with dew. Pale birch trees rose like icicles, encircling a vast lake that stretched out beyond my sight. Tendrils of light curled from its crystalline waters to spear the sky, its surface crowded with lotuses in vivid hues. At the far side, a large pavilion rose from the waters—an unusual shape, like three round pavilions joined together, the interior concealed by panels of brocade that hung straight down. The gilded roof was crowned with a sculpture of a dragon facing a phoenix, a luminous orb trapped beneath both their claws. How could such a place exist here? Yet after seeing the wonders of the realm above, nothing seemed impossible with the might of the gods.

The warmth in my chest intensified, my scar throbbing now. "This lake doesn't seem real . . . it doesn't feel a part of my world."

"Some believe this place was formed when a dragon and a phoenix fought over a pearl," Zhangwei told me.

"A pearl seems a small prize."

"Not when it possessed great magic," he replied. "These powerful creatures fought ferociously to claim it, crashing into mountains, gouging chasms with their claws. Evenly matched, they battled until the heavens shuddered. In the tussle, the pearl was dropped, striking the ground to form this lake. Desolate at the loss of their treasure, the dragon and the phoenix chose to remain here. According to legend, their bones lie at the bottom of this lake, their blood fused with these waters."

"Do legends exist in your realm?" I asked with a smile. "Or is this 'history'?"

"Our stories are more truth than myth," he acknowledged. "Dragons swim in our seas, phoenixes fly in our skies—yet they still strike awe into our hearts. It grieves me to imagine these majestic creatures losing their lives over such a thing, that the beauty here sprouted from strife. I would rather think of it as a legend."

I fell silent, mulling over what he'd said, the feelings this place roused in me. "The pearl's magic—was this how the Divine Pearl Lotus formed?"

"Yes, from the remnants of the jewel, watered in the blood of the dragon and phoenix."

If only the lotus could have healed them, too. My eyes were damp as I stared at the waters, imagining my grandfather standing here.

Zhangwei gestured to the pavilion on the lake. "Both the gateway and the way to the Ancient Grandmaster lie there, but we'll have to examine the gateway first."

"There is no bridge or pathway. Do we swim?" I asked.

In the silence, my gaze followed his, trailing over the lotuses. As a dragonfly landed upon the petals, a root sprang up, curling around the creature and dragging it below—the waters rippling in its wake.

"Let's not swim," I corrected myself hastily.

"I will carry you," he offered.

As I nodded stiffly, he slid his arm over my back and the other beneath my knees, lifting me effortlessly. Heat jolted through my body, as I stared ahead—anywhere but at him. With a powerful bound, Zhangwei leapt into the air. Wind surged into my face, thick with the intoxicating fragrance of lotuses. As we soared across the lake, my hands instinctively locked around his neck, my head pressed to his chest. A shudder seemed to course through Zhangwei as he tensed, his arms tightening around me. It felt like flying but for the dips in his rhythm, the feather-light steps he took upon the leafy pads—barely grazing them so they wouldn't sink beneath our weight. Magic was not his only strength.

He landed by the side of the pavilion, then set me upon the floor. My heart raced as I moved away, adjusting my robe. As we drew aside a brocade panel to enter, I was struck by the beauty of the ceilings, painted to resemble the skies—an azure blue, interspersed with clouds of white. The floor was tiled in an intricate mosaic pattern, circling a small hollow in the center, its border encrusted with amber. A solitary stalk rose from the waters beneath, silvery white, its tip withered like its bloom had been snapped off. Something slid into place inside me, a sense of knowing, the scar above my heart searing now. This was where the Divine Pearl Lotus had grown, the one Grandfather had harvested—then given to me.

I followed Zhangwei to the next chamber, where the ceilings were painted a deep midnight, set with glittering white stones. One of the entryways was connected to a slender bridge—hidden from where we'd entered—that arched over the waters toward the far side of the mountain.

We hurried across the bridge to a shimmering wall that was frosted over like a pane of ice. Here, the air gleamed as though suffused with magic, one that seemed to extend beyond the mountain itself. Thick ropes of vines hung over the surface, thorns glistening from their stalks, entwined with clusters of wisteria. As the wind blew, the petals quivered but did not fall. The place appeared untouched, almost pristine in its desolation.

"The gateway to the Netherworld." Zhangwei studied it intently. "The seal still holds—"

"Wait." I pointed to a scattering of petals in a corner. "They've withered here but nowhere else."

Zhangwei's brow furrowed at the sight. "While the gateway is intact, this part feels thinner, like a patch of fabric worn away."

"This must be how the Wuxin entered Tianxia." I stared at the gateway, growing cold inside. I'd imagined it to be more secure, stronger—not this translucent pane that appeared far too delicate, easily snapped. How could this hold back the Wuxin? If the gateway was broken, my kingdom could be engulfed in a day.

"Why weren't they sealed further away? Was there nowhere else the Wuxin could be held? Is this why the wall around Tianxia was erected—to keep us *all* in, mortals and monsters?" Fear made me lash out whether it was deserved or not. One thing was clear, that my people deserved better. "You immortals don't care what happens to us. We are dispensable, your first line of defense, paying the heaviest price for any conflict." I shoved at him, unable to control my anger, my pent-up resentment against his kind.

He caught my hand, holding it firmly. "Kunlun is the only way to the Netherworld, but it's not close, even though it might appear that way. The gateway bridges the distance between, like a fold. And the Netherworld was the only place the Wuxin could be sealed away, where they wouldn't starve, because the Wangchuan River fulfils their needs. As long as Her Majesty's enchantment holds, they cannot cross the gateway, whether above or under. She wove this spell at great cost to her own strength to keep them away, to keep Tianxia safe. Our guards patrol the grounds to keep watch—"

"Where are they?" I yanked free, stepping back from him.

"Maybe they couldn't come because the skies are sealed."

My anxiety spiked; I couldn't stop imagining the worst. "The Wuxin were in my land, my home. The immortals can't help us; we're facing this alone. How can there be a crack in the gateway now? What if it *breaks*?"

"The loss of the Divine Pearl Lotus could have weakened the seal; its magic was entwined with this place," he said. "Despite this, the gateway still holds—else the Wuxin would have already swarmed your lands. Their small numbers mean only a few can leave at a time. Once Queen Caihong learns of the situation, our warriors will come. Tianxia won't be left to fend for itself." He paused, before adding, "But we must get to the Ancient Grandmaster first. It's the only way to send word to her."

I nodded stiffly—what else could I do? Emotions warred inside me, my habitual caution rearing up. Were these soothing words part of his plan to gain the lotus? I wanted to trust him without reservation . . . but I didn't dare.

As we headed back to the pavilion, Zhangwei clasped my shoulder, drawing me to him. His hold was gentle but firm, soothing me despite the coolness of his touch. "I know you're afraid," he said. "But we will find the Ancient Grandmaster. We will get word to Queen Caihong. I will protect you and your people."

The last was spoken as a promise, one I drew strength from. But suddenly Zhangwei stiffened, releasing me, his hand flying to the hilt of his sword. Footsteps sounded from the pavilion. The brocade panels before us billowed, then parted, as a group of soldiers headed toward us. Sunlight glinted over their gold armor, that of the immortals, such relief filling me at the sight.

As they bowed to Zhangwei, he asked, "Where were you before?"

One stepped forward. "Lord Zhangwei, we were waiting for our replacements for the change of shift. When they didn't appear, we went to check if there was trouble. But we can't get word to the palace, like the skies are closed to us."

"Has there been any sign of disturbance around here?" Zhangwei asked, his hand remaining on his sword.

The soldiers shook their heads in unison. "None, my lord. All is well."

I edged closer to Zhangwei. Their manner seemed too calm. The sealed skies should have evoked alarm, curiosity at least . . . unless it was no surprise.

"Have you been on duty long?" Zhangwei's deceptively mild tone set my nerves on edge. "Since the last change of shift at midnight?"

As the soldiers nodded Zhangwei's hand swept out so swiftly, it was a blur—drawing his sword and pressing its edge to the guard's neck.

His eyes rounded in shock. "Lord Zhangwei, how have we offended you?"

Zhangwei's face seemed carved from ice, his tone of iron. "The change of shift here is always at dusk. Never midnight. Who are you? Where are the soldiers that guarded this place?"

They grinned insolently as their hair faded to white, their features morphing to form new faces as they discarded their disguises. One of them was Captain Rao, and others I recognized from the attack on my home—though Miss Lin was absent.

The captain's smile widened. "They offered little sport, not as well trained as we'd believed."

Zhangwei's jaw clenched, his throat convulsing. "You will pay for hurting them."

"No, God of War," Captain Rao replied, staring at the waters. "It is you who will pay today."

I spun toward the lake, once calm, now undulating like wind-blown silk. A monstrous serpent reared up, shattering the mirrored surface. Silver-bright scales, eyes glowing like embers. Crescent-shaped fins fanned from the sides of its head, as its jaws parted to reveal needlelike fangs.

Light gleamed from Zhangwei's hands, the air thrumming with his magic. Terror seized me; he hadn't recovered from the attack on my home. As the Wuxin advanced, his flames arced in front of them, forcing them back.

The serpent shrieked, its tail lashing the waters behind us. Zhangwei swung to face it, his blade outstretched. "Stay behind me," he warned.

I glared at him, trying to smoothen the tremor in my voice. "I didn't train to stand behind you."

He didn't reply, his attention on the serpent. The lake churned violently, waves cresting higher—then crashing down. Water sprayed all around, stinging and cold. As the creature darted toward us, the god slammed his sword against the serpent's body. Its scales fragmented like shells, shards flying up to scrape my face. It seared, but I tightened my grip on my sword, holding my ground.

The serpent reared back, gnashing its fangs. As it loomed above us, its jaws opened like it would swallow us whole. But Zhangwei leapt to thrust his sword into its neck, flames surging along his blade, pouring into the serpent's body. It shrieked—an eerie, high-pitched sound—as it swooped down to rake its fangs across the immortal's shoulder. Zhangwei did not flinch as he knocked the serpent's head aside with a brutal blow. Panic surged as I swung my sword at the serpent, trying to shake the numbing disbelief that I was battling this *monster*. My blade sank into its cheek, slicing through the scales even as I fought to remain steady, to stop my knees from giving way.

As the serpent spun toward me, diverted from the God of War, Zhangwei sprang forward, his sword raised in both hands as he plunged it into the serpent's chest in a seamless strike. His eyes flashed as he twisted the blade once, wrenching the flesh apart. There was not a trace of pity as he drove the blade further in until its tip slid from the other side, coated with blood. As he yanked it out, an unearthly cry erupted, riddled with anguish. The serpent shuddered as it fell back into the waters.

Yet the air thickened ominously around us. A movement from the side startled me, the Wuxin circling us now. Three soldiers blocked Zhangwei—another faced me. As his blade fell upon me, I blocked it with mine, my arms burning from the force of the Wuxin's blow. He drew back for another strike, but Zhangwei's sword arced high, slicing the soldier's throat. Blood sprayed wide as the soldier fell back, clutching at his neck.

Captain Rao struck then, his fist crashing against my head. Pain bloomed as I staggered back, my skin splitting as a warmth trickled down my cheek. As I stood there, dazed, Zhangwei swore viciously and lunged toward the captain. But more soldiers circled him now, forcing him back. A panel of thick brocade swung between us, blocking Zhangwei from my sight. The soldiers had divided themselves, most of them surrounding Zhangwei—Captain Rao and another two advancing on me. I stumbled back as they closed in on me, edging me farther away.

They're herding me, separating us. I couldn't see Zhangwei anymore. As the soldiers drew closer, a keen chill sliced the air, laced with an earthiness that was coupled with a metallic tinge. Was this the scent of the Wangchuan River? Hair sprang up along the back of my neck; I could not fight them all.

The clamor of battle intensified from within the pavilion. Zhangwei was fighting the soldiers, yet he was outnumbered, still injured—my blood hardening in my veins at the thought.

"Come with us," Captain Rao ordered me, a triumphant ring in his tone.

I took a step back toward the edge of the pavilion, desperately seeking a way out. But there was none, just the waters beneath, those murderous roots awaiting new prey.

"I will never go with you," I swore.

"Foolish mortal," the captain sneered as he moved toward me. "What makes you think you have a choice?"

"There is always a choice," I snarled as I sheathed my sword, leaping over the railing to dive into the churning waters.

27

Water, cold and dark, closed over my head. I flailed, sucking in a mouthful that seared as it clogged my nose. Panic flooded me, fragmenting my thoughts and stiffening my limbs—a death sentence to any swimmer. A frail disc of light shone above, the setting sun, the sight calming me . . . though soon it would be night, and the waters a hundred times more terrifying.

Lotus pads blotted the surface like spilled ink, their roots trailing into the murky depths. One coiled around my ankle, but I tore it away. As I glanced below, my insides twisted. There were just darkening shadows and those slender, vinelike roots tangling together like a net. As I imagined the fate of those unfortunate enough to be snared by them, I kicked a little harder.

I resisted the urge to surface till I was farther from the pavilion, grateful that I could swim without tiring as before. Once I relinquished the Divine Pearl Lotus, I might lose this strength. But I would regret nothing; the trade was more than fair. My mind wandered to Zhangwei—was he safe? He'd used so much of his strength already: battling the Wuxin, shielding my people, trying to unseal the skies. I halted mid-stroke, wanting to return for him—but it was safer for Zhangwei that I'd gone. The greatest danger to him was if I ended up a captive, the lotus in the hands of

256

the Wuxin. This way, they would be forced to split up in pursuit of us. And I assured myself that those soldiers were no match for the God of War now that they'd squandered the element of surprise.

My arms were beginning to ache, my lungs burning. My drenched clothes were heavy, though the sword strapped to my side seemed unnaturally weightless. I surfaced briefly for a gulp of air, then dove deeper. I didn't know how long I swam, my body leaden, almost numbed. The waters of the lake stretched without end, and I came up only sparingly for air, afraid of being discovered. Fortunately, the lotuses with their treacherous roots were left far behind.

Something floated in the water ahead—a small body. A round-faced boy in a white robe, his eyes closed, his arms curled around a log. I hesitated, keeping my distance. What had happened to him? How did he get here? Was he a victim of the Wuxin? They would be vile to prey on a child. His face was ashen, his body limp. As I watched, his fingers began slipping from the log—I couldn't let him drown. I swam toward him at once, then tucked my arms beneath his shoulders, pulling him to the surface.

The boy was startlingly light. A large bruise swelled on his forehead, split open with a trace of blood. His eyes were still shut though his throat convulsed, a welcome sign of life. I combed the lake desperately, searching for land. Night had fallen, moonlight glazing the waters with an oily sheen. My body was growing heavier, weighed with fatigue and the child in my arms. Each movement was a struggle. At last, something pale gleamed in the distance. Spurred by a burst of strength, I swam toward it. As my feet sank into the claylike earth, I stumbled upright, gulping in the air greedily, tears of relief mingling with the water sliding down my face.

I dragged myself and the boy to the shoreline, both of us falling to the ground. The boy's eyes were open now, hair plastered around his pale face.

"Where am I? What happened?" he asked.

"I pulled you from the lake. We're somewhere in Kunlun Mountain," I replied.

"Kunlun?" He shivered, clasping his arms around his knees. "I was told we weren't allowed to come here, that we'd die."

"You're still alive," I assured him gently. "How did you get here?"

"I was traveling with my father. We were attacked, close to the mountain." His lips quivered. "They struck my head. I fainted. And when I woke up, I was in the water."

I wanted to ask more questions, but the boy gripped my arm. "Where is Father? Did you find him, too?"

As I shook my head, the boy trembled, pressing his fists to his eyes. His grief wrenched me, a sharp pain burrowing into my chest. "When I get back, I'll send the soldiers in search of your father," I vowed. "They will find out what happened to him."

"Do you have many soldiers?" His voice was muffled like he was choking back tears.

"An army."

The boy nodded, his breathing steadying. Once he calmed, I helped him to his feet, but then he cried out, folding over. Kneeling before him, I examined his leg. A deep gash split his calf, his blood trickling down in rivulets. I ripped a strip from the hem of my robe, then wrapped it around the wound, knotting it tight. I didn't know what else to do, except I had to stop the bleeding.

A snarl ruptured the stillness, ominous and low. I looked up to find a pair of round, yellow eyes gleaming from between the trees. As the boy gasped, scrambling away, the eyes went dark, a twig snapping—

I hoisted the boy on my back and ran. My feet pounded the ground, winding between the trees. All the while, the beast bounded closer. Cold sweat broke out as I ran as fast as I could, desperately seeking a place to hide. As my legs were about to give way—I spied a large cluster of rocks. Racing to it, I lowered the boy behind them, then unsheathed my sword.

"Hide here," I told him.

Terror beat through me. Was this how Zhangwei felt whenever he'd cautioned me from danger? It wasn't that he thought himself *better*, but he was afraid I'd be hurt—he wanted to protect me, as I did the boy.

The beast prowled forward, the size of a tiger, its yellow eyes slitted with menace. Its fur was a startling white, fangs curled from its jaws, a chain of blue stones encircling its neck. Was this a collar? Was it hounding us for prey, or upon another's command? A low growl—my instincts screaming as I flung my blade up—but the creature leapt past me, over the rocks and lunged at the boy, who threw his arms over his head.

I rushed forward, slashing at the beast, only managing to shear its fur. It ignored me, its attention fixed upon the boy. His wound had reopened, leaking blood across the earth. The thick, metallic scent was entwined with a frail sweetness, like that of cloves. Raising my sword, I swung it at the creature again. As a terrified scream erupted from the boy's throat, the beast spun around to bare its fangs at me—then bounded abruptly into the forest.

"Are you all right?" I asked the boy. I was breathing heavily, my hair in my eyes, still clutching my sword.

"Are *you*?" The boy sounded surprisingly calm.

I glanced at the blood that had soaked into the ground. "Come, we must keep moving. The creature can smell blood—"

"Why are you here?" the boy interjected, his eyes wide. Only then did I see the flecks of gold in his pupils.

"I'm hiding from someone. Like you, I was attacked." I didn't want to lie to him though it might have been easier to.

Shadows played across his face as he shook his head. "I mean, why did you come to Kunlun?"

He sounded different, older somehow. But for some reason, I

felt no fear . . . though the boy was not who he seemed. "I came here to find the Ancient Grandmaster."

"As you have."

The boy's voice was resonant now, like the peal of a gong. The gravity of his manner jarred with the youthfulness of his appearance. Yet in his eyes shone the wisdom of the ages, his black hair lightening until it gleamed silver. A faint glow emanated from his skin, the unmistakable aura of an immortal. As he smiled, a warm breeze darted through the air, winding around me, my clothes drying at once. My aches faded, along with the swelling on my face where the Wuxin captain had struck me. At once, I clasped my hands and bowed to greet him.

"You have shown me kindness, and I welcome you to my home," the Ancient Grandmaster said.

Lanterns flickered to life from the trees above, their light spilling through the branches. A red tiled pathway appeared, flanked by trees. Clusters of jewels glittered between the leaves, the wealth of kings upon a single branch. The path ended in front of a mansion built from bricks of jasper and agate. The wooden entrance was painted with a tree that spread across both panels. As the Ancient Grandmaster approached, the doors slid apart, opening into a wide courtyard. There were no guards or attendants, yet the grounds were immaculately tended. I followed the Ancient Grandmaster into a large pavilion, where we sat down by the marble table. A tall brace of candles flickered to life as a tray of food appeared, gliding toward us at a steady rhythm.

"Who brought this here?" I tried to stem my unease. If I were not in the presence of the Ancient Grandmaster, I would have thought this place haunted.

"House spirits. They keep hidden from my guests. They are remarkably resourceful and obedient, as long as they are rewarded for their services."

As the Ancient Grandmaster gestured to the tray, the dishes

flew to our table: chicken stewed in wild herbs, beans fried with prawns, a whole fish, plump scallops.

I took a little of each dish, suddenly hungry. "What payment do they require?"

"Some spirits are caught between the realms—lost, unable to find their way. They no longer *feel*, their senses gone. Existing in eternity without aim, their earthly ties severed, their memories extinguished. It can be hollow, despite the peace. It is lonely." He opened his palm, a flame leaping within. "Here I give them the illusion of the living, a breath of mortality—whether to taste food, to hear music, or sense the warmth of another."

"They want to be mortal?" I asked, my tone lifting in disbelief.

The Ancient Grandmaster closed his hand, the flame dying out. "There is no greater gift. The happiness of a mortal is incandescent. A shame it is so fleeting—though maybe that is why it's so precious, so perfect, in the moment it exists."

"Our lives are far from perfect. What of loss, heartache, and grief?" I asked.

His gaze was clear and unwavering. "It means you were loved."

A sudden wetness surged into my eyes. I blinked, setting down my chopsticks, the emptiness inside me no longer for food.

"I have made you sad," the Ancient Grandmaster said. "It was not my intent." He gestured toward the porcelain cups, now filled with a clear liquid. "Drink this. It will improve your mood."

I took a sip, startled by the sharp tang. A warmth swept across my tongue and glided down my throat like perfectly brewed tea. The weight in my chest dispersed, my appetite returning in force.

"Now, eat," he said. "You'll have need of it."

I fell upon the food, resisting the urge to grab a chicken leg with my hands, to cram the rice into my mouth. Somehow, I managed to retain my manners, though part of me feared the food might vanish before I ate my fill.

When I was finally sated, I set down my chopsticks. The Ancient Grandmaster picked up the plate of half-eaten fish and placed it on the floor. Yellow eyes gleamed from a dark corner of the garden—just like those of the beast in the forest, but smaller. A creature padded out: a large white cat with a collar of blue stones. It swished its tail as it approached, ignoring us as it headed toward the fish with single-minded purpose. *Was this* cat, the beast?

"It was all an illusion," I said numbly. A trick. A trial. Another immortal game. But it had been real to me, the sweat and blood— the fear that choked me then. I should be angry, yet I could not wholly resent the Ancient Grandmaster. It was his choice how to bestow his favor when so many wanted something from him.

"An illusion implies everything is false." The gold in his eyes was startlingly bright. "But what matters is how you acted when you believed it was real." The Ancient Grandmaster inclined his head. "I have a gift for you, Lady of Tianxia."

He knew who I was; I hadn't told him. Part of me wanted to refuse. As the Ancient Grandmaster's guest, courtesy dictated that *I* should bring *him* a gift. But I would be stupid to refuse anything he wanted to give me. With the Wuxin a breath from Tianxia—we needed all the help we could get.

My chest tightened at the thought of Zhangwei. "The God of War was meant to accompany me to find you, but we were attacked and separated. Do you know where he is?"

Light glinted off the Ancient Grandmaster's silver hair. "He will come."

He spoke with such assurance, my fears faded. "Thank you."

"Do you wish to ask anything else?" he asked.

"I came here because we needed help, Honored Immortal," I began haltingly. I'd imagined it would be Zhangwei asking this, but the task had fallen to me. "The Wuxin sealed the skies. Without the immortals' protection, countless lives in Tianxia are at risk.

I would be grateful if you could send word to Queen Caihong, informing her of this danger, and requesting her aid."

He nodded. "I will ask the spirits to help. They have ways of traveling that are closed to the rest of us."

I hesitated, ashamed to ask for more, but I plunged onward. "Honored Immortal, could you undo this spell on the skies? The Wuxin are planning an attack—"

He raised his hand to stop me. "I do not interfere with such matters. My strength is reserved for the care of the Tree of Everlasting Life. There is nothing more important to me in the world."

Not even our lives? Anger flickered, but I doused it. It was as Zhangwei had warned, but I'd wanted to try. I was not entitled to his aid. I had no right to say one thing was more precious than another, my judgment colored by my own bias.

Before I could reply, the Ancient Grandmaster rose, motioning for me to follow. "Come. This gift I offer you is for you alone."

The trees around us rustled, the air sweet with the scent of shorn grass and a trace of cloves. A narrow stone path appeared between the trees, leading to a cave. It was dark within, yet as we entered, candles flickered to life. The earthen walls were coarse, the rough ground covered with a carpet that was worn and threadbare yet still gleaming with luster. The path curved until it seemed like we were walking in circles.

Scroll paintings hung from the walls, the earliest ones depicting a plant, from a seedling to the unfurling of its first leaves. As it grew to a young tree in its bloom, a round-faced boy tended to it now. When clusters of white flowers bloomed on the tree, it threw its shade over the boy—now a youth. In one painting, leaves fell in bunches as a man raked them into piles. In another, silver gleamed at the man's temples as he pruned the branches—until at last, in the final scroll, the tree bore nothing but silver flowers on its branches. The boy had gone, I noted with a pang, how quickly I'd grown accustomed to seeing him with the tree.

The boy in the painting . . . was he the Ancient Grandmaster? The shape of his face was the same, yet with the silver hair of his age. Had he lived and died by the tree, and if so, what was he now? A tremor ran through me, not of fear but uncertainty.

The sweetness in the air intensified, the scent of flowers giving way to the richness of cloves. The corridor ended in a clearing—grass creeping over the ground, the ceiling opening to the star-studded sky. A tree flowered in the center, crowned with silver-white blossoms. The same tree as in the paintings, except here . . . it was luminous, aglow with an unearthly radiance.

"The Tree of Everlasting Life," the Ancient Grandmaster said solemnly. "It sprouted with the first breath of life in the realms and will remain until the last."

As I stared at it, unsure whether to bow, the flowers of the tree quivered, startlingly bright, like the stars themselves had gathered in its branches.

Come closer, mortal. Step into my shade.

I started looking around. Where had that voice come from?

Mortal, do not doubt the truth before you. The voice sounded amused. *A tree is a living thing, too. Why shouldn't we speak?*

I stepped forward until the shadow of the branches wove across my face like a spider web. Its aura felt familiar, reminding me of the Ancient Grandmaster's. Had the spirits of the boy and tree entwined into one?

Press your hand to my bark.

I followed its command without hesitation this time. The wood was smooth to my touch, a current surging into my fingers, the smell of cloves thickening. Something clinked above. I glanced up to find a single dewdrop glistening like ice—falling from the branch to land upon my brow. A current jolted me, searing deep, rippling across my body like a warm embrace. Peace stole over me, of the priceless kind.

"A blessing from the Tree of Everlasting Life," the Ancient

Grandmaster said gravely. "One of protection, to seal your spirit from harm."

What did this mean? There was so much I wanted to ask, but my mind was growing sluggish. My eyes closed, a deep exhaustion sinking over me as I fell to the ground, wrapped in the unrelenting embrace of slumber.

28

Sunlight glided across my eyelids, stirring me. How long had I slept? A blurred silhouette appeared, gradually splitting into two. The Ancient Grandmaster . . . and Zhangwei. Such relief filled me at the sight of him—here, unharmed. My palms pressed the soft grass to push myself up as I cleared my throat to call out to him—

"I am in your debt." Zhangwei's words startled me as he bowed to the Ancient Grandmaster. "Thank you."

Instinctively, I stilled, pressing my eyes shut.

"Lord Zhangwei, there is no debt. I did not do this for you or Her Majesty; I did it for her." The Ancient Grandmaster's tone was formal.

"Does she know?" Zhangwei asked, his voice tense.

"She knows of the tree's blessing," the Ancient Grandmaster replied.

"Can she stay here, where it's safe?" he asked. "I must try to break the enchantment over the skies; I must return to get aid."

"Both of you can remain here one night, but no more," the Ancient Grandmaster said sternly. "The Wuxin are searching Kunlun. I won't risk them being drawn here to find the Tree of Everlasting Life."

Zhangwei sighed. "I understand. Nevertheless, I am grateful.

What was done—it was what I hoped for."

Something jarred, my gut twisting. It was becoming harder to feign sleep when I wanted to shake Zhangwei, to demand the truth. He had told me we'd be safe here, that the Ancient Grandmaster could help us send word to Queen Caihong. Were we here for another reason—one he'd chosen to keep from me? For this "blessing," whatever it was? His secrets teetered on the brink of lies.

I kept my breathing steady, my eyes closed to maintain the pretense. It grated, hearing them speak of me this way, but I needed to learn more.

A brief pause. "Ancient Grandmaster, could you remove it?" Zhangwei asked. "It isn't part of her."

My heart plunged, my mind clouding with suspicion. Zhangwei meant the Divine Pearl Lotus—what else could it be? Was this another scheme to seize it from me? Part of me flinched from this thought. After everything we'd been through, he couldn't be this devious, nor was I so stupid to be tricked by more lies. I should believe better of him and myself. But what if he no longer trusted that I'd keep my word? After all, he'd asked me twice to give him the lotus, and I'd refused.

"That is her decision." The Ancient Grandmaster spoke before my patience snapped, before I could demand an answer. "Neither you nor I, nor anyone in the realms, can decide this for her."

"It is what's best for her," Zhangwei said fiercely. "If there's a price, I will pay it."

An eerie whistling glided through the clearing, the air seeming to constrict as I found myself holding my breath.

"My honor has no price."

A stern rebuke from the Ancient Grandmaster, a taut silence settling between him and the God of War.

Some of my tension uncoiled, even as my mind worked frantically. What was Zhangwei planning? He claimed to be an ally, yet he had not shared this part of his scheme. How dare he decide what was "best" for me? How dare he keep me in the dark, a pawn to his whim?

No more lies and secrets, I'd demanded of him. As least he'd been honest when he'd replied: *No more lies.*

There was a bitter taste in my mouth. After how he'd defended us against the Wuxin, our kiss by the river, everything he'd said and done since—he'd almost made me believe in him again. If all this had been false, the Wuxin were more honorable than him.

Footsteps tread closer. Zhangwei was crouching down beside me, my senses attuned to him though my eyes were still closed. As he lifted me in his arms, I resisted the urge to push him away. He carried me with great care through the winding corridor, my body stiffening whenever it jolted against his.

I hated this uncertainty, just when I'd thought we could finally trust each other. And I hated that I didn't know what to do: whether to confront him or to conceal what I'd heard.

It was a long way back to the Ancient Grandmaster's home, or at least it felt that way. Once, Zhangwei stumbled, his hold tightening protectively around me. I stirred, intending to end the farce—but the Ancient Grandmaster's voice rang out.

"You may both share the chamber in this courtyard."

No.

"Ancient Grandmaster, separate rooms would be preferred. Otherwise, I will remain outside," Zhangwei said without hesitation.

My jaw clenched, my hands curling. I didn't want to share a room with him—but irrationally now, I was annoyed that he didn't want that either.

"As you wish, Lord Zhangwei." The Ancient Grandmaster sounded amused. "Take the chamber beside hers."

Zhangwei carried me into a room, the lamps flickering to life as we entered. Without warning, he dropped me unceremoniously upon a bed, my skirt tangled between my legs.

I sat up, glaring at him. "How dare you."

Zhangwei leaned against the bed frame. "If you wanted to be carried, you could have just asked."

"I want nothing less," I hissed, grasping at my pride—though it defied what I'd just done. "I don't want you to touch me."

His eyelids lowered, a corner of his mouth curving. "Shall we put that to the test?"

"No." I meant it. I wanted him, but every time I drew too close, I ended up burned. Fire was his Talent, after all.

I looked away from him, examining the room. It was simply furnished, the bed crafted of light-colored wood, the coverings softer than any I'd lain on. A fresh set of robes was folded and left on the bamboo table, though the shelves were bare.

He frowned as he studied me. "Were you hurt getting here?"

Such concern . . . was it real? I shook my head. "What about you? How did you find me? The last I saw was you fighting the Wuxin."

His voice thickened with suppressed fury. "Their plan was to separate us, to capture you."

"Do they know about the lotus?" I asked.

"It's likely," he replied tersely. "After the fight, I looked for you in the pavilion—all around the lake. You had gone, no trace of you left. Fortunately, I knew you weren't with the Wuxin because they'd been looking for you, too, searching the lake—at least until I found them."

As his eyes glittered dangerously, I asked, "Did you kill them?"

"Those who hurt you, are my enemies, too." The darkness of his tone sent a chill through me. "Some escaped, as did their captain—the one I most wanted." He added, "I knew you could swim, that you'd jumped into the lake, though I was worried you couldn't find your way here."

"I had little choice; they cornered me in the pavilion." Quickly, I told him about the boy, the beast who'd attacked us, the Ancient Grandmaster's disguise.

"I heard the Ancient Grandmaster tested the few mortals who reached his shores," he said.

"What of those who failed?" I asked.

"No one knows."

My throat tightened. Even though the Ancient Grandmaster had been kind to me, there was another side to him—the ruthless deity alongside the benevolent, childlike god. Yet mortals were not objects to be judged; we were more than a single choice. We deserved to be weighed for the sum of our deeds, rather than one plucked from a moment of urgency. Immortals could never understand the despair the threat of death roused in us, how much we wanted to live, to delay the inevitable end. To ourselves, we were everything—and yet our inevitable fate was to become nothing.

"Where do we go now?" I asked, breaking the silence.

"We can't stay," he told me. "The Ancient Grandmaster won't risk the Wuxin following our trail here. But he will send word to Queen Caihong. Hopefully she'll find a way to break the spell over the skies. We just need to keep hidden a little while longer."

"What of Tianxia?"

"The barrier I crafted is undisturbed." His gaze was penetrating. "I remember all my promises to you. Just as I hope you remember yours to me."

A reminder of what I owed him. I nodded slowly. There was a new urgency to return what I had taken if I could, to be free of these powerful beings and their deadly games. *Soon,* I told myself. Then I'd never see him again—the thought a stone in my chest.

He was staring at my robe, streaked with blood from where he'd carried me. Only then did I notice the gash across his palm, though the wound on his shoulder appeared healed. Plucking a handkerchief from the pile of garments on the table, I took his hand and wrapped the silk around the cut. He did not pull away, his large hand cradled between both of mine. As I bound his wound, blood seeped through the cloth.

"Is this what the mortals do?" he asked.

"We don't have your advantages." I released his hand, suddenly feeling foolish. "You could have just healed yourself.

"I like this more." A small smile played on his lips as he inspected my clumsy bandage. "Why did you do this for me?"

I didn't answer; maybe I didn't know why. "I don't like to see you bleed," I said at last.

He was studying me; did he sense a difference in my manner? Trust was not easily yielded, and even harder to restore. But I didn't want to just question him in my mind, to imagine the worst—I wanted to know, and for him to tell me.

"I heard you speaking with the Ancient Grandmaster," I began. "I heard what you asked. Was it about the Divine Pearl Lotus?"

He shook his head. "It's not what you think."

"Then tell me. Don't give me a reason to doubt," I told him flatly.

The corners of his mouth tightened like he was suppressing his words, or choosing them carefully. "I can't."

"Why?" I demanded. "Because you think I won't understand? Or because you're afraid I won't agree? Either way, how can I trust you?"

He took my hands, holding them between his . . . and I was so weak, I didn't pull away. "I swear on my life, you can trust me with yours—I will guard it better than my own. I will keep all my promises to you: those from yesterday, today, and those to come. One day, I will tell you anything you wish. But the time is not now."

He spoke quietly, sincerely, yet these words left me cold. I wanted to trust him; I wanted what we had to be real, but I couldn't let my desires color the truth. Somehow, I had to uncover what lay in his heart. And if I was wrong this time, if he betrayed me—he would learn that I could be every bit as heartless as him. I'd walk away and never look back, even if it broke my heart.

Even if it killed him.

29

The next morning, the mansion was deserted, the Ancient Grandmaster nowhere in sight.

"How do we thank him or bid him farewell?" I asked.

"When you have lived as long as the Ancient Grandmaster, you grow weary of farewells," Zhangwei replied.

We walked a long way through a bamboo forest, the leaves rustling with the wind. I was glad for the clothes left in my chamber last night: a blue silk embroidered with silver leaves on the hem and an outer robe in a darker shade. The climate here seemed colder than back home. Once I turned to find the trees swaying in our wake, the stalks weaving into each other until all trace of our path had gone. Even if I tried to return, I wouldn't know where to begin.

The path sloped down, a steep descent. I had to hold on to the bamboo to avoid slipping as we made our way. Ahead, a rock wall loomed, covered in moss. As Zhangwei placed his palm upon it, the stone seemed to soften, undulating like churned mud.

"We'll have to go through this."

"I prefer the way we came," I said faintly.

"That way is gone now," he told me, extending his hand.

I gripped it, holding my breath, trying not to think of what would happen should the stone solidify once more, entombing us alive. As we stepped into the rock, it felt slick over my skin, cool and heavy. Yet as we emerged on the other side, no trace was left on us, not even a fleck of dust. Sunlight fell upon my face as I dragged in a long breath. Behind us, the stone surface rippled, then hardened once more. It seemed impossible that we'd come through here.

Kunlun Mountain towered behind us, like we'd walked the length of a dragon this morning—from its head, along its spine, to emerge at the tail.

"The Ancient Grandmaster warned that the Wuxin are searching Kunlun," Zhangwei said. "We must get away from here, as far as we can—until Queen Caihong sends reinforcements."

Until we reach the wall. No matter how far we ran, we were still trapped.

"What if the Wuxin manage to open the gateway all the way through?" It was my worst nightmare, the one that preyed on me since I'd seen them in my home.

"It still holds; we have time yet." His face darkened. "Though their actions reek of urgency."

An unwelcome thought unfolded in my mind; my insides clenched with unease. "You said the gateway was weakened because the Divine Pearl Lotus was harvested. What if this is why they're seeking it? What if they've found a way to hasten the gateway opening?"

"Then you must stay out of their reach." He spoke gravely, without pause, like he'd considered this too.

We returned to where we'd left our horses. While they'd untied themselves, they had not left and were munching on a patch of grass. They seemed pleased to see us, trotting over without being urged. The stallion nuzzled Zhangwei, who stroked his mane. He had a way with animals, maybe because they didn't view him with the innate fear we did—maybe because to them, he was not the God of War.

Zhangwei and I rode along dirt-crusted paths, through grassy meadows and fields of wildflowers, heading away from Kunlun. As the sun sank lower, setting the skies afire, the hills threw their long shadows over us. Our pace slowed to a canter as we traveled along a winding river, aglitter in the dwindling light. Feathery reeds twined with blades of grass, swaying in the wind like dancers. We halted by a shady grove and dismounted, leading our horses to the river, where we tied them to a tree.

As the sky darkened to indigo, the air cooled, welcome after the heat of day. The fire we built crackled softly, the flames dancing low as they bent to Zhangwei's will. Magic was useful for concealing our trail. Glistening fish he'd caught earlier were speared onto a long stick and set over the fire. I sat on a rock watching him turn them over, a mouthwatering aroma lacing the air.

"How did you learn to fish?" I asked.

He grinned as his gaze swung to me. "I never did."

"Did you . . . *cheat?*"

"It was just a trace. A nudge," he protested. "How is it cheating when no one was wronged?"

"Just the fish," I remarked pointedly. "You should have bested it in a fair fight."

"If the fish had gotten the better of me, we would have no dinner," he replied. "But if your sensibilities are offended, I can always eat your share."

I scowled, my stomach rumbling in protest. Leaning back against the grass, I lifted my face to the sky. Even when clouded over, the boundless horizons infused me with wonder. Such freedom, if only we would reach for it. How long had I trapped myself in my palace, in the court . . . in my mind? Some walls were built by others, while others were of our own making. The hardest to escape were those we chose to remain behind of our own will.

Rising to my feet, I plucked several large leaves from a tree, then rinsed them in the stream. Once the fish were cooked, Zhangwei dropped them onto the leaves. I lifted one with my fingers—

still hot—and bit into it, tender flakes falling onto my tongue. Despite the lack of seasoning, it was delicious, the flesh tender and sweet. We ate in silence, picking over the fish until all that remained was a pile of bones.

Zhangwei's expression was unreadable as he rested an elbow on his raised knee. What we were doing seemed utterly mundane, sitting on the ground with the sky as our roof. Yet how full life seemed, how content my heart, as long as I reined in my wandering mind. He bent to pluck a flower, then leaned over to tuck it behind my ear, his eyes searching mine. I should have swatted his hand away, tossed the flower into the fire. Yet something in his gaze held mine fast, my heart quickening against my will.

"Have you decided?" he asked.

"What do you mean?"

"Whether you will trust me," he remarked. "Since last night, you've drawn away again."

I yanked out a blade of grass, twisting it around my finger. "Gods can lie as easily as mortals." It was what I'd told him once; it still held true. Yet now, even as my mind tried to pull me from him, my heart edged closer. "I want to trust you . . . I did. But after yesterday, I don't know what to think."

"Then you never really trusted me; real trust is not so easily shaken. Or perhaps you were just looking for an excuse to run away." His tone was unflinching, his mouth set into a hard line. "Stop being afraid. Stop running from me."

"Then give me a reason to stay."

The words slipped from me, my chest clenching. If he were not the God of War who needed the lotus from me, I would have trusted him long before—the moment he drew his sword to defend my people. I looked up at him, trying to gather the courage to speak, to give him the honesty that I craved from him. Lies were easier than the truth; they protected us, while the truth reached to where it hurt the most . . . to where there was the most to lose.

"I've been trying. There's nothing I want more," he said.

"But no matter what you say or do, no matter my feelings— the simple truth is that you *need* me to love you." My hand covered my scar. "You need this to live."

As he reached for me, I drew back—afraid that if he touched me, my resolve would fall apart. I needed more from him than these tentative declarations. "We already have an agreement. Don't play with my heart; I can't bear it."

"I've told you before, I'm done playing games." His voice roughened with emotion. "This is real for me; it's always been real."

"If I didn't have the lotus, would it be different?" I demanded.

"No," he said at once, light flaring in his eyes. "Because I'll always need you to live."

It was like I was walking into a storm, lifting my face to the wind and rain that beat down relentlessly. Reckless yet liberating, to embrace the intensity of the moment—to not care, hide, or run. I was tired of fighting, of struggling to do what was right. Right now, I wasn't thinking of the danger that lurked, of our enemies, or what the God of War needed from me. Just for tonight, I would be selfish, surrendering to my own desires.

Let the rain fall. The sun would rise tomorrow in its luminous, merciless clarity.

I shifted toward him, tilting my head to his. As my lips parted, his eyes flicked toward them.

"Will you stay?" he asked, his fingers grazing my cheek.

"I'm done running away."

Something glinted in his gaze, something unleashed. As he clasped my shoulders, drawing me closer—I leaned forward . . . and kissed him. A current sparked within me, stirring an elusive, glittering heat that reached into a part of me I never knew existed. My pride was forgotten, my caution extinguished. I pressed closer as he held me to him, his kiss deepening as my mouth parted beneath his, his breath hot against my tongue. As one of his hands slid down my back, the other buried into my hair, I wrapped my arms around his neck. His skin was as soft as silk, as cool as moonlight—a balm to the heat searing my body, the ache that swelled from deep within. He lowered me to the ground, hard against my back, yet I was numbed to all else but these awakening sensations. My robe was loosened then pulled apart, slipping over my shoulder, his lips moving along the curve of my neck. I arched with pleasure, a tightness coiled inside me, impatient to be released.

But even in this moment, my mind would not be wholly silenced. Desire was not enough; an immortal could never love me the way I wanted. I deserved more than what he offered, to be more than a brief interlude in his life, for us to belong together in every way.

My heart was pounding as I made myself push him away. He stilled, a tremor running through him as he lifted himself from me. My traitorous body protested as I turned from him, my shaking hands taking far too long to straighten my robe. How I burned with shame from what we'd done . . . with wanting to continue.

"This isn't right." I was thinking of the impossibility of our situation.

"Is it your betrothed?" he replied without a flicker of remorse. As I cursed myself for forgetting the farce of my engagement, he added in a somber tone, "I wouldn't do this if you loved him, but you don't—and he doesn't love you as you deserve."

Could you? The question hovered, but all I said was, "Chengyin is a good match for me."

"Don't marry him." He spoke with such emotion, it pierced the barrier around my heart.

"If not him, it would be another. Maybe someone from the court, or I'd have to hold a tournament to find someone to marry." I added the last in an attempt to lighten the mood.

A grave mistake.

"A *tournament?*" He spat the word. "Don't marry your First Advisor, don't marry any of them," he said wrathfully, light blazing from his eyes.

"Who should I marry then?" This was as close as I would go. If he didn't declare himself now, he never would.

Silence fell over us, my spirit sinking with each moment. But I would never show him my disappointment, or how this hurt.

"I can't ask you now," he said in a low voice. "But I promise you—"

"Don't say it." I swung to him, my hands clenched. "You demand that I keep myself free, yet won't promise yourself. You want everything on your own terms. But I want more than what you offer—what you have to give."

He opened his mouth, then closed it, like he was struggling with himself. More secrets? Would there ever be an end to them with him? But then he stiffened abruptly, his body shuddering.

"What's wrong?" But I already knew.

"The symptoms are worsening. It's becoming harder to control them, away from my realm."

He sounded breathless, like it was an effort to speak. My anger vanished as I took his hand, trying not to flinch at the ice of his skin. I reached for the lotus within, to lend him the strength as I'd done before—but he shook his head.

"It won't work this time; the damage is too far gone."

He stood, weaving on his feet. Blood trickled from the corner of his mouth, which he swiftly wiped away as though unwilling to let me see it. I'd seen him weakened before . . . but not like this.

The air shimmered around us, crowded with flecks of light that streaked from him—a beacon to those hunting us. "I can't control my magic. You must go. The Wuxin will sense this; they'll come soon." His words emerged unevenly, his body pulled taut as he stalked to the horses, then untied mine and thrust its reins at me. "Find someplace safe to hide, far from here. Queen Caihong will send aid once the skies are unsealed. Don't be afraid of her. Tell her what happened . . . she will protect you."

I shook my head. Not just because I didn't trust her but because I didn't want to leave him. The halting way he spoke frightened me, as did the wildness in his gaze—like his restraint was about to snap. "What about you?".

"I will keep the Wuxin away as long as I can."

"No!" My vehemence startled us both. "I'll not leave you defenseless and alone—"

My voice cut off as he raised a finger to my lips. The hairs lifted along my arms and the back of my neck, my skin prickling with familiar dread.

The Wuxin were near.

30

"We must go." I grabbed Zhangwei's arm, tugging at him, but he pulled my hand away gently.

"They are too close; I'll draw them to me." His magic continued to spill forth in a glittering stream, as he dipped his head to mine. "You have to go now. Think of Tianxia. If they find you, if they open the gateway—your people will be the first to fall."

My chest squeezed like a fist was wrapped around it. He was ruthless to make this argument, the only thing that could make me leave him. As Zhangwei drew his sword, a tremor ran through his hand that was abruptly stilled. How hard he fought to hide these symptoms; how long had he been suffering? How could he keep up this pretense against a pitiless foe?

Taking my silence as acceptance, Zhangwei handed the reins of my horse to me. "Head south; I'll lead them further up north. Your soldiers shouldn't be far—those your First Advisor sent—find them if you can." He looked away like he didn't want to see me leave. "I don't want you to be alone."

Something splintered in my heart. He was going to sacrifice himself . . . he was going to die.

"Not today," I whispered.

His brow creased. "What do you mean?"

My gaze slid to his, my emotions raging through me. "You will not die today."

I pulled out my dagger, the scar throbbing at my chest, a heat building within as though it sensed what I was about to do—like it was craving this, too. I silenced the last whispers of doubt in my mind, of unfulfilled promises and unpaid debts. I was done weighing the stakes; I would give him what he wanted of me.

It was the only way we'd all have a chance, I reasoned with myself. Right now, the God of War was the only one who could protect Tianxia. With the Divine Pearl Lotus, he could hold the Wuxin back until the skies were opened once more. But beyond the safety of my kingdom, beyond any debt or obligation—the simple, shattering truth was, I *wanted* him to live.

I clutched the hilt of my dagger, pressing its tip against my chest. He'd spoken once of opening a connection with it. This time, no token was needed because it was me wielding the blade. This time, it would work; the Divine Pearl Lotus would be his . . . gifted of a willing heart.

"Wait." His hand closed around mine, halting me. "Are you sure?"

How different from the first time, when he'd sought to seize it from me. Back then, if he'd succeeded, I would have cursed him and hated him forever. Had he changed? Had I? Maybe nothing remained the same, even in the realm of immortals.

"I want this," I said clearly.

His gaze locked mine, not letting go. "Do you know what could happen? You won't die, but you won't be as strong as you are now—"

A sliver of cold speared me, but I'd known this already. A price I would gladly pay to save us both. "I know."

"*Why* are you doing this?" He spoke intently, his voice ringed with a clear resonance.

I thought of the way his face filled my mind, how his words slid into my heart, of the heat he stirred so effortlessly inside me . . . and how I yearned for him, even when I should hate.

"Because I'm a fool."

His eyes blazed like fire and moonlight. "Then I am one, too, since the day we met."

I caught his hand with my other, wrapping his fingers across the hilt, pressing down until the dagger pierced my chest. A sharp sting, blood trickling from the wound.

Silence thickened, my breathing growing harsher. It wasn't easy to surrender; fear still gripped me, for myself, my kingdom. "Remember your promise," I told him fiercely.

His other hand touched my cheek, tilting my face to his. "I remember *all* my promises to you."

"Then take it from me. I . . . don't know what to do."

"Say it," he whispered, leaning closer until his breath curled into my ear. "Mean it."

"I give this to you of a willing heart." My chest ached, something struggling inside—then giving way like part of me was coming undone, a bond unmade. The Divine Pearl Lotus was detaching itself from me because I'd yielded it. Because I loved him . . . even if he didn't love me back. Even if he never knew it.

Light flared along the dagger, coursing over the hilt—the glittering flecks of the lotus scattering like starlight, arching away from me, toward him. The warmth in my chest subsided, leaving a hollow that gaped a little wider with each breath. My teeth sank into my tongue, the salt of blood spilling into my mouth. It was like the strength had fled my limbs as I slumped, fighting to keep standing, the ache swelling across my body.

Zhangwei's arm swept across my waist to steady me, our hands clasped around the dagger that was still pressed to my chest. His touch was warmer now, no longer glazed with the chill that had become so familiar to me. I smiled, relief surging, though I was afraid to move, to do anything that might break the spell.

The god's eyes closed, such radiance gliding over him—as though he was bathed in that golden hour of sunlight that gilds the mundane with rare beauty. Something stirred within me, an intimate awareness of our joined hands, a fleeting glimpse into him like a window thrown open—the scorching intensity of his emotions, the fire and passion that raged through him unabated. Just as quickly, this awareness closed. A heat steadily built, his touch warming me as I'd once warmed him, forging something new between us: fragile and precious, chaotic and untamed. We stood a foot apart, yet I'd never felt closer to another . . . like we were one.

It was done; he was safe. I closed my eyes briefly, the tumult inside me calming. There was a void within where the Divine Pearl Lotus had once pulsed. How I would miss it. Yet a profound peace now swept me high, the weightlessness of a burden relieved. It had worked; he would be safe. The symptoms I'd suffered from the waters of death didn't return, though I felt drained—an echo of that familiar heaviness in my limbs, the one that had plagued me in my childhood, but neither as deep nor as consuming as before. Yet now if I ran from the Wuxin . . . they would catch me.

As I pulled the dagger out, my blood trailed from its tip, sliding down to fall into the earth. Zhangwei collapsed to the ground, eyes wide, his body unmoving. Did he feel as I had when I'd first consumed the lotus, unable to move or speak as it bonded with me? I prayed this would pass soon, that the toll on an immortal body would be easier than on a mortal's—it was far too dangerous here. Though his magic no longer spilled free, his aura blazed, the force of his presence strengthening.

I bent, arranging his limbs into a more comfortable position. "How do you feel?"

He didn't reply, though his eyes were fixed upon me, startlingly bright. His mouth twitched like he was trying to tell me something.

I squeezed his hand. "This won't last long; you'll be well

soon."

The wind was glazed with a bitter chill, frost blooming across the ground like mold. My instincts recoiled, dread sinking over me.

They were *here*.

Terror spiked, sharp and cold. If they found Zhangwei, helpless, they'd kill him; they'd seize the lotus. I grabbed him under his arms, struggling beneath his weight. Panic yielded a burst of strength as I dragged him a short way to a thick grove of bushes—my breathing ragged with fear.

"Don't make a sound. I'll lead them away." The words clogged my throat. He was always telling me to run, and now I was protecting *him*.

His eyes widened, the veins in his arm bulging with the force of his strain. He didn't want me to go. I placed my hand over his, relieved at its warmth. "You can't move until the lotus has merged with you. Don't fight it, don't let this all be for nothing." I searched his face, wanting to remember every feature. "If I stay, we're both dead anyway."

I pushed myself to my feet, forcing myself to leave. I wasn't trying to be a hero; I just wanted to give us a chance, to lead the Wuxin away until he recovered. They would follow my trail, believing *I* had the power they sought. Once they learned I didn't, I'd pay a heavy price—but Zhangwei would come for me then. I only hoped it wouldn't take too long for him to recover.

I sprinted along the river, away from him, the wind tearing through my hair. The Wuxin were close, but I didn't let myself turn, afraid to waste a single moment. I was already tiring, my chest clenched tight. Yanking off my outer robe, I thrust a fistful of stones into its folds, then hurled the bundle into the river. Silk arced through the air, plunging into the waters with a splash, scattering the reflected moonlight. A decoy to draw my pursuers away.

Footsteps padded; branches creaked. Several shadowy forms flew forth, taking physical form as they neared the river. As they searched the waters, some diving into the depths, I backed away quietly, only turning to flee once I was out of sight.

I ran in a winding path, hoping to confuse anyone on my trail. Already my pace was slowing, my sword a burden as I fought the exhaustion creeping over me. If only Zhangwei were here, or my soldiers. They might be close, as he'd said . . . and if so, I had to warn them of the Wuxin.

Deeper in the forest I stopped to catch my breath, leaning against a tree as I fought the urge to retch. My mind urged me onward. In the dark, the trees seemed to close tighter around me, ominous and oppressive.

"Liyen!" It was Chengyin's voice. He dashed from the trees ahead, his eyes going wide at the sight of me. His dark-red robe was torn and stained, like he'd come in a rush. "You're safe. I was so worried."

I could have wept with relief, even as my pulse stuttered unevenly. "What are you doing here, Chengyin? Weren't you meant to stay at court? Is there trouble at home?" I kept my voice hushed as I glanced around. "The Wuxin are chasing me."

His expression turned grim as he whispered, "Our scouts reported more of them were sighted around Kunlun, searching for something."

"*Someone*," I corrected him after a pause.

"I suspected as much, which was why I sent more soldiers here and joined them myself." He hesitated. "I hope you're not angry. I didn't want to disobey your order, but I was concerned about you."

I shook my head, comforted by his presence. "Who is heading the court now?"

He grinned. "Minister Hu is appointed the acting First Advisor, leaving Minister Guo apoplectic with rage. He took to his bed in protest, and let's hope he remains there."

I suppressed a laugh. "Thank you for looking out for me, my friend."

"Always," he said somberly, his eyes bright. "If you die, who will appoint me as the Minister of Revelry?" He bent to study my face. "Are you well? You look pale."

"I'm fine," I assured him, though my nerves were still frayed. "Where are the soldiers?"

He jerked his head eastward. "They've made camp over there, but I came this way because I heard something. You made enough noise to wake an elephant." His mouth pursed as he asked, "Where is the God of War? Why isn't he with you?"

Chengyin and I had few secrets from each other. Yet what had passed between Zhangwei and me felt private, for us alone. And I dared not tell him that the god was vulnerable now, for who knew who was listening in the dark?

"We were separated. When the Wuxin came, I ran," I said.

A clash broke out from behind us, the night illuminated by shafts of fire. The familiar rush of Zhangwei's magic surged through the air—the force of his might far stronger, at last unhindered by the poison.

"Zhangwei is near." I grinned, trying to figure out where he was, wanting to rush to him. "We must find the soldiers and join him. We'll be safe now."

"Zhangwei?" Chengyin repeated, his eyes pinched together. "You're on familiar terms with the God of War."

"We've been through a lot. Let's find him first," I suggested. "He might need help."

Chengyin's lip curled. "It's unlikely the God of War will need any mortal's aid."

"Mortal?" I repeated slowly, the disdain in his tone jarring me . . . a hateful suspicion unfurling in my mind.

"Come, I'll take you to our soldiers first." He extended his hand to me. As his sleeve slid back, I caught sight of the scar on the underside of his wrist—the one I'd given him when we were children. It had never wholly faded, still a faint purplish red like it was newly inflicted.

I nodded at the scar, furrowing my brow. "Does it still hurt? You should be more careful when training with the soldiers."

Just the barest pause as he smiled. "I will. It won't happen again."

The most powerful Wuxin can even steal another's form.

This was *not* Chengyin. The scar was one *I'd* given him, years ago when we'd broken his mother's vase—and he'd never let me hear the end of it.

But I swallowed my terror, stamping it down, forcing my lips into a rictus of a smile. My only chance lay in being the better liar. "Show me the way. I'll follow you; I can't walk as fast."

As the imposter stalked ahead, I slowed my steps to fall behind, my hand closing around the hilt of my sword. I had one chance; I mustn't falter, recalling all Zhangwei had taught me. Drawing my blade, I raised it to strike—but he spun around, a flash of green light erupting from his hand. I ducked, then drove my sword at his chest. He swung back swiftly—my blade piercing his shoulder instead, a fierce satisfaction surging through me. The Wuxin hissed in fury, blood oozing from the wound. How vicious he looked, eyes slitted with malevolence.

"Try that again and I'll bring you back in pieces," he snarled.

"You need me alive, or you'd have killed me already," I shot back, caging my terror. If I gave up now, I'd stop fighting.

As I lifted my sword again—a whip appeared in his hand, seething with greenish light. He flung it toward me, wrapping around the length of my arm—the pain almost blinding, worse than the immortal queen's punishment. I gasped as my blade fell from my hand.

He was studying it, his eyes alight. "Your weapon is the companion blade to the God of War's. How did you get it?"

Impossible. I froze, staring at him blankly, dazed by this revelation. Why would Zhangwei entrust me with this sword? Was it because I had the lotus?

"I'll tell you nothing," I said with feeling.

"It doesn't matter." He picked up the sword—but as his fingers touched the black jade hilt, it glowed with an unearthly light. An unseen force shoved him back, red welts forming across his fingers. The sword shimmered, then abruptly disappeared. I hoped Zhangwei sensed this, that he was near.

The imposter was nursing his hand, still searching for the sword. I scrambled away—but he lunged at me, wrapping his hand around my throat. In the same move, he brought me to the ground, pinning me down effortlessly like I was a doll in his grasp. As I struggled, the pins fell from my hair, the coils unraveling down my back.

"Liyen!" Zhangwei's voice called out, ringing with urgency and fear.

Hope flared, even as despair mounted. He was close, yet I was trapped. I kicked wildly at the Wuxin, gathering my strength as I screamed—a piercing cry, the sole defense left to me. Zhangwei would hear it; he would come. My scream was cut off as the Wuxin's fingers squeezed my neck tighter, choking me. I was lightheaded, dizzy, yet his grip was relentless, his nails digging into my throat. His eyes shone, ringed with copper. How could I have ever thought he was Chengyin? I clawed at him, clinging to consciousness, but as his hands clenched harder, I was lost—the night rising up to drown me.

PART
THREE

31

I lay on a hard surface, my body numb, my head pounding. As I inhaled, an unfamiliar scent wafted into my nose of cedar-wood and earth. My neck was tender where the imposter had throttled me; when I swallowed, it hurt. Pain throbbed along my arm where his whip had struck, the welts still raw.

I opened my eyes, blinking against the sudden brightness. Sunlight fell in amber shafts through the window. A quick glance assured me that my garments were intact, the ones I'd worn yesterday. Yet the sword from Zhangwei was gone, vanished when the imposter had tried to take it.

The thin mattress beneath me was covered with a rough sheet, stained in places. Revolted, I scrambled up, fighting a wave of panic at the sight of my surroundings: the closed door, gray stone walls, a solitary window fenced with bars that gleamed with a strange brightness. I tried the door first, wrenching it—but it was locked as expected. Climbing onto the chair, I peered through the window. The sky beyond blazed with rose and vermilion like dawn and dusk entwined. It was beautiful, if only terror did not spear me at the sight.

I was no longer in my world.

Though I knew it was futile, I reached toward the window and yanked at the bars. A humming ripped through the air, the metal scorching my hands. I cried out, staring at the cuts crisscrossing my palms. How they seared, like I had scraped them against a bed of nails.

Footsteps sounded from outside. Something clinked, a lock unlatching as the door swung open. A man strode into the cell, his purple brocade robe trimmed with white fur. It was Chengyin—the false one. This monster had stolen my friend's body. My hands balled into fists. Anger was good; it helped me forget my fear and misery, the very thing these creatures thrived on.

When I lunged at him, he shoved me aside with brutal force, his hand as cold as ice. I staggered back, fighting the tears that threatened.

He straightened his robe, his expression irate. "You're not in your kingdom anymore. Mind your manners, if you care for you and your friend's safety."

"Where is Chengyin? Is he safe? Who are you?" I was struggling to steady myself.

His mouth curved though his eyes remained flat, ringed with that strange coppery glint. "Your betrothed is well—for now."

Betrothed? I kept my face blank, recalling how Chengyin had defended me in the palace. Had Captain Rao or Miss Lin reported this? By trying to help me, he'd ended up a target. I didn't correct the imposter, afraid to expose Chengyin to greater danger.

"How did you know so much about us?" The way he'd acted, the things he'd said back in the forest—I'd almost believed his pretense.

"His memories are useful, yielding valuable information, though he's grown better at concealing them. I was remiss to over-look the scar." He sneered, my insides tightening at the malice on my friend's face.

If you know someone, you can easily discern the true from false—as long as you're looking.

Zhangwei had been right. I'd been careless, seeing only what I wanted to, missing the signs. A mistake I was paying for.

"It's fortunate for him that you showed up. I was getting bored and tempted to dispose of the host."

My temper snapped. "You monster," I raged. "Hurt him, and I'll kill you."

"His well-being is in your hands; it depends on your behavior. When I'm angered, I tend to take it out on those closest to me." He tapped his shoulder where I'd stabbed him. "Try what you did before, and I'll carve him into pieces—the parts of him I don't need."

He raised his hand, nails sharpening to talons, then plunged them into his own arm, raking deep crevices. Skin slit, blood oozing forth. "Your beloved can feel this." Lines creased his forehead, then smoothed away abruptly. Could *he* feel it, too? "You have a sharp tongue. Guard it better, or he will suffer each time you defy me."

"Stop!" I cried, fighting my queasiness. "Please . . . just stop." How I *loathed* him, his delight in toying with us, the fact we were at his mercy.

He dropped his hand, ignoring the blood that trickled down his arm. "Next time, I'll slice his vein."

I shook my head frantically. "Let me speak to him."

"Try asking nicely," he suggested.

"Please," I said through gritted teeth.

"No." A laugh.

I drew a shaking breath. I wouldn't beg; it would make no difference. Glancing outside at the reddish skies, I asked, "Is this the Netherworld?"

He inclined his head. "You are the first mortal to have the honor of coming here."

And even though I'd already known, his confirmation came as a blow. I sat back down on the mattress, pressing my hands to my head, my palms stinging from the cuts. But I hid my discomfort, to conceal my attempt to escape.

"You have me trapped. Why don't you let Chengyin go?"

He rubbed the birthmark on his face. "I don't like this form, these flaws, but I have need of him yet. Don't forget, I protect him while I have use of him—while *you* are of use to *me*." He yawned as though bored. "It was not easy to secure this host. It took threats against his mother's life before he succumbed."

I bit back the curse that leapt to my tongue. "Where is Aunt Shou?"

"Why don't you stop worrying about everyone else and look to yourself? Do you know why we want you?"

The Divine Pearl Lotus? My gut hollowed, my pulse racing unsteadily. They didn't know I'd surrendered it to Zhangwei. My heart ached as I recalled how he'd called my name, searching for me even after he'd gotten what he wanted. Could he find me here? Regardless, I had to keep up the pretense, afraid of what they'd do to Chengyin and me once they learned the truth.

"Why don't you tell me?" I said, drawing him out.

"Not yet. You'll find out soon enough." He examined the chamber, wrinkling his nose. "The Lady of Tianxia should not suffer the indignity of such quarters. If you promise to behave, you will be treated as a guest."

Unease slithered over me. I didn't like accepting favors from those I did not trust, those who threatened and coerced to get their way. "What does 'good behavior' entail?"

"Act as your elders brought you up, treating your host with courtesy." His smile was viperous. "Remember this, and we'll get along."

A "guest" would have more freedom, while I'd gain nothing by being confined. I couldn't afford to anger him; I had to swallow my pride, hard though it was.

As I nodded in agreement, he bowed in a mockery of gallantry. "Follow me, my lady."

I gritted my teeth as I smiled. Still, it was a relief to leave the place, even as I dreaded what lay beyond. I let the Wuxin walk ahead of me, taking the opportunity to study my surroundings. He strode down a flight of stairs and entered a wide hall, its walls of gray quartz speckled with white. A row of latticed windows stretched along the side, offering a glimpse of the world beyond. I darted to an open one, gripping the frame as I looked out. A mountain loomed ahead, its jagged white peak tucked into a ring of clouds, a river coiled like a serpent around its onyx-like base. The Wangchuan River. I leaned farther out the window, seeking a way to climb down—

The flap of wings stirred the air, a shrill screech ringing out. I jerked back from the window just as a white-feathered bird soared past, its wings fanned wide. A vermilion plume adorned its head like a comb, its claws and beak glinting like iron. A long tail with needlelike feathers struck the window frame, scraping the wood. Dozens of these creatures circled the skies, and I went cold at the sight. These birds . . . I'd seen them before. In Tianxia, when the skies had been sealed. Was this how the Wuxin had done it?

"What are they?" I asked.

"Void birds. The original inhabitants of the Netherworld, though they have welcomed us and now guard our skies." The false Chengyin's voice rang with satisfaction. "A friendly warning: While you're welcome to explore, take care to stay indoors, or bring a guard when you go outside. These creatures are ravenous. While they leave my people untouched, they would relish the taste of mortal flesh."

My throat went dry as I backed farther away from the window, resisting the urge to slam it shut. We walked in silence along the corridor, down another flight of stairs, then halted by a closed door.

"Your new quarters." His gaze raked me, lingering on a tear in my skirt. "Find something better to wear for tonight."

"Why?" Suspicion thickened my tone.

"A banquet will be held in your honor."

There is nothing I'd hate more. "What gracious hospitality," I said, forcing a smile.

He straightened like my words pleased him. "To those who deserve it. If you need something—"

"I have a request of my host," I interjected, latching onto the opportunity. "Would you show me your real face? I want to know who I'm speaking to. I've heard only the strongest among your kind can take another's form." These vile words were chosen to stir his pride. I had to know if Chengyin was still there, if he was safe.

When his mouth pursed, I added, "If it's too difficult, there's no need. I understand some might be shy to show their true appearance, preferring to hide behind another's."

The imposter's eyes narrowed, rolling back until only the whites could be seen. His body shimmered as he seemed to split apart—another face rising from Chengyin's like mist, gradually solidifying. Handsome, almost beautiful with white hair and flawless skin, even as his hard gaze repelled me.

"What is your name?" I asked.

"Call me Lord Dalian. I am the ruler of this place."

I recoiled inside, hiding my fear. It was the name Miss Lin had spoken, the one the captain had flinched from. No wonder this person spoke with the unwavering authority of one used to being obeyed. The emphasis he set on his position was telling; he would have little tolerance for disrespect in any form.

"Lord Dalian," I intoned obediently, scrutinizing his face—except it wasn't him I was looking at. Just Chengyin, a flash of himself once more, though gaunt and pale. His mouth gaped in a soundless scream, then twitched as though fighting some inner battle—finally, forming a single soundless word: *Run.*

My hands curled. Even now he still looked out for me.

"Are you satisfied?" Lord Dalian's voice rang out.

I yanked myself back from the brink of rage, from making rash threats and unwise promises. "Let him go. Please."

"Not yet. Not until you prove yourself to me. I know there's little you won't do to save him." His face blurred as it settled back into Chengyin's like a shadow coalescing into its original form.

"Wait!" I lunged forward—but Chengyin's hand shot up, controlled by Lord Dalian, slamming against my shoulder to send me sprawling to the floor.

My friend's eyes closed as his body stiffened. When his eyes opened again, their pupils were ringed with that despicable coppery sheen. Lord Dalian's hateful expression returned, his lips twisted. I would have gladly clawed his face off if it wouldn't hurt Chengyin, too.

"Did you like what you saw?" He rubbed his chin with the languid complacency of one assured in himself. "Was my appearance as you expected?"

I expected a monster, and that was what I got.

But I nodded, unable to speak—still shaken by what I'd seen, by the weight of the unseen chains that snared me. As long as Chengyin was a hostage, I was bound along with him because I wouldn't leave him here. I had to find a way to free him, for us to escape before we outlived our usefulness . . . before they killed us both.

32

Once Lord Dalian left, I pulled at the doors—surprised when they came apart. I'd expected to be a prisoner, locked up like before. As I stared down the empty corridor, the tip of a boot at the end caught my eye. A guard? A spy? Maybe this was a test, and until I knew for certain, I would tread carefully. After closing the doors with a decisive thud, I turned back to the room.

It was spacious, with large windows—so different from the cell I'd awakened in. Gossamer silk flowed from the canopy over the bed, tied back with strands of amber beads. Willow branches clustered in porcelain vases were arranged around the chamber. The light from outside spilled through the windows, melding into those of the candles mounted upon bronze stands. At the sight of the copper bath already filled, I disrobed swiftly, then sank into the steaming water. It was a relief to scrub the dirt from my skin and hair, though my wounds stung. After I dried myself, I pulled out a set of clothes from the closet, one of the more elaborate designs. Appearances seemed to matter to Lord Dalian. The dark-blue brocade was embroidered with waves, flecked with gold and pearl, and while the work was not as fine as the immortals', the colors shifted seamlessly from turquoise to midnight.

Someone knocked on the door. An attendant entered, her white hair gathered into a plait down her back, her gray robe fastened with a red sash. "Lord Dalian sent me to help you prepare for the banquet tonight."

"I am ready. Would you show me the way?" I fell in stride with her as we walked, trying not to think of the vicious stories I'd heard of the Wuxin. "What is your name? What do they call this place?"

"I'm Mingwen," she said with a small smile. "This is the End-less Dawn Palace."

A lovely name, surprising for those who dwelled by the river of death. But even here there was beauty to be found in the jeweled skies.

The girl was staring at my arm, frowning. "The marks left by Lord Dalian's whip go deep. Do they hurt?"

"Not as badly as these." I lifted my palms to show her the cuts from when I'd yanked at the window.

"It means you've touched something you shouldn't. I wouldn't show those to Lord Dalian," she advised, then looked down like she'd said too much.

"I won't," I assured her. "I'm grateful for your advice; I'm still learning the rules."

She glanced behind her, then took my hands quickly, touching the torn flesh. I winced, unused to the chill in her fingers. As a soft gleam passed through them, seeping into my skin, the wounds closed a little, the pain dulling. It still hurt, but no longer with the fiery agony of before.

"Don't tell anyone I did this." Her tongue darted nervously over her lips. "This is the best I can do; our healing abilities aren't strong. There are a couple of healers in the palace, but you'd need permission from Lord Dalian to see one."

"Thank you, Mingwen."

Her unexpected kindness moved me, more so because I had no right to it. I was a stranger and she'd risked herself to help me. She was nothing like the brutal Captain Rao or the malevolent Lord Dalian. I'd thought all the Wuxin were bloodthirsty monsters, hungering for strife. Were those like Mingwen the rare exception, or were most like her—just trying to make a living, no more evil or good than my own people? Acts of violence or war were often dictated by those in power. For those who had to struggle each day, what was a crown when weighed against a loved one? What did they care for the varnish of glory when all they wanted was to survive?

My perception of the Wuxin had been colored for so long, it was hard to shift my perspective. I didn't know enough yet . . . but what if they weren't all enemies here? Maybe, I might find an ally. The thought buoyed me; it made me feel less alone.

"Do you know how your people came here?" I asked. Stories changed depending on the narrator; sometimes what remained unsaid was as vital as what was shared. Learning more might help answer some of the questions in my mind.

"Once we lived among the immortals in the Golden Desert, until the grasping Queen Caihong seized power. She claimed she united the tribes—yet those who disagreed were persecuted under her rule." Her expression clouded, her lip trembling. "When they murdered our beloved heir, it was Lord Dalian who protected us, who led us to fight back."

It was the first I'd heard of their heir's death. I frowned, reminding myself that the Wuxin had killed the queen's consort and wounded the God of War. If what Mingwen said was true, the waters of vengeance ran deep on both sides. Was this how Lord Dalian maintained control over his people rather than being blamed for what his ambition had cost them? Or had the immortals glossed over their own history, plucking only the truth they'd wanted to share. When neither side could be wholly trusted, it was vital to keep an open mind.

"Why did the immortals attack your people?" I asked.

"Our ruler refused Queen Caihong's demand for an 'alliance'—a mask to her desire to rule." She twisted a lock of white hair between her fingers. "They said she needed a villain to unite the others, and we were an easy target, different from the rest."

I didn't know the truth; I hadn't been there. Yet history had not been kind to the Wuxin. As Mingwen walked ahead of me, maybe tiring of my questions, I chose an easier one. "Are you happy here? Do you miss the skies?"

She shrugged. "Most of us barely speak of it anymore. It's beautiful here, and our people are together. The Wangchuan River sates our hunger—at least for now." She glanced at her waist, her forehead puckering. Only then did I see her bronze bell adorned with a tassel, just like those the other Wuxin wore.

"What is that bell?" I asked curiously.

Mingwen ignored my question as she pointed to the doors ahead, flanked by soldiers. Their armor was a coppery red, black-tasseled spears in their hands. "We're here," she told me, as the doors were thrown apart.

The skies had deepened to garnet, speckled with stars that glittered no less brightly here. A cool breeze threaded the air, the scent of leaves mingling with the distinct earthiness of the river. Beneath my feet, the ground crumbled like sand. Plants bloomed unlike any I'd ever seen, purplish vines with wide, flat leaves trailing the earth, climbing upon the branches of trees. Clusters of flowers hung from their tendrils in luminous purples and reds. Just ahead, a wide river glistened as it snaked around the base of the mountain.

A large barge was moored by the pier, two stories high, round lanterns strung along its roof. Its lacquered railings were a deep red, the sloped roof a brilliant yellow. A carved gilded bird with a jeweled crest ornamented the prow, its shining wings tucked around the sides of the vessel.

An eerie whistling split the air—the void birds circling the skies, their plumes as bright as flame. I shuddered at the sight of their needle-like feathers, recalling the ease with which they'd sliced through wood. At the sight of me, one swept down, eyes glinting, its beak parted menacingly. I leapt back, just as Mingwen moved in front of me, shielding me from the creature. As she called for the soldiers to escort me to the barge, sweat broke out along my back. I was sorry when Mingwen returned to the palace, a rare friendly face in this hostile world.

A low fence was built along the banks of the Wangchuan River, sharp stakes of wood thrust into the earth at an angle, sliding against each other to form a cross. From the distance, they appeared a nest of spikes, aglow with a subtle sheen—just like the bars of my cell. My hand curled instinctively at the memory. The waters beneath were streaked with greenish lights, glittering like beads of jade. Were these the tormented spirits, unable to find peace, adrift forever in these cold waters? Were they now the sole source of the Wuxin's strength?

I touched my lock of white hair, the mark of the waters that flowed here—those that had almost stolen my life, forcing Grandfather to betray the immortal queen. Who could have obtained such a thing in Tianxia? Unless it had been given to them.

As I followed the soldiers to board the barge, it swayed to the rhythm of the river. They led me up a f of stairs to enter a large chamber. Rosewood columns were carved with birds, a red carpet thrown over the floor, gold chrysanthemums woven into the wide border. As a musician in a corner plucked his pipa, a delicate melody rippled from the lute. Brightly painted wooden tables were arranged around the room, laden with cups of wine, though only a little food: plates of walnuts, crisp seaweed, small cakes and pastries. No one seemed to be eating; their appetites not for food—my own stomach churning with unease and hunger.

Wuxin crowded the place, not the wraithlike forms that had invaded my home. The ones here wore finer garments, dressed in muted shades of blue and brown and plum, a foil to their surroundings that were flushed with color. Despite the crowd, the tables closest to the dais remained empty, as was the gilded throne upon it. Strange, when the places nearest to the seat of power were usually the first to be filled. Were the Wuxin afraid of their lord?

Just one woman stood beside the throne, draped in violet brocade, a long strand of pearls around her neck. Snow-white hair framed her face that she lifted to me—a scream catching in my throat.

Aunt Shou.

33

It couldn't be her. Had Aunt Shou been possessed, too? But while Lord Dalian's control of Chengyin was a precise mirror, there were unsettling differences here: Aunt Shou's gray hair was now pure white, though still coiled in her preferred style, her clear eyes devoid of the filminess of age, and the spots that had speckled her face and arms were gone like they'd been washed away. Worse yet was the way she looked at me with such knowing—she *was* Aunt Shou, if time had reversed itself.

"How is this possible?" The question slipped from me; I was still grasping for any other possibility—that she had a twin, that she'd been tricked or even bewitched? Because the alternative, that she had betrayed my grandfather and me all these years, sent a shaft of unimaginable pain through my chest.

Aunt Shou clicked her tongue as she always did when she was impatient. "Trust your eyes, Liyen—the truth before you."

Her hard tone, her cool gaze . . . she didn't seem like Aunt Shou anymore, her softness cut away like the flesh of a fruit, revealing its stony pit.

"Who are you?" My voice fractured over the words.

"This is my real home; these are my people. Dalian is my son," she replied.

I shook my head in confusion. "I thought you had a daughter

before Chengyin?"

Her eyes clouded as though she still struggled with these memories. "My daughter is dead. I just never mentioned Dalian; it would have raised too many questions."

I stared at her, feeling a tightness within, a hollowing despair. Grandfather and I had trusted her, we'd loved her—and all this while she'd been working against us. We were fools to have trusted her, never questioning how she knew so much of the immortals and her dislike of them, how she'd nudged Grandfather to confront them, her interest in the lotus and even the God of War. It was so with those we grew up with, who came into our lives before our hearts were bruised and hardened. Before we knew better.

Anger surged, breaking through the disappointment and shock. "It was you who poisoned me with the waters of the Wangchuan," I said flatly. "You sent the Winged Devils after me, both at the wall and the queen's palace. Why did you want to kill me?"

She sighed, shaking her head. "If I wanted to kill you, I could have done it a hundred times before. While the waters of the Wangchuan would bring death to any mortal, there is one cure—"

"The Divine Pearl Lotus," I finished, almost choking on my rage. The threads were falling into the place, weaving a picture far more tangled and intricate than anything I could have imagined. "You knew about it from the start—when it bloomed, because Grandfather confided in you, and that he was going to surrender it to the immortal queen. Is that why you poisoned me, to make him give it to me instead? Why not just take the lotus for yourself?"

"It had to be you." Her tone dipped with something like regret. "The Divine Pearl Lotus grew from your grandfather's care, a treasure of the Mortal Realm, maybe the greatest one that ever existed. Your grandfather was the only one who could harvest the flower without it wilting, he was the only one who could *gift* it."

"And he would only give it to Queen Caihong, or to me." How painful this choice must have been for him.

"Why do you want the lotus?" I demanded. "Was it because you didn't want Queen Caihong to have it? Or because of its link with the gateway?"

"The immortals don't *deserve* it; they don't deserve the cure, especially not the God of War. Let them all die," she said bitterly. "They murdered my people. They are wicked and false, wearing a mask of benevolence when they are as greedy, ambitious, and conniving as those they accuse."

"The immortals helped us," I argued. "It was your people who invaded my kingdom, who were killing us."

"We had no choice. We were dying," she said. "Wasting away to nothing but dust. It's why we took physical form, because it strengthened us. We had to fight for our own future."

A weight sank over me. Maybe that was the tragedy—both sides believing unflinchingly in their own rightness, that they'd been wronged by the other. Maybe they'd fought so relentlessly because they believed it was for their survival. And my kingdom had paid the highest price of all.

"Aunt Shou"—it didn't feel right to call her that, but old habits were hard to break—"was everything false? What about Chengyin? Did you plan for Grandfather to die?" The possibility revolted me.

Her mouth quivered, the harshness fading from her expression. "I was still grieving for my child when I saw Chengyin for the first time, abandoned and helpless, reviled for nothing more than superstition. I couldn't bear it." She drew in a long breath, her chest heaving. "As for your grandfather, he was a true friend to me. I didn't think the immortals would kill him; I didn't expect his heart to give out. His death is one I will forever regret."

Her sorrow did not blunt my anger; it would not bring my grandfather back. "How could you disguise yourself all these years? Why did no one in Tianxia know who you were?"

"Such magic runs in my bloodline," she said. "It's why Dalian can usurp another's body, a rare ability among us."

"*Another's body?*" I repeated scathingly. "Chengyin is *your son.*"

Her face fell but she said nothing. I wanted to ask more, to learn all I could. But I was drained, sick to the heart. I would never forgive her betrayal, for abandoning Chengyin to her vicious son.

Lord Dalian—the false Chengyin—strode into the hall, his hair pulled into an ornate gold headpiece. Two women followed him bearing weapons, one of whom was Miss Lin, the short-haired Wuxin who'd attacked my home. The other was a taller woman with curly hair, though they shared similar features. Were they his personal guards? Captain Rao followed after them, a sneer on his face as he passed me.

Silence trailed Lord Dalian's entrance, all bowing as he stalked onto the dais, then sat on the throne. His turquoise robe was a flash of brightness amid the somber garb of his court. I wondered why the other Wuxin wore such dull colors. Was it their natural preference or because their lord preferred to be the center of atten-tion—a peacock among the sparrows?

"Long live Lord Dalian, the Eternal Ruler over the Nether-world," they intoned.

I dropped my head but did not bow like the others. He hadn't earned my deference. As Aunt Shou beamed at him, I bit down on my tongue. Didn't she care what he'd done? Chengyin loved her as a mother, and she must have cared for him, too—though what did it matter when she refused to help him now?

As Lord Dalian leaned against his throne, I tensed beneath his scrutiny. "I see you've become reacquainted with my mother?" he remarked.

"An unexpected surprise." I managed to say, though I hated seeing him in my friend's body, the way he made Chengyin seem terrifying and vicious.

"Do you know how your betrothed was snared by me?" His smile was coated with malice. He wanted to see me hurt; he wanted to break me.

"I heard it's not easy," I said through clenched teeth. Let him talk, let him teach me what I needed to know to fight him.

He laughed sharply as he nodded at Aunt Shou. "It was a fine act, Mother, when you pleaded for him to help you. You acted so convincingly, he didn't hesitate, believing you were in danger."

Aunt Shou went pale, her lips pursed into a knot. I hoped Chengyin couldn't hear this, trapped in his own body. Lord Dalian seemed to relish tormenting not just me, but his mother, too.

"Better this than Chengyin's death, if he didn't surrender," Aunt Shou said in a low voice.

"Did you know he would sacrifice himself willingly?" Lord Dalian needled. "Is my 'brother' such a paragon of virtue?"

Aunt Shou lifted her head. "He is a good person. Goodness should not be scorned; there's far too little of it in the world."

"Enough, Mother," Lord Dalian drawled, though his eyes glinted dangerously. "I know I'm your greatest disappointment. I know how you prefer *all* my siblings to me—even the dead."

"Don't say such things." Aunt Shou pressed a fist to her forehead. "Damei's death was a great loss for us."

"We all know how you mourned for her, Mother—your precious heir. You even relinquished your throne because of your grief," he said with an edge to his voice.

"Not just my heir; she was your *sister*," Aunt Shou hissed.

"And it's why you hated the immortals, willing to do whatever it took to seek vengeance." He jerked his head at me. "Even living with the mortals."

I ignored his intended slight. "Why did the immortals kill your daughter?" I asked Aunt Shou, wanting to learn more, seeking a weakness to exploit.

She didn't answer right away, blinking like there was a haze over her eyes. "Before, we didn't hurt anyone, we took what no one noticed. But after we protested Queen Caihong's rule, her soldiers began attacking us, unprovoked. Damei was killed in one of the skirmishes."

"They thought they could dominate us. They were wrong; they made us stronger." Lord Dalian raised his voice so all could hear him. "Power keeps us safe; it keeps us alive. Though we lost the war, we never forgot the lesson. This time, victory will be ours."

Aunt Shou nodded woodenly. "We must talk, my son. I've been away too long in the Mortal Realm. What are these barriers erected along the Wangchuan River? Has the situation worsened?"

"The barriers are to ensure the river is protected, that no one can harm it or steal from it. It became necessary as there was discontent before, from those who didn't understand why the restrictions were in place." Lord Dalian nodded at Captain Rao, who approached Aunt Shou and held out a bell on a tray. It was just like those I'd seen the Wuxin wearing, except this one was crafted in gold—almost the twin to the one on Lord Dalian's waist, though his was a darker shade.

"Take it, Mother," he urged when she remained still. "You won't be bound to the same restrictions as the others."

She frowned as she looked from the bell, to him. "This is not the way, my son."

"Are you questioning me, Mother?" Lord Dalian's tone grew harsher. "I don't need your approval; I rule our people now."

"I only want what's best for you and our people," she argued calmly. "A good ruler thinks of *all* his people, not just those who are closest."

"Save your sanctimonious lectures for the mortals like her." As he glanced at me, I itched to slap him for his disrespect to his mother—even though I should despise her.

Captain Rao bowed to Aunt Shou, pushing the tray a little closer. "Great Lady, the Wangchuan River weakened in potency shortly after you left to the Mortal Realm. It was unable to sustain us as before. Lord Dalian erected the barriers around its banks to help preserve it, restricting its use to ensure there was enough for everyone."

The bell the captain wore was of shining gold, unlike the bronze ones worn by Miss Lin and the others. It seemed unlikely that he suffered any of the restrictions he spoke so glibly of.

"Is this true, Dalian?" Aunt Shou asked.

"This is why it's imperative to secure the Mortal Realm for our people," Lord Dalian replied curtly. "Take the bell, Mother." The last was spoken almost as a command.

The other courtiers were watching as Aunt Shou finally nodded, reaching for it. "I didn't know about these troubles."

"I didn't want to worry you," he replied. "Rest assured, I didn't act lightly. I will secure our people's future and avenge my sister."

My mind whirled. They were not attacking our realm out of vengeance, ambition, or greed—but desperation. If the Wangchuan River fulfilled them as before, would they still invade us?

Aunt Shou touched Lord Dalian's shoulder where I'd stabbed him. "How is your wound?"

"The healing is slow. Her blade was no ordinary one; it vanished before I could retrieve it." He scowled as he adjusted his sleeve, his cold gaze flicking toward me. "I grow bored of this weak body. With her here, maybe this vessel has served his purpose."

Panic flared, along with hate. Before I could protest, Aunt Shou cast me a warning look.

"We still need him," she said. "Their bond is strong. He will tether her to us, ensuring her obedience. And as importantly, your healing will be quicker in the mortal's body."

He nodded. "You are right, Mother."

It struck me then, Aunt Shou knew there was no engagement between Chengyin and me, yet she hadn't told Lord Dalian. Was she trying to protect Chengyin in this way? Or was she keeping her own secrets because she didn't wholly trust him? Either way, this was a divide I might be able to wrest wider apart.

"How was I brought here? Has the gateway been opened?" I desperately hoped to be wrong, even as I sought a way out—suppressing a rush of longing to go home.

Lord Dalian's expression darkened. "Not entirely. Only a few can cross each day."

I feigned a look of surprise. "Why not open it all the way through? Is it hard?"

"Prying just this sliver is an immense strain—who else would dare to undertake such an endeavor? It is far more complex than anything you might conceive," he snapped, almost baring his teeth. "While there are restrictions to the crossing, while it is dangerous for now—it's a worthwhile risk to secure our future."

Easily said, when another paid the price instead of him.

"You have accomplished what no one else could do, my lord," Captain Rao flattered him in a fine display of how he'd earned the gold bell. "Soon the gateway will be open and our forces in place to invade the Mortal Realm." His eyes gleamed like he was eager for war, but Miss Lin's expression was tense.

She hesitated, then moved forward to bow to Lord Dalian. "Perhaps an invasion may not be necessary if the Wangchuan River can be restored?"

Several courtiers nodded, not all as hungry for war as the captain.

Lord Dalian's eyes slid toward me. "Of course. It's why she's here."

"What do you want from me, Lord Dalian?" I braced for him to ask about the Divine Pearl Lotus, to demand its surrender.

"A simple task." He stretched his arms along his throne. "You've heard how the waters of the Wangchuan have weakened in potency. We believe they've been tainted."

The hall had gone quiet; everyone staring at us.

"We've traced the taint to the pond in the Temple of the Crimson Moon. It is connected to the Wangchuan, and we believe this is causing the river's power to wane." Lord Dalian's gaze hardened. "I need you to purify the pond, to restore the Wangchuan River. Only one who wields the power of the Divine Pearl Lotus, as you do, is allowed into the temple."

No longer. At last, he'd mentioned the lotus, but questions still crowded my mind. I'd thought he wanted it to open the gateway. Had I been wrong? Did he *only* want to use me—the lotus—to restore the Wangchuan River? To help their world instead of destroying mine?

It would be infinitely preferable to end a war rather than to start one.

I bit the inside of my cheek, concealing my unease. If they knew I'd surrendered the lotus, Chengyin and I would suffer. "Is it safe for me to enter the temple?" I asked carefully.

He smiled as though I'd already agreed. "There is no danger. Once you are inside, your task will become clear."

"If I do this, will you let Chengyin and me go? Will you swear to leave the Mortal Realm alone?"

His eyes gleamed. "*If* you succeed in restoring the Wangchuan River's power, we won't need your realm."

Unease thickened. He'd agreed too quickly, without even negotiating the terms. His answers seemed too convenient, too smooth. I didn't want to agree, yet how could I refuse? There was little choice, but what if I could delay it? Even now, Zhangwei might be searching for me, even gathering reinforcements. I just needed a little time.

"Why the urgency, Lord Dalian? My arm is still injured from your whip; I don't know if I can do what you ask." I didn't usually play the victim, but I'd say anything to buy a reprieve.

He stiffened, maybe expecting unflinching obedience. "Lin, see to her wound," he barked.

Miss Lin stalked forward, her bearing taut with annoyance. I don't think she liked being spoken to this way, or maybe she thought this task was beneath her. As she reached for my hand, I hesitated before giving it to her. She inspected the wound, frowning—did she notice someone had tried healing me? My eyes met hers, a silent plea in them. I couldn't expose Mingwen; Lord Dalian would take her help as an insult to his authority, not the simple act of kindness it had been. As she nodded slightly, relief flooded me.

Light flickered from her fingers, gliding over my arm and wrist, even the cuts on my palms that she said nothing of. The last of my discomfort vanished, along with the marks.

"She's healed, Lord Dalian," Miss Lin said, returning to his side.

"Will you do this?" Lord Dalian asked me sharply, an order veiled as a question.

When I hesitated, he plucked a dagger from his waist, pressing his finger on its tip until it pierced the skin. His brow tensed as his blood spilled. I recoiled, suppressing my rage. Wanting to strike him, yet afraid to.

Aunt Shou spoke before I could, her face pale. "Be careful, my son," she said in a voice that I strained to hear. "This form helps you to recuperate, but while you're connected to the host, you are bound to their weakness—"

"Silence, Mother." He glared at her, his mouth twisted in fury.

As she shrank away, I quashed my pity, reminding myself of her betrayal—that she deserved this and more. But it still didn't make this right.

Lord Dalian was waiting for my answer, toying with the blade in his hands. A vise tightened around me. I had tested him as far as I dared. If I didn't yield, Chengyin and I would suffer the consequences. And even if I refused, from the look on his face, he'd just drag me there by force.

"I will go."

He settled back against his throne, his smile as false as mine. "Then let's not waste any more time."

34

The air was still, the waters calm. When had the barge stopped?

My gut twisted as I followed Lord Dalian onto the deck. The silhouette of a cliff loomed ahead, a temple perched on its edge, as luminous as if carved from a sliver of the moon. Blood-red tiles gleamed from its roof, shining like they were wet with rain.

"You brought me here? What if I'd refused?" Anger crept into my voice, though I buried the spike of alarm.

"You don't seem like a fool," Lord Dalian said with deliberation. "I would hate to be proven wrong."

I quelled a sharp retort. He'd already shown that he was not averse to using force. For now, there was no choice but to obey him, or at least pretend to.

When I didn't reply, Lord Dalian nodded to Captain Rao. "An escort will accompany you to the temple, so you don't get 'lost.'"

Soldiers surrounded me at once, led by Captain Rao. As I left the barge with them, the winged predators of the Netherworld circled hungrily above our heads. If I ran, they'd devour me whole. And even if I fled, what about Chengyin? Where would I go, where could I hide?

A long flight of stairs was cut into the slope that led to the temple, the wooden boards narrow and steep. Golden larch trees flanked the path, their bright-yellow leaves brushing my shoulders as I passed. Above us loomed the temple, clad in shadows and star-light. The dark-red roof was almost black in the night, the ridges adorned with small sculptures of birds. At the top of the hill, the grounds were immaculately tended, flowers blooming in culti-vated profusion. The place was desolate—unsurprising, as Lord Dalian had said no other could enter.

What would he do to me if I failed, if I was no longer of use to him? My legs were shaking as I approached the temple. I held my breath as the doors slid apart—to my intense relief and dread. Maybe the trace of the lotus left inside me sufficed, the bit that had healed me. It was dark within, not a single candle or lantern lit. My insides twisted as I glanced at the soldiers who had formed a ring around me, fencing me in.

"Go in," Captain Rao ordered with a malicious grin. "Lord Dalian said we could help hasten you should you waver." His hand grazed the hilt of his sword.

I wouldn't give him the pleasure, my smile hiding my gritted teeth. "You are most *obedient*, Captain Rao. Lord Dalian is fortu-nate to have such a loyal servant."

I relished the flicker of wrath in his eyes, my satisfaction van-ishing as I forced myself to stalk into the temple, fear beating wildly in my chest. The doors closed, entombing me in darkness. I swung around and tried to pry them apart, but they were locked. Would they open once I'd completed my task? A scent wafted in the air of incense mingled with an earthiness that reminded me of the Wangchuan River. They must be connected, as Lord Dalian had said. Was everything he'd claimed true? If there was a small chance of restoring their river to avert a war, I had to seize it.

Lanterns flared to life, casting their light across the walls, which were as smooth as the hollow of a shell. A whisper of music glided through the chamber, although there was neither instru-ment nor musician in sight. Thoughts of ghosts crowded my mind.

They aren't real, I told myself harshly. Yet after all I'd seen in the skies and beyond, the lines between reality, nightmare, and myth had irrevocably blurred.

In the far corner, a round pond gleamed. As I walked toward it, the music faded. Shafts of light fell from a hole in the ceiling, the waters glistening. Bright-green algae bloomed over the pond evenly, like a silk sheet pulled taut. Were the waters tainted as Dalian had said? His story seemed to fit, yet a shard of unease lodged in my chest. What was I missing? What had I overlooked? For these immortal beings, nothing was ever as it seemed.

I approached the pond cautiously. My senses prickled, the air thick with the unknown. Bracing myself, I glanced into the pond. A whispering rustled through the silence, a strange force enveloping me—drawing me closer until my face hovered just above the water.

The algae dissolved abruptly and sank into the depths. My reflection looked back at me, as clear and still as though I were looking at myself through another's eyes. Except now copper ringed my irises—just like those of the Wuxin—my hair all glittering white. Ice clung to my veins as a desperate terror mounted. Something loosened inside me, breaking away, darkness crashing down like waves of night. Screams bottled up, an emptiness ripping through my head like something vital was being torn away . . . an invasion, a theft of what was most precious.

It was a trap. This task was never about restoring the Wangchuan—was it to seize the Divine Pearl Lotus? I cursed Lord Dalian, shivering as sweat beaded my skin, the cold sinking into my flesh worse than any fever. Closing my eyes, I grappled with these vicious sensations tearing me apart. The stars above glittered like a crown of light, bathing me in their pale glow. Would I die here? A pang struck as I thought of Zhangwei. What lay between us felt unfinished—a story without an ending. And what of Tianxia? Would he honor his promise to me? Somehow, I knew he would . . . if only I could see the walls come down.

My head fell back, as I closed my eyes, on the cusp of succumbing to despair. Faces flashed across my mind: Grandfather, my parents, Chengyin—and Zhangwei, his eyes of midnight flame, his voice urging me to *fight back*. Something sparked in my core, morphing into a deep warmth that surged through my body. The shivering stopped, my breathing calmed, the turmoil settling like dust falling to the earth. Such sweetness spilled into the air, of cloves . . . the scent transporting me back to the Ancient Grandmaster's courtyard, when I'd lain beneath the shade of the Tree of Everlasting Life—when the glistening drop had fallen to my brow. The deep peace that had suffused me then was enveloping me now.

A blessing from the Tree of Everlasting Life . . . One of protection, to seal your spirit from harm.

Tears pricked my eyes, those of gratitude. I still struggled to understand, yet sensed I'd been protected from something terrible. I'd almost forgotten the tree's gift, only now awakening to how precious it had been—the only thing keeping me safe, keeping me whole.

As my pulse slowly steadied, the unfamiliar sensations fading, my eyes flicked open. Above lay the gap that opened to the skies, void birds circling as though sensing the disturbance. Though they were far away, specks in the night, their shrill whistles pierced my ears.

A strange tingling rippled through my body as a sudden awareness crashed over me—the ends of countless threads coiling around me, some tangled, others knotted, a few merging together seamlessly. Images drifted into my mind of things I'd never seen yet were familiar somehow, like a shadow of the past, their fragments and broken shards, an echo of a melody I'd almost forgotten:

Clouds floating across the sky. Mountains of turquoise, nestled amid the glittering sands. A woman was holding me in her arms, her long hair obscuring her face, the gold thread on her brocade gown rubbing against my skin. There was such love in her embrace, my heart ached.

"Mother," I whispered, looking up into her face.

The Queen of the Golden Desert.

A scream burst from my lips, my heart racing. Queen Caihong was harsh and cruel, the bane of Tianxia. My own mother had died long ago, along with my father. Was this some trick? If so, it was a twisted and vicious one.

As I pressed my hands to my head, more recollections swept through me as if a dam had burst open, too many to weave together, leaving me grasping at shreds: the immortal queen picking me up when I fell, wiping tears from my eyes, smiling with pride at my accomplishments, scowling when I misbehaved. How she'd tucked me into my bed, whispering my name in her clear voice. And once, when she'd hugged me as we'd both wept, grief hollowing our hearts—and though I couldn't recall what we'd lost then, tears fell from my eyes now at this echo of unspeakable sorrow.

What was happening? What did this all mean? I was no longer afraid, just filled with a fierce longing to *know.* "Is this a trick? A test?" My voice resonated through the empty chamber. If it was, just let it end. My heart could bear no more.

The waters of the pond shuddered, as a disembodied voice rang out: *Those who come here claim one future, but two lie before you.*

My eyes darted around frantically. "Who are you?"

The Mirror of Destiny—of the past, the present, and that which has yet to come.

I stared into the dark waters, light flickering over the surface like fireflies. My reflection looked back at me: the copper gone from my eyes, now as black as my hair, just the sliver of white remaining.

"What are you? Are you . . . alive?" I asked carefully, suspecting a trick.

No. Neither am I dead. A long pause. *Will you claim your destiny? Choose, and the other will be no more.*

"I don't believe in destiny, nor do I believe a puddle in the ground." I spoke vehemently—afraid of what was happening, of what might be unveiled.

You are insolent.

"I am cautious. It comes from knowing too many liars."

Destiny bears as much weight as you yield it. Sometimes hope can forge your path, sometimes fear can divert you from it.

"Hope is not the same as blind faith," I said.

Just as you should not deny what you are ignorant of.

I flushed, feeling justly rebuked. The mirror was right; I shouldn't close myself off to any possibility simply because it might be hard to hear.

"Who are you to the Wuxin?" I asked.

Neither their ally nor their foe. I take no sides, revealing only what lies in my domain.

"Are the waters here tainted at all?" Part of me was still hoping for the slightest chance of a peaceful solution. "Is the Wangchuan River weakening?"

The waters here are untainted. Yet the power of the Wangchuan River has waned. Before one attempts to restore it, one should learn the cause.

Dread sank over me. It was as I'd suspected; Lord Dalian had lied just to bring me to the temple. "Why do the Wuxin want me here?"

To complete the ritual, to become one of them.

I jerked back in horror. "Impossible."

It should be, the mirror agreed. The way it spoke, so dispassionately, eased some of my suspicion. *Except they found a way. You are no ordinary mortal, your spirit from the realm in the skies.*

I was frozen with shock, certain I'd heard wrong. In the silence, it continued: *You* were *immortal. You* are *mortal now. What you will become—that is yet to be determined.*

"I was immortal?" I repeated in disbelief. "What of my life in Tianxia? My family there? Was everything false?" My words tripped out as I tried to piece everything together, all I knew . . . at least, all I *thought* I'd known. The one thing I held on to was my memory of Grandfather—he was real, as was his love and care for me.

One truth does not cancel out the other. Just because one element is real, doesn't make the other false.

These words calmed me. It didn't matter how something had begun, but what it had grown into. "Why don't I recall any of this—of my immortal life? Why only now?"

As a mortal, you wouldn't remember anything of your life before; these memories are only restored once you regain your immortality. But entering the temple, looking into my depths, reveals who you are meant to be.

My head was spinning. Was this a dream or a nightmare? For some inexplicable reason . . . it felt right. Memories were trickling into my mind, those I couldn't decipher, like reading a book in a language I didn't understand—that I desperately wanted to.

I knelt beside the mirror. "Please tell me what happened. I can't decide if I don't know what this means."

A sigh rustled, the waters rippling. *During the war, the Wuxin cast a powerful curse over their enemies—including you, the immortal daughter of the queen they hated. For the cure, you had to become mortal.*

"Because of the Divine Pearl Lotus," I whispered.

Once it had been harvested, once you'd been cured—they'd planned to restore your immortality. Except the Wuxin's poison concealed you from the immortals, leaving your core vulnerable. The Wuxin were able to stake a claim on you in your mortal form, by feeding you the waters of death. This would have secured your transformation had you come here without the blessing from the Tree of Everlasting Life, or if the immortals had attempted to restore you without it. You would have lost your memories forever then, your immortal self, erased.

My heart was racing—fear and grief, anger and relief bound up and tangled. If I weren't kneeling, I would have fallen. I should be lost, yet there was a clarity in my mind that hadn't existed before, like a fog had dispersed. Pieces were falling into place, those that had never quite fit together, of unanswered questions and unexplained coincidences: my weakness and unabating chill that were a remnant of the Wuxin's attack, why Aunt Shou had given me the waters of death. Even Queen Caihong's behavior when I'd met her—and what of Zhangwei? He'd been poisoned, too; had we been attacked together? I shrank away, my mind clouding suddenly as I wrestled with these revelations.

"Why did the Wuxin want to do this to me? Why transform me into one of them?" I asked.

A pause. *Who knows the desires that dictate such action? Maybe it was vengeance—to steal the queen's heir after they'd lost theirs? Or maybe it's because the key to the gateway lies in your heritage, in the power you possess.*

It had never been about the Divine Pearl Lotus after all—they just didn't want the God of War to have it, to be healed. All this time, the Wuxin had only wanted *me*. Dalian's promise of vengeance made sense now: I'd been one part of his vile plan—the other, to destroy my realm.

"What happens now?" I asked.

That depends on which path you choose.

More riddles, more unanswered questions. The urge to lash out swelled, except the mirror was not my enemy. Those harbored far more devious and cruel hearts, and I would never let them win.

I will reveal my secrets only once. Will you learn your destiny and claim your fate—or remain in endless ignorance?

In the pond, my reflection quivered, breaking apart into two distinct forms, side by side. They no longer followed my movements, remaining still, as though frozen. Fear hovered, yet I cast it aside. No longer would I be afraid.

Slowly, I lifted my head. A deep sense of purpose filled me, laced with foreboding and anticipation. "Show me what you will."

35

The water glittered as the twin reflections of me lowered their heads in an eerie greeting—one I returned as I folded into a bow. The reflection on the left fragmented, sinking into the dark depths. The remaining image tilted her head to the side. Her hair gleamed, morphing into the silvery-white of the Wuxin, the copper rings shining in her eyes—the reflection I'd seen when I first looked into the pond. Her smile sent a shiver through me, a stranger's, sharp and almost predatory—then the waters churned, breaking the reflection.

"Wait." I reached out to her. Though she frightened me a little, she *was* me, and I didn't want her to go.

The ripples stilled abruptly, the surface a clear mirror once more. A scene formed: the dark silhouette of the mountain against the radiant sky of the Netherworld. Hundreds of pale boats glided across the Wangchuan River, halting before a narrow stretch of land. Something shimmered in the distance: a white marble archway against obsidian stone, draped with thick vines. Was this the gateway that led to Kunlun? As my reflection strode forward, a roar went up from among the Wuxin. Light gleamed from my hands, the vines of the gateway falling away, the shimmering wall vanishing—leaving the path to Tianxia unhindered.

"No." My hands clenched until they hurt. "You don't want

this." Of course she couldn't hear me. Illusion or prophecy, this was not real . . . *not yet*. The thought calmed me; there was still a chance to stop this.

My reflection showed neither doubt nor remorse, watching coldly as the Wuxin marched through the opening. The mirror shifted to span a vast field, bordered by a river, the red wall of Tianxia gleaming in the horizon. A battle was under way between the Wuxin and the mortals. Aunt Shou fought beside my reflection, along with Lord Dalian and Captain Rao. Captain Li led the Tianxia troops, her face already streaked with blood. My image raised her sword, cutting through my own soldiers without remorse—those who'd have given their lives to protect me. How heartless this manifestation was. Did she not remember? Or maybe to her, the mortals stood in her people's way. I hated her; in that moment I hated myself. This was an uneven battle, cruel and unjust. Where were the immortals? Were the skies still sealed? Without them, it was a massacre—the Wuxin overcoming the mortals with ease, their weapons and magic scattering my people like sand. As my people wept and screamed, some pleading for mercy—the Wuxin fought with greater vigor, their movements swifter, their magic shining brighter.

"Monsters." My eyes were damp as I struck the stone floor in frustration, cutting my knuckles. I forced myself to keep looking at the reflection, though my stomach roiled. I had to see this through; I had to stop it.

Flashes of light illuminated the skies in the mirror. Clouds were descending to Tianxia, bearing immortal warriors. Zhangwei rode at the front, his great sword unsheathed, his armor gleaming darkly. When he landed, he froze at the sight of my reflection—a deadly mistake when facing a ruthless foe. *She* did not hesitate, attacking him relentlessly with her sword. Each move she made was one he'd taught her, that he'd taught *me*—the realization a punch to the gut. Zhangwei did not fight back, his expression anguished as he tried to reach for her, but she struck him aside viciously. How I wished he'd strike her, too. Again and again, her sword thrust at him—and while he evaded most of her blows, those that landed drew blood. Meanwhile, Zhangwei's attacks were halfhearted—to deflect, not to injure.

It sickened me, wrenching me apart. From behind Zhangwei, Lord Dalian appeared—had he been lying in wait all this while? My blood turned to ice as Lord Dalian raised his whip, lashing Zhangwei. As it coiled around his neck, Zhangwei clawed at it—but Lord Dalian yanked it harder, the whip glowing malevolently as it snapped Zhangwei's head back.

I was screaming; I would have struck both Lord Dalian and my reflection if I could. She just stood there, a stony smile on her face as Zhangwei raised a hand to her, his fingers curled—a moment before he collapsed to the ground, the whip still biting into his neck. Dalian drew his sword then, and drove it through Zhangwei's throat with enough force to pierce his skull—

I curled over and retched, unable to control myself. I'd never believed some fates worse than death . . . until now. Tears were running from my eyes, my chest heaving, my heart breaking apart.

"No more," I whispered, almost pleading, my voice raw.

The mirror faded to an oily sheen, erasing the devastation it had shown. Relief swept through me that this needn't be my destiny, that there was a choice—and after what I'd seen, it would be an easy one to make.

The other reflection, the one that vanished before—now resurfaced. This manifestation of myself was clad in the gold armor of the immortals. Her black hair was pulled high, the ends curling around her shoulders, not a fleck of copper in her pupils. Zhangwei appeared in the mirror and took her hand. A smile lit her face, such fierce joy, it warmed me inside. A glow emanated from her skin, akin to his—an immortal's aura. The reflection undulated, shifting to show a battlefield in Tianxia once more, Kunlun towering in the distance. Immortals fought alongside my soldiers, battling the Wuxin. Zhangwei and my reflection fought together, their swords gleaming as magic flared from their hands. Screams tore the air, an agonizing refrain— this time as many wrenched from the Wuxin as from my people. Zhangwei's sword flashed, cutting down Captain Rao—that young soldier avenged at last.

A savage satisfaction curled in my heart, though the violence repelled me even when inflicted on those I should hate. They were our enemy; they'd killed so many of my people, tried to transform me against my will into one of them. But then my gaze fell upon the body of a young Wuxin attendant—Mingwen. The one who'd helped me. A coldness enveloped me, deepening as I found Miss Lin next, her eyes vacant, a gaping wound on her neck. The bodies were piling onto one another, their limbs twisted, their anguished faces blurring. Were they immortal, mortal, or Wuxin? In death, somehow, they all looked the same. Who among them truly deserved this vicious end?

Someone was weeping, the sound—the voice—piercing my heart. Aunt Shou clung to a limp body: Lord Dalian's. His pale skin was mottled with blood, his eyes closed. I should have felt triumph; I should rejoice in his defeat. But there was just a numbing emptiness within, a grief that had no name.

The reflection shifted once more, cheers erupting across the immortals. The soldiers bowed as Queen Caihong came toward me. Her bloodstained sword fell from her hand as she folded me in her arms. Such pride shone in her face, such love. In this moment, I almost believed she *was* my mother. On the surface, all seemed as it should be: I was among my people, our victory against the Wuxin was complete.

Yet why did it feel *wrong*? Why did this triumph feel hollow? Was the price of victory too high?

The answer lay before me among the bodies of the fallen, the earth dark with their blood. A dawning horror set in that most of the dead were *mortals* . . . those of Tianxia: not just soldiers but the elderly and children, splayed on the ground, curled in terror, some still shielding their loved ones in their lifeless embrace. Death shrouded the land that I would have given my life to protect. The greatest losers of this war were my people after all—what I'd always feared. Vengeance had sown this field of death, and its cruel harvest should never have been reaped.

The nightmare faded, my two manifestations appearing side by side once more. But I could not unsee the devastation—weeping silent sobs that racked my core, tears that never fell. My arms wrapped across my stomach, trying to banish this chill within me.

One fate was preferable to the other, but both felt wrong. Death marked them in despicable measure; both culminating in the destruction of Tianxia. What would be left of my kingdom? Just the ghosts of the dead. The banks of the Wangchuan River would overflow with their tormented spirits, their cries ringing through my conscience forever.

How could I choose any path that led to this end? How could I live with myself?

"Why?" I asked numbly. "Why does the future diverge this way?"

You are marked by both—a curse in its burden, a gift in its choice. The blessing from the Tree of Everlasting Life shielded your core, giving you the choice of the destiny you wish. Without this gift, the Wuxin would have claimed you entirely. You would not know anything of your life before . . . in some ways, maybe an easier choice, never knowing what you'd given up?

"No," I replied furiously. "A coward's choice, a despicable one. I'd rather know than to live as a fool in ignorance."

A brief silence followed my outburst. *Then choose well. Choose wisely. Once made, this decision cannot be undone.*

It should be clear. The choice to become one of the Wuxin—to slaughter my people, both mortal and immortal, to kill Zhangwei—was utterly horrifying. Yet both fates were cruel, the death of countless innocents staining my hands. If war broke out, Tianxia would be destroyed. If these were the fates written for me—I wanted neither.

Then write your own.

Zhangwei's words resonated through me as I straightened, raising my chin. A calm spread through me, a precious clarity. "I claim neither fate. Return my memories, all of them—and I will make my own destiny."

I tensed, expecting the mirror to rebuke me, to demand a choice—yet only a sigh rippled through the temple. A wind stirred, the waters of the pond frothing and churning, the two images of me shuddering—as they shattered, vanishing like they'd never existed.

So be it.

Closing my eyes, a tingling sensation rushed through my blood, into my head. An awareness surged to life deep in my mind, unleashing what was once bound—my body warming with a trace of my power. Neither borrowed nor stolen but my own, answering to my command. Had my immortal lifeforce been restored along with the awareness of my true self? Gone was the confusion and uncertainty, my knowledge of magic returning in force—yet something felt different about it . . . a restraint, where once it had flowed free. I was weaker; my power diminished. Was it because I'd been poisoned and taken only part of the cure? Or was it because I was no longer wholly immortal?

The sensations softened into a glittering warmth that darted through me. Azure light flickered from my hands as I reached out to touch the pond. The water stilled at once, cold to the touch—my pale face staring back at me. I looked almost as before: just a slight shimmer to my skin, a brightness to my eyes, my lock of pale hair shining as it curled down my face. Yet inside, I was forever changed.

It is done, the Mirror of Destiny said solemnly. *You are all, yet you are none.*

"Then what am I?"

This time there was only silence. Maybe, at last, this was a question the mirror could not answer.

My mind was suffused with memories, too many to decipher at once. I struggled to piece my past together from the glimpses I'd caught, an unfinished book to be filled in. "There are still gaps in what I remember," I said haltingly. "Many things I don't understand or recall, yet I know something is missing—memories that haven't been regained."

If you were restored through the Elixir of Immortality, it would be a smoother transition. Yet you regained your immortal awareness here. Your memories are still fragmented; it will take time to recall your years. Rest will hasten the process.

"Thank you," I whispered.

A brief silence. *Don't thank me; I gave you nothing. This path is of your own making.*

THE GUARDS WERE WAITING OUTSIDE. THEY CLOSED around me when I emerged from the temple, though I was relieved to find the loathsome Captain Rao had gone. We walked in silence down the stairs, back to the pier. Lord Dalian's barge was no longer there, a small wooden boat in its place, the prow carved with a bird, its plume painted bright orange.

Aunt Shou sat within. At the sight of me, she rose to her feet. "Is it done?"

Her knowing tone hurt. She was Dalian's accomplice; she'd plotted to take my choice from me, too. But I hid my emotions, fixing a smile on my face. Aunt Shou would be hard to deceive; she had known me since I was a child.

"Yes," I told her, stepping onto the boat.

It set off at once. The vessel was small but swift as it glided along the river, heading back toward the palace.

Aunt Shou's eyes flicked to my hair. A frown lined her forehead, but she returned my smile. After all, she had no reason to doubt; she knew nothing of the gift I'd received. "This is for the best. You are powerful now. Eternal."

She was careful not to say "immortal," careful to avoid any mention of my true heritage, the one they'd try to steal from me. I swallowed my anger; I had to convince them their scheme had worked. It was the only way to gain their trust, to secure a chance for Chengyin and me to escape.

The void birds shrieked, a pair breaking away to soar toward me, their beaks and talons glinting like spear tips. I cursed in my mind, afraid they would attack me, revealing my farce—but light shot from Aunt Shou's hand toward them, the birds flying away at once.

"They might take a while to get accustomed to you." She pressed a small amber bottle into my hand. "It's our scent that they're attuned to. Yours might differ from ours, given your transformation. Wear this fragrance for now; it will keep them away."

"Thank you, Aunt Shou." Her expression did not waver, though I searched her for any sign of suspicion. I uncorked the bottle and shook out a drop of clear liquid, then rubbed it over my wrists—an earthy sweetness rising in the air.

"It reminds me of the fragrance of the desert," she said, a trace wistfully. "I miss it sometimes. Though we've made a new home here, part of us was left in the skies."

As another void bird circled us, I stiffened—but it ignored me this time.

"Do you feel well, child?" Aunt Shou asked.

I pressed a hand to my forehead, trying to hide my unease. "I'm tired, Aunt Shou. The mirror said I needed to rest."

She patted my shoulder. "Let's go home."

Home? A chill shot through me. I fell silent, staring at the reddish skies in the horizon, the glittering waters of the Wangchuan River beneath us.

"There was no taint in the pond." I was careful to keep the accusation from my tone.

"Not in the Temple of the Crimson Moon," she admitted, touching the bell by her waist. "But it's true that the power drawn from the Wangchuan River has diminished of late. No one knows why, but this affects us all. Once, these waters satisfied our needs—yet now it must be rationed. We will weaken if this continues; this is why we need the Mortal Realm."

I looked ahead, straining to appear indifferent. "How are the waters rationed, Aunt Shou? How do you feed from it?"

Aunt Shou bent to dip her hand in the river as she closed her eyes. The bell by her waist glowed, a soft chime ringing out as specks of greenish light rose from the water to settle over her skin. When she opened her eyes, the copper rings around her pupils gleamed brighter, her skin flushed. "Once you grow more adept at this, you can choose the emotions you wish. The Wangchuan River holds many memories—not just sorrow, but also joy and love so great it was hard to relinquish."

Aunt Shou reached into her pouch, drawing out a gold bell like hers, like the one Lord Dalian and Captain Rao wore. As she tied it to my waist, it clinked against the seal of Tianxia. I suppressed the urge to tear the bell away. It did not belong there, just as I didn't belong here.

"Why are ours crafted of gold?" I asked. "Most of the others wear bronze ones."

Her expression clouded, her mouth pursed. "Dalian devised this scheme to ration the river's power. Different restraints are set upon the different bells. Once we reach our limit, we cannot feed from the river until the next week."

"Who sets the limits?" I already knew, but wanted her to acknowledge it—sensing how much she disapproved of this.

"Dalian." She continued quickly, not wanting to dwell on this. "Your hunger may be different because you were mortal; you may not suffer the same cravings as us. Let your body guide you. When you feel weak, you should feed as I did."

"What if we don't feed?"

"We fade. We lose our physical forms. We become little more than these spirits in the river." She glanced at the cuts on my hands where I'd struck the ground in the temple. "We have a few healers in the palace. Their power is limited but they can treat such injuries."

"Can't you heal me?" I asked curiously.

"It's not a skill many of us developed. What need did we have to mend flesh and blood before?"

Silence fell over us once more. "Why was I sent to the temple, Aunt Shou? Why was this done to me?" I wanted to hear her answer.

"Now you are a part of our family forever." There was such warmth in her voice, I might have believed her—if I didn't know how well she lied.

"I want the truth," I said bluntly.

She sighed. "That was only part of it. We need you to open the gateway. Dalian has almost exhausted himself in his attempts. The crack he's pried apart won't hold for much longer. As the Lady of Tianxia, as one of us—you can open the gateway to secure our people's future."

I looked away to hide my revulsion. She was both cunning and careful in her answers, speaking only of my mortal past. But it wasn't my mortal heritage they wanted. I was Queen Caihong's daughter, the only one who had a chance of lifting the enchantment crafted with her magic—the one that ran in my veins. And they would never let me go, not until I'd done what they wanted.

"Can I open it?" I asked.

"Yes, with the power you now have." She spoke like she knew, like she'd already sensed it. "Do you know how to use it?"

"A little," I said carefully. "It's unfamiliar, though the God of War instructed me before, showing me his magic." I had to pretend I knew nothing of my powers, that they were new.

She nodded. "I will help you. What matters most is that you're safe and well. I kept my promise to your grandfather to look after you; he would have been pleased at how things worked out."

He would not. She was deluding herself, trying to excuse her deception. Grandfather would have throttled her for what she'd tried to do to me.

Live a good life, Liyen, he'd told me. He would not have wanted the blood of countless mortals and immortals on my hands.

"What of your appetites? How else do you feel different?" she probed.

I repressed a shudder. "I don't feel much right now. I'm more tired than hungry. My head hurts, my body aches."

Aunt Shou reached out to brush the side of my head. The affectionate gesture sent a pang through my chest. "You are the first. No mortal has ever become one of us. If anything confuses you, come to me."

So, she could craft more lies? The less I said, the better. They had no reason to believe their plan had failed—unless I gave it to them. Beyond Zhangwei, no one else knew of the Tree of Everlasting Life's gift, the only thing that could have kept me safe.

"I'm not confused," I replied with a smile. "I remember Grandfather and Tianxia. You and Chengyin, too."

She nodded gravely. "That is good. We should cherish such ties."

"What of Chengyin?" I pressed. "Will Lord Dalian release him?"

"I will protect Chengyin. You must trust me," she said. "Now that you are one of us, Dalian will feel more at ease."

Despite her many lies, I believed this. We didn't speak for the rest of journey, and I was glad for the silence. Memories descended relentlessly, a confounding stream . . . years of recollections unfolding at breathless speed, one merging into the other until I could not pick them apart.

One question echoed in my mind: Who was I now? What had I become? Not even the Mirror of Destiny knew. Was I a mortal with an immortal's spirit, or an immortal with a mortal's heart? And as I touched my lock of silvery hair, I also wondered at this lingering trace of the waters of death that had marked me by the Wuxin's treachery. It didn't matter; none of it would control me. I was my past and my present—and I would forge my own future.

36

Once in my room, I closed the door, then pushed a heavy desk in front of it. A mortal habit, for what could keep these powerful beings out? I scrubbed myself in the copper bath, inhaling the rose-scented steam. All the while, flashes of memories darted without order or meaning, yielding more questions than answers. After the bath, I dressed myself quickly. The robe stuck to my damp skin, my wet hair blotting the silk as I stared at myself in the mirror.

It was my face; it had always been my face. Any similarities had just been obscured when I was mortal, like a veil now torn away. My name came back to me, too . . . except I wasn't her anymore: I was Liyen. There was a humming in my body, a reverberation that reached into my bones, a newfound warmth coursing through my veins. I reached instinctively for the energy, bracing for a tussle—but it flowed into my grasp effortlessly. Everything I'd learned from before was returning to me now—my training, the remembrance of my magic as familiar as swimming after a long break. Some things, one never forgets.

"Ice," I whispered, my magic drawn like shining threads from the lifeforce buried in my mind. Frost speckled my fingertips, aglow with an azure light—yet I did not feel cold; our own magic could not harm us. "More." I was eager to test my boundaries, to feel that rush of power through my body. Spears of ice formed at my fingertips, breaking off to slam against the wall before me.

As I released my hold, the ice melted away, leaving scratches in the stone. Power was a heady thing, especially after being without it. Yet I sensed the difference—my magic blunted, not as strong as before. Part of my lifeforce had been irrevocably damaged, which the Divine Pearl Lotus could not undo. But I wouldn't regret the little I'd lost. I was alive; I was myself.

I breathed deeply, fatigue pressing on me. Maybe I was still unused to channeling magic, or I had to learn to adjust to my new limits. As I lay on the bed, I slipped my dagger under the pillow—a necessary precaution in an enemy's home. And when I closed my eyes, sleep claimed me at once.

I WAS STANDING ON THE EDGE OF A BATTLEFIELD. MY gold armor was stained with blood, the black jade hilt of my sword in my grasp. Shouts rang out, blades clashing all around, magic surging through the air. The Wuxin were fighting against us, hate curling inside me at the sight of them. What did they want? Chaos. Suffering. They thrived on it.

A broad-shouldered warrior in a gold helmet battled the creatures. Beside him was Queen Caihong—my mother—the recognition twinged, still edged with the unfamiliar. Wuxin soldiers surrounded the pair, isolating them from their own. Was it a trap? I ran toward them—Zhangwei rushing to join me, his sword in his hand. Just ahead, a hooded warrior raised his arms, greenish lights crackling between his palms. The air thickened, rife with ominous energy. What power was this? I hurled my sword at the Wuxin just as Zhangwei released an arrow—but they rebounded against an unseen shield. The Wuxin did not look our way, focused instead on his prey: my mother. As I shouted a warning, he hurled the lights at her. Her companion had swung around at my cry, pushing the queen to safety. The malevolent lights struck him in his chest, crawling over his neck and face. His eyes went wide, his body thrashing, snared in the throes of this brutal curse. Soldiers rushed to him but were flung aside by the force. Some of the glowing streaks fragmented from the warrior—to come, hurtling toward me. At once, Zhangwei covered me, using his body as a shield—stiffening as the ominous lights plunged into him.

"No!" I shoved at him, wanting to get him to safety, but he held me like he'd never let go. Despite his protection, a scattering of the spell struck me, too—the pain as excruciating as nails being hammered into my flesh. A bitter cold sank over me, spreading throughout my body like ice. Yet Zhangwei's skin was ashen, colder even than mine—he'd shielded me at the cost of his own safety. As we fell to the ground, my gaze fixed on the warrior who'd protected the queen. He'd borne the brunt of the vicious attack, those lights devouring his body like a ravenous beast—only fading once he went deathly still.

A cry split the air. Such anguish . . . it wrenched me within. Queen Caihong pulled away from those restraining her, weeping as she fell by his side, clasping him to her. I was crying, too, grief crashing through me at the sight of my mother embracing the warrior's body, shuddering in ceaseless grief. She tore the helmet from his head, cradling his face between her palms. He was striking: a broad chin, a sharp nose, dark-brown hair. Recognition was a bolt to my heart, a surge of pure joy that was drowned by despair.

Father.

He was dead . . . they'd killed him. I curled on the bed, awake now, my pillow wet with tears, a fist crammed against my mouth. A cruel thing to relive the death of your loved ones—to lose them all over again, just when you'd found them.

A shadow fell across the floor; someone was in my room. My skin prickled as I seized the dagger under my pillow. Why wait to be attacked? Silently, I rose from the bed, raising the dagger—then I sprang toward the intruder.

He towered over me, but I shoved him against the wall, the edge of my dagger to his throat. The man was well built and strong, but I was quick, my grip firm as I held him fast—or was it that he didn't struggle? As he slanted his head away from me, a shaft of moonlight illuminated the smooth planes of his face, the column of his throat.

"Zhangwei," I breathed.

Wonder stirred in me—both shock and relief. And something else, warm and bright and endless. Yet in the same breath, terror struck. What if this was another imposter? I didn't drop my dagger; I didn't dare. Instead of trying to break free, he leaned closer until the tip of my blade was tucked beneath a fold of his flesh. The barest touch, and his skin would tear. My hand shook as I shifted the dagger slightly.

His lips stretched into a smile. "I expected a warmer greeting, Liyen."

"How do I know it's you?" I desperately wanted this to be real.

In a flash, he spun me around, until my back was against the wall, his arms fencing me in as his dark gaze pinned mine. Somehow, I felt no fear. His presence seemed to fill the room, the air tightening with the force of his aura—more potent than before. The last time I'd seen him, he'd been weakened by the poison, incapacitated by the lotus. And now . . . he was here.

"How do you want me to prove it's me?" he asked in silken tones, his face cast in shadow. "Shall I show you where my dagger pierced your chest the first time? Shall I tell you what you said when you yielded the lotus to me? Or shall I show you how I kissed you when we were in the river—"

The dagger fell from my hand, clattering softly on the carpet. As he reached for me, I threw my arms around his neck. This was him; I knew it in my heart. Tears blurred my sight, those of joy, a lightness filling me. He was here, he'd come for me. He clasped me tightly as I buried my face in the curve of his neck, his large hands stroking my back in a soothing rhythm, a warmth kindling inside me.

"Why were you crying?" he whispered, gently brushing the tears from my face.

"A bad dream." My voice was hoarse, my pain still raw.

He nudged the fallen dagger with his boot. "Is that why you almost stabbed me? After all the trouble I took to find you?"

"What did you expect? Praise and grateful tears?" I mocked, even as I wiped my eyes.

"At least I have the tears." His gaze was startlingly bright. "But I'll take a curse from you any day, over praise from any other."

"A bad trade."

"No trade is bad between us." He tucked a lock of hair behind my ear. "With you, it doesn't matter whether I win or lose."

I grinned at him. "It matters to me."

"I know." He laughed as he spoke, his tone jolting something in me—something elusive that slipped from my grasp. "Then let me be a fool."

At his slow smile, heat surged through my veins. How close we stood, my leg wedged between his. As I stepped back, his hands slid around my waist, holding me lightly in place. "I'll even take your dagger through my heart if you stay."

My pulse raced as I traced his chest slowly. "Is that a challenge?" There was a new assurance in speaking to him, my body attuned to his—like something had awakened inside me, like I'd been asleep all this while.

He bent his head to mine. "I'm yours to do with as you will."

My face burned from the intensity of his stare. I wanted to linger in this moment, to savor it—but I made myself move away, regretting it as his fingers slid from me, my body still craving his touch. There were too many questions in my mind, and he was far too potent a distraction.

"How did you find me?"

"The moment I could move again, I searched for you. The skies were still sealed. When your sword returned to me, when I heard you scream, I rushed toward you—but it was too late. You were gone." His face darkened. "There was only one place they would have taken you, for the reason they wanted to seize you."

"The gateway. How did you get through it?" I asked. "Lord Dalian said there were restrictions on who could pass through it, that it was dangerous."

"The Wuxin attacked me on my way back to Kunlun. I left one of them alive. He proved to be most informative, and not entirely fond of their ruler."

"You killed the rest?" I tried to recall the viciousness of their schemes, but found no satisfaction in their deaths.

"They took you from me," he said with deadly calm. "I was not inclined to mercy, nor did they seek it. One agreed to help me in exchange for his life, letting me take his place through the gateway, showing me how to slip through it unharmed."

"You could have died." Though he stood before me, I went cold at the thought.

"Some things are worse than death. If I couldn't get to you, you would have been lost to me. I couldn't bear that again."

"Again?" Something stirred in me, something that slipped further away the more I tried to grasp it. "The way you speak to me sometimes . . . it's like we've known each other long before we met."

Zhangwei searched my face, light flaring in his eyes. "What do you recall? What happened to you?"

"I was taken to a temple. I looked into the Mirror of Destiny there, regaining some of my memories. Fragments. Disjointed pieces. I was an immortal, like you. My mother was Queen Caihong." I laughed; it seemed ludicrous when spoken aloud.

"She *is* your mother," he corrected me gravely.

"Does she hate me now?" I asked haltingly. "Why did she try to hurt me?"

"She never hated you; she loves you," he replied. "When you were mortal, she couldn't show her feelings. She had to pretend, even as it hurt her, because you weren't meant to know—not until you'd regained your memories. Otherwise, our plan would have failed."

It hadn't been anger or loathing in her face, but pain? My heart ached, and I did not realize until that moment just how much I'd missed her. "What was the plan?"

"You and I both needed the Divine Pearl Lotus, the antidote to what we suffered. But there was only one, and it hadn't bloomed yet. We had to wait. And the only way we could share it was between a mortal and an immortal; there wasn't enough otherwise. If you'd regained your memories too early, before you'd given me the lotus—you wouldn't be wholly mortal anymore. We wouldn't be able to share it."

"And you'd have died." I recoiled, unable to bear the thought. When had my feelings for him grown so deep? They frightened me a little, because I didn't quite understand them.

"At least you would have lived," he said.

Silence fell over us as we stared at each other. Was he thinking of all we'd almost lost? All we'd regained?

"It was fortunate our scheme failed the first time," he said somberly. "We didn't know you'd been given the waters of death then. If we'd tried to restore your immortality without the gift from the Tree of Everlasting Life, your immortal self would have been irrevocably lost. You would have become Wuxin, your past a blank sheet of paper to write whatever they chose."

I drew a long breath. "They plotted this all along, trying to turn me into one of them. Fortunately, they knew nothing of the tree's gift."

"Who gave you the water from the Wangchuan?" His voice dropped dangerously low.

"Aunt Shou. She is one of them." It hurt to say it aloud. "She did it to force my grandfather's hand into giving me the lotus."

"She always kept a distance from me; I couldn't sense her. Her powers of concealment must be strong." His expression was grave. "I sensed the lotus when I first healed you by the wall, but I only detected the taint of the Wangchuan River later—when my enchantment bound us in the palace. I'd hoped the Ancient Grandmaster could remove it."

"Was that what you asked him? What you couldn't tell me?" It all made sense now.

"I wanted to, but I couldn't then. It was hard to keep everything from you."

"You shouldn't have tried to take the lotus from me the first time," I said, recalling the hurt when I thought he'd betrayed me.

"A mistake, that I ask your forgiveness for," he admitted. "I thought you loved me then. I wanted to believe it, impatient for us to reclaim our lives. There was nothing harder than pretending you were a stranger, seeing your mistrust and resentment whenever you looked at me."

"There is nothing to forgive." I meant it, too. I now understood that he hadn't wanted to harm me but to help us.

"If only we'd found you earlier. We'd been searching for you for years, the moment you descended to the Mortal Realm," he told me. "Discreetly, not to alert our enemies of your vulnerability—not just the Wuxin, but many at your mother's court would leap at the chance to dispose of the heir. It should have been easy to find you, but our search was thwarted by the mortals' fear and suspicion of us. Many lied, concealing their children's birthdates, obscuring any information they shared."

"Immortals have done little to earn our trust," I said, defending them. No matter what, they would always be my people. "The

Wuxin also concealed me from you."

"It was fortunate we met by the wall of Tianxia."

"Fortune had nothing to do with it." I grimaced, recalling the spilled offerings and broken incense sticks. "Don't you remember what I did to your shrine?"

His eyes narrowed. "Was that intentional?"

"For survival," I explained quickly.

"The Winged Devils were there to snatch you away, to hand you to the Wuxin." His face darkened as he added, "It terrifies me how close they came to succeeding. At how I almost lost you forever."

"Fortunately, it didn't work," I reminded him. "I was given a choice."

His fingers brushed the streak of white in my hair. "You aren't immortal—not entirely. What did you choose?"

I raised my chin. "Do you think me a monster?"

"Never," he said vehemently. "You are more than your face, more than your name. With you, I am whole."

My heart was so full, I thought it might break. "The mirror showed me two destinies—one of the Wuxin, one of the immortal." I braced, afraid of disappointing him to not have chosen the latter. "I rejected both; I could not bear either: the war, the deaths, the loss of countless innocent lives. Tianxia would be destroyed. There must be another way."

Zhangwei took my hands, lacing our fingers together. "Whatever you choose, I will be with you from now on."

I couldn't speak for a moment; I couldn't find the words to describe this unadulterated joy. How I loved him—even as I marveled at the depth of our emotions, jarring a little with what I knew. What could I not remember?

"I have my magic now. Some of my memories," I said haltingly. "But I feel I'm missing something about us—something important."

"Do you remember *me*?" he asked fiercely, his intensity searing me.

I searched for any recollection of him, yet nothing emerged beyond the glimpses I'd seen. We must have been close before—all the signs were there, those that had teased my mind: our inexplicable connection, our matched swords, the way he spoke to me that slipped into familiarity, the feelings that didn't feel wholly earned from him, those I felt for him in turn.

Why couldn't I remember? Had I truly forgotten? Or was it because these memories were so precious, so vital . . . I'd buried them far too deep.

"Not yet," I said, biting my lip. "The Mirror of Destiny said it would take time for all my memories to return, to make sense of them."

Light flared in his eyes like midnight fire. "Then let me help you."

In one step, he closed the distance between us. He pulled me to him—not roughly, but not patiently either. It was like he was at the end of his tether, on the brink of snapping. I wanted this, too, my heart racing as his fingers cradled my face. His eyes glittered dangerously bright—and then he kissed me. Our breaths mingled as his lips parted mine, a current running through me at the intimacy. I pressed myself against him, my arms arched around his neck, fire scorching my veins. Nothing mattered in this moment except the touch of him, his taste and scent as I inhaled, half-delirious with pleasure.

When he broke away, I wanted to protest—even as I was suddenly conscious of the thin robe I wore, the neckline gaping to reveal the curve of my chest. His gaze shifted, then darkened as he swung me into his arms and strode to the bed. This time, he did not toss me upon it but laid me down gently—almost reverently. His breath warmed my cheek, the scent of him suffusing my senses. His skin seared mine, hot or cold I did not know . . . just that I was burning all over, aching with need, craving more.

He lowered himself over me, leaving just a breath of air between us. "Liyen?" There was no sweeter sound than my name on his lips. "I want you."

Yearning twisted me at his confession. I wanted him, too, but the words stuck in my throat. I reached out instead, pulling him to me. His body covered mine, pressing me against the covers with his weight. My hands sought his, our fingers lacing as he kissed me again and again, our legs tangling between the silken layers. Hunger built within me, kindled from the moment he touched me. I drew back, tugging at his belt. Unsure of what I was doing, driven by a primal urge to be as close to him as I could. A low laugh rippled from him, one that was almost a growl. If he was amused, I did not care. What was pride in this moment, buried beneath this relentless desire? Whatever this was . . . even if my memories were still hazy, I knew deep down that it was *right*.

I clasped him tighter, arching against him. One of his hands slid around my body again, the other sweeping the curve of my neck, his thumb brushing the sensitive hollow. His lips were soft yet firm, his breath hot against mine. Our tongues brushed, then entangled with hunger. We kissed as though it were our first and last time, and I never wanted us to stop. I wanted more; I would always want more of him, my heart beating to his. As his nails dug into my waist, I relished his roughness, his urgency. Beneath his hands, my sash broke away like a strip of paper. My robes were pulled aside, his mouth moving to my bare shoulder, seeking and hot. I curved closer, running my fingers along his back, winding into his hair that draped like silk over my face. I yanked his head back as I kissed the column of his neck, gripping his broad shoulders, feeling the raised ridges of old scars upon them—almost familiar, like I'd touched them before. How beautiful he was, how perfect. A guttural sound slipped from his throat, his hold tightening as he pressed me closer, one of his hands sliding up my leg, near the part of me that burned like liquid fire.

Only once, my mind surfaced from this haze as I clasped him tightly, moving to his rhythm. His breathing was as rough as mine, my heart pounding like his, my palms against his bared chest—his skin like sun-warmed silk. A headiness consumed me like I was drunk on wine, in a dream I never wanted to awaken from, a divine moment when reality is more wondrous than fantasy. We were so close, so intimate—we were as one.

"I know you." My gaze searched his with aching certainty. "I knew you even before we met."

He looked into my face, his eyes shining as the stars at dusk. "Welcome back, my beloved."

Beloved.

The word resonated through me, healing wounds I didn't know existed, making me whole once more. There was no doubt left in me, all of that had cleared away like the clouds after a storm.

This was happiness.

37

Afterward, in bed, his fingers traced the length of my body, stirring my hunger with ease. I should have been sated but was far from it; it didn't seem possible to have enough of him. Zhangwei rose, lighting a brace of candles. They flickered to life, casting a warm glow around the chamber.

As I pulled on a thin robe, he returned to my side and cradled my cheek in his palm. "I want to see your face. I want to see all of you."

I swallowed, my mouth going dry with desire as his fingers trailed lower. I caught his hand and held it tight.

"You've regained your strength, most of it," he remarked. "When you were mortal, I was always afraid of hurting you."

Some men thought of women as delicate flowers to be shielded and tended when it suited them, and pruned when they grew too wild. "How do you feel about it now?" I asked.

His slow smile sent a shaft of pleasure through me. "I like touching you the way I want to, without fear or restraint."

"I like it, too," I admitted, lifting my face to his.

His lips brushed mine, softly at first, then more urgently. How I wanted him. As the familiar heat built, I pulled away with regret. There were still answers I needed, and we weren't out of danger yet.

"I have many questions," I began.

"I have one," he countered. "Do you remember me now, do you remember *us*—all that we are to each other?"

"That is more than one question," I said with a laugh.

"They mean the same thing." His expression was grave, intent. After all, he'd been waiting for this answer for a long time.

"I remember you, Zhangwei. I remember us." I took his hand in mine. "I will never forget again."

"What about your fiancé in Tianxia?" he wanted to know.

Was he still jealous? He had never been in the past, always so annoyingly assured. Maybe our separation had made him anxious, when he couldn't find me in the Mortal Realm. An urge rose to tease him as my eyes slid to our discarded clothes. "Do you feel remorse now?"

"No," he said bluntly, holding my gaze. "Because you were mine first. Because I'd claimed you as you'd claimed me—for eternity—and I will hold you to that."

I wanted this, too, yet something knotted in my chest at his words. "What if I don't have eternity?" I didn't know what awaited me; no one did.

"Then, for as long as we live. Or until the day you want to be released, knowing all we are to each other." His tone hardened. "Now, tell me, are you going to marry another?"

The knot loosened, my fears dissipating. "No. I love Chengyin—but as a friend. A brother."

"Yet you are engaged?"

"It was a ploy to divert the ministers who were trying to marry me off."

He smiled even as his jaw tightened. "Tell me who proposed a groom, and I'll silence them on your behalf."

For a moment, I contemplated the pleasure of unleashing the God of War upon Minister Guo and his allies. Shallow, yet undoubtedly satisfying. But if I didn't establish my own authority, it would forever be bound to his.

"I can silence them myself," I told him.

He nodded. "You never had any trouble standing your own ground, not since the day we met."

I sifted through the recollections that crowded my mind, filling the void like the strokes of a painting. Zhangwei and I had met when we were students, long before he'd become the God of War. Back then, he was a rival in my studies, the only one who'd matched my ability. Whenever he'd bested me, he'd flick his eyes my way as though making sure I was watching, asserting his victory. I'd loathed him then . . . maybe I would have gone my whole life believing I disliked him, when the truth was I'd thrived on his challenge and he'd fascinated me. For years, I'd ignored my feelings, burying them away—it was easier that way. What a fool I'd been.

I hid these thoughts; he was arrogant enough. "Back then, you were the teacher's favorite," I said.

He grinned. "It was the only way to get your attention. I studied hard because I noticed how annoyed you were whenever someone beat you."

I'd been competitive in my youth—I still was. But I'd wanted to earn each victory, disliking those who tried to gain favor by letting me win. Zhangwei *never* did, throwing himself entirely into each challenge. Once, we'd sparred so intensely, he'd cut my arm with his sword, though bloodshed was frowned upon by our instructor. I'd left in anger then, returning to my room where I had healed myself clumsily—cursing him loud enough to be heard down the hall, and from the other side of the door that he'd knocked on.

I remembered opening it, staring at him stonily. "What are you doing here?"

His gaze went to the rip in my sleeve. "I'm sorry. I didn't mean to hurt you."

"Oh, I think you did." I jabbed him in his shoulder, knowing I'd bruised him there earlier. "But I would have done the same if I could," I added grudgingly.

He'd looked down then as he shoved a handful of jasmine at me. The fragrance was my favorite . . . had he noticed? I'd stared at them blankly, unsure of myself. "What am I supposed to do with them?"

"I read in the books . . . I thought you might like them."

I had snorted then, not cruelly but because the idea of him wanting to please me was absurd. As a deep flush crept up his neck, the wall around my heart crumbled a little. I moved from the doorway. "Come in."

He hesitated, touching the wound on my arm gently. His energy surged into my body—unfamiliar, yet potent and warm. The pain eased, the wound closing. "I've finally found something you're not good at," he said with a smile. "If you ever need healing, come to me."

"What is *your* weakness?" I demanded, annoyed at his sharp assessment.

He looked at me directly. "I thought it was obvious."

Silence had fallen then. It felt like something new had sprung between us; something precious and rare. "Do you play weiqi?" I shifted the conversation to safer ground.

The way his smile had widened—I'd almost regretted my invitation, even as part of me was eager for a good opponent. None of the other students wanted to play with me after I'd won all the matches. Our game was the first of many—infuriating, demanding matches, where the days melded into nights, when I almost forgot who my opponent was. Respect tangled with frustration, resentment at his skill even as I admired his game. He played like he fought—unyielding and ruthless, his brilliance shining through each move. A victory against him meant something because it was hard-won. Perhaps it was inevitable that after spending all that time together, we had become friends. And then so much more.

I wanted to laugh now, recalling how badly I'd played against him in his library—before I'd known who I was. My pride was still bruised as I nodded toward the weiqi board in the corner. "Do you want a rematch?"

He caught my meaning at once. "This time we'll need higher stakes, so you don't surrender as easily again."

"I didn't surrender," I said through gritted teeth. "I was distracted—"

"By me?" His mouth curved in bold assurance.

"With trying to figure out why you were interrogating me then," I retorted.

"I was trying to find out how much you hated me," he admitted. "And how I could change your mind."

"I don't think I ever truly hated you," I said slowly, my mind too rational to blame him wholly for things beyond his control—though I'd certainly disliked him, resented him, and even feared him, too.

I paused, then added, "Maybe after you stabbed me I hated you a little."

"I deserved it," he said. "But we were trying to restore you, not hurt you. We'd already procured the Elixir of Immortality and believed it was safe." His expression grew thunderous. "We were wrong."

I was teasing him, and yet the echo of his betrayal still stung. No matter the farce, the emotions had been real. "I wish you could have told me the truth from the start."

He tilted my face to his. "The Divine Pearl Lotus complicated matters. I could not reveal anything about your immortal life before you gave it to me, because it could have triggered the start of your transformation. You had to surrender the lotus of your own will as a mortal—to love me again, though you'd forgotten me."

"But you failed then," I said, needling him, selfishly wanting to hold on to these precious moments of discovery.

He sighed. "And you said *I* had the heart of ice."

I colored at the memory, of all the terrible things I'd thought and said of him. "You were too impatient, too sure of yourself," I teased mercilessly. "But I yielded in the end."

A moment's hesitation and it might have been too late. Zhangwei, dead. While I would be lost to my own past, never knowing the life I had left in the skies. I shuddered at the possibility.

He lowered his head to mine. "We didn't foresee the Wuxin's schemes. If they'd succeeded in spiriting you away, we would have failed you."

"No, Zhangwei. You saved me, we saved each other. For all the things that went wrong, as many went right."

As my hand tightened around his, he said, "It should have been me who went to the Mortal Realm."

I struggled to remember, the memories still blurred. "What do you mean?"

"The Divine Pearl Lotus could only cure one immortal. I wanted you to have it, but you refused—you never gave up on us, researching relentlessly. It was you who learned that a mortal and an immortal could share the lotus. While neither would be entirely restored, while we would each give up a little of our strength—this way we both would live. We agreed that I would descend to the world below."

Only now did I recall how I'd argued passionately against him, wanting to go instead. He was hurt more than me from the attack; for once, I was stronger than him. While Zhangwei usually yielded to my choices even if they went against his own—when my life was at stake, he became domineering, ruthless, and stubborn. The foe I must outmatch.

"I did not 'agree,'" I reminded him. "Your injuries were worse than mine. I was afraid you wouldn't survive the transformation, that you'd die before the lotus even bloomed. It was safer for you to remain with our healers, sustained by the magic of our realm. Don't forget, the curse carried over into our mortal forms, too." The constant fatigue, the deep cold—only dissipating after I took the lotus.

His face darkened. "And so *you* went instead."

Our last night together blazed through my mind. We'd been in his home, in the courtyard that had been forbidden to me. "The South Courtyard was mine," I murmured in wonder. "All this time, you kept my things just as I'd left them."

"I would let no one touch what belonged to you," he said. "All that is mine is yours."

The courtyard had been our haven, away from the demands of duty. No one disturbed us there, none daring to incur the God of War's wrath. We had played weiqi in our room, eaten our meals in the garden. I had read while he played the qin. And at night, we'd slept entwined. There were also quieter moments of simple companionship, the kind when your soul is at peace, when your heart is whole. When you want nothing more from life . . . content to simply exist. This was how I felt when he was with me.

"I couldn't let you enter the courtyard because I was afraid it would jolt your memory too early—before it was time. It was also why parts of your mother's palace were closed to you," he explained. "I didn't expect your mount to break free of its restraints to chase you the day we visited the Phoenix Kingdom."

The qilin. The recognition struck now: Red Storm had been my faithful qilin since my youth. No wonder Zhangwei had not wanted to hurt her. How loyal she was, helping me flee. How I wished she were here now.

"Once you entered the South Courtyard, it became too dangerous for you to remain at my home. Your mother wanted you back at the palace. A pity, as I'd planned a different courtship."

"Was Mother very angry—about this, about my leaving?" I asked tentatively, like I was a child once more, afraid of her disapproval.

"More shocked and scared, than angry," he replied.

A half-smile. "She must have been glad to punish me that day on the Dragon Platform."

"Never think that," he said solemnly. "She did everything she could to protect you."

Something weighed on my mind, unsettling me. The stories I'd heard of her from my people and the Wuxin . . . I had always known she was ambitious but never truly understood its cost. "Mother can be harsh but isn't cruel. Why did she inflict suffering on the mortals?"

"When Her Majesty lost your father and then you—those were dark days. As the years passed and we found no trace of you, she began to wonder if the mortals were plotting against us. She was furious, unable to control her temper and grief—spilling forth, often without intent to harm. But the slightest shift in the weather in our kingdom bore drastic repercussions upon Tianxia. Something we should have been more aware and careful of, yet our efforts were focused on finding you."

Mother had not meant it . . . yet those actions had spawned cruel consequences. Many lives had been lost, much suffering wreaked. This should not have happened—and as long as I was the Lady of Tianxia, I would fight to offer my people a better future. How it also hurt that Grandfather had died out of fear of my mother's reprisal. Guilt stabbed me that both, in their own way, had just been trying to save me. I would never forget Grandfather's sacrifice; I would honor *all* my family for the rest of my days.

"I swore to my grandfather that I'd keep our kingdom safe. This vow is as precious to me now as it was then." Such bonds tethered our lives, gave it meaning. And I couldn't help wondering whether I'd have felt the same had I not lived a mortal's existence—where time mattered, the legacy one left behind.

My hands curled. "Mortal lives are as vital as ours; they cannot be sacrificed upon a whim. Tianxia must be free."

"I know," Zhangwei assured me. "I remember *all* my promises to you."

It was what he'd told me before, the true meaning of his words sinking in. All he'd suffered for me . . . no one would ever love me like he did. How hard it must have been for him to pretend indifference, hiding his hurt that I'd forgotten him, that I seemed to no longer love him. The heart could not be guided, forced, or coerced. Love and hate could not be taught.

"That day on the Dragon Platform, the punishment inflicted on you was real." I flinched at the memory. "Your wounds, your suffering—why?"

He sighed. "I'm not proud of it, but it seemed the surest way to win your heart. Time was running out. You had already taken the lotus, you'd entered our courtyard—we only had one chance."

And he was dying.

"You were too guarded around me," he continued. "Resentful of what had happened in Tianxia. I had to make you see me in a new light—to help you find your way back to me."

I remembered how he'd looked the night I left, sleeping so peacefully. I had brushed his hair from his face, drinking in his features, imprinting them in my mind. Soon, I would forget. His eyes had flicked open, his instincts for danger ever acute—but I was prepared. My magic had surged, locking him in an enchantment, and it worked only because he was severely weakened, because I knew him so well. His eyes had blazed furiously, but I was doing it for him.

The God of War protected the realms, but all I wanted was to keep *him* safe.

"Wait for me. Find me," I had told him. "No matter where I am or who I become, my heart will always be yours."

I had forced myself to walk away then—one of the hardest things I'd ever done. Outside, I'd summoned a cloud, then flew to the Celestial Kingdom. As the Jade Palace loomed ahead, dread had sunk over me. What if our plan failed? What if they couldn't find me? What if I could never return?

I'd pried away the claws of fear. At least Zhangwei would be safe. When the Divine Pearl Lotus blossomed, he could take it then. He would guard our realm, our memories, my mother— even if I could not. But I *would* return; I had to believe it.

I'd made my way to the north of the Jade Palace, where the chasm lay, how immortals were sent to the realm below with the permission of the Celestial Emperor. One of the soldiers there had frowned at the sight of me. "You're early. It's not yet dawn, as scheduled for your descent."

"I couldn't sleep. I'm impatient," I'd said.

Another had smirked. "To become mortal?"

I had not liked his tone. I didn't know much of the mortals then, but they did not deserve to be disdained that way. Yet I held my tongue; it was not my kingdom. I couldn't risk them stopping me.

"The sooner I get this over with, the sooner I can return," I'd said.

They had laughed, waving me through. The ground inside was paved with malachite and marble. Mist rose from the center, coiling in the air. Stepping to the brink, I'd hesitated, staring into the chasm beneath. Swirling lights of amber and ruby, ripples of luminescence. The power thrummed like a hundred lutes plucked at once.

As I looked down, a gust of wind tugged at me. Terror had gripped me; the unknown looming, far from my loved ones. Yet it was the only way Zhangwei and I could have a future together. What was a mortal lifespan but a handful of decades? My memories and power would be restored once I regained my immortality. How I'd reasoned with myself then—but the truth was, I had done this because I loved him. I could bear whatever the world below had for me; I was strong enough for us both.

As I'd stepped forward, a desperate cry rang out: "Stop!"

Zhangwei was racing toward me, pushing his way past the Celestial guards. There was no time left, my feet moving toward the edge.

He called my name, his voice ringing in my ears. Holding my breath, I took the final step—plummeting into the void of emptiness. The air shrouded me, erupting across my skin. Such agony . . . even now I flinched from the memory. Hairpins tumbled from my head as the coils of my hair unraveled, streaming behind me like lengths of ribbon, my robe twisted into trails of crimson silk. The pitiless wind lashed my face, my neck—any bared part of me till they were raw. Zhangwei's roar faded, along with the shouts from above.

My eyes had darted up. Zhangwei was struggling against the Celestial soldiers who were restraining him. Had he tried to leap after me?

"Only one can go at time," a Celestial told him harshly. "If you follow her now, she will die—you both will."

When he had stilled, relief filled me—he would be safe. I'd closed my eyes then, my ears filled with the deafening roar of wind, slamming into every pore. Pain erupted across my body, my power stripped away like a layer of skin. I had clung to the memories of home, my parents, my love—I didn't want to forget, struggling instinctively—yet they were plucked from my mind like petals from a flower. Tears spilled, a void opening—all of me, all that mattered, swallowed whole. And then it had ceased abruptly, a loathsome peace stealing over me.

Even now my chest ached at the memory. "I did not want to forget you," I told him softly.

"I know." He pulled me to him, holding me tight. "It was a struggle to keep myself in check, to leash my emotions. Your hostility made it a little easier for me to pretend, to remind myself of why I was doing this. Though there were times I doubted whether I could win your heart all over again."

I smiled through the tears in my eyes. "But you were never one to walk away from a challenge."

"I would never give up on you," he said steadily.

I rested my head against his chest. "You plotted everything so elaborately, with the precision of setting out to war."

"This was the most important battle I'd ever fought. The one for your heart, our lives, our future."

"I'm not immortal any longer," I said slowly. "What if I can never return to our home?"

"We will make a new one," he replied without hesitation.

He kissed me again—deeply, searchingly. My lips met his with equal hunger, my hand pressed to his chest as he clasped me tighter. With a swift move, he spun me around until I lay pinned beneath him. One of his arms was coiled around me, his other hand braced against the side of my face. His mouth slanted over my mine with a languid deliberation. Heat surged, scorching bright. His hands moved to the silk folds of my robe, pulling them apart. I was too impatient for tenderness, my lips moving across his throat, eager to taste him. We were breathing heavily, my insides ragged with wanting as my legs twisted and writhed beneath his.

We kissed again, melting into each other. I should stop, draw away again—letting reason prevail. But I wanted to be reckless; restraint was hard after our long separation. After all we'd endured, I was greedy and jealous of our time together. I had drunk deep of the well of loss, and had no desire to taste its bitterness again.

38

The skies had blossomed into a radiant rose—beautiful, unexpectedly so. As I got up and pulled on a new robe, Zhangwei heated the water in the teapot, then prepared a cup for me. There was still an edge of newness in seeing him do such mundane things, though he'd done them for me countless times before.

"We must be careful." I glanced at the doorway. "They think I'm resting, but their patience won't last much longer. Lord Dalian is impatient; he'll want to see me . . . and I don't know if he'll believe my lies."

"I won't let them hurt you."

"I don't want them to hurt you either." When he stiffened, I squeezed his hand. "You are the God of War; there's no one your equal in battle. But we're not in our world anymore. We're in theirs—and no matter how brave or strong a warrior is, no one can win against such odds."

"Don't go to them, it's too dangerous. We can leave now." He handed me my sword, the one Dalian had tried to seize.

The sight of our blades together sent a shaft of warmth through me, their similarities threaded between their differences. Mine was of black jade and silver; his of white jade and gold, the scrollwork carvings on the hilts of a similar style.

"You gave this sword to me when we pledged ourselves to each other." I shook my head. "Anyone else would have offered me a hairpin or bracelet as a token of our promise, but the God of War gifted a sword."

He shrugged unrepentantly. "You never showed much interest in jewelry. The sword kept you safe; it helped me identify you by the wall in Tianxia."

"Because I was the only one who could draw it."

"Yes. Even if you'd lied about you who were, it would not matter. I crafted your sword myself; it was meant for your hands alone."

"Just as I crafted yours," I said, another memory falling into place. "It's why I could carry your blade, why it recognized me." It struck me how everything twined and wove together, the lies he'd so skillfully told.

"No more lies," I reminded him.

"No more secrets, either," he agreed.

"I can't take the sword now. Lord Dalian knows what it is—if they find it, they'll suspect you're here," I said. "How can we escape? Is the gateway the only way out? It will be heavily guarded. What about through the Wangchuan River?"

"Only those who have surrendered their memories forever are allowed to board the Eternal Boatman's vessel, and his is the only one that can cross the realms."

"What happens to those who don't yield their memories?" I asked.

"They don't get on the boat. They drift in the river."

"For eternity?" My throat tightened at the thought.

"Until their burdens are lightened, until they can surrender their regrets and cares. In a way, the Wuxin might help them, too. Though some are still unable to find their path, and a few choose not to."

To never know Zhangwei again . . . both of us to forget each other forever. Even if it was the safest way out, I could not do it.

"Then we must go through the gateway." I frowned. "But I won't leave without Chengyin. He is still a hostage, under Lord Dalian's control."

"If he was really your betrothed, I'd be tempted to leave him." Zhangwei's expression turned grave. "Your family is mine, as are your enemies. We will save him."

"Thank you. For not trying to convince me otherwise."

"It won't be easy," Zhangwei told me. "If we use force, we might hurt your friend. It would be safer if we found a way to make Lord Dalian relinquish his hold over him."

"I must convince him that I'm on his side, that his plan worked. Only once he trusts me will he release Chengyin," I said. "Lord Dalian expects me to be one of them. He'll be harder to deceive than Aunt Shou—more suspicious, and far more dangerous."

Zhangwei's gaze clouded the way it did when he was thinking. This was a different type of fight from the battles he usually led. "Let me come with you. I'll follow at a distance."

"No," I said flatly.

"I don't want you to face them alone."

"It will be more dangerous for us both if they find you," I reminded him.

He didn't like this—nor did I. But he was unable to come up with a better solution. It wasn't as simple as taking my place for a dangerous task; any slip on his part would endanger me tenfold.

"Can Lord Dalian force me to open the gateway?" I asked. "What if he needs just my blood or my presence?"

"It's more than your blood alone, else he'd have already slit your throat. The gateway will only respond to the imprint of your magic. That must be why they wanted to transform you into one of them, to access your power."

My hands curled in anger. "Then he won't kill me, at least not yet."

"Not while you remain useful to him," Zhangwei told me.

"From what I've heard, Lord Dalian only ever thinks of himself; everything and everyone else is only an accessory. He needs the gateway opened because to launch an invasion, he requires the full force of his army, not just a sliver that can slip through the cracks."

"I won't do it, no matter what he does." Yet fear needled me that he might find a way to force my hand.

"What if you do open it?" Zhangwei asked, with an intent expression.

"No." I knew how his mind worked, that he was already scheming to ambush the Wuxin. "What if the skies are still sealed? What if the immortals cannot come to our aid? And even if you could somehow escape to gather the immortals—war will be inevitable then." My insides twisted as I recalled the horrors in the temple's mirror. "Even if we win, many will die. I won't let my people pay this price."

He sighed. "You're right. Nor will I leave you alone here."

"I will be safe," I assured him with more confidence than I felt. "I'll pretend I'm his ally. It will be easier to escape if I'm not behind bars, if his guard is down."

Zhangwei's fingers deftly set the pieces on the weiqi board in preparation for a game. I was in no mood to play, but remembered he liked to play by himself on occasion, experimenting with different strategies—probably because there were also few opponents of his ability.

"You must convince Lord Dalian that you're one of them," he said.

"How can I?" I glanced at my reflection in the mirror. "I look just as I did."

"Your aunt was convinced," he reminded me. "They want to believe their scheme worked, which is in our favor. Moreover, they know little of this supposed transformation; you're the first Wuxin transformed from a mortal. You set the rules. In their minds, nothing could have saved you."

"Should I change the color of my hair? My eyes?"

He tilted his head like he was considering it, flipping a black counter between his fingers. "Act like there's nothing to hide. If they sense any drastic attempt to alter your appearance, it will raise their suspicions. It will do more harm than good."

"I've had some practice pretending to be someone I'm not. But if I don't look at all like them, it will reinforce any doubt in their minds, a constant reminder of my difference," I told him.

He nodded then, brushing a finger across my eyes, a tingling warmth gliding across them. As I glanced into the mirror, I started to see a thin copper ring around my irises. "A small illusion, one they can't sense clearly with the aura of your magic."

He took my hand, holding it to his chest where I could feel the thud of his heart. "Be careful. Don't trust anyone, especially your aunt. She's already proven her treachery."

"Not all Wuxin are evil," I said slowly, thinking of Mingwen and Miss Lin.

"Perhaps," he agreed. "But we cannot trust any of them. Being good and being brave are not the same. A compassionate coward can inflict as much damage as any villain. We also don't know what they've been told about us, what set them against us. In a war, the first battle is for our people's hearts. If they do not believe, they do not fight—and the war is already lost."

"The Wuxin believe the immortals are the wicked ones, usurping their domain in the Golden Desert, banishing them to this place," I told him. "They claimed to be attacked and persecuted when they refused to support Mother's bid for the throne. They saw it as ambition and greed, while Mother believed this was necessary to strengthen our kingdom." Part of me had always longed for her clarity, even as I dreaded the rigidity of her purpose.

After all, it had cost us dearly: my father, her husband. Zhangwei and me, poisoned by the Wuxin's curse. All those lives lost across the realms. "I don't think I could have done that," I said in a low voice. "I could never pay the price she did." Still, I loved and admired her, respected and feared her. Even now I wished I could feel her hand on my head, even as I shied from her anger and disappointment.

"Many saw it as ambition, but it was your mother's vision for our future. The Golden Desert needed to unite, to maintain its position among the immortals. The Phoenix Kingdom was eyeing an expansion of its domain, as were the monarchs of the Northern and Southern Seas." He paused. "They might have swallowed us whole if we remained fragmented."

"If only the Wuxin had been left in peace." Regret stabbed me at how events had unfolded, bringing us to this point where both sides demanded blood. "Aunt Shou's daughter, the beloved heir, was killed during one of the attacks. The Wuxin were determined to seek vengeance. This was how Dalian ascended the throne."

"I remember," he said slowly. "I demanded an accounting of that incident. One of our soldiers was struggling to control his magic—he was still young, new to our army. His magic spiraled out of control, striking the Wuxin heir. Their soldiers attacked in retaliation, and ours struck to defend themselves . . . just as the Wuxin believed they were doing."

"A tragic accident. Yet it changed the course of the realms," I said heavily.

"Life is often a chain of small events with large consequences," Zhangwei said. "We can never predict any outcome."

"They had their cause, and so did we." I closed my eyes. "Hatred cannot be uprooted as easily as it was sown."

"Regardless, they are now our enemies. We must escape as soon as we can, the moment we've freed your friend."

"His name is Chengyin," I reminded him. "When I returned to the skies as a mortal, no one there bothered to know my name."

Zhangwei nodded. "I will not forget."

"I must go now," I said reluctantly. "If I remain in my rooms, they will think I have something to hide. If they send someone here, it will be worse for us."

His jaw clenched, his grip tightening before he released me. "It will be dangerous."

"Only if they don't believe me."

"I don't want you to go," he said tightly. "What if something goes wrong, what if I can't get to you in time?"

"There's no choice; we can't hide here forever." I pulled on an outer coat and combed my hair, trying to hide the tremor in my fingers. "Is it safe for you to stay here?" How I wished he could, but I wouldn't risk his life.

"I will stay until I know you're safe—that you convinced them."

"Then leave as soon as you can. I will meet you afterward, away from here."

"There is a bridge east of the nearest town that I'll mark with a lantern. Cross it, and I'll find you in the forest. If you don't come by nightfall, I'll return here for you."

He spoke like it was a simple matter, like there wasn't the entire force of the Wuxin Army between us.

I uncorked the bottle Aunt Shou had given me, then rubbed a few drops of the scent over Zhangwei's wrists and neck—then over myself, too, as a precaution. "This should shield you from the void birds," I explained. "In any case, stay out of their path."

He touched my white lock of hair, curling the ends around his finger. "Being mortal has made you worry more. I can handle a few birds."

"I've always worried about you," I told him honestly as I strode to the door. "And now I know all the things that can go wrong."

39

My life depended on my lies.

A sobering thought as an attendant showed me to the hall where Lord Dalian was, the last place I wanted to be. Tall windows flanked the chamber, opening to the skies beyond, the void birds circling in the distance. The floor was covered with thick carpets edged in silver, intricate wooden carvings of flowers hanging from the walls. Rosewood lanterns swung from the ceiling, gleaming in the afternoon light.

A trio of dancers swayed in the center of the hall. Their outstretched palms bore flames that curved to their movements, flaring higher as they spun gracefully. Those bronze bells hung from their waists, eerily silent. Musicians accompanied them, one strumming a lute, another playing a bamboo flute. The guests were seated at low tables, each one set with jars of wine, though only small servings of food: jellyfish, pickled cucumbers, pastries the size of coins. The Wuxin picked idly at them, their hungry gaze darting around the room. Some were gaunt, almost ashen. I would have thought them ill if they were mortal. As a thin woman raised a cup to her lips, her fingers seemed almost translucent. They were weakening, fading . . . starving? I smothered a flicker of pity. Maybe they weren't wholly evil, yet they'd chosen their survival at the cost of my people's.

Lord Dalian and Aunt Shou were seated upon the dais. His gilded throne was so wide it could have sat two across, while his mother's chair was smaller, crafted of precious zitan wood. I strode toward them, stifling a burst of anger that he wore Chengyin's face so brazenly, twisting his features with spite.

As I approached, Lord Dalian's eyes thinned. He raised his hand seemingly in greeting, yet light darted from his fingers through a window. A void bird with a saffron plume soared into the hall, its body the span of my arms spread wide. As its wing caught a low table, porcelain cups were swept onto the floor. I stumbled back, instinctively reaching for a weapon I didn't have. Yet the Wuxin remained calm, some glaring at the bird like it was a petty nuisance rather than the monster it was.

It wouldn't hurt them, just outsiders like me. As the bird cocked its head at me, studying me with its beady eyes—my pulse stuttered evenly. At last, it turned away as though bored. Lord Dalian flicked his hand toward the window again, the bird spreading its wings to fly out once more. I sagged with relief, silently thanking Aunt Shou for the fragrance.

Lord Dalian was examining me like I was a book he was forced to study. "Welcome," he said at last. "Our newest member of the family."

I tilted my head to the windows, letting the sunlight catch my eyes, hoping the coppery illusion shone through. "Did I pass your test, Lord Dalian?" I smiled to blunt the edge in my tone, concealing my fear. "If you'd like to call another of your pets in, maybe we should move the tables away from the windows."

He returned my smile, though there was no warmth in it. "More an affirmation than a test. Best to clear up any doubts before things get complicated."

"Enough with the games, Dalian," Aunt Shou said. "I told you last night, everything went according to plan. Her transformation was secured the moment she entered the Temple of the Crimson

Moon. Now it's best to deal openly with the Lady of Tianxia."

"Is she still that?" he scoffed.

"Yes," I replied with emphasis. "I don't relinquish my duty to my people that easily. You would understand, wouldn't you, Lord Dalian?"

As an uncomfortable silence fell, I looked around the room. "Am I interrupting a celebration?"

"You are welcome here." Lord Dalian lifted a cup toward me in a toast, though he did not drink from it. "We would have invited you earlier, except Mother mentioned you needed rest. Her advice was sound; you look refreshed."

I fought back a laugh. They could never imagine what I'd done last night. "I am grateful for your consideration."

"Are you grateful for the honor bestowed on you as well?" He leaned forward, resting his elbows on his knees. "It is a great gift to become one of us. Eternity lies before you, power and glory."

He was trying to place me in the position of a supplicant; the better for him when he made his demands. Yet all I wanted was to stab him for trying to take away my choice. "I was confused at first—uncertain," I said. "But I now have a new appreciation of my abilities."

His eyes gleamed. "Yes, I sense your magic. Can you use it?"

A dangerous question. My magic was of Water, rare among the immortals who grew up in the Golden Desert. Lord Dalian believed that part of my life was extinguished; I couldn't admit to remembering my past training. Yet I had to be of some use so he wouldn't hurt Chengyin. A thought struck: was this a chance to delay his plans?

"Only a little," I said, furrowing my brow. "I might need more training—"

"No training is needed for your task," Lord Dalian cut me off. "I believe Mother has explained it to you?"

Before I could reply, his gaze shifted to the back of the hall.

A stout, bearded Wuxin warrior wearing an ornate helmet strode forward and bowed to the throne. "Lord Dalian, I bring a message from the Winged Devils trapped in Tianxia. They are unable to return home because the immortals are hunting them."

"What do they want, General Fang?" Lord Dalian asked, leaning back against his throne.

"Permission to cross the gateway to enter the Netherworld," he replied.

Lord Dalian shook his head. "The gateway has grown unstable of late. We must secure the passage for our own people."

General Fang frowned. "My lord, the Winged Devils are our faithful allies. They are in danger after attacking Queen's Caihong's palace upon our request. They expected our aid then, but—"

"Then they were fools," Lord Dalian snapped. "How could we reveal ourselves back then? Tell them to be patient. Once the gateway is opened, they can rejoin us."

General Fang exchanged a look with a tall woman, who stepped out from the side. Her long hair was braided and tucked into a helmet. "My lord, what of the Winged Devils in the Immortal Realm, imprisoned by Queen Caihong?" she asked.

"They will have to wait, Captain Lai. Our priority is to secure the Mortal Realm. Once we are strong, the other realms will fall."

She stiffened, her jaw tensing. "General Fang and I gave our word to the Winged Devils that we would protect them in return for their service—"

"Captain Lai, it's not my concern what promises you made," Lord Dalian said harshly.

"These promises were what *you* told us to make." General Fang's gaze slid to Aunt Shou. "Great Lady, surely you see the importance of keeping our word?"

"My mother no longer rules here, General Fang." Lord Dalian's tone was sharp with threat. "If you need a reminder of who wields the power now, I'd be glad for a demonstration."

His gaze shifted to the general's gold bell that glowed with an eerie light. A strangled sound slipped from General Fang's throat, sweat glistening across his brow. The color drained from Captain Lai's face as she fell to her knees, clasping her hands before her. "My lord, General Fang spoke in haste. We will respond to the Winged Devils as you commanded."

Aunt Shou touched her son's hand. "Dalian, enough. General Fang is a brave and loyal warrior."

"Maybe, but he needs to be cleverer, unless he wants to be replaced." Lord Dalian glanced at Captain Rao, whose hungry expression reminded me of Minister Guo whenever he scented opportunity.

A heavy silence cloaked the hall as General Fang and Captain Lai left. I was beginning to understand why few wanted to sit closer to the throne, but I couldn't let that deter me.

"I have a favor to ask of you, Lord Dalian," I said.

An eyebrow quirked up, the expression so reminiscent of Chengyin that my heart quailed. "You may ask."

"I am here now, one of you. Will you release Chengyin?"

His fingers crumbled a pastry upon his plate. "Do you still care for him? Your mortal betrothed?"

"Our bonds are not so easily broken." I turned to Aunt Shou, adding, "Just as he's still your son."

A miscalculation. Lord Dalian scowled, displeased at the reminder. "I'll keep him a while longer, until you prove yourself to me."

I cursed inwardly, for it meant Zhangwei and I were trapped, too. But a direct challenge would only set him against me when I needed him to think I was on his side. "Lord Dalian, haven't I already done that? I did as you asked, going to the temple. Why are you still holding him captive?"

He studied me through hooded eyes, as though trying to see

beneath my skin. "Come, let's speak as equals."

It rankled that he hadn't thought of me as one before. "Very well, Dalian," I replied, intentionally misunderstanding him as I discarded his title—he didn't deserve the courtesy.

Anger flickered in his gaze. "Things might be different in your mortal court, but here, you will adhere to the formalities. I am the ruler and will be acknowledged as such," he said cuttingly. "As you know, I want you to open the gateway to Kunlun. A small matter for the rulers of Tianxia who are its guardians."

He was lying. Just as he'd lied to get me to the Temple of the Crimson Moon. It was my *immortal* bloodline he was after. My mother, Queen Caihong had trapped the Wuxin here with her magic—and only with mine could they be released.

"How do I know you're telling the truth this time?" My tone was soft yet firm. "You said you'd free Chengyin before, too."

He sighed as though I'd become tiresome. "I swear before all present—once you open the gateway, I will leave this mortal husk."

My hands clenched but I forced them to loosen. "Why do you want to open the gateway?" Aunt Shou had told me, but I wouldn't give him the satisfaction of thinking I obeyed him unquestioningly.

He looked around the hall. "Because we need the realm beyond. My people grow hungry; the Wangchuan River can no longer sustain us."

Several nodded, as did the woman with the translucent fingers—but as many or more remained still, their silence emboldening me.

"Why not leave the mortals alone?" I asked. "Why not channel your efforts into restoring the Wangchuan River, to rebuild rather than destroy? The mortals are not your enemy—"

"They should serve *us*," he snapped. "We are stronger than them, greater than they could ever hope to be. Our existence is infinite, not measured in paltry years. Our lives are worth *more*."

Revulsion bloomed in my gut like mold in dank air. I could understand ambition, the drive to aid one's people, the desire to rise high—but to enslave others out of greed, because one imagined they were "inferior" . . . it was wrong. More than wrong, it was *vile*. But I had to hide my thoughts, to give Dalian no reason to suspect me.

"If I do this, your people must leave Tianxia untouched." I would never let him get that far, but I had to pretend we were aligned—to act like his promise mattered.

"Of course," he agreed magnanimously. "You may have Tianxia, as long as they submit to my rule."

He was not being generous. With the gateway opened, he would have the entire Mortal Realm to feed from.

As he smiled, my stomach churned. "But first, a small trial, to demonstrate your new abilities. Let me gauge your strength."

As I stiffened at his suggestion, Dalian gestured to the two women behind him who stepped forward. "Lin, Mei—both of you will challenge her in a test of magic. One of might, not combat—do not hurt her. If you win, you'll be rewarded. Fail, and you'll be flogged."

He offered such vicious punishment so easily, like it was commonplace. A tyrant ruling through fear.

"Mercy shows the strength of your heart, my son," Aunt Shou advised.

"How dull you are, Mother," Dalian replied scornfully. "Do you take pride in acting like a virtuous do-gooder?" He was on edge; anger unsettled him. I was beginning to realize that when he was calm was when he was most dangerous.

Lin and Mei turned pale as they bowed. Like me, they had no choice. Together, we crossed to the center of the hall, though my mind was distracted. I wanted to win, angered by his condescension—yet didn't want the women to be flogged. As Lin raised her hand, light hurtled forth to slam into my shoulder. It seared as I staggered back—caught unaware. At once, she caught my hand to steady me, her face grim.

"I didn't know you weren't ready," she said by way of apology.

I shook my head. "I should have been."

Her fingers probed my shoulder before I could protest—afraid that she might sense I wasn't who I claimed—but her power flowed, healing my wound.

Mei called out to her, "Sister, are you ready?"

We resumed our positions. Light blazed from my hands to form a curved barrier of azure light, while Lin's power formed a yellow shield that collided against mine. I stumbled from the unexpected force, still unused to channeling my magic. Digging my heels in, I forced myself to steady—as Mei raised her hand, a reddish light flowing into her sister's shield. The pressure intensified, my breathing growing hoarse. Frost formed across my hands, the other guests murmuring in surprise. But I was already tiring, these enchantments taking a toll.

It was a relief that I could hold my own against these two seasoned fighters. I grasped more of my power, eager to clinch victory, to catch them off-guard. As I braced to strike, the sight of their faces stalled me. Lin was sweating, Mei was pale; their expressions twisted with strain. They were exhausted, yet afraid to fail.

If I lost, I'd earn Dalian's insults—but he wouldn't hurt me, not yet. Meanwhile, a brutal thrashing awaited them. I'd tasted the violence of his whip once, and it was Lin who'd healed me. And maybe it would be better if Dalian thought me weak, if he underestimated me.

Slowly, I released the hold over my magic. Lin frowned as though sensing my intentional weakening. I inclined my head, waiting a moment longer—then gasped, falling to sprawl upon the floor. Their magic surged toward me, but Lin leashed it swiftly before it struck. The trial was over . . . and I'd lost.

As they bowed to me, I folded my body in return.

"Your guards are impressive, Lord Dalian," I said deliberately.

He was glaring at me like I was a prize he'd won that wasn't worth as much as he'd thought. "You're not as strong as I expected."

I shrugged. "I've never been strong. Maybe I can't do as you asked."

His mouth pulled taut. "For your sake, I hope that you can."

And though he smiled at me, it reminded me of a viper parting its jaws, biding its time as it contemplated *when* to strike. Even if I did everything he asked, he would kill me anyway . . . once I was no longer of use.

40

Rain fell in heavy waves, dark clouds sheathing the skies. I sheltered beneath a lacquered umbrella; it was easier than channeling magic into a shield.

"Which direction leads to the town?" I asked the guards at the entrance.

A woman gestured ahead. "Follow the pathway lit by the lanterns. Would you like an escort?"

I paused, pretending to weigh the suggestion. "Not in this weather. But if you have a recommendation for a good teahouse, I'd welcome it." An excuse, in case Dalian had sent spies.

"Phoenix Nest Inn has excellent tea and wine." She grinned at me. "If you mention Soldier Yung sent you, you'll get a fair price."

"I'll keep that in mind." I jangled the pouch taken from my room, filled with the smooth stones that the Wuxin used as money. Each bore a flicker of emotion: a purple gem pulsing with excitement, an aquamarine heavy with grief, pieces of amber bright with joy.

As I walked, the rain lightened to a drizzle. Stars glinted, violet streaks carving the crimson skies. An unearthly beauty enveloped this place like a midnight sunset. As the wind blew, the oblong lanterns that were strung up swayed. Birch trees flanked the path, their bark peeling in patches to reveal an underside of white. All the while, the void birds circled above.

Some of the Wuxin chatted as they walked, others were silent. A few held the hands of children. By each waist hung that soundless bronze bell, a tether they could not unfasten—not if they wanted to survive. Without seeing them as I now did, it would be easy to think of them all as monsters, to fear what I didn't know. And I couldn't help wondering if all this strife might have been averted had there been a little more compassion on both sides . . . if our minds had been more open, if pain had not been twisted into opportunity and suffering into ambition. A great pity that it was easier to hate than to understand.

Lights glimmered ahead, voices rising from the town. The liveliness was in stark contrast to Lord Dalian's court, where even the music could not veil the silence. The streets were flanked by buildings of light-colored wood, their sloped roofs tiled in dark reds and greens. As I turned east toward the bridge Zhangwei mentioned, unease darted over the back of my neck. Someone was following me—was that why I'd been allowed out?

I ducked into a store selling tea. Jars were filled with dried osmanthus, jasmine, silver needles. There were also plants I'd never heard of: five-century bark, winter lilies, fire-leaf tea. I lingered over my purchase, yet when I left the shop, the prickling sensation of being followed remained.

Unlike the villages of my kingdom, there were only a few food stalls along the streets. I stopped by each one, choosing candied fruit, a box of dragon-beard candy, steamed buns, and a paper cone of roasted chestnuts. Did the Wuxin eat purely for entertainment, or did a small part of them crave our food once they took our forms?

"Why did you buy so much?" A small girl, her white hair braided, pointed at the bags in my hands.

I crouched down to look into her face. "I like to eat. Have you tried these?"

She shook her head. "Father said it's a waste of money. We don't need it."

I grinned as I lifted the chestnuts, their rich aroma wafting in the air. "If you'd tasted these, I'm sure you'd like them, too."

Drawn by her clear voice, more children surrounded me, staring openly. An idea sparked. "Would you like to try the food?" I asked them.

A boy scowled, his thin face tugging at my chest. "Not if it will turn my hair black like yours."

I laughed. "I promise it won't."

When he nodded eagerly, along with the others, I approached the hawker selling sticks of candied strawberries, grapes, and hawthorn. "I will buy each child here one," I declared loudly, offering him a handful of stones.

The children cheered as they began jostling for their place in the line—more streaming in from the street, drawn by the crowd. The vendor's expression alternated from panic to glee as he handed out the sticks. In the chaos, I slipped away, hurrying into a narrow lane. An unpleasant stench rose like rot and mold, but at least the sense of being watched had gone

I crossed the bridge with the single lantern, then ran into the forest. Zhangwei was close, I could sense him. A flock of void birds circled the forest, ignoring me as they swooped down toward other prey. As a thin screech rang—abruptly muffled—my blood turned cold. Zhangwei—were they attacking him? Had his scent washed off in the rain? I raced ahead, darting between the trees. The curve of a blade glinted as it whistled through the air, magic coursing in ripples and waves. Fortunately, we were far from town, unlikely to draw attention. Following the trail of the birds, I sprinted onward, wishing I had a weapon.

Ahead, a shield gleamed around Zhangwei as he fought several void birds. Their feathers gleamed ash and white, their talons emitting a clicking sound as they surrounded him.

His head darted up, his body stiffening at the sight of me. "Stay back—"

A moment's distraction, a costly mistake. One of the birds lunged at him, its beak plunging into his shoulder. As blood seeped through his robe, his shield broke. These creatures were powerful, possessing magic of their own.

I dropped my bags and grabbed a rock to hurl at the bird closest to Zhangwei. It hissed as it swooped toward me—but Zhangwei sprang forward, bringing his sword down upon the creature's head. Swiftly I wove a shield over us, just in time, as two birds tried to claw at Zhangwei, scraping at my barrier. I flinched beneath their unexpected force but held steady. As a large bird flew at me, Zhangwei kicked it aside, then drove his blade through the neck of another.

His face was grim; there was no pleasure in this. He had learned to fight without emotion, to win at all costs. Yet each loss weighed on him, leaving its mark like the rings on a tree. He was the God of War, not the God of Death.

Swiftly I uncorked Aunt Shou's bottle, shaking the fragrance over Zhangwei, praying it would still work. As another bird dove toward us, it stopped, cocking its head like it was confused—then flew away. A moment later, the others followed after it.

Zhangwei sheathed his sword and came to me. His strong hands caught me around my waist, lifting me to him. He held me like he had not seen me for a year, like he was afraid I'd be taken from him again. I buried my face against his neck, inhaling his crisp scent, trying not to look at the feathered bodies around us.

"You were right to worry." A hint of humor lifted his voice.

I smiled, too relieved to even gloat. "These birds have a power of their own. I think Dalian used them to seal the skies over Tianxia."

Zhangwei's aura seemed to waver. Leaning away, I tugged at his bloodstained robe, revealing claw marks, bleeding and raw.

Without thinking, I released my magic into his body, healing him even as he tensed.

He inspected my work dubiously, but there were just darkened streaks where the wounds used to be. "You've improved your abilities."

"I take more care with you," I admitted.

A shriek rang out, more birds circling the skies. Zhangwei cursed under this breath, raising his hand to strike them down, but I grabbed his arm. "Leave them. They won't disturb us now."

"I don't like the way they look at us." His gaze narrowed as he stared at them. "Nothing is as it seems here. The skies are red, the birds thirst for blood, the river glows with the dead. Clouds crowd the skies, yet they don't answer to our summons."

"We aren't in the Immortal Realm anymore," I said gravely, staring at the silhouette of the mountain in the distance.

How I wished we could escape now—to go home and not look back. But if I left, Chengyin would die. I'd never forgive myself, and I was glad Zhangwei didn't try to persuade me.

We headed deeper into the forest, the trees concealing us from the birds. Zhangwei led me to a cave ahead—well hidden behind a rocky outcrop, obscured by bushes. As he set down the bags he'd carried for me, I inspected the place. Lush green moss covered the earth, dotted with tiny blue flowers that reminded me of violets. Rivulets of glistening water streaked across the uneven ground, the rock walls glimmering with an iridescent sheen. Here, the air was cool, infused with a woody fragrance.

Without a word, Zhangwei pulled me to him. His mouth sought mine, his lips hard and impatient, like I was a craving he needed to sate. Slowly, he edged me against the wall until the rough stone pushed against my back, his body pressed to mine. My arms wound around his neck as I kissed the column of his throat— his eyes going dark with desire. As he bent down, his teeth grazed the delicate skin of my neck and bit down. A gasp slid from me as

I went taut with wanting, thrusting a hand through his hair as a melting heat spilled inside me.

"Wait," I whispered before I lost my last tether to sanity. Before I sank down with him upon the floor and cast all caution aside.

He stilled at once, his heart pounding against mine. "You're right—it's too dangerous." His mouth curved into a smile, though his breathing was still harsh. "Later. When we're home."

I no longer knew where that was. To lighten my mood, I handed him the food from the town, keeping the candied fruit for myself. I bit into its sugared shell, chewing with more enthusiasm than true relish. The sweetness blunted the edge of desire, a diversion from the fear that shadowed me. As I ate, Zhangwei inspected a piece of dragon-beard candy, parting the fine sugared strands to reveal a core of crushed peanuts.

"What happened today?" he asked.

"It was eventful." I spoke lightly, concealing the turmoil I'd felt, the fear that pierced like an arrow in my gut. "Dalian summoned a void bird to test me, pitted his fighters against me, then demanded that I open the gateway."

"I will kill him," Zhangwei swore, his body clenched with rage.

I wanted Dalian to suffer, but I wouldn't let vengeance rule our heads. "All I want is for us to escape," I said in a low voice. "Once we're away from here, out of his reach—we can stop him then."

Zhangwei took my hand, threading his fingers through mine. "What did you tell him?"

"I had to agree." A sinking dread settled over me. "If I'd refused, he might have locked me up. He promised to leave Tianxia unscathed, that he'd release Chengyin—if I did as he asked."

I closed my eyes, seeing before me the green plains of my kingdom, the shining rivers and blue gray mountains in the distance. It was my home as much as the Golden Desert was; one did not diminish my love for the other. To imagine destruction descending upon either—I could not bear it.

"I won't do as he wants; I can't." Despite my resolve, my fear remained because Dalian had a hundred ways to threaten me, to force my compliance.

"We'll stop him," Zhangwei assured me. "Until then, stay on your guard. Do nothing to provoke him. Are you safe in the palace?"

"I don't think Dalian trusts me fully. He keeps testing me, needling me . . . hoping I'll slip. Even if I do as he asks, he'll likely kill me after."

"He'll never get the chance." Zhangwei's tone was rife with menace, like he was ready to challenge the entire Wuxin army.

"Maybe he doesn't trust *anyone*, not even his own mother," I added. "Nor does he seem to listen to his people. Some of his soldiers spoke for the Winged Devils who were deceived by Dalian's promises. But he resorted to threats, forcing them to submit. Many don't seem to want war, yet they're convinced it's the key to their survival. If there is another way, I don't think they'll want to invade."

"Will Dalian give them a choice?" Zhangwei asked.

"No. Maybe it's why he now controls who can feed from the Wangchuan River, to stem dissent." I touched the bell at my waist. "This is a collar, not a gift."

Zhangwei's lip curled with disdain. "A ruler that is tolerated and feared, rather than respected or loved. He wears a hollow crown."

"As do I," I said slowly.

Zhangwei shook his head. "You're not the same. The venom in your court stems mainly from the ambition of others. They *want* to believe you incapable because it gives them a reason to seize power. You are untested; he is unfit."

"Dalian has his supporters, too." I thought of Captain Rao, the nobles who were quick to agree with his every command. "But there are others who value peace more than ambition." Part of me wanted to help them except I didn't know how, and my desire to escape—to protect my own—was greater.

"We must get him to relinquish his hold over your friend—Chengyin," Zhangwei said. "But Dalian is cunning; he'll want you to open the gateway before releasing him."

I thought back to what Aunt Shou had said before Dalian silenced her. "In Chengyin's form—he's vulnerable, too. I heard the Wuxin who possess another are also exposed to their weaknesses."

Zhangwei fell silent as a line creased his brow. "If Chengyin is injured, will Dalian be, too?"

"He cut Chengyin to threaten me," I recalled how he'd grimaced. "But when he did it, he also hurt himself."

"Then this is the only way," Zhangwei said decisively.

"No." I recoiled instinctively from the loathsome thought—hating the hope that flickered.

His hand tightened over my mine, his other wrapping around the back of my neck to tilt our heads together. "You must trust me. If I have to wound him to help us all escape, I won't endanger his life."

A pause, my emotions warring within. "I do trust you . . . I just don't want him to be hurt."

"He's hurting now," Zhangwei pointed out steadily. "Whatever Dalian is doing to him, your friend is suffering. Ask yourself, would he want you to take this chance?"

Run. Chengyin had told me with his first breath of freedom. He'd wanted me to be safe; he'd wanted me to get away. And I would, but not without him.

As I nodded, fighting down a wave of despair—Zhangwei's arms wrapped around me, holding me until his heart beat against mine once more. "We will get out, all of us. Trust me in this. Keep up the pretense that you're an ally; go with Dalian when he commands you to. You won't be alone."

"He'll be impatient, his hold over the gateway is waning. He said it's unstable."

"Then we must be ready," Zhangwei replied. "I'll head to the gateway and wait for you there. It will take some time, as I must go through the mountains, not along the river." His hand slid to the small of my back. "The moment Chengyin is freed, you must take him through the gateway first. I'll make sure it's safe—"

I pushed away from him, meeting his gaze. "I'm not going without you."

"The Wuxin who helped me said only two can cross at a single time, and no more than a handful in a day. It's too risky otherwise," he said adamantly. "Both of you must go ahead; I will follow. There is less danger for me—"

"You're immortal, but you're not invulnerable." I spoke with deliberate measure. "I'm not leaving without you. Chengyin will leave first—and then, we will go *together*." As he opened his mouth to protest, I placed my hand over his heart. "Where you go, I go."

We glared at each other for a long while, neither of us yielding. Then he pulled me to him again and kissed me—his lips pressing against mine, not with hunger alone this time but with a tender sweetness that curled into my chest.

"Where you go, I go," he whispered into my ear. "Now, and always."

41

The Endless Dawn Palace loomed in the distance, its silver-gray walls of quartz gleaming. Someone called my name, hurrying toward me—Lin, clad in a close-fitting brown robe. As she slung an arm around my shoulders, I stiffened at her unexpected familiarity.

Before I could speak, she muttered through clenched teeth, "Smile. We're being watched. Lord Dalian wants to know where you've been, since you eluded the guard following you."

A chill slid through me, though I smiled as she'd suggested. "Why don't you tell me where I've been?"

Her eyebrows arched. "We just spent the evening in a teahouse. Eating. Drinking. What else might we do there?" she said in a teasing tone. "Though you *are* to my liking, I sense you're taken?"

As I nodded, a flush creeping over my face, she sighed as she dropped her arm. "A pity."

"I'm sure you have no shortage of partners," I said, adding, "Is Lord Dalian always this on-edge?"

"The void birds reported that an intruder was sighted," she said in hushed tones. "Lord Dalian uses them to keep a close watch on us."

I don't like the way they look at us. Zhangwei was right; I should have let him kill them all.

"They spy on you, too, not just strangers?" I was trying to test her loyalty, to see if it might be pried apart. From what I'd seen, she didn't seem to share Dalian's vicious inclinations, unlike the malevolent Captain Rao.

"Lord Dalian is cautious. There have been murmurs of disquiet recently. As you saw earlier, many don't want to go to war with the immortals again."

"You don't miss the skies? Your past home?"

"If you keep yearning for all beyond your reach, you'll end up wasting a lot of time, blinding yourself to the good that's here." She spoke with a calm pragmatism. "We are content here, with the Wangchuan River, at least until its powers waned. Here we can even keep our physical forms easier—whereas in your world, in our old one, we had to fight harder to retain them."

"Has anyone tried to reason with Lord Dalian?" I asked.

"Do you think he takes well to 'reasoning'?" Her mouth curled. "In the beginning, some tried, but they were harshly punished. And now, when Lord Dalian controls our access to the Wangchuan, we have no choice but to obey."

I glanced at the wooden stakes along the riverbank, the tips glinting darkly. "Can these barriers be removed? These restrictions?"

"They seem impervious to our efforts—they keep us from the waters, except to feed. Lord Dalian claims this way, no one can tamper with the river to cause mischief."

Except for him. But I kept it to myself, letting her speak.

"He also decreed a harsh punishment for anyone who tries to remove the barriers. According to him, the Wangchuan's power must be rationed, though he hoards most for the army and those close to him." Her eyes flashed with suppressed anger.

"The Wangchuan River doesn't belong to him alone," I said.

"Who will dare tell him? Only fools would risk getting their allotment cut—not just for themselves but their families, too?"

Her gaze flicked to the bronze bell by her waist. "I spoke up once, and my sister and I suffered."

"Why are you telling me this?" Though I wanted to trust her, I had to be careful. We weren't friends, and it was not just me at risk.

"Because you helped my sister and me," she replied. "Not many would have chosen defeat to aid a stranger."

"You helped me, too—not just when he asked you to heal me but for what you didn't tell him."

"Many of us keep secrets from Lord Dalian; it's safer that way. And if anyone valued that little help I gave, it means they were worth helping. Someone who appreciates the gifts of others rather than just seeking to take." Her expression turned serious. "Even here, you're still fighting for your people. You *want* to help them; you don't just think of what they can do for you."

I studied her, trying to decide how far I could trust her. "Why did you stop Captain Rao from attacking us in Tianxia?"

"Something didn't seem right with the God of War, but it wasn't a risk I was prepared to take. Needless slaughter turns my stomach. Unlike what you've been told, we don't only want to feed on suffering."

We walked slowly, nearing the entrance with the guards. There wasn't much time left. "What do you want of me?" I asked bluntly.

Her gaze was bright. "Swear that this discussion will remain between us. If you repeat any of this, I'll carve your tongue out."

"I'll tell no one, whether you threaten me or not—as long as you swear the same," I said tersely. "I have as much to lose."

"I didn't mean to offend you; we're used to threats here," she said with a half-smile. "Threats, bribes, and coercion."

"It shouldn't be that way."

She sighed. "It didn't used to be. Lord Dalian's mother was a good ruler, if only her son took her advice. You remind me a little of her—someone who cares for their people, who listens rather than punishing all who question."

"If I do, it's because I had the benefit of her advice," I admitted—though it was hard to remember how Aunt Shou had once guided me, without resentment or anger.

"So did Lord Dalian. The difference is that you listened," she pointed out.

"Why did no one protest Lord Dalian's rule before?" I asked.

"In the turmoil of our exile, we grew reliant on our leadership. Those who disagreed were easily silenced, and we became accustomed to obeying." She frowned. "But now the stakes are too high. With this invasion, Lord Dalian risks us all. And we don't even know what we're really fighting for."

My pulse quickened. More vital than their discontent was their mistrust—an ember to be stoked, an opportunity to seize. "With the Wangchuan weakening, isn't the invasion vital for survival?" I asked, still guarded, even as I wanted to draw her out.

She chewed her lower lip as though weighing her words. Were they treacherous? How I hoped so.

"Where is the proof that it's weakening?" she asked softly. "All we have are Lord Dalian's claims, and those of his trusted advisors. Many of us doubt, but we don't dare say anything. And even if it's true . . . if Lord Dalian shares the wealth of the Wangchuan River rather than hoarding most for his select few, there should be enough."

I glanced at the gold bell fastened at my waist. Guilt pricked that while others were going hungry, I didn't even need it. "If only the power of the river could be restored, or shared—this war could be averted."

"If not, many of us will die," she said. "If the Immortal Realm unites against us this time, the Wangchuan River will run red with our blood."

"Are there others who think like you?" I probed, thinking of the general and captain who'd argued with Dalian.

"Yes." She didn't elaborate, as cautious as me. "However, Lord Dalian has the support of most of the army. Captain Rao is a favorite, as they share the same ambitions."

"If you weaken his standing in the army, you weaken his position."

"They will need a firm reason to turn against him. He guards their favor well, ensuring all their appetites are met," she said.

"It won't be easy. It will be dangerous," I told her.

"Is anything worthwhile not?" she replied.

"How can we help each other?" I asked carefully, thinking that even as I'd been hoping she might be of use to us—she'd been doing the same of me

"We want what you want; we want the gateway to remain closed. We don't want this war." Before I could protest, she continued: "I saw your face when he asked you to open the gateway. You're doing this for the mortal Lord Dalian holds captive."

"Is it true keeping mortal form helps his recuperation?" I wanted to know. "When he captured me the first time, I was surprised I was able to hurt him."

"He was already weakened from opening the crack in the gateway. Sustaining it drains his strength—as did sending the void birds across to seal the skies." She added then, "I don't know how he was able to do all this."

A thought slipped into my mind, something the mirror in the temple had told me about the Wangchuan: *Before one attempts to restore it, one should learn the cause.*

"What if he's using the powers of the Wangchuan River for this?" I asked slowly.

Her eyes blazed with fury. "It would be a grave betrayal—but not an unthinkable one."

A brief silence fell over us. "Don't open the gateway," she said flatly. "We'll create a diversion so you can escape back to Tianxia, you and the mortal. Once you're through, summon the immortals for aid. Seal the gateway again. Put an end to Lord Dalian's ambitions."

I kept a smile on my face as a guard walked past us. "If you help me, what happens to you afterward? Won't Lord Dalian unleash his anger on you?"

Her eyes glinted. "Maybe he won't be in power for much longer."

Did she intend to *kill* him? Before I could ask more, Dalian himself stalked around the corner, his guards following close behind.

"Where have you been?" he demanded of me.

I was glad for Lin's warning. "I visited the town. Was I not meant to?"

His gaze flicked to Lin, then back to me. "You seem friendly with my personal guard."

Lin bowed, interjecting smoothly, "Lord Dalian, we met by chance in the town. She was lost and I showed her the way back." She added in a low voice, "It was preferable to having her wander unaccompanied."

As he nodded, she quickly moved behind him, out of sight.

"Why were you looking for me?" I asked, to divert his attention.

"The fleet has assembled. The gateway must be opened tonight," he said.

Inside, I was winter and ice. It was too soon; how could I get word to Zhangwei? "Why tonight?" I studied his pallor, recalling what Lin had told me. Was he strained from sustaining the gateway? Eager to gorge on mortals to restore himself? I'd never let that happen.

"The enchantment over the skies is waning." He raised his voice, letting it carry to the soldiers nearby. "We must strike quickly to secure a foothold in the Mortal Realm before the immortals descend."

He meant Tianxia; what else lay on the other side of the gateway? Dalian's promises were worthless. His forces would descend upon my home like locusts, devouring everything in sight.

"Come with me," he ordered.

My mind spun, grasping at straws—but he was not asking, he was *commanding* me. If I refused, he'd drag me there anyway. Any protest would raise his suspicions, and I had to remain his ally for now. I followed him along the path that led to the pier, my breath struck from my lungs at the sight before us.

The river curled around the mountain like a sleeping serpent, streaked with those glowing bands of green. Hundreds of pale boats were moored upon the riverbank, gleaming like the shards of a shattered reflection. An endless stream of soldiers boarded the vessels, armored in red and gold, weapons glinting from their hands. They moved with swift purpose as the void birds circled above them, the skies rife with the promise of violence.

I had fallen into a war and ended up on the wrong side.

"Tomorrow, the sun will rise on a new order. The strong will rule, the weak will yield. Such is the way of life." Dalian's eyes bored into mine. "Will you do as I ask?"

Out of the corner of my eye I saw Captain Rao approaching, his hand on his sword.

"I will." I bowed my head, hating this, and hating myself for it.

But victory was not always a straight path, the one of honor and glory. In a storm, one had to bend with the wind to remain standing—to live, to fight another day.

And the storm was upon us now.

42

The barge rocked to the rhythm of the water as a thin breeze wound through the air. This time there were no musicians, food, or wine. Aunt Shou sat in a chair, clad in dark purple brocade. Her eyes followed Dalian dully. Did she see just her son or also my friend whom she'd abandoned?

Soldiers surrounded the room, quelling all thought of flight— though the only way off this barge was to plunge into the Wangchuan River, these lethal waters that had almost claimed my life. For an immortal, though, it was said just one cup would steal a lifetime of memories, and I dreaded to think what immersing oneself in their waters might do.

Dalian strode to his throne, Lin and Mei trailing behind him. He was staring at me with the appraising look of a farmer considering the purchase of a beast. I found myself folding inward instinctively.

"I confess to being disappointed," he drawled. "Mother spoke so highly of you, I expected a great beauty, someone with more impressive abilities than what you've shown." His eyes glinted with malice. "Mother hoped that I would consider you for my bride."

I'd rather die. I suppressed my retort, the anger that choked me. But I couldn't entirely ignore his slights; the Lady of Tianxia would never stand for such humiliation. After all, he'd said we were "equals" now, though he'd meant none of it.

I smiled brightly like his insults didn't sting. "Lord Dalian, I don't think we'd suit either. Moreover, I'm already spoken for." To him, indifference would be the greatest affront.

His eyes thinned. "Do you prefer a weak mortal?"

"I am *agreeing* with you," I said innocently, leashing my temper with great effort. "Given your disappointment, it should be a relief that you don't have to tie yourself to me."

His jaw tightened, his lips rolled almost all the way in. He didn't want me; but he'd wanted to hurt me with the taunt. Behind him, Lin's shoulders quivered like she was suppressing a laugh.

Tired of being around him, of the constant mask I had to wear in his presence, I rose and bowed. "Excuse me, Lord Dalian. I would like some fresh air."

Without waiting for his reply, I headed to the prow, relieved when the soldiers did not stop me. Tonight, the skies burned like the fires of a forge. A flapping sound rushed through the air, the void birds leading the way, their pale feathers gleaming. Despite the barge's size, it swiftly outpaced the other boats, which trailed after us like fireflies in the night. The waters of Wangchuan rippled beneath, beautiful yet haunting—those green lights twining through the inky waves like strands of onyx and jade.

The lines of an old rhyme surfaced in my mind:

Wangchuan waters, a curse and a gift,
A sip eases strife, casting sorrow adrift.
A cup erases the past, severing all ties,
To swim in its depths is to forget, to die.

If I were a stronger person, more valiant—I should dive into the river. Without me, Dalian could not open the gateway. But I was afraid for myself, and for Chengyin. While some might think it was a worthwhile sacrifice—our lives for many—I could not do it, not while there was a chance I might stop this. I wouldn't sacrifice my kingdom—but neither would I stop fighting for Zhangwei, Chengyin, or myself, for the future we all deserved.

Yet now, trapped on this vessel in the bleakness of night—it seemed hopeless. I closed my eyes, reaching for calm. Zhangwei would be making his way toward the gateway. While he hadn't anticipated us arriving so soon, few things caught him off guard—he wouldn't miss this trail of boats. And I was not wholly alone here; Lin and Mei would help me if they could.

Footsteps padded from behind me. I braced myself to endure Dalian's loathsome presence. It was wearying to strike the balance between not challenging him outright and not caving either—to act like I was one of them, his ally rather than his enemy.

But maybe to him the distinction was blurred; I'd seen how he treated his allies.

"Child, when you have that look on your face, I worry."

It was Aunt Shou. I wished I didn't think of her that way still, but I couldn't help myself. She came to stand beside me, her presence familiar, though it was like we were strangers.

"There's nothing to worry about, Aunt Shou." I smiled warmly to ease her suspicions. "Sometimes I just like to be alone. Particularly when the company grows . . . stifling."

"I did hope you would like each other," she said, shaking her head. "You would be a good influence on him."

My laugh was real; it was hard to pretend with her. "Aunt Shou, do you believe anyone could influence him against his inclination? I'm sure you've already tried." I added, "If Chengyin had behaved like this, you'd have thrashed him till he couldn't sit down. Yet you make far more allowances for Dalian."

Her lips trembled as she mashed them together. "It's not easy to be a ruler, as you know, to bear the weight of your people's future. Dalian is strained from his efforts because he tries to do too much. Since his childhood, he's been sensitive to criticism, it makes him lash out."

Convenient excuses for bad behavior.

"Aunt Shou, do you agree with what he's done: erecting the barriers over the river, distributing its power in this manner, punishing those who disagree with him? The invasion?" I was careful to keep my tone calm like I was seeking her opinion, rather than trying to influence it.

When she didn't reply, I lifted the bell by my side. "You would have advised me better; you wouldn't have let this happen in Tianxia."

"He has his reasons," she said tightly.

"Or do you want the invasion, to avenge your daughter?" I asked.

"My thirst for blood has been long quenched." Her voice thickened with emotion. "I am sick of death; I've lived and breathed it for far too long."

"Why don't you stop him? Find a way to make him listen?" I said slowly. "You were very good at making yourself heard back in Tianxia."

"Dalian is headstrong, yet he has his own strengths. I should have tried to soften some of his edges earlier, before he grew too set in his ways." She looked down into the river. "I didn't bring him up right, focusing my efforts on his sister because she was the heir."

Was guilt behind this? Because she felt Dalian had been neglected in his childhood, she blamed herself for who he'd become? If so, she should stand up to him now rather than allowing him to continue along this treacherous path. It was never too late to become a parent. In some ways—much as I hated to admit it—she was still mine. My guard was up, yet I couldn't wholly shake the ease of familiarity. Sometimes being around her was harder than being around Dalian.

"How did your daughter die?" Part of me wanted to help her

unburden this ancient grief—and another hoped she'd let something slip so I could secure an advantage. I was neither as compassionate nor as heartless as I should be.

"I was away when Queen Caihong's soldiers came to our territory; they'd been patrolling more often, seeking to quell dissenters. Insults were exchanged, but then they attacked without warning—killing her."

"I heard it was an accident," I said, recalling Zhangwei's words.

"Does it matter?" she asked harshly. "My daughter is dead. The immortals took her from me."

Maybe it was easier to believe in villainy than in the cruel accidents of life. Anger and vengeance struck outward, while the wounds of grief remained within. It was harder to look inward, but in the end, this was how we healed.

Aunt Shou continued, her voice dulled: "Dalian was gravely wounded, but he survived. He carried her body back to us. Since that day, he was never the same, nor was I—the day we'd learned to hate."

"I'm sorry for her death." My tone gentled, her pain reaching me, too.

"I blamed myself for not being there. In my grief, I relinquished the throne to Dalian when he asked. He had a plan to secure our vengeance, training in powerful magic that the immortals knew nothing of. He just needed the support of the court."

And the army. I wondered at this magic he'd learned. Was that how he'd sealed the skies? Erected these barriers along the river?

Aunt Shou shrugged. "The rest you know. We lost the war. We were exiled here, though there was a kindness to it. In the beginning, we thrived here, supported by the wealth of the river. We were almost happy again."

"Except for Dalian," I guessed.

"He yearns for what we lost. He's always wanted *more*." The lines deepened along her forehead until she almost looked like the mortal aunt I'd loved. "I thought I was giving him his freedom in his childhood, while he imagined my neglect. This planted the seed in his mind that he was unfavored, unwanted—why he craves assurance, his inclination to dominate rather than persuade. How can you sway others when, deep down, you doubt your own worth?"

"We are more and less than what we've been taught, Aunt Shou. If one's mind is closed, lessons fall on deaf ears. You can teach someone to shoot an arrow, but you cannot guide where it strikes."

A long pause fell as she tilted her head back. "You don't speak like you used to."

"Maybe I've grown up," I said quickly, to divert any suspicion. "I've lived more in this year than my entire lifetime."

Her eyes slid to me, bright with knowing. "I know when you're hiding something, Liyen. I know you're not what you say."

Was that why she'd given me the bottle of scent? Was she trying to protect me in her own way? "I don't know what you mean, Aunt Shou." It was safer this way, no matter her intentions. "If I'm different, it's because of what was done to me."

"I won't tell Dalian," she assured me. "I care for you, too. I just hope you'll see reason. You're clever; you must realize there's no way back for you. Your mother would never accept you, what you've become." She didn't sound spiteful or angry, just resigned.

I went cold inside, her words wounding deep—was it the truth in them? But I reminded myself that Aunt Shou didn't know my mother. Hate had a way of twisting one's perspective.

I frowned, feigning confusion. "Aunt Shou, my mother is dead, along with my father."

"I know you don't trust me, but just listen to me." Her voice turned persuasive. "This can be your home. Marry Dalian, share the burdens of his throne. Help him become the ruler I know he can be."

"Aunt Shou, even if I wanted to—which I don't—he doesn't want any help. He rejects even you, so why would he listen to me? This is something neither of us wants," I said gravely. "When I marry, it will be for love—because of who they are, not what they might become."

Aunt Shou fell silent, looking into the horizon. The mountain loomed ahead, the gateway to Kunlun. How close it was—fear creeping over my heart.

"Do you miss Tianxia?" I asked. I wanted her to remember, if there was a chance that she might help us later.

"Every time I see this place, I think of it and your grandfather. He was a good man, a kind one." A tear fell, which she let slide down her cheek. "But my first loyalties are to my people and my son."

I took a deep breath, caging my resentment. Regardless, I needed her support in one matter, one I didn't think she'd refuse. "Aunt Shou, will you help me keep Chengyin safe?"

Her gaze was piercing. "Will you keep your word to open the gateway?"

No.

"Yes," I lied. "But if things don't go to plan, do you promise not to let Dalian hurt Chengyin?"

And though she nodded, I couldn't help wondering if she was lying to me, too. We were on dangerous ground, both of us making promises we had no right to make . . . that we weren't going to keep.

43

Ahead, the river forked, one side continuing into the Wangchuan—the other flowing into a narrow inlet that our barge turned into. The landscape shifted, towering cliffs flanking us, their jagged peaks clawing at the skies. The other boats did not follow us, instead heading toward a wide stretch of land on the far side of the river.

Dalian strode out to the prow, joining Aunt Shou and me. He was smiling, and in that moment he almost looked like my friend again.

"Where are the other boats going?" I asked.

"Only one vessel can enter this passage at a time. The rest of our soldiers will make their way through the mountains," he replied, gesturing at the steep cliffs.

This must be the same path Zhangwei was taking. The slope appeared treacherous, and what if he encountered the other soldiers? As Dalian's gaze shifted to me, I turned to conceal my anxiety.

"Don't worry." His lips curved wider. "There are more than enough soldiers on board here, my finest warriors to ensure everything goes to plan."

Was that a threat? Maybe he knew only one way to make people obey him.

The deeper into the inlet we sailed, the narrower it grew, pressing us between the dark mountains until their shadows engulfed us, until it felt like we were being squeezed between two giants. Here the waters gleamed with an oily opacity, the green lights of the Wangchuan fading away.

The air sharpened abruptly, frost creeping over the wooden floorboards, the cold seeping through my shoes and my robe. As I shivered, mist shrouded the barge like a gossamer sheet. Just ahead, land gleamed, my pulse thudding as we neared it.

The barge glided onward, finally halting by a slender stretch of earth at the foot of a mountain ringed by cliffs. My throat tightened at the sight of the shimmering gateway ahead, just as I'd seen in the Mirror of Destiny.

That was not my fate, I reminded myself. It was not the future but a possibility—one I had denied, one I would not let come to pass.

Upon Dalian's order, we left the barge together. Aunt Shou walked beside him as Lin, Mei, and I trailed after them. The soldiers followed us closely, more than fifty of them, including Captain Rao. My steps dragged, my gaze darting around for a sign of Zhangwei, but there was none.

A silent scream was building inside me. My choices were rapidly narrowing. Lies would no longer suffice; the only chance of survival lay in doing what Dalian wanted. I wouldn't—but I also wasn't ready to die. Who was? It wasn't about being a coward . . . but wanting to live, holding on to each frail moment. Maybe I'd become more mortal than immortal.

"Walk faster, or I'll help you along," Captain Rao snapped from behind me.

At once, I feigned a stumble, kicking a lump of dirt over his feet. "My apologies, Captain," I said brightly. "I'm clumsy by nature. When I hurry, I tend to trip."

As his mouth twisted, I resisted the urge to laugh. My triumph was short-lived as the captain barked a furious command to two soldiers, who grabbed my arms to yank me along. Their fingers dug so hard into my flesh, bruises were already forming.

"Release her," Lin called out. "Don't manhandle Lord Dalian's honored guest."

"We'll see how long she remains a guest," Captain Rao flung back, an ominous prediction of my future.

I wrenched free of the soldiers' hold, striding out of reach. As the gateway loomed before me, my heart plunged. The mountain gleamed like obsidian, a white marble arch set into the stone. Just as in Kunlun, ropes of vines were twined around the archway, thorns dusting their stalks. Thick clusters of wisteria hung down in rich shades of violet. A shimmering pane of liquid cascaded within, its ceaseless rush muffling the cry of the void birds above. It flowed seamlessly, without pause, obscuring what lay on the other side—jagged lines streaking across the water as lightning illuminates the skies. Closer to the ground, a small part of the pane thinned—just as I'd seen on the other side.

The air rippled with powerful magic, infused in each drop, petal, and thorn. Something about this place called to me, anticipation coursing in my veins, an inexplicable urge to draw closer that battled with my terror. Was it the imprint of my mother's magic? If I closed my eyes, I could almost imagine she was here, the familiar thrum of her aura winding around me. But she was not; I was alone.

Wings fluttered as a bird swooped down to snare a dragonfly in its beak. As the tip of its wing brushed the liquid in the gateway—a crackling tore through the calm. The marble arch blazed, the lights from the gateway surging along the bird's wing, spreading across its body like a web of fine cracks. It flapped its wings desperately yet could not take flight, caught in the throes of this merciless spell. As it shivered, the creature folded in on itself, bones crunching, feathers scattering—like it was being crushed alive. Piteous cries rang out, then faded abruptly as its struggles weakened, until all that remained of the bird was its mangled form.

I shuddered; many of the soldiers turned pale. A gruesome death for any who touched the gateway, and this might be our fate should we fail to cross it safely.

Dalian grinned like he sensed my fear. "You're wise to be afraid. Don't make any careless mistakes; just do as you're told."

I wrestled with my anger, to keep my tone soft. "I don't know what to do," I said, trying to draw this out.

Dalian offered me a scythe with an amber hilt, nodding toward the stairway that was cut into the wall, wide enough for one. It led to the top of the arch—close enough to touch it—though who would dare after seeing the bird's end?

"Cut the vines away. Once they are cleared, channel your power to break the archway." When I didn't move, he seized my hand, thrusting the scythe into it. My skin was as cold as his.

"Don't fail me," he growled before releasing me.

I gripped the scythe, wishing I could thrust it into his chest. *Not yet.* I turned, wrenching my mind from the terror that tangled my thoughts. With the weight of all eyes upon me, I forced myself to climb the stairway. My foot slipped once as I fell, intentionally, the scythe clattering to the ground.

As a soldier rushed to hand it back to me, Dalian's face creased with rage. "Another 'accident,' and I'll have Captain Rao accompany you."

My stomach churned at the thought. Not daring to falter again, I ascended the stairs steadily this time. At the top, I looked down, my head swimming. Soldiers swarmed this pale wedge of soil, the boats that had landed away from the inlet, dotting the river behind like beads of foam. I was surrounded, trapped. Despair sank deep, digging its claws into my heart.

"I'm afraid," I whispered to myself.

Saying it aloud was a release . . . an admission, a forgiveness of myself, my flaws and shortcomings. Fear need not be a burden when it could be harnessed into a desire to live. Hope possessed a magic of its own—rare to manifest, yet wresting miracles within one's reach.

Calm spread over me, my mind clearing. The sweetness of the wisteria was stronger here, almost intoxicating. Each petal was veined with silver as though traced in stardust. Thick vines looped and curled in front of me, each culminating in a cluster of flowers. My hand shook as I lifted the vine closest to me, ignoring the thorns that pricked my fingers—their tips stained with my blood. I lifted the scythe gently to the vine, a tentative touch to appease Dalian. Yet the moment the blade brushed it, light rippled from my fingers—the scythe drawing my magic against my will, flowing into the plant. A clump of wisteria fragmented, petals drifting away like dandelion seeds. A segment of the vine fell into my hand, heavy and limp, like uncoiled rope. The gateway shuddered, the darting lights in the water stilling as a metallic scent thickened the air—the scent of *my* blood. With a wrench, I halted the flow of my power, numbed with horror at what I'd done—inadvertently weakening the gateway I was trying to protect.

A cheer rose from the Wuxin—the sound bringing me back to the Temple of the Crimson Moon, the moment my despicable manifestation destroyed the gateway. I swallowed hard, fighting down a burst of queasiness. This had to end now; I'd drawn it out for as long as I could. But suddenly my skin warmed with a new awareness, my heart lifting though I didn't know why. As I glanced up, something on the far side of the mountain caught my eye: a flutter of black brocade.

It was Zhangwei, standing on a ledge across from me. Relief swept through me that he was safe; he was here. Yet there were too many soldiers to fight—even more making their way through the mountains. I needed to create a diversion, something to give us a chance.

The curtain of liquid flowed like molten crystal through the gateway, light dancing over its surface. A sliver of an idea un-raveled, barely enough to be woven into any coherent plan, but I would grasp at the thinnest thread.

Magic flitted from my fingers toward the gateway, this time upon my command. Yet the waters did not shift, nor did the lights flicker. If they couldn't be manipulated by magic, what about something of its own? My fingers tightened around the vine, al-most welcoming the sting of the thorns, jolting me from my numb-ing fear. I grasped my magic, my gaze sliding to Zhangwei's, then to Lin and Mei—praying they would catch my meaning—while Aunt Shou and Dalian remained a distance behind. Drawing a deep breath, I hurled the vine down, right through the shimmer-ing gateway. It sank through the liquid, splashing the surface, deli-cate sprays of water arcing wide. Dalian and Aunt Shou scrambled further to safety, while Lin and Mei had shielded themselves. And Zhangwei had vanished.

Screams of anguish erupted, punctured by a ferocious crack-ling. The soldiers closest to the gateway collapsed, clawing at their faces, tearing at their armor. Yet the lights of the gateway swarmed mercilessly across them—as they had over the bird—blazing with vicious brightness, devouring the soldiers whole. As they twisted and writhed in the throes of death, I looked away, sickened by their torment, wanting to weep. Most were simply fol-lowing orders, but they would have killed me without hesitation if commanded to. I would not trade my life for theirs.

Captain Rao sprinted forward, unfortunately unscathed, his sword drawn as he headed toward me. Lin and Mei raced to block him, but more soldiers closed around them. As Dalian and Aunt Shou hurried to the shoreline, I rushed down the narrow stairway—but Captain Rao blocked my path.

I backed away, trapped—my only weapon, the scythe. Swiftly, I channeled a shield over myself as Captain Rao reached the ledge, advancing toward me menacingly. "I always knew you were lying about the transformation. I told Lord Dalian as much, but he was blinded by his desire to open the gateway."

"And I always knew you were a vicious snake, the day you tore out my soldier's heart," I spat.

His eyes slitted with rage. "Let's see what color your heart is once I've ripped it from your chest."

Fury roiled, eclipsing my terror. "You'll never get that far."

As he slung his sword at me, I ducked, slashing out with the scythe. It was too short—Captain Rao evaded with ease as he thrust his blade at me again. I threw my scythe up to catch his blow, straining beneath the force. He was stronger, more skilled, with the better weapon—but I couldn't give up.

I dropped my arm without warning, darting to the side. As he staggered forward, thrown off balance, I raced for the stairs. He lunged at me, grabbing at my ankle—but someone sprang between us, flinging the captain aside with brutal force. Zhangwei stood there, his eyes blazing with rage. Such relief swept through me, such joy. Without looking away from the captain, Zhangwei tossed me my sword, my fingers closing gratefully around the familiar black jade hilt.

"The God of War," Captain Rao snarled, pushing himself to his feet.

"Touch her again and you'll die." Zhangwei's voice was dangerously taut as he lifted his blade, pointing it at the captain. "For what you did, I'll kill you anyway."

I straightened, unsheathing my sword. "I'll kill him myself."

Captain Rao's eyes fixed on Zhangwei's weapon, shining with power, the color draining from his face. When the captain charged at him, Zhangwei didn't evade, instead slamming a fist into his face. The captain went sprawling to the ground, blood oozing from a cut on his cheek. He blinked wildly as though stunned—the ferocity of Zhangwei's blow shocking me, too.

As Captain Rao fled down the stairs, Zhangwei leapt from the ledge to land gracefully on the ground. His sword arced to slash at the captain again and again, Captain Rao swinging his weapon in defense—his movements growing clumsy and frantic. As the captain turned and ran away, Zhangwei stalked after him—but other Wuxin soldiers surrounded him now. As they closed in on him, he kicked one, then punched the next, the shove of his elbow sending a third flying. He brawled as well as any mortal, like he'd been born to it.

I rushed toward him, my pulse racing. A soldier leapt into my path but I didn't halt, swinging my sword wide as light crackled along the blade. It slammed into the soldier who fell to the ground. This weapon had always felt like it fit my hand, and now it was almost a part of me, seamlessly melding with my power. It felt like a lifetime ago when I'd fled from the Winged Devils, their helpless prey—and in way, it had been. At last I reached Zhangwei. Lin and Mei were close by his side as they fought Wuxin soldiers together. The distant shore beyond the inlet was crowded with boats, most having landed. Soon, Dalian's reinforcements would arrive through the mountains. We were running out of time.

Zhangwei flung aside the soldier battling him, to come to my side. His eyes raked me, as though searching for injuries—then flicked toward Dalian in the distance. "You know what has to be done."

I nodded even as my insides recoiled. "Be careful with him."

"As I would with myself," he promised.

The remaining Wuxin soldiers surrounded Dalian and Aunt Shou protectively, their swords pointed our way. Lin and Mei advanced to attack them, with Zhangwei joining the fray. He edged closer to Dalian with deadly purpose, forging a path with his merciless blows. As Dalian turned toward the barge, fear struck me. If he left, Chengyin would remain trapped—Dalian would kill him after what I'd done. I couldn't let him escape, not while he had Chengyin's body.

"Lord Dalian, I was surprised you were so easily tricked by a simple disguise," I called out mockingly as I discarded the illusion over my eyes, letting the copper fade

His face was white with fury. "*What* are you?" he taunted me. "Not one of us; not one of them. You're nothing."

"Fortunately, I don't care what you think." I unclasped the bell at my waist and tossed it toward him, the gold glittering as it landed by his feet. How liberating to no longer hold my tongue.

"What did you do? How did you halt the transformation?" he demanded.

"Try asking nicely." I smiled as I repeated what he'd said to me in the cell. He'd hate that. I made myself look at him, not at the others—especially not Zhangwei who was drawing closer to Dalian.

"Don't you dare condescend to me," he seethed.

"Enough, Dalian." Aunt Shou tried to pull him away. "We must go. It's too dangerous here with the God of War."

He swung to face her. "Did you know about *her*, Mother? That she was lying?"

A protest sprang to my lips, the instinctive urge to defend her—but I smothered it. If Dalian thought he'd been betrayed, he might be incited to rashness. Aunt Shou had shown Grandfather no mercy either, sending him to the immortals to confess. Shame flooded me; this was ruthless—cruel, even. And for the first time, I thought Mother and I might not be so different after all.

As Aunt Shou nodded jerkily, Dalian went pale. "You betrayed me."

"I was trying to convince her—"

As she reached for him, he shoved her back. "You lied. You told me her transformation was complete." A sharp laugh. "Why did you protect her? Did you care for her more than me, your own flesh and blood?"

"No." Her voice broke, her expression haunted. "Let them go, my son. Enough suffering has been caused." She gestured at the river behind us. "We don't need the realms beyond; we can build a great kingdom here. I can't lose you as I lost Damei—"

Dalian's eyes slitted with rage as he drew back and struck her across her face. Aunt Shou pressed a hand to her reddened cheek, the hurt in her eyes piercing my heart.

"Never compare me to my sister. Never question my decisions. Nothing is over until *I* command it," he snarled.

He stiffened abruptly, his hands clenched. The mask of Chengyin's face quivered, his body shuddering as though he were struggling with himself.

I stared at him, holding my breath, willing my friend to appear. "Fight him, Chengyin!" I called out, on the fragile hope he could hear me. "You are stronger than him."

Dalian laughed, a breathless rasping sound. "This weakling will never escape. Once I'm done with him, I'll flay the skin from hi—"

His words died. His teeth bared, the veins pulsing along his arm. His body jerked wildly—as he pulled a dagger from his waist and thrust it into his own gut.

Aunt Shou's scream rent the silence, my own ringing in my mind. Chengyin . . . it was Chengyin. It was *his* eyes that flicked to mine, warm and bright, devoid of the malevolence that had stamped Dalian's domination over him. Somehow Chengyin had wrested back control over his body, though the price had been too high. How had he done it? In a flash I understood: It was Dalian's cruelty to his mother that broke the hold. His mother—*theirs*.

The Wuxin stilled, all eyes on their leader—but all I saw was my friend, fear gripping me as blood spilled from the gaping wound in Chengyin's side. A peaceful smile stole across his face; he looked like himself again. I pushed my way through the others, to drop down beside him.

Chengyin's hand grasped mine, his skin icy. "I don't want to die." How frail his voice was.

"I won't let you. Not until you're old and gray and can barely walk—"

His laugh cut off as he gasped for breath. I clasped his hand, trying not to look at the deep gash in his body. The eyes he turned to me were gentle and knowing. "You were always a terrible liar."

I bent my head, fighting back tears. "Only because you knew me so well."

Aunt Shou rushed toward us. Her hands glided over Chengyin's injury as she tried to stanch the blood flow, magic gleaming through her fingers as she muttered feverishly. Tears fell from her eyes, but his wound did not close—healing was a rare skill among the Wuxin, much less for an injury this severe.

I grasped my magic, but Zhangwei shook his head in warning. Where was Dalian? He hadn't emerged. Tears of fury pricked my eyes; I couldn't help Chengyin yet.

"Heal him!" Aunt Shou cried to me, almost pleading. "Why are you hesitating? There is nothing Chengyin wouldn't do for you."

My throat clogged, my nails biting into my palm, but I forced myself to play this despicable part, to not waste the one chance Chengyin had wrenched for us. If we didn't force Dalian out now, it would all be for nothing.

"Chengyin would not have wanted this, Aunt Shou. He would *never* want us to sacrifice the kingdom for his life, to be used as a puppet for evil." The words left a bitter taste, but I couldn't relent.

Aunt Shou seized my arm. "You can't let him die."

I steeled myself, though inside grief racked me, terror clawing that it might be too late. "You know, deep down, that Dalian won't release Chengyin—and if he does, it will only be to kill him. Dalian is cruel, vicious, and envious—especially of those better than him." I hurled each insult, hoping they'd strike to pry him loose.

I bent to touch Chengyin's cheek, loathing myself in this moment. "I love you . . . but I won't save you."

My heart twisted until it was on the cusp of breaking. I wanted to take back these vile words, but Aunt Shou's gasp rooted me to the spot. My eyes darted to Chengyin, his form wavering as I'd seen it do once before. A mask seemed to split from his face like a shadow separating from a body—the features settling to form Dalian's, solidifying to flesh.

He loomed over Chengyin, who was curled on the ground, the earth dark with his blood. "Why do you weep for the mortal, Mother?" Dalian spat, his white hair falling over his face.

"I weep for your brother *and* for you." She wasn't hiding her feelings anymore, like something inside her had snapped, too. Had she realized that no matter how she loved him, Dalian would only see the ill in the world?

As Dalian lunged toward me, Zhangwei blocked his path, his sword thrust out. The Wuxin soldiers rushed to protect their leader—just less than twenty remained, but their reinforcements would arrive at any moment.

I swooped down to Chengyin, freed at last from the cruel captivity. Gathering my magic, I laid my hand on his wound. He was cold, his skin ashen. Each breath came shallow and weak. He was fading fast. Our magic could not heal injuries formed by age, or from natural causes. But this tear of flesh, I could heal, if it wasn't too late.

My magic flowed in a ceaseless stream. But although Chengyin's wound was closing, it wasn't fast enough. I held him tighter, channeling as much of my power as I could into him—until at last he stirred, the bleeding stemmed. Yet he was still weak, gravely so. I had to get him back to Tianxia, away from the danger. But I couldn't do it alone, almost exhausted from the strain.

I caught Aunt Shou's eye. "Help me get him home."

She nodded without hesitation. Her eyes shone as she bent to kiss Chengyin's pale cheek. As his eyes fluttered apart, his face twisted with the awakenings of pain.

"Mother," he whispered. "Are you well?"

"I am now, my son. Remember that I love you—always." She touched his face tenderly. "The soothsayers called you unlucky when I brought you into my family. How wrong they were. I was *lucky* to have you in my life."

A gentle smile stole across his face, tears shining in his eyes before he closed them once more. I was crying, too, pierced by their sorrow—their love. Aunt Shou's power coiled around Chengyin, melding with mine to form a powerful barrier around him. Her magic summoned a wind that rose up to bear him away, through the slit in the gateway, back to the safety of Kunlun.

A howl of rage erupted from Dalian—his gut still bleeding, a mirror to the wound Chengyin had inflicted on himself. Captain Rao and his soldiers were still fighting Zhangwei, yet he held his ground against them with ease, closing in on Dalian with each soldier he brought down. If we could kill Dalian now, this would end. An eagerness seized me, an impatience for this to be *over*—for us to be *free*.

My resolve hardened as I advanced toward Dalian, my sword raised. He didn't seem to notice as he threw his head up, gripping the bell at his waist—not of gold as I'd originally thought but streaked with bronze, too. As light flowed from his hands, the bells of the soldiers surrounding him chimed once—then shattered with a startling crack. Captain Rao's eyes went wide as he groped for his bell, but it was too late; the metal breaking apart like the others.

Glittering streams of copper and gold glided from the shards of the bells, flowing into Dalian's like rivers merging into the sea. It blazed like living flame, the light seeping into Dalian—the color returning to his face as his wound healed, his hair gleaming like polished silver.

Lin and Mei backed away, exchanging wary looks. Their bells were intact, a shield cast over them. After all, they'd never trusted their ruler. Aunt Shou's remained untouched; even Dalian wasn't as heartless as to hurt his own mother.

A groan rose from the Wuxin soldiers, collapsing to the ground around us. "Lord Dalian," Captain Rao rasped through clenched teeth. "Why are you doing this to us? We are loyal to you. It's forbidden to harvest our strength; you are killing us."

"Your sacrifice will be honored." Dalian's voice rang with a new resonance, a cruel indifference.

"Just as you honored the Winged Devils?" the captain raged. "You promised to help them if they attacked the immortals, that they would rule the Golden Desert. You sent them to their deaths—a sacrifice that you did nothing to honor. You lied to win their service, just as you lied to everyone about the Wangchuan River—"

"Enough!"

Dalian flung his hand out, a flash of green light striking the captain right between his eyes. They went white at once, then closed, his body going limp.

The other soldiers shuddered, their expressions of fury and sorrow. "We are your own people," one gasped. "We don't want this."

Already they were fading to watery reflections of themselves. Hollows caved in their cheeks, their hair turned translucent, their skin papery and thin. Their cries melded into the whistling of the wind, their bodies disintegrating, leaving just the shells of their armor.

"Dalian!" Aunt Shou cried, her body shaking. "This is forbidden; a heinous deed. What will the people think?"

He sneered as he glanced at me. "We will tell them the 'truth,' Mother. That *they* killed them."

I was shaking my head as Zhangwei took my hand. "We must go. Now."

Together.

A small part of me didn't want to go yet, but he was right. We turned to race to the gateway—but then bolts of green light hurtled down, fencing us in. As we sprinted the other way, Dalian appeared, blocking our path, the copper in his eyes spread all the way through, his power rippling like a cloak of shadow.

We were out of time.

44

Dalian was studying Zhangwei, his skin alight with an eerie sheen. He seemed larger somehow, the veins along his neck and arms more sharply defined, his nails pointed like spear tips. "I have been curious to test myself against the God of War's might."

"You did once," Zhangwei reminded him coldly. "And you ended up here."

"Was this why you reaped your loyal soldiers' strength, killing them all?" My voice fractured; I was still shaken by Dalian's horrific deed, worse than anything I might have imagined of him.

His eyes flashed like pools of molten copper. "You will open the gateway now, else I will wring every last drop of your cursed blood into it as a parting gift to your mother."

I raised my head, glaring at him. "Do your worst. I'll never open the gateway for you."

Dalian's hand shot up, the air quivering as a wave of light crashed over me—my shield shattering like glass. I scrambled to form another, but he raised his whip now, writhing in his grip. As he flung it at me—Zhangwei moved between us, blocking the blow with his sword. The whip wrapped around the blade, but Zhangwei slashed it clean through, flinging the pieces aside. As light surged from Dalian's hand, the whip re-formed, blazing as bright as new.

Zhangwei attacked him again, his sword flying so quickly it was a blur—but Dalian evaded him swiftly; he was faster and stronger than he'd been before. His whip gleamed as it slammed down again, but Zhangwei dipped back—the lash curling harmlessly over his body. Dalian didn't pause, lunging forward again, twisting at the last moment to avoid the tip of Zhangwei's blade.

I glanced around, unable to find Lin and Mei—had they retreated to the barge? They had helped us enough. Aunt Shou was slumped on the ground, her face in her hands. It hurt to see her misery, part of me wanting to comfort her—but I dared not move, desperately seeking a way to aid Zhangwei. Their blows landed with dizzying force, such brutal lack of restraint, my blood turned to ice.

Zhangwei's sword swept toward Dalian's head—but the Wuxin spun out of reach, summoning waves of blinding light to engulf Zhangwei. As he struck at them, Dalian's whip hurtled forth, coiling around Zhangwei like a snake. He struggled wildly, the binds tightening with each movement, tearing his robe, his flesh, his blood spilling to the ground.

"You're not as strong as before, God of War," Dalian mocked him as he stalked forward. "You should have taken the *entire* Divine Pearl Lotus for yourself rather than sharing it with another."

Sick with horror, I rushed between them, raising my sword to hack at Zhangwei's binds. As I struck at the whip, a greenish light flashed across my arm, the pain tenfold worse than when Dalian had lashed me before. I cried out—unable to stop myself—my fingers stiff with fright, but I wouldn't stop sawing through the binds though they were as hard as stone.

"Go." Zhangwei's eyes slid to the gateway then back to me, his eyes ink dark. "I'll follow."

Liar.

"I'm not leaving you," I said fiercely.

Dalian's laugh was one of disbelief. "What is this? Does your

betrothed know?" Lines creased his brow. "*Were* you even betrothed?"

"Only ever to me." Zhangwei's gaze was still fixed on me alone.

I blinked through the sudden brightness in my eyes—though
I cursed him in the next instant for clouding my mind with his declaration. If we escaped, I wouldn't let this pass. He had never asked
me to marry him before, and this was *not* the time for a proposal—
God of War or not.

Dalian's eyes thinned to crescents. "How easily you've tamed
the God of War. There is no greater chain than love."

"You're wrong, and I pity you for it," I said scathingly, knowing how he'd detest that. "Love is the greatest freedom in the
world, but you have to be capable of yielding it, to grasp its true
meaning."

I aimed my sword at Dalian. He grinned, not bothering to
raise his weapon—knowing I would lose, that I was far from his
match. As I lunged at him—I spun around at the last moment to
slam my sword against Zhangwei's binds. As it struck, I channeled
a burst of magic, surging through the blade, coating the whip in
a layer of frost. It held fast, but as I bore down harder the whip
began to crack. Zhangwei's jaw clenched as he struggled harder,
forcing his binds apart, even as he tore his wounds wider—

Dalian flew at me, his teeth bared, grasping my throat to lift
me like I was a doll. As I kicked wildly, he knocked my sword from
my hands. His nails gleamed, arched like talons, his grip tightening to puncture the skin of my neck. Choking now, I clawed at
Dalian, reaching for my magic to fight back. But as his grip tightened, my composure broke, my power slipping away like I was
snatching at water.

I kicked at Dalian, again and again, my legs colliding with his
chest, his gut and thighs. If he hurt, he gave no sign of it, his hateful grin widening. Mustering my strength, I raked my nails across
his face, digging as deep as I could. At last, he flinched, uttering a

vile curse. I seized my power, summoning darts of ice that hurtled into him, scraping his cheeks and neck. With a hiss, Dalian flung me aside as though scalded—

Zhangwei broke free to catch me, then set me down. His wounds crisscrossed his arms, his robe shredded in parts, wet with blood. As he swung to Dalian, his eyes glinted dangerously, his guttural tone sending a chill down my spine. "I promised you death, but now you will *suffer*."

I seized Zhangwei's arm, glancing at the gateway. Who cared for vengeance or retribution; I just wanted us to escape. Yet Dalian's power erupted in a violent onslaught, crashing against us— forcing Zhangwei and me to shield ourselves, trapping us in place.

Behind him, a large group of soldiers was heading toward us—Dalian's reinforcements that had come through the mountains—my heart sinking at the sight. Yet it was Lin and Mei who led them onward, General Fang and Captain Lai among them, those who'd challenged Dalian on behalf of the Winged Devils. Their approach was silent as though their presence had been shielded. Zhangwei tensed at the sight of them, but when Lin nodded at us, some of my fear dispersed. They stopped a distance away, observing us intently rather than attacking. Had Lin convinced them to listen?

The first battle is for our people's hearts. If they do not believe, they do not fight—and the war is already lost.

Dalian remained oblivious to the soldiers, his back to them as he faced us, blocking the gateway. His attacks were intensifying, his magic a viperous green as it slithered through the air. Sweat slid from my face, the veins along Zhangwei's arms bulging as we shielded ourselves. Dalian would never let us go; he'd kill us, unless we destroyed him first.

Raising my voice, I asked, "Lord Dalian, you say the invasion of the Mortal Realm is necessary because the Wangchuan River is weakening. Have you investigated the cause? What has been done to restore it?" I needed to distract him so he wouldn't notice the soldiers.

"You have no right to question me," Dalian said with a sneer. "All know the river's powers have waned."

Zhangwei frowned, his mind falling into stride with mine. "The Wangchuan River's force should not diminish. It is eternal, constantly replenished through the cycle of life and death. It would not wane—unless it was being *drained*. As the ruler of the Netherworld, Lord Dalian, you should know this." He spoke with such authority, few could have doubted him.

"You did this, Lord Dalian," I said loudly, so all could hear. "You're the one draining the power from the Wangchuan River—first to pry apart the gateway, then to seal the skies. This invasion isn't the cure but the cause."

I paused, letting my words sink in. "That's why there isn't enough for your people, because you've been *wasting* it, hoarding it for yourself and your chosen. You control your people, keep them obedient—by keeping them hungry."

Dalian's eyes burned with rage; he was shaking with it. While I'd been forced to tread cautiously before, afraid he'd lash out at Chengyin and me—now I wanted to shove him to the brink, to reveal his true face to those who served him, who deserved better.

I pushed aside my terror, gesturing to the piles of scattered armor around us, all that remained of the soldiers he'd killed. "You drained the Wangchuan River for your own selfish ambition, just as you drained your own soldiers for their strength—you *murdered* them, even Captain Rao, a vile betrayal of those most loyal to you. Their bodies are no more, turned to dust."

Silence fell, only interrupted by the sound of weeping. Aunt Shou's body was folded over, her shoulders heaving. Though the wrinkles had vanished from her face, she had never appeared so worn.

General Fang broke away from the crowd to stride forward. "Lord Dalian, is this true?" His voice reverberated with disbelief and fury.

Dalian swung around, freezing at the sight of the soldiers behind him. He blinked uncertainly, his magic dispersing as outrage twisted his features. "How dare you question me, General Fang?"

The general did not cower, his expression hardening. "You didn't answer my question, Lord Dalian. Did you murder our soldiers? Are you hoarding the power of the Wangchuan River?"

Captain Lai moved to stand beside him, her white hair flying in the wind as her hand grazed the hilt of her sword. "Lord Dalian, silence is an answer in itself. Refusing to answer or even defend yourself, is akin to an admission of guilt."

Dalian looked around at the soldiers, a hunted look in his eyes. General Fang and Captain Lai were not easily silenced. Their presence had purpose; their voices bore weight.

"Captain Lai, remember your place. Apprehend these traitors and kill the God of War. I'll need the Lady of Tianxia a while longer," Dalian ordered. His tone was harsh yet there was a wildness in his eyes, a frantic unease.

"Lord Dalian, I am beginning to wonder who the real traitor is," Captain Lai countered as she raised her chin.

"You are treading dangerously close to treason," Dalian hissed.

"While Your Lordship is already waist-deep," General Fang replied.

Dalian's face turned white. "Traitors—all of you! You will be executed, your bodies torn apart and scattered into the Wangchuan River, where you will suffer endless torment."

Despite these threats, General Fang showed not a flicker of trepidation. "Lord Dalian, we ask you to return with us to answer our questions," he said steadily

More soldiers had drawn closer, approaching from the mountains. They stood behind the others, whispering among themselves as they looked uncertainly from their ruler to their commanders.

"Kill any who oppose me!" Dalian shouted to them. The copper in his eyes shone so bright, it hurt to look at him. "They have been plotting with the villainous immortals to usurp my throne. They will lock you away to starve here while they reap the wealth of the Mortal Realm for themselves!"

"He is lying to you." Somehow, my voice emerged calm. Zhangwei stood beside me, his sword drawn, guarding me from attack. I gestured to the abandoned armor once more. "The proof lies before you."

"You're the liar! You bribed them to your side," Lord Dalian roared as he rounded on me. "She and the God of War killed *all* your comrades."

Several of the soldiers glared at us with suspicion, their whispers gaining strength. Why should they trust us? Even though he was the monster, we were the enemy.

"Some, certainly," Zhangwei replied solemnly, "But these soldiers, including Captain Rao, were killed by their lord—the one they defended with their lives."

General Fang crouched down among the piles of dust, touching a gleaming breastplate. "It wasn't the immortals. Only one of *us* could have done such a thing."

"Have you not wondered about the Wangchuan River? Why it fulfilled our needs before but no longer?" Lin cried. "Lord Dalian told us we needed to invade the mortals to feed our families, but it was a lie. The barriers he erected along the river were not to help feed us but to *starve* us, so he could keep its power for himself."

"General Fang, is this true?" a soldier asked hoarsely, her eyes rounded in disbelief.

"Captain Rao was in charge of constructing the barriers. We knew the river was weakening, but we didn't know why. We didn't investigate as we should have, accepting his word," General Fang said, touching the gold bell by his waist. "I am ashamed to admit we didn't feel the same urgency, we grew complacent—a mistake we will not repeat."

"Traitors!" Dalian raged as he pointed at the general, his face blotched with fury. "Those who will not obey me will die!"

As his hands gleamed once more, an eerie light enveloped the bell at his waist. Fear shrouded me, the memory of the withered Wuxin still fresh in my mind. "Shield yourselves!" I cried out. "Your bells are bound to his, he controls them. It's how he killed the others."

As shining barriers formed around the soldiers, Dalian's power surged—an immense force, yet the soldiers held steady. Again and again he lashed at them, until at last, he faltered, lowering his hand as sweat slid down his face.

Aunt Shou walked toward him slowly, her eyes red. The side of her face was swollen where Dalian had struck her. Yet her expression was calm, devoid of resentment, as she reached out a hand to him. "Come, my son. It is over. Let me look after you now."

Dalian's voice was almost hollow, his shoulders hunched. "Why pretend that you care for me, Mother? You only love Damei. You'd rather she was alive and I was dead."

"Never," she swore vehemently. "We don't trade or weigh those in our hearts. You are both precious to me in your own way."

"What if I told you that I let her die?" His eyes were wide, his last tether to sanity fraying.

Aunt Shou stared at him, the blood draining from her face. "No. Don't say it. You couldn't—"

"The immortals wounded her, but I *let* her die. The others didn't realize she was still alive, despite her wounds. While they were all fighting, I could have saved her had I brought her back sooner, had I summoned aid. We will never know. When she lay hurt and bleeding, I just kept thinking how much better my life would be without her. She was weeping, whispering my name. But after a while, she stopped." His voice hitched, an echo of regret. This act haunted him still—and maybe he had been punishing himself all this while.

Aunt Shou closed her eyes. "It's not true. *They* killed her."

"None of the spirits of the Wangchuan bear a greater burden than me," Dalian said, closing his eyes. "I am tired, Mother. I'm tired of trying to be better than I am, to prove to you, to everyone—that I deserve the throne more than my sister."

"We never asked you to." Aunt Shou's hands balled to fists. "How could you, Dalian? Your sister *loved* you."

His face hardened. "Because of her, nothing I did was ever good enough. *I* was never good enough. But now I am greater than all of you—and you will suffer for doubting me."

All around, the air twisted unevenly like it was throttled, a great force roaring through as blinding light erupted from Dalian's palms. A blazing pillar streaked into the heavens, crackling like a storm of lightning—a heartbeat before it hurtled into the depths of the Wangchuan River, setting the waters and the barriers aglow.

"The river!" Lin shouted. "He's destroying it!"

A rustling sprang up, the sound creeping down my spine. In the distance, the green lights of the waters writhed, moans rising from the river, melding into a cry that broke across the heavens—no longer of regret but of unfathomable suffering.

Lin, General Fang, and Captain Lai rushed forward, their hands alight with magic, channeling it into the waters—but the barriers along the riverbank gleamed brighter, towering like the tentacles of some monstrous sea creature. Their power rebounded sharply, the Wuxin soldiers thrown onto their backs, blood trickling from the corners of their mouths.

"We can't remove the barriers," Lin cried in despair

Dalian laughed, a vicious sound. "Only I control the Wangchuan River; none of the other Wuxin can touch it."

"Stop!" I shouted at Dalian. "You're killing your people. You don't want this."

A cold smile stretched across his face. "They betrayed me. If I die, let them die with me."

He flung his arms out, light now plunging toward the gateway—his body jerking violently from the force. The shimmering pane shuddered, then crumpled like paper. "A final gift for taking everything from me. A choice: Stay, to help your enemies, or flee and leave us to our fate." He smiled cruelly, one last game. "You were never one of us anyway."

As he collapsed to the ground, Aunt Shou rushed to embrace him. She was weeping as she channeled her power into him, but it was too late. He had spent himself—a final breath slipping from his chest as his eyes flicked toward his mother. How bright they shone, his mouth stretched into a faint smile as his body went still.

A thunderous sound tore from the gateway. It was closing— the marble archway shuddering as chunks fell away, the wisteria wilting on the vines that had shriveled and browned. Petals fell in a shower like rain.

"Liyen, we must go," Zhangwei said urgently. "The gateway is unstable, destroying itself. If we don't leave now, we will be trapped here forever."

My insides turned to ice, my mind engulfed by the cries rising from the Wangchuan, the shouts from the soldiers desperately fighting to restore the river—even as their efforts rebounded and hurt them in turn. It would be so easy to flee now, leaving the Wuxin to fend for their survival. They had killed my father; I would be avenging his death. Zhangwei's grip on my hand tightened as though pulling me away. He had no bond to the Wuxin, knowing them only as enemies. While I had lived among them, learned from them, tasted their compassion. Even in this short time, I'd seen the many faces they possessed . . . not just the mask they showed to their foes.

I was selfish . . . but I wasn't a monster. I couldn't let this tragedy unfold, the destruction of an entire kingdom. I couldn't close the door on them all to save myself—to preserve my own joy, precious though it was. My heart was breaking as I turned to Zhangwei, memorizing his face. This time, I would forget nothing.

"I can't leave them to die. There is good here, too." I drew a ragged breath, yet the weight in my chest did not lessen. "The Wuxin can't touch the barriers, but maybe I can."

Zhangwei clasped my shoulders, his eyes so dark yet dazzlingly bright. "Once the gateway collapses, there will be no way out, no way home."

"*You* must go." It was the hardest thing I ever said, my heart cleaved apart as I pushed him toward the gateway. "This is my choice. Tell Mother I miss her . . . that I'll find a way back." I didn't want him to leave, but I could never ask him to stay.

"Don't be a hero; they don't have happy endings," he said quietly.

"I'm no hero."

He pulled me into his arms tightly. "You have always been stronger than me."

I let myself stay in his embrace for a heartbeat, for one last perfect moment. Then I broke away, turning to the river—the pain so sharp, I couldn't breathe.

Zhangwei caught my hand, a fierce glitter in his eyes. "Where you go, I go."

I wanted to tell him to leave me, that we would be strong whether we were together or apart—that we weren't the romantic fools who would die of heartbreak without the other. But if I was honest, I wanted him with me.

"You would stay here, with me?" Tears fell, sliding down my face—when had they formed?

"Forever," he said. "If you'll have me."

"I want you for longer than that," I whispered.

His fingers slipped between mine. "Keep your word."

Zhangwei and I raced to the shoreline. Lin's face was white with fear as she stood with the other soldiers, channeling their magic into the distant barriers though it seemed futile.

A loud crash erupted behind us, the gateway to Tianxia collapsing. Our only way home had gone . . . but there was no time for regret. Magic surged from Zhangwei, weaving into mine—scarlet fire, white bands of ice, braiding in chaotic harmony as it streaked toward the barriers of the Wangchuan. It struck, not rebounding like the magic of the others—the barriers quivering but holding fast. My pulse raced; could we do this? Or would Zhangwei and I die here with those who were meant to be our enemies? Except they weren't enemies anymore.

Zhangwei and I clasped our hands, our power sweeping from us, as much as we could grasp. Our breaths came harshly, our energy spilling in violent force, twining and writhing together. At last, the barriers cracked, then shattered into fragments—the bells the Wuxin wore falling soundlessly to the ground. The cries from the Wangchuan River softened to rustling murmurs, the roiling waters calming, settling into a soothing rhythm.

I swayed on my feet, overcome by a wave of exhaustion. Zhangwei caught me, sliding an arm across my shoulders, though his heart was racing, too. I couldn't speak for a long while, our arms locked around each other, a lightness and weight crashing through me all at once.

"You stayed." My voice shook with disbelief once reality began sinking in.

"How could you think I wouldn't?" He tilted my face up to his, his voice pulsing with emotion. "I've chased you across the skies and earth, to the Netherworld itself. I will never let you go again."

A lump rose in my throat, my joy laced with pain at his sacrifice. "I wish I didn't take you from your home."

He pulled me closer, running his hand along my back. I rested my head against his chest, listening to the sound of his heart beating to mine. There was nothing more beautiful in the world.

"I *am* home," he whispered.

45

Zhangwei held me for a long time, and I was in no hurry to break away. These days of ceaseless strain had exhausted me. All I wanted was to sleep, and to awaken to him beside me.

Aunt Shou was slumped on the ground beside Dalian's body, his hand still clasped between hers. The tears had stopped, but the haunted expression in her eyes remained. How calm his face in death, stripped of bitterness, regret, and spite. I felt no pity for him. Dalian had died as he'd lived, sowing hate and fear. His legacy was devastation, wreaked upon his own people after the realms beyond were out of reach. This quiet death, in the arms of his mother, was far better than he deserved. Part of me hoped that he'd found peace at last, though the other part didn't think he deserved it.

Captain Lai approached Aunt Shou and knelt respectfully. "Great Lady, now that Lord Dalian is dead, we ask if you might reclaim your position? The Wuxin prospered under your reign; we seek the peace you once brought us."

Aunt Shou shook her head, her gaze almost vacant—dulled with pain. "I have no wish to rule, I have no heart for it . . . it died with my children."

General Fang, Lin, Mei, and the other soldiers fell to their knees before her, their red-gold armor gleaming like the setting sun. "There is no one else, Great Lady," General Fang said. "Chaos lies in Lord

Dalian's wake; we fear an opportunist will take advantage. Who can we trust with the throne during these precarious times? The people need a steady hand to settle the unrest and rebuild our kingdom."

I broke away from Zhangwei reluctantly, walking toward Aunt Shou. My body tensed as I sat beside her, my resentment still unquenched. Yet in her own way she had loved Chengyin and me—she had tried to keep us safe here, hiding my secret, defying Dalian to help Chengyin escape. For that, I would always be grateful, and my heart was not so hard as to be numbed to her pain.

"Aunt Shou, when I took the throne in Tianxia, I did not want it either. It was you who guided me until I found my way. Your people need you now, as you need them."

Aunt Shou remained silent for a long time. If she heard me, she gave no sign of it. At last she released Dalian's hand and rose to face the soldiers.

"I will accept the position, but only until another leader is elected. Choose wisely—one who will serve the people rather than themselves alone." She spoke quietly, yet her voice resonated. "Power should not be inherited but earned."

General Fang frowned. "It's never been done this way before."

"What if the leader is unfit?" Lin asked.

"Then choose again," Aunt Shou said. "The mandate to rule should no longer be determined by bloodline alone, it should reflect the voice of the people. We cannot afford a recurrence of what happened before." She glanced at Dalian, her expression unreadable. "Don't be afraid of change; it's what helps us grow."

The soldiers folded over in a bow, pressing their foreheads to the ground in an obeisance. As they rose, they dispersed, most heading back toward the mountains to begin their trek home. General Fang, Captain Lai, Lin, and Mei remained, speaking to Aunt Shou in hushed tones. Her words lingered in my mind, her wisdom awakening something in me. She had given her people a wondrous gift—of freedom, of choice, a voice in their own future.

"We will return now," Aunt Shou said. "We must prepare for my son's funeral."

As we made our way to the barge, Aunt Shou stumbled once as she walked, but she refused any help offered. It wasn't easy to feign strength when one felt weak—but sometimes, pretending was easier than reality. Sometimes you might even fool yourself.

"Will Chengyin be all right?" she asked me dully.

"Yes. His wound is healed, he just needs rest."

She frowned. "Our barrier will protect him, but how will he make his way home from Kunlun?"

"Once the skies are unsealed, the immortal soldiers will return. They will bring him back safely," Zhangwei assured her.

Aunt Shou bowed her head, her shoulders heaving. "What must Chengyin think of me? I'm not the mother he deserved."

"He loves you, Aunt Shou. As you love him." I reached out toward her—hesitating—then took her hand.

"Thank you, Liyen." Her fingers tightened around mine as she turned back to glance at the ruin of the marble archway, the shattered remnants of the gateway. "What will you do now?"

"Zhangwei and I will have to stay here until we find a way back." How heavy my heart was. We had won, yet lost so much. "Can we get a message to the Golden Desert? If the immortals know we're trapped, could they restore the gateway?"

Aunt Shou shook her head. "There is no way to send a message between our realms."

Zhangwei's arm drew me close. "The magic that helped create the gateway is no more. Queen Caihong—your mother—was only able to craft the enchantment because the archway existed in the first place, the one that linked Kunlun to here."

As we boarded the barge, the skies above were lightening to rose, the first shafts of daylight spearing the heavens. We traveled the rest of the way in silence, until the palace loomed ahead. As we drew to a halt, the shining lights of the waters beneath us caught my eye.

"What about the Eternal Boatman? Could he help us?" I was grasping at threads, but I wasn't ready to give up, still fighting to find a way back.

"Only those who have surrendered all their memories are allowed to board the vessel," Aunt Shou explained, confirming what Zhangwei had told me before.

A bitter trade—to give up the one thing that gave home its meaning.

"How can we find the boatman? Maybe we can negotiate with him? Offer something else instead of our memories?" I suggested.

Lin glanced at Aunt Shou. "The ruler of the Netherworld can summon the Eternal Boatman. However, he does not do their bidding—the choice to bear a passenger is his alone, and he is bound by his own rules."

Aunt Shou's eyes were bright as she turned to me. "Why not remain here with me? I will find a place for you and the God of War. You will want for nothing; we will be as family again." Her voice trailed away. The truth was, nothing could replace the family we'd lost.

"My home isn't here, Aunt Shou. Just as yours was never in Tianxia—your heart was always here." I spoke gently, not wanting to be cruel; she had lost so much already. If there was the slightest hope of returning, I would not turn my back on it.

"I understand."

Aunt Shou's smile was sad but resolute as she strode to the bank of the river. Bending down, she dipped her hand into the water. White light trailed from her fingers, forming a silvery trail. Foam frothed on the surface, the fragrance of incense springing into the air. The delicate peal of a wind chime rang out, one that folded into the stillness instead of shattering it.

The wind strengthened, shifting its direction, tearing strands of my hair loose. Something gleamed on the horizon. A golden boat curved like a wedge of the sun floated upon the surface. The only vessel that could traverse the rivers and oceans across the realms, unhindered by any barrier, whether of stone or magic. It was ferried by a nameless boatman said to be as old as death— neither immortal, nor mortal, nor demon. A broad bamboo hat covered his head, leaving a silver beard peeking beneath. His cheeks were hollowed, his eyes as pale as pearls. A cloak covered his shoulders, the cloth so fine it seemed to be woven of ash and mist. His callused fingers gripped a long pole that he thrust into the water with rhythmic strokes.

As he approached, Aunt Shou inclined her head. "Honored Boatman, thank you for answering my call."

"Why have you summoned me, ruler of the Netherworld?" His voice was rich and deep.

Aunt Shou gestured to me. At once, I stepped forward, Zhangwei beside me. As we bowed in greeting, my hands were clammy, my stomach knotted. "Honored Boatman, could you bear us back to the Mortal Realm?"

"There is nowhere I cannot take you, if you both will pay the price." He pulled out a pair of jade cups that he dipped into the river, now brimming with glistening liquid.

I fought the urge to recoil, the white lock of my hair tingling.

The boatman held out the cups to Zhangwei and me. "The water from the Wangchuan River consumes all memories," he said. "It gives as much as it takes, offering peace in place of misery— for many of the spirits trapped here suffer from the same thing: a broken heart. Whether a loved one lost, dreams unfulfilled, or betrayal—they are unable to move on, unable to forget."

"Why would anyone want to forget someone they love?" I asked.

"Memories are cherished when they bear joy, but what if one was never loved in return? What if you lost a loved one in a great tragedy? Wouldn't it be kinder to forget?" The boatman's lips stretched into a knowing smile. "The Wangchuan waters are a boon for those who need it, a curse when it is forced. Which will it be for you?"

"All memories have value," Zhangwei said. "They form our character, give our lives meaning. Even the parts that hurt."

The boatman's hand remained raised, the jade cups gleaming. "If you do not drink, you cannot cross the realms." There was no cruelty in the harshness of his demand, yet I sensed no kindness in him either. Maybe he had grown numbed to it, after all he had seen and heard and done.

He turned to me then, tilting his head to one side. "Who are you—with the waters of the Wangchuan in your veins, yet neither quite mortal nor immortal?"

I lifted my chin. "Why does it matter?"

The boatman studied me before he replied, "Two sets of memories exist within you: the mortal and immortal. For you, I will only ask for the payment of the former, in return for safe passage to your realm."

Ice formed in the pit of my stomach, spreading like a merciless winter. To give up one part of myself . . . it was like being in the Temple of the Crimson Moon again, except without the threat of war on the horizon, the clarity of my path then. In a way, this choice might be harder.

When I didn't reply, the boatman pushed the cup closer to me, sensing capitulation. How many desperate mortals had he faced? How many proud souls had wept before him? "The choice must be made, here and now. I never make the same offer twice."

"What of Zhangwei?" I asked the boatman hesitantly. "Will this cover passage for us both?"

"My price remains the same. It did not change for you, just that your situation is unique." His pale gaze bored into mine like he could see everything inside me. "If your hearts are connected, if you remember him—you will find each other again, whether in the skies or earth."

As we had. Even as a mortal, without knowing anything of him before—I had fallen in love with him all over again.

430

"Can we do this?" I asked Zhangwei, my heart undecided—the sliver of hope the boatman offered, clouded by fear and doubt. "What if you forget me? Us?"

"Even if I do, I will know you once we meet. Wherever we are, my heart will always be yours." His eyes pierced mine as his knuckles brushed my face gently. "But I do not want to forget."

I let my mind drift to our future if I accepted the boatman's offer. If I yielded my mortal memories, Zhangwei and I could return to the Immortal Realm together, to be reunited with our families. Even if he forgot me, I would find him again—we would make new memories, building a new future together. It would be a good life, one that might even be worth this sacrifice.

My fingers reached for the cup—then stilled, as my grandfather's face slipped into my mind. His love for me, how he'd nursed me throughout my illness, protected and fought for my place in Tianxia. How he'd risked everything to save my life. Love was the greatest gift any child could receive, and I had been blessed twice over. Even though my time in the Mortal Realm was fleeting, a ripple in the span of our existence—everything I had undergone there had been real. It had mattered. And how could I relinquish my duty to my people? They were a part of me, too, they gave meaning to my life—not just a toy I picked up, then tossed aside when I grew bored.

Sometimes it wasn't the number of years that gave something significance, but how deeply it marked one's heart. Grandfather. Chengyin. Even Aunt Shou. These bonds were precious, not easily discarded. There were other memories, too, those of Zhangwei. Our brief time in my mortal life was as precious to me as the years we'd spent in the skies. I had fallen in love with him again; we were bonded in a way we'd never been before. Our love and sacrifice, joy and hurt—all these were a part of me that I could not, that I *would* not relinquish.

"I don't want to forget either," I said in a low voice.

His strong fingers closed around mine, his eyes dark and knowing. "Not a day, an hour, or a single moment with you."

The warmth—the knowing—that seeped into my chest was as bright and clear as summer. "Honored Boatman, we will not accept your offer. We cannot pay your price." Even though this decision felt right—it hurt to refuse, both doubt and regret gripping me. "But if there is another way back—"

The boatman shook his head. "The toll must be paid. This is the rule since the start of time."

Silence fell over us, shadowed by despair.

Aunt Shou stepped forward. "As the ruler of the Netherworld, I ask you for one favor—to allow another to pay their price. In return, you may ask another favor of me, at a time and place of your choosing."

I stared at her in shock, unable to believe my ears. "Aunt Shou . . . why?" Even if the boatman refused, the fact she'd tried was enough—more so because she wanted me to stay.

"We don't cage those we love, we set them free," Aunt Shou said quietly. "Keeping someone against their will isn't love but selfishness, weighing your happiness above theirs."

The boatman bowed to her. "A favor from you, Great Lady, is not to be disdained."

Aunt Shou nodded. "There is much I wish to forget."

"I can't let you do this, Aunt Shou," I protested.

"My children's faces are dear to me, as are their memories. But their deaths . . . I would gladly wipe from my mind," she said fiercely.

"A sip, then, for a fragment of a remembrance. If there are enough here willing to drain the cups, I will bear these passengers," the boatman offered. "Only once will I allow this, as my gift to the new ruler of the Netherworld. One who I believe is worthy of the title."

Aunt Shou inclined her head as she accepted the cup he offered her. "I will remember your generosity, Honored Boatman."

Lin called out, "I will take a drink, too."

"As will I," Mei echoed.

More of the Wuxin stepped forward, my heart swelling. "How can I let all of you bear this burden?" My question emerged hoarse with emotion.

"The Wuxin pay our dues," Lin said with a smile, glancing from Zhangwei to me. "You saved us, protecting the Wangchuan River. We were your enemies, yet you stayed when another would have left us to our doom."

I blinked back the haze that descended over my vision How strange life was. For as long as I could remember, I'd hated and feared the Wuxin—and now, somehow, we had saved each other.

"I don't need payment—"

"A gift, then," Aunt Shou said. "In exchange for yours to us."

"Thank you." On impulse, I hugged her tightly, then bowed to the others. Tears fell from my eyes, trailing into the river. "Thank you all."

They lined up one by one, each taking a drop from the cups the boatman held out. Their expressions shifted, from surprise to peace to a trace of doubt. At times, there was a flicker of grief before it eased.

At last, when the cups were empty. Zhangwei and I boarded the golden boat. The boatman pushed away with one strong stroke of his pole. The waters were smooth and calm, the current unbroken. We stood there staring at the faces of those who remained to bid us farewell, staring at them until I could see them no more. I was going home, yet why did grief still cling to my heart?

Zhangwei wrapped his arms around me, holding me close. Together, we glided along this river of lost hopes and dreams, the stars fading with the promise of a new dawn, aglitter on the horizon.

46

That night, I went to sleep in Tianxia—and when I next opened my eyes, I was standing amid the clouds. The glittering sands of the Golden Desert stretched out like a bolt of silk, encircling the Palace of Radiant Light. Jasmine dotted the grounds, the air thick with its sweetness. Aquamarine bridges arched above, melding into the heavens. A cry rang out, a qilin flying through the skies, her mane the hue of flame, her body sheathed in copper scales. My chest twinged. Would Red Storm still acknowledge me as her rider? As she glanced at me, her jaws seemed to part in a smile, dispelling my qualms. Drawing a breath, the familiar fragrance evoked a deep calm inside me—of peace, of belonging.

A tall woman walked toward me, her violet robe embroidered with orchids. Pearls encrusted her headdress, jade bangles encircling her wrists. The tilt of her chin, the set of her mouth, the way her fingers curled—all these sent a shaft of remembrance through me, one that went deep. How could I have forgotten my mother? How could I have forgotten it all?

We stood there, staring at each other as I shifted nervously. I was not the child who'd left, nor was she the parent I remembered. Though the Queen of the Golden Desert looked just as when we last met, I now saw her through new eyes: no longer the terrified mortal before her sovereign but with the guilt of the daughter who'd defied her parent—one respected, feared, and loved.

"Mother." My heart beat unsteadily as I greeted her, clasping my hands before me, unsure whether she would welcome or spurn an embrace.

She did not move, keeping a distance between us. "My daughter, you finally remember who you are."

"Forgive me for forgetting you, Mother."

We had always spoken with such formality; she had always been the queen first, and my mother second. I wished things were different between us; that I could just hug her and know she would embrace my weakness, instead of fearing she would scorn it. And remorse filled me too, for the years lost, for not grieving by her side . . . for being part of another family, cared for by others whom I'd loved in turn. One did not replace the other but filled a different place in my heart, one that was wholly their own.

"You shouldn't have descended to the Mortal Realm," she rebuked me, her eyes unusually bright. "You should have let Zhangwei go."

"Why? Because he's stronger than me? More capable?" The words slipped out before I could stop myself. Maybe I was tired of her expectations, her attempts to mold me into the perfect daughter—of trying to be more than I was.

She took a step forward, narrowing our gap. "No, my child. Because I didn't want to lose you. It was a selfish decision. There was risk on both sides, but far more unknown for the one who descended to the realm below. After all, we couldn't find you for years; I thought you were lost to us."

I stared into her face, seeing at last the tenderness and relief as she looked at me, the hurt that clung to her still. Reaching for her hand, I held it tight, relieved when she didn't pull away. Mother didn't like public displays of affection, but maybe she allowed it now because we were alone . . . or was it because this wasn't real?

"Zhangwei was too badly injured, Mother. I couldn't let him go; he might have died. I didn't do this because I was being reckless or foolish or rebellious. I did it because it was right for us."

"Yet look at what you've become——" Her voice broke then, lines forming around her mouth as though she were silencing herself.

I flinched at her words, Aunt Shou's previous claim ringing through my mind: *Your mother would never accept you, what you've become.*

While Mother had taken pride in my accomplishments, she'd never shied from expressing her disapproval that I wasn't as strong, clever or ruthless as her. "You could never have seized the throne as I did," she'd often told me. And she was right. I could never have done it . . . nor paid the price. Mother had united our kingdom, rewrote the fate of our people, inked her place in history. She was the blazing sun, and for a long time I believed it was enough to be her moon—reflecting her light, destined to be forever in her shadow.

But I was wrong. We each shone brightest in our own lives, unless we allowed our light to be dimmed. Our differences did not make us weaker; we were strong in our own ways. I had grown to know the mortals and the Wuxin in a way Mother never could have. This might have been a weakness in her eyes, but I believed it was my greatest strength.

I should not cheapen my accomplishments, letting them tarnish unseen. I had protected those I loved, saving countless lives—immortal and mortal. There was no glory in war, each side paying an unforgivable price, reaping a harvest of strife. The violence of the past should serve as a warning for the future; its cost was far too high to pay again.

And so I had ended the cycle of vengeance, extinguishing the embers of war.

But standing before my mother, doubt assailed me anew, along with the creeping insecurities of my childhood that I would never match up to her hopes. Yet the most important thing was that *I* regretted nothing. Life was not about right or wrong but finding our own way, learning what made us happy, what filled our lives—instead of looking to others for it.

My time as a mortal had altered me forever. Once, I'd pitied the mortals, imagining them lesser than us—such short-sighted, insufferable arrogance. There was a wisdom among them that the immortals lacked: a courage to face the unknown, the drive to make the most of themselves, to live life to the fullest. In some ways, they knew better than us how to live . . . and maybe it was because they were prepared to die. It mattered less how long one walked the earth or flew among the clouds—but what one did with their time, the legacy that remained.

"Mother, do you accept me for who I am? Can you love me this way?" It hurt to ask, just as it hurt to be unsure of her answer. After all, I was no longer her accomplished immortal daughter, a jewel in her crown.

Maybe love was less about perfection but acceptance, in a way—our flaws alongside our strengths, the beautiful with the ugly, all those parts we tried to hide. Maybe we should stop expecting perfection from those we loved, which was the surest path to resentment and disappointment.

When she finally spoke, there was a softness in her voice that I'd never heard before. "My daughter, I never stopped loving you."

The shell around my heart broke, the one I'd built out of fear of being rejected. "I've missed you, Mother. How I wish I could come back." As I stared at her, at the shining palace of my childhood, I wondered aloud, "Is this a dream? Am I with you now?"

"I am with you always, even if you cannot see me." Her eyes lingered on my face. "In your heart, you know whether this is real or not."

She cradled my cheek, her eyes sliding to my hair. Did she

see the mark of the waters of death? "You faced such trials in the Mortal Realm and the Netherworld, such hardship. I wish I'd been there with you, to help you through it."

"I wish that, too." There was a rare closeness in this moment, one of priceless honesty. "But this made me stronger, Mother. Though my power is weaker . . . I don't miss it." I struggled to form my thoughts. "Somehow, with less, I am more."

"While I have never felt like it's enough." Her smile was tinged with sadness. "I would give everything up if I had your father back. But there are things not even magic can accomplish, wishes that even the gods can't grant."

"I'm sorry, Mother. I couldn't kill them." My voice hitched. "I didn't want to."

"What do you mean?" Her gaze was penetrating, like she saw my deepest secrets.

"The Wangchuan River was being destroyed." My confession spilled from me, though her spies might have already told her everything upon our return. "I could have escaped with Zhangwei, letting Lord Dalian destroy his people. The Wuxin would have been obliterated without sacrificing the life of a single immortal. But . . . there is good there, too. Most just want to live in peace, to protect their own. Just like us."

When she remained silent, my chest clenched. "Do you hate me? For not avenging Father when I could have? I know it's not what you'd have done—"

Her arms went around me, holding me tight. "I could *never* hate you. I am proud of you, my daughter. For doing what I could not—for learning a different way, one you weren't taught." She pulled away to stare at me. "There are days when my regret is so heavy, I cannot stand. When I think peace would be better for us all, rather than ambition or vengeance. Nothing good ever stemmed from hate; its price is always higher than one imagines."

I sagged against her, hugging her back. "I've missed you,

Mother. I'll always miss you."

"Are you happy, Liyen?" she asked, searching my face. "Cherish what you have, don't wait until it's too late, like I did. Life is a lot easier when you don't just dwell on what you don't have."

I nodded, thinking of all I'd lost, yet all I'd gained, too.

"What will you do now?" she asked.

"I want to come home, but I can't leave yet. My task in Tianxia is unfinished." I added hesitantly, "*Can* I even return? A mortal cannot live in the skies, and . . . I don't know what I am."

"You are *my daughter*. If anyone questions or insults you, they will regret it," she said darkly.

I smothered a laugh. "Mother, you sound like Zhangwei—always threatening first."

"That's why we need you," she replied. "You make us better than we are."

Something in her manner moved me deeply—this new softness. Though we'd spent all these years apart, I felt closer to her now than ever before.

"As for whether you can come home, that will take time," she said solemnly. "We are bound to the rules of the Immortal Realm; as it stands, you cannot return. I will have to negotiate new terms with the Celestial Emperor." She sighed. "He's a cunning one; he'll exact a high price for any concession on his part."

My mind worked quickly, thinking of my people. "You can offer for Tianxia to rejoin the rest of the Mortal Realm. To return our shield and bring the walls down, as was promised in the treaty." I braced for an outright refusal.

"Tianxia strengthens us." Her mouth tightened. "Do you know how hard it was to wrest it from the Celestial Emperor? It was only because we won the war without their aid."

"Tianxia is not a pawn. The mortals deserve to live their own lives, not subject to our demands and whims—or our anger." I stared at her unwaveringly. "The storms must cease. Rules must be set to protect them from the immortals. Mortal lives are as precious as yours."

Her eyes flashed. "Are you negotiating with me, Daughter?"

I clasped my hands and bowed, sensing I'd pushed her as far as I could. It was enough for now to have seeded the idea, though I wouldn't give up. "I will submit a formal petition through the God of War."

Gently, she touched the lock of white hair tucked behind my ear. I recoiled, expecting revulsion, but her eyes were warm and bright. "I've asked the gardeners to plant lotuses in our garden. They are waiting for you to see them bloom—as am I."

My eyes stung. I cried then, raw gasps breaking from my throat. Such longing filled me to walk in the hallways of my childhood, to sleep in my own bed. How it hurt that I couldn't.

Not yet. But one day, I promised myself.

Silence fell over us, the wind blowing through our hair, our skirts fluttering. I would always remember this moment, carved into my heart: our closeness, our unflinching acceptance of each other . . . what made us different. What made us family.

At last she pulled away, wiping a hand over her eyes. I pressed a kiss to her cheek, my hand still clasped in hers—no longer ashamed of what she might see in me, of what I had done, of what I was.

"We will find a way, Mother."

When I awoke in the morning, sunlight was streaming through the windows. My chest was at once hollow and filled to the brim. This was not the end; I would see my mother again.

47

The candlelight wavered, close to the end of its wick. I sat by my desk beside a pile of unread scrolls, my mind wandering. Where was Zhangwei? He'd returned to the skies over a month ago; he had his duties as I had mine—but his absence left a hollow in my heart, one that only he could fill.

After everything, I should be secure in his love. Yet when I was tired and alone, as tonight, doubt slunk in like a thief through an open window. What if he'd changed his mind? What if he'd tired of me? I was not the immortal he'd fallen in love with, not even the mortal he'd pursued. There were times I no longer knew who I was.

Yet there was so much to be grateful for. Zhangwei and I had escaped. My people were safe, the threat of the Wuxin no longer darkening our horizon. Soon, I would begin negotiations with the immortals to release Tianxia. And Chengyin had recovered, though he was still shaken from the ordeal. I had spent many mornings sitting with him in his garden before heading to court.

"Do you remember anything of your time in the Netherworld?" I'd asked him once.

His face had shuttered, his body flinching.

"You don't have to tell me," I said at once, regretting having upset him.

"I want to," he assured me. "I was there, yet I couldn't control anything I said or did. When I tried to fight, it would hurt—the pain only easing when I stopped resisting. It was like being trapped in a nightmare, one I couldn't awaken from, my mind endlessly screaming for release."

I took his hand, holding it firmly. "I'm sorry you suffered this."

His voice dropped as he added, "The worst part was when he used me to threaten you, to hurt my mother."

"You stopped him. Without you, we'd still be trapped in the Netherworld."

"Only because you wouldn't leave me." His eyes were haunted as he raised them to mine. "Do you think Mother is well?"

The question was an echo of what Aunt Shou had asked me when I'd thought we were trapped in the Netherworld. "She is stronger than any of us knew. Wiser, too. And I know she is thinking of you every day."

"No matter what she is—Wuxin or mortal—I love her," he'd said in a low voice. "She will always be my mother, the one who took me in when no one wanted to."

Aunt Shou had been part of my life for so long, sometimes I found myself looking for her when I was uncertain, expecting to hear her voice ringing out when I said something I should not.

"I love her, too," I admitted, for the first time since learning who she was. My anger and resentment toward Aunt Shou weren't because she was a Wuxin but because of her deceit. Deep down, she was the aunt I'd always known and loved, the one who'd set us free in the end.

When I first returned home, suspicious looks were cast my way, a few of the ministers whispering among themselves. Was it the subtle glow that cloaked my skin, the faint thrum of magic in my presence, the hardening in my manner? I was no longer the mortal girl they'd condescended to, who'd tried to fight back in her own way—though I missed her at times. When Minister Guo led the furtive calls to cast me from the throne, I'd moved swiftly, stripping him of his position and banishing him from the palace.

The courtiers no longer made me feel nervous—their quarrels, once my bane, were now a nuisance. The threat of war, of death, being trapped in Lord Dalian's court had shifted my perspective. It didn't matter how good a ruler I was if those who were meant to support me chose to undermine me instead, if my rulings failed to be implemented. This court held the future of Tianxia in its hands, and those who did not value the honor had no right to be there. While the court was still in turmoil in the wake of Minister Guo's departure, I ruthlessly appointed new ministers, those on merit alone, ignoring family connections or influence. Tradition and history should be a guide but not a yoke. If something was wrong, the past was not a reason to keep it so.

Some at court undoubtedly hated me for it, but as long as it was good for my people—so be it. As my grandfather had said: *Rulers aren't just meant to be liked . . . what's most important is doing what is right.* Why please those who wanted to believe the worst of me, those who cared only to further their own ends? My harsh treatment of Minister Guo quelled the lingering murmurs of disquiet— his previous allies adjusting to his absence with remarkable ease, his rivals clamoring to fill the gap in power.

My efforts were centered on the people's safety and happiness, not pandering for the favor of the disgruntled few, those accustomed to privilege. No calamity had descended from the heavens, whether storms or floods, which added to the tranquility in Tianxia, to the illusion that my reign was favored by the gods. I let them believe it; it was easier that way. But I worked hard to build a foundation for the kingdom that would last beyond the current peace, one that would thrive even in adversity—even beyond my rule.

After all, I wouldn't live forever. I would not always be the Lady of Tianxia. The kingdom needed a steady hand while we adjusted to the changes, while I secured my people's freedom from the immortals. Only then would I hand the reins of power to another, one chosen by the people. A dream that had taken root from Aunt Shou's wisdom.

And then . . . I would live for myself, with the one I loved.

If he returned.

I scowled at the reminder of Zhangwei's absence. Immortals had poor sense of time—weeks felt like days to them, while I had learned impatience in the Mortal Realm. And there was the irksome matter of my betrothal. Now that the need for my false engagement with Chengyin had passed, the ministers had redoubled their efforts to get me married off. Maybe they didn't like seeing a woman alone on the throne. I would need to resurrect the threat of the betrothal tournament soon, if only to silence those more daring. I shouldn't have cared, yet each time one of them brought it up, my mind inevitably flitted to Zhangwei, my annoyance growing at his absence.

A thought struck as I picked up a brush and swirled it into the ink. A smile played on my lips as I wrote a message to Zhangwei, then folded the paper and pressed my jade seal upon it. If he was playing a game with me, I'd just rewritten the rules. This would bring him here before another week was over.

I was wrong.

The next morning, while the court was in session, chaos erupted outside the hall. I looked up, glad for the distraction. Minister Dao had grown more insufferable of late, emboldened by his rival's absence, insisting on the election of his eldest son to the court despite his having failed the entrance exams twice. While I'd never ordered an execution before, he was sorely tempting me.

The doors swung open as an attendant rushed in. "Lord Zhangwei, the God of War, the High General of the Golden Desert, requests an audience with the Lady of Tianxia." The use of Zhangwei's formal titles was unexpected, and several courtiers exchanged guarded looks.

I glanced down at my red robe embroidered with white camellias, suppressing the ridiculous urge to change it to one more flattering. "He has no invitation," I said. Zhangwei had kept me waiting this long, a few minutes more was no hardship for him.

"Do I require one to speak to the Lady of Tianxia?"

He stood in the entrance, sunlight gliding across his armor. His deep voice sent a shaft of pleasure through me, though I schooled my face into indifference, suppressing the urge to run to him. The problem with having too much pride is that you end up making yourself suffer.

"My time is precious," I replied in an aloof manner. "Unless you're here upon matters of state."

"Today, I would speak on both."

My heart quickened as he strode forward—though he looked ready for battle, not courtship, with his sword, the daggers sheathed by his waist, a large wooden bow slung across his back.

My eyes narrowed. "What brings you here, Lord Zhangwei? Why are you attired for war?"

He halted before the dais, indifferent to the stir he'd roused in my court. A sheet of paper was crumpled in his hand, the letter I'd written to him just the night before. "Did you not summon me?"

"I did not," I replied smoothly. "I merely informed you of my plans out of courtesy."

"Cancel the tournament." His voice pulsed with barely restrained anger. Had I provoked him too far?

"Afraid you'll lose?" My tone dropped, edged with challenge. I was enjoying this immensely, more than I should—my pleasure honed by the nights I'd spent waiting for him.

"No," he replied arrogantly, unslinging his sword. "As you can see, I've come prepared. If another happens to win, I'll just make you a widow."

He was calling my bluff, drawing this farce out. I cursed him in my mind, my hands clenched in my lap. "You're a bad loser, Lord Zhangwei."

"The worst." His mouth curved in a way that made me lean instinctively toward him, but I drew back, fighting a rush of heat.

Zhangwei turned to address my court. "There will be no tournament for the Lady of Tianxia's hand in marriage, nor will any suitors be entertained."

I glared at him, both fascinated and infuriated at his high-handedness. "That is not for you to decide."

"It is, when you've promised yourself to me, as I have promised myself to you. Or have you already forgotten?"

As whispers rustled around the court, I was torn between reaching for him and throwing something at his head. Chengyin stepped forward, ever vigilant when guarding my interests, braver than most to confront the God of War. "The Lady of Tianxia's betrothal is a matter for the entire kingdom."

Zhangwei's jaw tightened, his gaze pinning mine. "It is between *us* alone. I have a proposal that requires your immediate consideration. Would you prefer I speak now . . . or later?"

The way his voice had lowered—I bristled at his presumption. After weeks of unexplained absence, how dare he storm into my court and make any demands? I would not surrender so easily, running to him the moment he beckoned.

"State your terms," I said curtly. "What is your proposal?"

Zhangwei took a step closer, a fierce light in his eyes. "Marriage. To me."

My throat went dry. How could he declare himself before everyone? Though such intense pride surged through me that he had.

"Is this just to stop me from marrying another?" I had to know.

"No, I want you for myself. I want all of you."

He spoke with such certainty, the last of my defenses crumbled. I raised my hand to dismiss the court, but Chengyin cleared his throat.

"As the Lady of Tianxia's First Advisor, I would like to hear more of the God of War's offer," Chengyin said with feigned solemnity. "All proposals must be weighed by her advisors before anything is decided."

It was his way of protecting me, offering a diplomatic excuse to decline anything I did not want. Yet right then, a small part of me was tempted to throttle Chengyin. There was nothing I wanted more than to marry Zhangwei, even if he offered nothing but himself.

"My offer has three parts." Zhangwei cast a meaningful look at me. "Such delicate negotiations took time, hence my delay. The first part of my dowry—"

"Dowry?" Minister Dao repeated, his surprise infused with malice. "The dowry is usually paid from the bride's family." Maybe he sought to secure the God of War's favor, since it was clear he had lost mine.

Zhangwei's frigid expression sufficed to send Minister Dao scuttling back. "I need nothing else but the lady herself, as long as she is willing."

Warmth coursed through my veins like a thousand shards of sunlight. He had come to me, his heart in his hand. "I would hear your terms," I said.

The air glittered, a bronze shield appearing before me, inlaid with sapphires, amethysts and pearls—the one I'd seen in Queen Caihong's throne room.

"The Shield of Rivers and Mountains." My voice shook; this didn't feel real.

He nodded. "As promised, Tianxia will be released from its service to the Golden Desert."

Gasps erupted among the minsters, smiles spreading across their faces as their shock gave way to joy.

"What of the wall?" I asked quickly.

"It will be brought down. Those who wish to remain are welcome, but none will be stopped from venturing beyond. The people of Tianxia will be free to choose whether to rejoin the Mortal Realm or not. However, we ask that a troop of soldiers be posted at all times to watch over Kunlun."

I rose, forcing myself to walk to him when all I wanted was to run. "I need nothing else. This is everything to me."

He spoke clearly, for my ears alone. "I would give you everything I have, all that I am—and more."

As he extended his hand, a fine sword appeared on the ground between us. Gleaming with power, crafted with the magic of the realm above. I looked up at him in confusion, fighting back a smile. "More weapons?"

"The soldiers guarding Kunlun will be equipped with immortal blades."

Chengyin's mouth fell open. A few of the ministers' faces lit up with avarice. Were they already plotting how to use this to their advantage?

"These blades cannot be used for ill, else the magic will turn inward, upon the wielder themselves," Zhangwei warned.

"Typical dowries are gifts of gold or precious stones, offerings of food or wine," I said, a thread of humor coiled in my tone. "While you have given me a kingdom's freedom and outfitted an army."

"I am only the messenger," he told me gravely. "You won these yourself."

I blinked back the brightness in my eyes. "Then what do you offer?"

"My heart for yours," he said quietly, oblivious to the stir in the court.

His black eyes shone with the light of the stars. Such deep joy swept over me . . . with him by my side, I would never be cold again. We were surrounded by people, yet he was the only one I saw. A sudden impatience filled me to be alone with him, to claim every part he had offered me today.

I raised my voice. "I have urgent matters to discuss with the God of War. The court is adjourned for today—"

"For the next week," Zhangwei interjected, his eyes alight.

My face flushed, but I wanted him, too. Chengyin cast a pointed look our way before leaving, the other attendants and ministers following him swiftly, closing the doors after them.

As Zhangwei reached for me, I shook my head. "I cannot return to the Golden Desert," I began haltingly.

"Then I will make my home here. I would cross the Netherworld again, should you desire. Heaven or hell depends on whether we're together or apart."

Still, I hesitated. Not because I doubted the strength of his devotion but because he had given me so much, I dreaded taking more. I wanted him, but I didn't want him to suffer for being with me.

"I don't know how much time I have left, or what lies ahead in my future," I confessed. "I don't even know who I am anymore."

"You are *you*. You are all I need, whether we are together a year or a hundred." He stroked the hair from my face, looking into my eyes. "Never doubt my heart. I have loved you since we met—as I will for the rest of our days."

He pulled me to him and kissed me, his lips moving over mine with hunger. I closed my eyes, yielding to the heat that pulsed through my flesh, the rush of emotion as unrelenting as a storm. How I loved him—our love tested beyond imagining, transcending time, heaven and earth, even crossing the river of death. Unlike Zhangwei, I didn't know the years left to me, nor did I possess the certain end of a mortal. And so I would treasure each day like it might be my last.

Write your own destiny, Zhangwei had told me once. And I would, together with him. I would follow him to the ends of the earth as he had followed me once—and we could make our home anywhere, even in the Netherworld. Across the realms, each life-time, my heart had found its way back to him. He was my past, my present, and my future, and I would place all my days in his keep-ing. At last I had learned one of life's elusive mysteries, that the true meaning of eternity lay not in the endless years but in having someone to share them with.

A question slipped into my mind, one that had plagued me since leaving the Temple of the Crimson Moon, when I'd faced my destinies and defied them both—neither mortal nor immortal, with the waters of death in my veins.

You are all, yet you are none, the mirror had told me. I'd thought I belonged nowhere, untethered to the world, that I would never find a place to belong again—but I was wrong. The answer came to me, as clear as the skies after the rain. I would not be defined by a single decision, or by my name or title—whether the Lady of Tianxia or the Princess of the Golden Desert, daughter, grand-child, or the beloved of the God of War.

I was all of them . . . and I was more.

ACKNOWLEDGMENTS

TK

ABOUT THE AUTHOR

SUE LYNN TAN writes fantasy inspired by the myths and legends she fell in love with as a child. Her books have been nominated for several awards, are *USA Today* and *Sunday Times* bestsellers, and will be translated into sixteen languages.

Born in Malaysia, Sue Lynn studied in London and France before moving to Hong Kong. Her love for stories began with a gift from her father: her first compilation of fairy tales from around the world. When not writing or reading, she enjoys exploring the hills and forests around her home.